MANY WATERS

Stories

by Daniel Luther Olson

*"Many waters cannot quench love,
neither can the floods drown it."*
—Song of Solomon

Norway Pine Press
Athens, Ohio

To Steve Rudolph, Steve Mowrey, Thomas Doherty,
Scott Reber, Ann Marie Olson, and
as always, my wife, Sharon

Cataloging-in-Publication Data
Olson, Daniel Luther.

MANY WATERS: STORIES
by Daniel Luther Olson

"What the Surface Hides
Belies What The Eye Spies."

1. Water – Fiction. 2. Redemption – Fiction.
3. Black River Falls (Wis.) – Fiction.

"Upper Kensington" was adapted from the novel
DOUBLE EUCHRE and "Fifty-fifty" from
the novel COURT AND UNION

ISBN 979-8-9870067-2-6
www.daniellutherolson.com
Cover design by Enzo Varrie
First edition

Table of Contents

Ill Wind

"God, no!" Doug begged and flung the plastic shaver into the trash can. A nick, right off the corner of his mouth, and already oozing blood. He snatched a clean hotel towel, ran cold water on it, and pressed the fabric against his cheek. "What am I supposed to do now? Cancel the visit?" No way was he going to show up at Raymond's with a cut on his face, no matter how far back their friendship went.

Outside, the December wind howled down the Loop's skyscraper canyons, plunging the temperature close to zero. Another Alberta Clipper, according to *The Sun-Times* he had read on the El from O'Hare. Thank goodness southeast Ohio rarely got this frigid. Though Wisconsin indeed did, the home state he had left the year Ronald Reagan became President—and now his second term was nearly over.

Holding the cloth against his skin, Doug studied the haggard face mirrored in the fluorescent light. Wan, wrinkled, dark circles beneath both eyes—as if he were sick instead of Raymond. No wonder as poorly as he had been sleeping of late. That day he'd had to get up before six to catch a flight in Columbus, and after checking into this Hilton had been unable to nap. Not with the constant rumble of Lake Shore Drive and Michigan Avenue traffic. How dumb to have imagined a room on Grant Park would be quiet.

Doug felt guilty for not staying with Raymond this trip. If the situation were reversed, would Ray have kept his distance? Look how he had reacted four years ago, when Doug had called to say Liz was filing for divorce: "You sound terrible, kid. I'm coming down there for a visit." And he had done it too. His emotional support and their good times together had indeed lifted Doug out of his funk. Nobody else had stepped forward like that, not even closer friends who lived just across town.

Raymond certainly had the space for him now, in fact an entire vacant bedroom. In the past, Doug had been perfectly happy sleeping on the couch. Not that he had ever needed to save the money. No, comfort had always yielded to seeing as much as possible of his old college buddy. Though Ray wasn't so good a friend as Mike and Lenny, two faculty colleagues in Athens. But ever since he and Raymond had met in graduate school in Madison, they had felt close. Though exactly why, Doug couldn't say, because on paper they didn't have all that much in common. But when his marriage started foundering, who did Doug call? Ray of course. Or when that mysterious lump appeared in his groin that turned out to be a swollen gland, he was phoning Chicago even before his own doctor. Somehow it had always been so easy to confide things to Raymond he would never reveal to Michael or Leonard. Raymond had always been equally frank with him, that is, up until his lover, Danny, got sick.

While Doug stood there waiting for the cut to dry, his left eyelid began to twitch. Just as it used to in grad school, when the relentless stress almost forced him to quit. He tried to hold the flap of skin still with a fingertip, but it kept fluttering like a trapped mouse's heart. "To hell with it," he said and grabbed his leather bomber jacket. Why not just head straight to Raymond's now and take his chances, even if he wasn't expected for hours? Besides, the sooner he got the initial awkwardness over with, the quicker he could start enjoying this visit.

After only three blocks, his forehead and cheeks were already burning from the cold, but Doug trudged on. He turned up State Street and crossed the Chicago River, the wind raking his exposed face like razor blades. When he finally reached Marina City's twin corn-cob towers, he stopped and pressed his hands against his stinging ears. And there he stood, flinching with every new gust, just sixty stories below Ray warmly ensconced in his apartment. He took off a glove and gently tapped the nick. It didn't feel wet, but a wound was still a wound. Maybe he should buy himself some Band-Aids. But first go to a bank and cash a couple of traveler's checks. His aching fingers fumbled with his wallet and counted only thirty-six dollars.

"Beautiful building, isn't it?" a woman greeted, sidling close. In garish makeup as thick as a mask, she was shivering under an ankle-length mink coat.

"Yes," Doug said, edging away.

"I bet it cost a bundle. The good things in life don't come cheap." The crimson gloss of her lipstick was disgusting.

"Uh-huh," he agreed. She could have been forty-five. Or maybe only twenty-eight, but whatever her age she terrified him.

"A hundred bucks could buy a lonely guy a pretty nice time."

"I'm very sorry, Miss—or I mean, Ma'am—but I have to meet a friend." And with that, Doug darted out into traffic and a careering taxi just missed him.

He cursed himself for not having brought his old parka. It was much too warm for one in Athens, but this was a genuine winter. He debated whether to walk right in to the high-rise elevators. His growling stomach decided for him that no matter how unappealing food sounded, he simply had to eat some lunch. Besides, it'd be impolite to arrive at Ray's starving. So he hurried back down State Street, clutching the bridge railing for balance against the gale's buffeting.

A buttery three-egg omelet and home fries at a Wabash Street diner with a Dukakis-for-President poster in the window more than filled him up. After finishing the meal, he lingered until the ache left his half-frozen fingers and toes. Once back outside, he set out for his hotel only soon to halt, the tiny facial cut smarting in the swirling snow. What would be the point of returning to his room? He covered his freezing ears with his unlined leather gloves.

A black panhandler in greasy jeans and a torn coat cut off his path. "Hear no evil?" the guy said with a three-toothed grin.

"What?"

"You be Hear No Evil, right?"

Doug jaywalked to escape this pesky stranger and turned toward Ray's, but the stiff wind so stung his face he flipped around and let the brutal blast of air push him south. Soon he was loping down Michigan Avenue along Grant Park past his hotel. The famous Field Museum came into view. Dinosaurs! He simply had to go see those creatures again, the ones he had so adored as a kid. Back when his mother and father had brought him here. Did he ever miss his deceased parents, especially his mom.

Doug bounded up the stairs and through the geology display as an attendant had directed. Sure enough, there the critters stood, arrayed around a long, narrow hall. Another good look and he scurried right back out. Because those weren't dinosaurs—they were dinosaur *bones*. The skeletons of species that once had thrived, but now were long since gone. So what if extinction was perfectly natural? So what if ninety-nine per cent of all the species that had ever lived no longer existed? If some day we learned that they had been killed off by a comet or unstoppable viruses, would that bring a single one back? He wandered downstairs into the dioramas of Homo sapiens' ancestors. Australopithecus, Neanderthal, Cro-Magnon Man—

nothing but effigies one and all. Because they too were no more the living, breathing originals than had been the remains of Stegosaurus and Tyrannosaurus Rex. The ancient Egyptian artifacts—the mummies and the sarcophagi especially—were even more upsetting.

Flushing with nervous sweat, Doug rushed outside and stood coatless. Only after the wind had cooled him off, did he slip his jacket back on and head north into the gale, fighting for every step, while dwelling on Ray's plight. When had their last conversation been face to face? Sure, they had talked plenty on the phone and exchanged letters, but when was the last time in person? Before Danny got sick three years ago, wasn't it? When Raymond had invited himself down to Athens right after Liz moved out.

As comatose as the Ohio college town mostly was throughout the school year, it had been a veritable cemetery in August. But clever Ray had skimmed the local papers and come up with a slew of things to do. First, he had dragged Doug to a ladies' mud wrestling contest in nearby Nelsonville—actually, the competitors had all been stocky high school girls—and contrary to his misgivings, Doug had had a ball. Later that afternoon, they had taken in the National Jigsaw Puzzle Championship held in the Ohio University basketball stadium. Recalling the queer ripping noise of cellophane wrappers being torn off hundreds of virgin Hallmark boxes at once brought a smile to Doug's face even now.

That night's dinner turned out both stranger and funnier— free vegetarian pizza eaten cross-legged on the floor inside the pink Hare Krishna house. Hilarious for Doug anyway, because the suffocatingly sweet incense and lurid altar finally freaked Raymond out. "This isn't exactly pre- or post-Vatican Two," he had joked in racing for the door, close to retching. Though Ray's Catholicism had long since lapsed by the time Doug met him, he still remained oddly loyal to what he regarded as the one true faith.

Their next evening together, Raymond ate Doug's unimaginative chef's salad without complaint and then hauled out a fifth of Kentucky sour mash. Sipping the whiskey neat, they chatted about old times in Madison till they were guffawing over memories of the grad school grind and their eccentric profs. Schofield the Skywatcher, who lectured gazing up, as if his notes were written on the ceiling. Heinz the Hopper, who did toe-lifts to stress every dubious point. Van Dyke the Vise, who pressed his palms into his temples, as if that helped squeeze out longer strings of trivia.

After midnight, they lowered themselves from the couch onto the living room carpet, just as they had so often during the Seventies. As they knelt beside flickering candles, their thighs an inch apart, Doug confessed to the selfish preoccupations that had eventually driven Liz away from their marriage. No matter how bad his old friend let himself look, Raymond's sympathy and affection never flagged. Then Doug made the mistake of bringing up Ray's lover. "You've hardly mentioned Danny at all," he said.

Raymond drew up his knees and buried his face in skinny thighs. "Danny and I are getting along fine."

"Great. I mean, since you hadn't said anything about him that's what I assumed." When Ray didn't reply, Doug asked, "Is something wrong?"

"Not yet." Ray jumped up, saying, "Let me freshen both of our drinks."

Doug could only cringe to contemplate all the months he had allowed to pass without having repaid such faithful friendship. But at least he was here now in Chicago, even if he hadn't yet gotten himself inside Raymond's place. By slouching and leaning into the wind, he quickened his pace.

His ears had passed from pain to numbness when a pedestrian up ahead shouted to a companion, "There's no line!" Doug's squinting gaze followed an outstretched arm pointing at a huge banner proclaiming, "GEORGIA O'KEEFFE." Of course—the Art Institute. How could he come to Chicago and pass up such a major exhibit?

Inside, clumps of admirers had coagulated in front of every masterpiece, bringing the flow of visitors to a halt. Doug sidled and excused his way through the throng, skipping what he had paid to see before stopping. A wheelchair was blocking his path. In it sat what at first looked like a hairless, albino monkey. Could a person really look this bad and still be alive? Though he was probably no older than Ray. One glance at what the poor guy's glistening gaze was fixed upon—a cattle skull painted in stark tones—and Doug twisted away, eager to bolt for the coat check. But he restrained himself. He turned back around and studied the sickly man's face. Head tilted back, lips slightly parted, eyes wide open—like the epitome of contemplative serenity. And without a hint of self-pity or fear. Doug faced the painting and soon also lost himself in the admiration of its contour, color, and clarity.

At a throaty, "Excuse me, Sir," Doug stepped aside and let the wheelchair pass, reciprocating the plucky fellow's nod and smile. It was high time he got himself to Ray's.

He trotted all the way to the Chicago River and by clutching the railing pulled himself across the bridge. The outside door to Marina City's lakeside tower was indeed open just as Ray had promised. The husky elevator attendant checked Doug over askance while pretending to read a scribbled note.

"I'm a guest of Raymond McNulty," Doug told him. The guy's poker face relaxed into a toothy grin, and he grabbed a telephone from the wall and dialed. "Who should I say is calling, Sir?"

"Douglas Borrud."

Doug overheard a tinny, old man's voice croak, "Send him straight up."

As the elevator ascended the sixty stories, Doug's heart thumped, as if it wanted to escape from his chest. He gently fingered the shaving nick, the dried blood crumbling like loam. The lift eased to an almost imperceptible rest, the doors opened, and he led himself off like a condemned convict, but then hesitated. And there he stood staring at the rough stucco wall, as if trying to decipher a cryptic message written upon it.

A full five minutes he lingered in the circular hallway, lightly tapping the tiny cut. It was trivial, he kept telling himself, nothing really, a stupid accident he made every other week, so why was he making such a fuss? Because like the tiniest breach in a Dutch dike, it threatened to let in all the ruinous seas. But it wouldn't, would it, if he kept enough distance from Raymond? Say, by not sharing the same couch or drinking from the same cup, or using his silverware, and, above all, by not giving him an embrace.

The elevator doors split again, and a trim woman about his age in scarlet jogging clothes got off, key already in hand. Pointedly avoiding his gaze, she stepped behind him, and with a deft insertion, opened the adjacent door, and darted inside. After slipping on her chain lock, she inched the door back and gaped at Doug with one large, hazel eye. "May I help you?" she asked.

"I'm looking for the apartment of Raymond McNulty."

"Oh, we're so sorry about what happened to Danny." Her lone eye kept scrutinizing Doug, especially his slender torso and pale face. "It's that door to your right. Please give Ray our condolences. We hope he's doing okay."

Long after the neighbor had shut the door and snapped the dead bolt, Doug still stood there, mentally rehearsing all the measures he would take to remain safe. Scenes from his mother's funeral drifted to mind. He deeply regretted not having spent that last year by her side, even though he had managed to get there at the end. Sure, he had called her daily from Ohio and avowed his love, but in retrospect that felt so paltry.

But was where she had gone that awful? In light of how she had lived and what kind of person she had been, he sensed not. By example, she had shown that leaving this world was as natural, and no more frightening than entering it. But what if it occurred among strangers, no matter how kind they might be? Doug rapped on the door.

A frail voice on the other side wheezed, "Yes?"

"It's Doug, Ray."

A latch clacked, a chain lock clicked, and the door edged halfway back to reveal a long, narrow, emaciated face. "Raymond?" Doug ventured. This old man's moist eyes appeared to be sinking into a shriveling head, yet their dark chestnut color and piercing gaze were unmistakably Ray's.

"You're early," Raymond rasped. He looked like a human scarecrow in pleated charcoal gray woolen slacks and a Brooks Brothers button-down pink shirt.

"No," Doug said, "I'm late." All of a sudden he burst forward and hugged his dear friend with all his might.

"Careful, careful," Raymond whispered, but Doug wouldn't let go—his neglect of their friendship through Ray's ordeal was racking him with guilt. Minutes after pressing his cheek into Ray's tears, Doug remembered the shaving nick he had resolved to protect. Too late. But at least he had finally shown his friend how he truly felt.

"Where'd all the furniture go?" His last visit this place had been stuffed with antiques.

"Danny and I had to sell most of it to pay his medical bills."

Doug squelched an automatic "I'm sorry" for fear of sounding inane.

"Where's your suitcase?" Raymond said, squinting his rheumy eyes.

"Oh, the airline lost it. I mean, they misplaced it. I'm sure it'll turn up."

Ray paused a full minute to take that statement in, as if his quick mind had at long last slowed. "Let me show you to your room," he finally said. Doug dutifully followed. How was he going to break the awkward news about already checking into the Hilton? "I'm sure I have a spare toothbrush for you somewhere. Your towels and a washcloth are lying on the pillow."

It was Danny's bed and Danny's room, though the only trace of him left was a high school graduation picture on the wall. Dark, neat, Princeton-cut hair and smooth skin years from its first wrinkle and a disarming, guileless smile. Danny's natural warmth and constant good cheer had been easy to like, yet his utter lack of irony or sarcastic wit had always made him seem an odd partner for Raymond. No matter, they had gotten along famously throughout their brief years together, and Ray had stood by him all the way to the end. For a fleeting moment Doug envied Danny for not having had to die alone. Because if he didn't find himself a good woman and pull his life together soon that would be his own fate.

"He was handsome, wasn't he?" Ray said. "A gorgeous saint. But was his death ever miserable."

"Raymond," Doug said, facing his friend, "United didn't lose my luggage. It's sitting in my room at the Hilton."

Ray's gaze locked on Doug with a fierce glare.

"My flight got in this forenoon, and since then I've been touring Chicago. Or at least, I've been trying to."

Raymond's stare was merciless.

"Ray, please forgive me. I know I've been a shitty friend."

Raymond kept silent until tears began to trickle from Doug's eyes. "You never did like Danny much, did you?"

"No, I liked him. Really. He was one of the nicest guys I've ever met."

Ray snorted, revealing a flicker of a grin. "One thing you and I have always agreed upon is that nice is not enough. He was a sweet dweeb. And, boy, was he sweet."

Doug stood there quietly crying over the pain Raymond had gone through without his support. "Please don't hate me," he said, "for not having been there for you with Danny."

"Hate you? I've cursed you, I've damned you, I've reviled you, but I"—Ray paused as his own eyes filled with tears, and he lifted his skinny arms and reached out—"but I could never hate a dear, old friend. Besides, I don't have time to hold a grudge."

Doug jumped into Raymond's embrace, and in each other's warm grip they both freely wept.

Finally, the soft tenor Doug had been hearing on the phone for years, if not face to face for far too long, murmured into his ear, "Consider yourself forgiven."

"God bless you."

"Don't forget you're not religious. Now I have two favors to ask."

"Certainly."

"First of all, may we sit down? I don't have the energy to stand very long anymore."

So they seated themselves close on the couch, and Ray went on, "I recently made an appointment in Amsterdam." Doug glanced at the coffee table and spotted a stack of Hemlock Society magazines. He picked up the topmost issue and skimmed its table of contents. Alas, these periodicals were precisely what he feared.

O Lord God, have mercy.

"So my second request is this," Ray said. "Will you fly with me there, carry my ashes back, and place them in the family niche?"

Doug folded his hands as if in prayer and uttered a barely audible, "No."

"No?"

"No, I won't go with you to Amsterdam. But I'll tell you what I'll do." Doug hesitated before continuing. "You know that I've got an empty bedroom back home in Ohio. Ray, will you come live with me?"

Raymond blinked, bit a lip, took a deep breath, and whispered, "Okay." And then quipped, "But not indefinitely."

They both chuckled.

Midway

"King! King!" echoed inside Dean Haugen's mind, the insult lashing the thirteen-year-old boy like slaps across the face. Yet his nimble fingers never quit plucking strawberries without squeezing and placing the precious fruit into six quart boxes inside his wooden tray. If there was one thing Daddy couldn't stand, it was blowing money on fancy food. But Dean had never asked to eat cube steak, though he did relish the chewy beef.

He glanced up ahead at a grove of spindly pines, concealing a cooing mourning dove. He felt a crazy urge to sprint for the Black River, flowing just behind the trees, and plunge straight in. But what about the drop-offs, water snakes, and snapping turtles Daddy kept warning him about? Still, just once in his life he'd love to take a dip in that murky stream. Just like he ached to turn sixteen so he could apply to become stock boy at the Piggly Wiggly or IGA groceries. But till that day came, picking strawberries in June like this for Mr. Halverson and string beans next month for Mr. Jessup were the best jobs available. The place—rural Jackson County in west central Wisconsin. The year—1958, midway through President Eisenhower's second term.

Okay, Deanie Boy, he told himself, think about something more pleasant while you work. But what? Janet Bue's curly blonde hair, azure eyes, and toothy grin came to mind. Hadn't General Science been his favorite class the past year because his desk sat right beside the cutest girl in the whole junior high? Alas, stuck-up Janet knew just how pretty she was.

His red-stained fingers never stopped moving among the saw-toothed leaves of the ground-hugging plants. When he finished stripping the half-row on his right, he did the same for the bushes on his left. Once all the vines within reach were picked clean, he slid his tray ahead three feet, scooted forward on his knees, and resumed picking. So it would go all that Saturday. So it went every day of the week during strawberry season except for Sundays.

He peeled his jeans off his sweaty thighs. Too bad Janet wasn't out here working too. Not that the daughter of a hardware store owner like Mr. Bue actually had to earn money to help buy clothes for school, not like Dean and other kids from poor families. Which meant Janet had all the time in the world to play with her snooty friends like Bonnie Larson. Dean's scalp prickled to recall how Bonnie and Janet had laughed last winter when Lenny Quick had mocked Dean's worn-out shoes. But his folks couldn't afford to buy him a new pair, not with their high heating oil bills. Of course a snot like Lenny never had to think twice about stuff like that, not when his dad was President of the Jackson County Bank.

Okay, thinking about Janet was a mistake. Still, try as he might, Dean couldn't stop seeing her adorable face, even though he was actually on Mr. Halverson's farm, five miles outside of his little hometown, Black River Falls.

Dean popped a strawberry in his mouth and sucked on it. The firm Beaver variety the kids were harvesting that day tasted tart, not like the softer, smaller, more delicious Sparkles they had picked midweek. Not that Dean swiped many from Mr. Halverson's crop, not when he wouldn't get paid for whatever he ate, but every picker sneaked at least a few.

A fly buzzed near his ear. Like the drone of propellors, only higher pitched. He shut his eyes and pictured a tight formation of U.S. Navy Douglas Dauntless dive-bombers, heading for the Japanese fleet bearing down on Midway Island in World War Two. Though Dean knew full well how the key battle would come out from reading *The Miracle of Midway*, he still relished replaying the details of the improbable American victory. On June 4th, 1942. Sixteen years ago that very month, three years before Dean was born.

He frowned at the fruit stains on his denim knees. But what else after crawling up and down a patch all day? The half dozen boxes in his tray were already filled level, but Mr. Halverson insisted the berries be heaped close to the handle to allow for what he called settling. Which was a lot of bull, because that meant Mr. Halverson ended up with seven quarts per tray, while only punching a picker's card for six. Like last summer, the pay was seven cents a box, as long as you stuck out the entire season and waited till the very end to get paid. As a result, Dean was earning up to three bucks per day. Good money, enough eventually to buy himself new school shirts and slacks and maybe even a pair of shoes. "Br-r-r-r," Dean softly trilled, vibrating his lips in imitation of the Navy planes about to wreak havoc.

Long after four Japanese aircraft carriers—the *Akagi*, *Hiryu*, *Kaga*, and *Siryu*—were sunk yet again, Dean was still picking away, only now with a grin. He prided himself on picking the fastest, just as he did on earning the best grades in school. Miss Hart, his fifth-grade teacher, had impressed upon him the need to earn straight A's every year, if he had any hope of making it to college, since his parents couldn't help him out with the expenses. Because without scholarships, he'd never go.

To get his mind off that bleak prospect, he thought about baseball. The Milwaukee Braves were having another strong season after defeating the New York Yankees in seven games to win the World Series of 1957. Above all, thanks to spitballer Lou Burdette then, after their southpaw ace Warren Spahn faltered. Herky-jerky Lou's pitching heroics made Dean yearn to stand up right there in the patch and go into the stretch like he was holding a runner on first base. Of course he did no such thing, not while working out here. Some day he hoped to see the Braves play in person. But till then he'd follow the team on the radio and study the box scores and batting averages in *The La Crosse Tribune.*

"Here you go, Deanie," straw boss Mrs. Torgerson piped up out of nowhere and dropped a handful of ripe berries into his tray with a kindly smile. His stomach sank. He'd missed that many in his pair of half-rows?

"Dean?" Brenda Bakken said from three rows over and behind him, once Mrs. Torgerson had moved on. Like Sally Bills on her right, Brenda lived on the rundown Eastside. Only twelve years old, both girls were a class behind Dean, and still short and scrawny. Not like Janet Bue, who had filled out nicely during the seventh grade. "You going to the Strawberry Festival tonight?" Brenda asked. The annual affair was held every June in nearby Alma Center, an even smaller town than Black River Falls. Shirley Whitedeer didn't even look up, but then Winnebago Indians never went to such doings. They wouldn't feel comfortable there nor would they be welcome.

Glancing away from Brenda's bashful grin, Dean shook his head. Of course she and Sally weren't going either. How could they when their folks, like his, didn't own a car? He supposed he could ride his bike the twelve miles to Alma Center, but then he'd have to pedal that same distance home. After dark, it'd be dangerous biking on the highway. Just as well, since he was ashamed of being seen on his rusty, one-speed Schwinn anymore. But he was willing to bet Janet Bue was going with her folks, just like that jerk Lenny Quick. Had a one of those spoiled kids ever earned a red cent? Had any of them ever bought their own clothes? The more Dean thought about his tormentors, the more he yearned to ask Mr. Halverson for all the pay he had coming, hop a freight train like Billy Johnson's older brother had done, and ride it to kingdom come.

Instead he jerked to his feet with another heaping tray and hustled to the packing stand without spilling a single berry. If only things could be like they'd been back in the sixth grade. One recess then the week Dean turned twelve, kids in his class had gotten sick of playing Kickball and Pom-Pom-Pullaway and decided to give Girls Chase the Boys a try. The rules were simple—the girls chased the boys till they tagged every last one. When that turned out to be too easy, they switched to tackling them on the grass. As the fastest runner in grade school, Dean ended up the final boy caught. Of course no girl could catch him by herself. Eventually though, Donna Glover, Barbara Mattson, Mary Alice Nelson, Sharon Bergdahl, and Nancy Nemec surrounded Dean, grabbed hold, pulled him down, and dogpiled atop him—till Mrs. Severson put a halt to the squirming fun.

Had that really happened? You betcha. Back when he still felt comfortable around girls. Not like now, when he could barely bring himself to talk to them. Not like the old days, when he'd always had a girlfriend, who in fact was merely a special recess playmate.

How could there be such a huge difference between twelve and thirteen? One year a grade school big deal, the next a junior high nobody. All because he had grown eight inches and gotten clumsy and slow afoot. And Daddy had lost his job at the plastic factory, and the family was forced to move out of the decent house they had rented up on Price Hill into their current dump in the Grove. Dean still hadn't made any new friends in their low-lying neighborhood near the river. But then had he honestly tried?

Finally, the long day of berry picking came to an end, and Dean and the other kids climbed into the open back of Mr. Halverson's pickup for the ride home. While the truck bounced and swayed and Brenda and Sally giggled and sang, "You Are My Sunshine," Dean closed his eyes and imagined those U.S. Navy dive-bombers, peeling out of formation to launch their devastating attack on the Japanese carriers. The Battle of Midway, the turning point of World War Two in the Pacific theater.

When Mr. Halverson dropped off scrawny Brenda and Sally at the Texaco station on the Eastside, they both gave Dean a big wave and skipped off. Hardscrabble folks called this part of town, because it was even more rundown than where the Haugens lived. Mr. Halverson drove across the lone bridge spanning the Black River, a block down Main Street, turned left into the Grove, and stopped in front of a shabby, little house with a gray, asphalt-shingle exterior. "See you Monday, Deanie," Mr. Halverson told his prize picker. Which meant Dean was free for the rest of that Saturday and all day Sunday.

The first thing he did inside the humble Haugen home was climb into the tub for his weekly bath, taken with only a couple inches of hot water, to save on bills like Daddy insisted. He had to scrub hard to get all the strawberry stains off.

Supper was a simple meal of buttered blueberry muffins and whole milk, eaten in gloomy silence with his parents. Dean frowned at his father's frayed blue bib overalls and his mother's faded flower-print house dress. "We can't afford cube steak every night, King," Daddy snarled.

Dean knew better than to reply. He sure wouldn't mind if Daddy went back to eating on his own out in the garage, like he'd done all that spring.

"The Strawberry Festival's this weekend," Mom piped up with her cheerful, chirping voice. Like Daddy, Dean didn't respond. Sure, he'd love to attend, but without a ride how was he going to get there? So the real question was what was he going to do instead between now and Monday morning? If they'd still been living up on Price Hill like last year, he'd have played with his old gang—Bobby, Glenn, Dave, and Tom.

After supper, he mixed eight cups of water and one of sugar together with a package of grape Kool-Aid flavoring. The resulting purple solution he poured into an aluminum ice cube tray and balanced toothpicks at an angle in a corner of each square to use as handles for homemade popsicles. Once he had slid the concoction into the freezer, he joined Daddy in their cramped front room furnished with a ratty davenport, pair of worn-out easy chairs, and bulky oil stove, and turned on the small black-and-white TV. Dean set his feet on the oval throw rug Mom had woven from rags and waited for the picture tube to warm up. Soon he and Daddy were staring at a flickering Coulee Region weather map on a snowy screen. Like everybody else in town with a television, the Haugens had one antenna on their roof pointing southwest toward La Crosse and another northwest toward Eau Claire, the two available stations. Towns of fifty thousand each, La Crosse and Eau Claire were as big as cities got in Dean's world. Both an hour's drive from Black River Falls, he had visited each once, thanks to riding along with Uncle Nordahl and Aunt Stella.

After a local report, the NBC evening news came on with Chet Huntley and David Brinkley. Thank goodness it lasted only a quarter hour. Because no matter what the announcers said about President Eisenhower or Secretary of State John Foster Dulles, Daddy clenched his fists and cursed under his breath in Norwegian, while Dean squirmed. If only he could get himself to the Strawberry Festival, but how?

"Why don't you go for a dip at the city pool, Deanie Boy?" Mom chirped from her perch atop a stool at the kitchen sink, where she was washing dishes. Admission there was free.

Dean stared at the President on TV, bald on top as a baby. But only little kids used the city pool. And whatever he was at thirteen, he certainly was no longer one of those, not at five foot ten inches and growing. Mom just didn't understand, and he wasn't about to explain. Still, he loved swimming as much as ever. Because even if he had lost his once tremendous foot speed after shooting up in height the past year, he could still swim like a fish. But where, if not in the public pool? Most folks swam at Lake Arbutus, as far away from Black River Falls as the Strawberry Festival, and so just as out of reach.

"How about going to the show, Deanie?" his mother said.

The Falls Theater was only a couple of blocks away. But Dean had already seen *The Creature from the Black Lagoon* and wasn't about to spend another fifteen cents to see the horror film again. Though he had sure had liked the scene where the monster swam underwater and ogled beautiful Julie Adams in her tight, white swimsuit.

"You could get a cherry coke at the drugstore fountain," his mother tried next.

That'd only cost a nickel. After all, other kids wasted fistfuls of coins on Topp's bubble gum with baseball trading cards or little wax coke bottles containing sweet syrup or boxes of Good and Plenty licorice candies. But Dean refused to blow any of his hard-earned dough on junk. Because he knew full well his folks needed help buying him school clothes. He glared at the holes in his Converse sneakers and the black spots worn in the linoleum underfoot.

Dean groaned when *Father Knows Best* came on, and Daddy threw him a nasty glare. Boy, that was one stupid program, more unreal than a Tom and Jerry cartoon. *Perry Mason* was on the other channel, but Daddy would never watch a show about a big-shot lawyer. Dean quietly stood up, climbed the steep, narrow stairs to his room, plopped down on the bed, and stared at the ceiling. Through the open register, the phony TV father said, "Pumpkin, don't ever doubt that your mother and I love you dearly." Dean grabbed his public library book, *The Miracle of Midway*, off the floor. Miraculous because the victory was so unlikely in light of Japanese superiority in carriers and planes. Yet the Americans had pulled it off.

He could never read enough about World War Two. Even as a little kid, he had no interest in silly children's literature, not when there were books about soldiers, sailors, and airmen to devour. Uncle Donald, the relative he seldom saw was actually serving on the carrier *Lexington*, when the Japanese sank it during the Battle of the Coral Sea, and had to swim for it to survive.

"Deanie Boy!" Mom hollered up the staircase. "You could go to the A and W for a root beer!"

That he could. But right now he would rather read about the doomed *Akagi*, *Hiryu*, *Kaga*, and *Soryu*, and the great American naval triumph, only six months after the sneak attack on Pearl Harbor. What most appealed to Dean about World War Two was how much went wrong early on, but everything still turned out well in the end.

Come to think of it, he was thirsty. A baby mug would only cost a nickel. Still, he hated the idea of folks seeing him drinking a kiddy-size root beer. "Bud, just call Mary Jane and invite her to the prom," the phony TV father told his fake son downstairs. "You can use my car." That did it. Dean stomped down the stairwell and headed for the front door.

"Don't go anywhere near the river!" Daddy yelled. "Not with all the drop-offs, water snakes, and snapping turtles!"

"You listen to your father, Deanie Boy," Mom told him, only her tone was sweet.

Dean sure wished his dad could be more like his mother's father, a nice old man who smelled of cigars and spoke English with a thick Norwegian accent. Grandpa Simonson used to give Dean a nickel every time he visited. Grandma was just as kind. A shame both grandparents had passed away.

Dean carefully closed the front screen door behind him so the spring didn't snap shut. A swift three-block walk through downtown and he was marching across the bridge that slanted uphill to the opposite bank. Midway, he paused to admire the dam upstream. None of its six gates were open, but dark brown water, the Black River's true color, was pouring over the spillway and smashing the red granite boulders beneath it.

"Out of the way, Slick," a kid called out. Bristling, Dean pressed himself against the railing and let Lenny Quick race past on the sidewalk atop a shiny, new, three-speed English bike. Smart of the nincompoop not to ride on the road here, not when the bridge handled all the traffic from Highways 12, 27, and 54 combined. Highway 12 saw the most cars, but then it was the main link between Chicago and the Twin Cities.

To Dean's relief, Lenny kept pedaling past the A and W at the top of the bridge. When Dean reached the root beer stand, his stomach sank to see a big, black Buick with three little side vents parked beneath the elms. No mistaking that car, not in little Black River Falls. So the Bues had come for a cold refreshment too. Before the family headed to the Strawberry Festival, he bet. Sure enough, there sat Janet in the back seat, looking cute as ever. Wishing he hadn't worn his slacks with the knee patches, Dean just stood there, forcing the hustling carhops to detour around him.

"Oh, no," Dean said when Lenny Quick came riding back this way and turned into the parking lot. Lenny pulled up beside the Bues' Buick, and Janet gave her pal a toothy grin and a big wave. Dean considered heading straight home, but that would look dumb after coming this far. So with a prickling scalp he walked up to the stand window and ordered a large frosty mug, even if that cost a dime—twice as much as he had planned on spending. He lugged the thick glass to the farthest picnic table and sat down with his back to Janet and Lenny, giggling together like fools. The fizzy root beer burned all the way down, especially as fast as Dean was gulping it. Out of the way, slick? Didn't that numbskull Quick realize he was yay far from a knuckle sandwich right in the kisser?

The instant Dean downed the last drops of his root beer, he jumped up, leaving the empty mug on the picnic table instead of politely returning it as usual. Muttering to himself about thumping Quick's head so hard the jerk would think it had stopped a Hank Aaron line drive, he charged back down the bridge. For a passing moment, he had the crazy notion of grasping the railing and flinging himself onto the rocks below. Instead he jammed both hands into his pockets and hurried on.

Back home in the Grove, Mom and Daddy were watching *The Lawrence Welk Show* on TV. Talk about old fogey music. Dean stomped upstairs to his room and tuned the radio to WLS in Chicago. The Everly Brothers' hit, "All I Have To Do Is Dream," came on, their crooning harmony so sweet it was almost sickening. Dean snapped the radio off and grabbed the library copy of *Huckleberry Finn* off the floor and lost himself in the story. If only he could float down the Mississippi himself. Fifteen pages later he laid the book across his chest and stared at the flowery wallpaper. The novel wasn't all made up, was it? Mark Twain had put much of his boyhood into the book.

All of a sudden Dean lowered himself onto the linoleum and reached far beneath his bed for the spiral notebook he had written half-full just since spring. He turned to the blank page after the last story he had created and began scribbling a new tale entitled, "No Defects," about a rich couple named Mr. and Mrs. Crick, who bought a new-fangled robot to do their housework. The inventor assured them the machine was perfectly safe, but because it lacked human feelings, it mistakenly butchered their darling son, Kenny, and served him for supper. Did the parents ever find the unusual pot roast delicious. Dean cackled.

"What'd I tell you about burning lights, King?" Daddy barked up the stairwell.

Dean didn't reply. If there was one thing Daddy couldn't stand, it was anybody talking back to him, especially when he was in a bad mood, and when was he anything but lately? Dean didn't turn off the lights either, not while the words were flowing so freely. Daddy's mood sure could improve though, whenever Uncle Nordahl stopped by and took his sister's brother fishing. Daddy's brother-in-law drove a rickety 1949 Dodge that barely ran well enough anymore to reach the cranberry marshes in eastern Jackson County full of crappies, sunfish, bluegills, and perch. Dean tagged along once, but so hated putting a minnow wriggling for its life in his grasp onto his hook he never went again.

Dean kept writing away, while downstairs Daddy barked, "King!" and cursed in Norwegian till Mom began to weep. Finally, Daddy shut up, and the back screen door groaned, which meant he had gone out to the garage for the night. After finishing the new story, Dean lay in his bed and stared at the ceiling, while only seeing Janet's adorable grin. Even if she stopped being so stuck-up, what exactly would the two of them do together? Since he wouldn't feel comfortable talking to her, though he had chatted easily with other cute girls from kindergarten through the sixth grade. But now whenever he tried, he felt like he was standing on a gigantic stage and the whole world was watching. Which didn't make sense because two years before he had stood at the foot of the Black River bridge in plain sight of everyone beside the old cannon and counted out-of-state license plates passing by and not minded in the least how many people had seen him. Some drivers had even smiled and waved.

He turned the radio back on and dialed it to the soothing voice of the Braves play-by-play announcer. "Outside, ball four," Earl Gillespie said, the disappointment in his voice a sign Milwaukee was out in the field. "Spahnie looks the runner back," Earl said when the next batter came up. "Here comes the pitch. Strike one. Screwball, outside corner." The hubbub between pitches from the unseen stadium crowd was such a comforting sound, so unlike the long silences in the Haugen household, where Daddy lashed out over the least noise. Which is why Dean had long since learned control every bit as good as the southpaw pitching ace, only what Dean controlled was himself.

He kept listening till the bottom of the ninth when Earl Gillespie crowed, "Going, going, gone! Eddie Mathews hit it out! Braves win! Braves win!" Dean fell asleep to visions of the home run. Soon he was dreaming about kneeling between two rows of strawberries and plucking fruit so fast his quart boxes filled faster than an ice cube tray under a faucet. He glanced up and there came Janet Bue, crawling toward him with a huge grin. They met knee to knee and gazed into each other's eyes. She took the biggest berry from his tray, bit off half, the juice reddening her pale pink lips, and handed Dean the rest to devour. No berry ever tasted sweeter.

Dean awoke before dawn like he'd done Monday through Saturday, only this time with a blissful smile—till he realized that had only been a dream about Janet. Worse, today was Sunday, his least favorite day of the week. Because Janet was Lutheran too, and she always sat up front in Sunday School with her nose high in the air, refusing to give Dean the time of day. He wrapped the pillow around his head and dozed back off—till the radio blaring downstairs startled him awake. Mom had turned on the first of the Sunday services she always listened to. "There is no salvation but through the blood of Jesus!" a man was hollering over the airwaves. Obviously no Lutheran to be ranting like that—or Methodist or Roman Catholic, for that matter. The three main churches of Black River Falls.

"Time for breakfast, Deanie Boy!" Mom called up the stairwell.

He stumbled out of bed and got dressed. Down in the kitchen he ate a fried egg, two pieces of toast, and a glass of whole milk. What his mother served him every morning. Daddy didn't show his face, though of course he was long since up out in the garage. Dean didn't mind. Once he finished the meal, he took out his modeling clay, knelt down on the front room linoleum, and rolled and kneaded and flattened his favorite toy till he had made himself four red, oblong rectangles—the *Akagi*, *Hiryu*, *Kaga*, and *Siryu*.

"Brothers and sisters in Christ, let's get one thing straight," Pastor Downing shouted from the kitchen. Though the man called himself a minister, everybody knew he was really a roofer and handyman. But at least the guy had a steady income. "Nobody can enter the Kingdom of God with a Bible in one hand and a bottle of beer in the other."

"Amen," the radio congregation responded.

"Amen," Dean's mother echoed from atop a stool at the kitchen sink. Once she finished washing dishes, she would mop the floor and bake bread. And that night baby-sit for the Bergstrom kids, while their big-shot folks ate out at Castle Hill—like she did every Sunday evening. And Dean would be stuck at home alone with nothing better to do than watch *The Ed Sullivan Show* on TV with Daddy or read alone in his room.

"Br-r-r-r," thirteen-year-old Dean trilled, vibrating his lips in imitation of the approaching Douglas Dauntlesses. Would the U.S. Navy dive-bombers achieve complete surprise? Yes, as long as the clouds pictured on the front room wallpaper didn't break up before they launched their assault. At that moment the Japanese planes were up on deck getting armed with torpedoes for attacking the American carriers. Talk about lucky timing.

"Rock of ages, cleft for me," the radio congregation wailed. "Let me hide myself in thee." If Mom couldn't walk up to the church on Price Hill on account of her bum knee, at least she could listen to broadcast services, be they Holy Roller or Methodist or Lutheran.

"Br-r-r-r," Dean trilled as the dive-bombers emerged from the clouds in perfect formation. His open hand, representing one plane, rolled out of formation into a steep dive. "Wah-ooo! Wah-ooo!" he wailed in imitation of the sirens sounding on board the Japanese ships. But it was too late for evasive action. He swooped his dive-bombing fingers a foot above the make-believe ships on the linoleum floor and dropped a clay bomb that barely missed. Darn. But the second plane landed its ordnance midship. "Bull's-eye!" he shouted and gleefully inflicted damage by peppering holes in the carrier with a toothpick.

"Look at King! Playing on the floor like a little kid!" Daddy yelled from the kitchen doorway and cursed in Norwegian. Dean swept up the clay ships and bombs and squished them together. "Why isn't King in church?" his father hollered.

Because there wasn't any Sunday school over the summer. Because no kids attended actual services without their parents. "I said why aren't you in church?" his father bellowed.

Dean shrugged. He supposed he could have asked Daddy the same question, but of course didn't. He hustled into the kitchen, away from his father's snarling, "Listen to me, King!" To judge from the deep fat sizzling in the frying pan on the black, cast-iron wood stove, Mom was making doughnuts, one of Dean's favorite treats.

"How's Deanie Boy?" Mom asked sweetly, her high-pitched voice barely audible over the bleating radio choir.

"Fine," Dean muttered and took out the metal tray of frozen Kool Aid from the freezer. He pressed down hard on its long handle and crunched the big cubes free. After grabbing one by a toothpick handle, he put the rest back, stomped upstairs, flung himself on his bed, and sucked on his homemade popsicle. Why'd Daddy have to come into the house and spoil his fun? Since he spent most of his time of late out in the garage, fiddling in his workshop, lying on his cot and listening to the Braves or reading biographies borrowed from the public library. Better that than have him in the house bawling Mom and him out. Sure, Daddy was mowing lawns around town and doing other odd jobs, but still not earning much. Which was why Mom had to keep washing big-shots' floors and babysitting. Dean's face burned with shame at the thought of his parents' menial work. Especially when Janet's dad owned a hardware store and Lenny's ran a bank.

The past year Dean had done the grocery shopping for Mom at the nearby Piggly Wiggly on Main Street, since Daddy refused to help out. When your family didn't own a car, you had no choice but to go on foot and lug what you bought home. Which was why the Haugens lived so close to downtown, two houses past Langley's funeral home.

At the groan of plumbing pipes downstairs, Dean's face lit up. Because that meant Daddy was drawing a bath. He grabbed a plastic pill-bottle cap and a baseball bat broken in half lengthwise from his closet and slipped out the back door, taking care not to let it snap shut. If there was one thing Daddy couldn't stand, it was sudden loud noises. Though he hadn't always been like this, not while they lived up on Price Hill, back when he had a steady job.

Holding the bat in his left hand and the bottle cap in his right, Dean faced the gravel driveway. "Eddie Mathews steps to the plate," he said just like the Milwaukee Braves announcer. "Drysdale looks the runner back to first base. Here comes the pitch." Dean tossed the stopper two feet up into the air, shouted, "Eddie takes a wicked cut! And connects!" He thwacked the plastic piece hard, sending a line drive arcing toward the garage. "Going, going, gone!" Dean cheered. But instead of hitting its door harmlessly as expected, the plastic cap curved and landed right in the potato patch. "Oh, no," Dean moaned, since he couldn't simply go and retrieve it. If there was one thing Daddy couldn't stand, it was anybody but him stepping in his garden. Which meant Dean had no choice but to leave the cap where it was for now. But he'd definitely have to get it before Daddy weeded again. Maybe after dark with the help of a flashlight.

Inside, Mom was still at the kitchen sink, her stool planted right on the linoleum piece cut out around the door to the tiny root cellar for storing raw potatoes and rutabagas and canned tomatoes, pears, apple sauce, and pickles. Dean grabbed a hot, greasy doughnut and darted up the steep staircase to munch away on his bed. It embarrassed him that their old house lacked both a basement and a furnace. Though at least he had this crummy room all to himself, even if it was freezing in winter and sweltering in summer.

He picked up his book on the Battle of Midway and again immersed himself in the unlikely victory. He dozed off to the acrid smell of burning flight decks, only to be startled awake when downstairs Daddy hollered, "King has really done it now!"

"Deanie Boy was just playing," Mom pleaded.

"King thinks he can do whatever he wants!" Daddy bellowed.

"What harm can there be in a plastic bottle cap?" Mom shouted back.

"King!" Daddy taunted again and again, like Dean was hopelessly spoiled. It must have been truly awful for his father growing up with eight siblings on a hardscrabble homestead west of town. But what about as an adult now with only a fourth-grade education? "I don't want King anywhere near my garden again!" Daddy yelled. Which was the same as saying don't ever play in the yard since every place else the lawn was so narrow. Dean wrapped the pillow tightly around his head till all he could make out was the angry tone, but not the words. That American torpedo bomber pilot, who survived being shot down to bob alone out in the ocean and witness his dive-bomber buddies' devastation of the Japanese carriers was one lucky guy. On one lucky day, June 4th, 1942.

Dean unwrapped the pillow. Daddy now was cursing in Norwegian and mixing in "King" every few words. One thing for sure, Dean couldn't stick around home that Sunday. Early Monday morning, Mr. Halverson would pick him up and take him back to the strawberry patch, but till then he needed a different escape.

The city swimming pool wouldn't be open till two that afternoon, not that Dean would go there again, no matter how much he used to relish it. Because only little kids swam there, and he was no longer one of those. Just like he no longer read comic books. Though back when he was small, he had truly enjoyed reading *Batman, Blackhawk,* and *Uncle Scrooge.* In fact, he had loved comics long before he learned to read them, hadn't he?

The Strawberry Festival was still on, but of course there was no way to get himself to Alma Center. He pulled the yellowing lace curtains aside and watched the Petersons next door pile into their Studebaker. Mary Ann Peterson, a high school freshman almost as stuck-up as Janet Bue, though not so cute, was lugging a stack of towels and suntan lotion. Which meant the Petersons were driving to the beach at Lake Arbutus.

All of a sudden Dean stuffed his faded swimsuit into a jeans pocket and hustled downstairs. Mom was on her hands and knees scrubbing the kitchen floor, while listening to a Methodist service. "Where you going, Deanie Boy?" she chirped.

"To get some fresh air," he said and darted out the front door. Since the Peterson car hadn't yet left their driveway, he headed the opposite direction, even though this meant he'd have to march past the funeral home. Thank goodness, snotty Mr. Langley wasn't fussing with his immaculate yard or strutting around in a fancy black suit, a sure sign the jerk had a new stiff. At the corner, Dean turned right toward the IGA and kept going around the block down First Street, before cutting toward the dike. Whenever the snow and ice melted in the spring or rain fell for days, the Black River always swelled, but the low-lying Grove never flooded thanks to this protective wall.

He climbed up onto the dike and loped along the solid mound of earth around the big bend till he was overlooking a beach with a rainbow ribbon of gravel at the river's edge. He gleefully ran down to the water, stuck a hand in, and shivered at its frigid temperature. He grabbed a piece of driftwood roughly the size of a baseball bat, tossed a small chunk of quartz into the air, and whacked it hard with a two-handed swing. The rock flew upstream and knifed into the current with a nifty pfft. A dozen more solid hits followed till he thudded one into the opposite bank. Raising his arms in triumph, Dean circled the bases like Eddie Mathews after that game-winning homer.

He flung his driftwood bat end over end high into the air and watched it stab into the water, only to bob right back. He grabbed stones big as baseballs at his feet and bombarded the floating stick, each kerplunk of a miss sending up a plume. "The *Akagi* is getting away!" Dean yelled, running down the beach and barraging the enemy carrier. Finally, a piece so large he had to heave it like a shot scored a perfect hit, and the Japanese flattop snapped in two. "The *Akagi* is sinking!" he shouted and jumped for joy.

Afterwards, he strolled along the gurgling stream with a huge grin, till he came abreast of a tiny island, growing white birch saplings. Nobody else in sight, Dean whipped off his clothes and tugged on his swimming trunks. He slowly stepped out into the auburn shallows, where glassy minnows emerged from the chilly depths and gave his feet tickling kisses. Little by little, Dean walked out into the river dark as rich dirt, the squishy bottom muck oozing between his toes. The water still felt chilly, but not so freezing as at first. So far not a sign of any drop-offs, water snakes, and snapping turtles. Though the riffling up ahead looked threatening. But couldn't a person swim around any boulder hidden beneath the surface?

Bit by bit he moved farther and farther out, slipping once on a slimy stone, but not falling, as the river crept up his shivering torso. When it finally reached his chest, he dipped his shoulders with a gasp and stayed under till it no longer felt so icy. He marched on till he hit a dreaded drop-off and sank out of sight. Holding his breath, he opened his eyes, but couldn't see a thing in water this murky. No matter. He paddled to the surface with an explosive exhale and swam straight for the swiftest part of channel, where he swung around feet first, relaxed his entire body, again shut his eyes, inhaled the river's rich aroma, and let the surge carry him along like a bobber, free from hook, line, and sinker—at long, long last.

Sensing a change, Dean opened his eyes at the approach of a jutting boulder and met the gaze of a cat-eyed, grayish-brown snake with a banded neck, swimming inches from his nose. The fellow creature stared back without anger or fear. No threat, no danger from either. A dip of its head and the river serpent disappeared.

Two strong strokes sent Dean around the big rock and the snapping turtle sunning itself atop it. Like darning needles with glistening wings, dragonflies hovered close to his face before darting off. "Kee-aah!" a red-tailed hawk, soaring overhead, shrieked. Closing his eyes with a blissful grin, Dean gently bounced with the current—just as he once had as a little tyke on Daddy's knee, back when his father read comic books and adventure tales aloud to him every day till little Deanie couldn't wait to learn to read himself and before long easily did. So now thanks to Daddy, he adored reading and would continue to do so for the rest of his life. And what about the delightful stories that Daddy had made up, yarns like "Walt's White Thing," "Dog Gone," and "Red Horse"? These inspired young Dean to make up his own tales, which he recorded as soon as he learned how to write and was still doing it. And that is why—despite everything since, especially of late—he truly loved Daddy as much he did Mom or Grandpa and Grandma. Miles to go before this modest river meets the mighty Mississippi, but it surely will. All streams flow into the sea, yet the sea is never full.

Twelve-Point Buck

I'm staring out my dorm window at the white caps the bitter November wind is whipping up on Lake Mendota and playing my clock radio to drown out the noisy Euchre game across the hall. I know I ought to be cramming for my chemistry test, but I can't stop stewing about what happened earlier this year, back home up north in Jackson County, Wisconsin.

"Eldon Onstad?" Mr. Jacobson read last May from my job application and made a face like his bare foot had just stepped on a tack. I squirmed.

The assembly line a thin wall away quit stomping and clanking, and a foreman barged in, shouting, "Another breakdown, Al!" The muffler plant manager jumped up and left me sitting there in his office alone. I seized the chance to spit on a finger and give the scuff on my new oxfords a quick swipe, but it didn't help.

On the wall facing me, a mounted deer with a ten-point rack was hanging alongside a portrait of John F. Kennedy. All squinty-eyed and toothy-smiled, our President looked like Gil Moe, that cousin of mine, who got killed when he rolled his car on a straightaway. Both the picture and the buck head gave me the creeps.

A vehicle came roaring into the parking lot outside. Who should jump out of a beat-up Chevy Bel Air, but Rodney Smith. Before you know it, Rod was plopping down on a chair right beside me. "What you doin' here, Onnie?" he said and flicked a hand through my waxed flattop. "You flunk out of college already?"

I chuckled, glad to have the company. I'd always liked how Rodney called me Onnie from my last name, and not Eldon like everybody else. He and I were only two weeks shy of graduation from Black River Falls high school. After classes together in sophomore Biology and junior English, our senior year we'd been in the same American Problems section. Not that I could ever be close pals with an East Side boy. That's what folks like my Dad and Uncle Oscar called those guys anyway. I'm talking about boys from the wrong side of the river, over in the part of town people call Hardscrabble. Parents claimed those guys were wild, meaning they drank beer, smoked cigarettes, and raised general heck, instead of going out for Boy Scouts and Student Council like my friends and me. But those of us who studied a lot and got A's and B's knew they were good kids at heart, no matter how much adults might rake them down.

When Mr. Jacobson finally returned, he gave our applications a quick onceover and checked out our shoulders and arms. "Okay, you're both hired," he told us. "We work 7:00 to 5:00, Monday through Friday, with an hour off for lunch. Pay is a buck thirty an hour. With time and a half for the overtime."

Rodney smoothed back the sides of his greasy ducktail with his stubby fingers. "So that comes to sixty-one dollars and seventy-five cents a week," he said. "Counting the five hours over forty."

"To the penny," Mr. Jacobson said with a grin. Me, I just shook my head. That was one heck of an arithmetic trick, especially since Rodney had never been known to crack a book or get good grades. You have to admit those are decent wages for a small Wisconsin town in 1963. I planned on saving pretty near every cent I made to help pay expenses at the "U" here in Madison, where I was heading at summer's end. Poor Rodney though got himself hired at the muffler plant for good. Everybody knew he'd be turning most of his dough over to his mom, because ever since his dad passed away when Rodney was only twelve, that's what he'd always done. Whether he'd delivered newspapers or picked strawberries and beans or trimmed Christmas trees or stocked the shelves at the Piggy Wiggly, he'd given his mother and younger brothers all the help he could with rent and groceries, while luckier kids like me were pocketing allowances, what with my dad's Rambler dealership and all.

High school commencement came and went without much of a fuss, and the muffler factory jobs began. My assignment from the start was to move around the plant, filling in for the regular guys, taking turns with their annual two-week vacations. I unloaded sheet metal and cut it. I drove pipes into flanges. I ground welds smooth. I rounded out tubes. I built and filled pallets. I drove the finished mufflers onto the loading dock with a fork lift. Whatever needed doing, I did.

But as a new permanent employee, Rodney didn't rotate anywhere. First thing, he replaced the painter promoted to welder, and off the end of the assembly line was right where he stayed. I can still see him standing there spraying a string of dangling mufflers and grinning over every stoppage that gave his aching shoulders a break. He refused to wear the mask the foreman gave him, not when older guys weren't using them around welding smoke and acid baths.

When I rotated near Rod to wash new mufflers hot off the assembly line, he took to teasing, "Hey, College Boy, can't you keep up?" Actually, I was having occasional trouble. But I didn't mind the razzing, not the way Rodney laughed whenever our gazes met. Then on breaks he began picking up coffee for me.

That's one drink I'd never touched, figuring it was intended only for adults. But it really did perk me up, so I learned to like it.

By the end of June, Rodney and I were not only spending every break together, but lunch hours too. Then the Army sent in a big order for jeep mufflers, and we began putting in evening overtime and eating suppers together on the loading dock. There he started telling me stories about chasing women and hunting deer and buying a wrecked 1957 Bel Air on the cheap and fixing it up himself.

"It looks a lot like Gil Moe's old Chevy," I told him.

"Most likely because it is," he said, cackling.

But then to hear Rod tell it, everything was hilarious. Though when I thought about his stories later at home in bed, they dug under my skin like wood ticks and kept on burrowing. I mean, my cousin Gilbert got killed when he rolled that car. And his funeral was ten times sadder than my grandma's on account of him being so young. I'd like to know how deer hunting's a sport. You tell me how often the deer ever win. As for chasing women, well, in my innocence that sounded like fun, but it bugged me too that what for Rodney was easy as falling off a log for me was impossible.

Still, he kept inviting me to come along, and I kept begging off. Not that I doubted he could show me a heck of a good time, but if my parents ever got wind of it they'd give me a whole lot worse than heck at home. Shoot, they'd blow a gasket if I just got in the same car with an East Side boy, especially without their approval. Which they'd never give.

To tell the truth, I was scared to go out with Rodney. Not on account of his fast driving so much or even the beer drinking, but, well, to be frank, because of his hustling. It wasn't just that he ran around with the wrong kind of girls, but that there were so many of them. To hear him tell it, he was constantly picking them up not just around Black River Falls, but in nearby Melrose,

Hixton, Merrillan, Alma Center, Neillsville, and Hatfield. In other words, practically everywhere in both Jackson and Clark Counties. And if he didn't have his fun with them first try, he did by the second or third. If even one-fourth of his stories were true, that made him the nooky-king supreme where we lived. And where did that leave dorky old Eldon?

Still, if Rod loved chasing girls, there wasn't a one he truly cared for. Sure, some he found more fun than others, but that was the closest he came to saying any were special. Barb, Peggy, Diane, Sharon, Sally, Janet, Shirley, Gracie, Denise, Cindy, Jodie, Sarah, Beth, Kathy, Julie, Vickie, Joanie, Nancy, Ruthie, Mary Alice, Carolyn, Becky, Terry—who can keep track of all their names?

Though I wasn't a total cherry myself, since my junior and most of my senior year I'd gone steady with Marla Amundson. But Marla was a far cry from any of Rodney's gals. Not that she and I didn't really like each other, but she was a good girl saving herself for the man she married. Which once she made it clear could never be me broke us up pretty quick.

But if I'd been around at least some, still I hadn't done much. So that was why I hated it when one day Rod got sick of talking about himself and said, "Okay, let's hear about you and your chicks."

"There's nothing to say," I replied. "Besides, I'm not the kind of guy who kisses and tells."

To which he said, "Skip the kissing and get straight down to the nooky." Somehow I managed to laugh along. Though I suspected Rod knew the shameful truth of my innocence, but was too nice a guy to rub it in.

After Marla and I split up last March, I wasn't really up to dating anyone else, and for the time being that felt okay. Besides, Mom preferred it that way, while Dad didn't dare disagree. But the more I listened to Rod's stories, the more stupid my virginity struck me. If it was so darned great as my Mom claimed, then how come it made me feel so dumb? I mean, I wasn't a cherry due to morality or courage or anything noble, but simply because of cowardice. And I knew Rod was right, when he said some of his women were plenty willing to go out with me too. Say, if I borrowed one of my Dad's new Ramblers and offered to take them out for a ride. So what was holding me back?

I was working on getting up enough nerve to ask out Denise Bailey, a classmate who'd always been friendly, when one Friday behind my back Rod snuck a couple safes into my lunch bucket. One glance at those rubber rings laying on my ham sandwiches scared the bejesus out of me. If Mom spotted those anywhere near me, she'd not only put the kibosh on me going to college, but probably lock me up in a closet for who knew how long.

First thing at work Monday, Rod asked, "Did you use any of the safes?"

"Not yet," I said. Talk about feeling dumber than dirt. Actually, both of them got flushed down the toilet.

After that he and I kept our distance out at the plant for much of the summer, not that we didn't still say hello or smile when greeting. Then one day halfway through August, Rodney made a point of sitting beside me at a picnic table inside the break room. Between bites of his peanut-butter-and-jelly sandwich, he asked, "What if I come by your house this Friday about seven, and I'll show you what's what?"

"I don't know," I replied.

A hurt look came across Rodney's eyes. "You don't think you're better than me, do you, Onnie?"

"No, it's not like that at all. Okay, I'll go." Right away I wanted to take the words back, but it was too late. It was one thing to be afraid of going out with Denise Bailey, but fearing Rodney Smith was nuts. Besides, all we were going to do was ride around and maybe drink a brew or two. Even though I'd never tasted beer before. All I'd do otherwise was sit home with Mom and Dad and watch TV. Or maybe go to a show with Jerry Homstad.

Sure enough at 7:00 on the dot, Rod's beat-up 1957 Bel Air pulled up in front of our Cape Cod with the aluminum siding. My mother took one look out the window and asked, "Why's Jerry Homstad driving that heap of junk?" The dented fenders and rust did look a heck of a lot worse in our neighborhood than out at the plant. I'd never said it was Jerry I was going riding around with, but if that was what Mom wanted to believe, it was fine by me. Not only because Jerry had been our class valedictorian, but also because he never smoked, drank, or chased girls. Even better, his parents belonged to our Evangelical Lutheran Church, the biggest in a county largely settled by Norwegians. I wasn't sure about Rodney's mom, but people said she was a Holy Roller, the only thing worse in my folks' eyes being Roman Catholic.

"I'll have to ask about the car," I said and bolted outside.

Just my luck, Rod's darned passenger door was stuck shut. He let out a cackle, stretched over from behind the wheel, and jerked it open. "Just apply a little elbowgrease next time, Onnie," he said, revving up the engine. "And it'll slip open nice and easy. Just like the chicks are gonna do for us tonight."

Fighting the urge to jump right back out, I tried to laugh, but my mouth was so dry I instead coughed.

Rodney slapped my back. "You gotta cut back on the ciggy-butts, Onnie!" Though he knew full well I never smoked.

"Let's get out of here," I begged, not daring even to glance in the direction of my house.

Rod shifted into gear, hit the gas, and squealed his tires. And swerved off Second Street onto Main Street and zoomed up the bridge across the Black River and along Highway 27 toward Sparta. Not far outside city limits, he steered into the sandy parking lot of a country bar and slid to a halt. "Wait here," he said, so that's what I did. Thank goodness. Like Rodney, I had turned eighteen that spring, so according to Wisconsin law could legally drink inside the state's beer bars, but of course couldn't carry any brews outside of them till I reached twenty-one.

Five long minutes later, he popped back outside with a you-know-what-eating grin and a six-pack of Hamm's stubby throwaways in each hand. It didn't surprise me that the bartender had mistaken him for somebody of age, because he did look older than he was. Just like Mom and Dad both look older than President Kennedy, though they're in fact a year younger.

"This ought to get us started," Rodney said with a wink, fishtailing out of the lot.

"I didn't know these old cars had so much horsepower," I said.

"A '57 Bel Air? Come on, Onnie! Maybe it don't look like much anymore, but it's still got a helluva V-8 engine. Ready for a brew?" He opened himself a bottle with his teeth and took a hearty swig.

"Nah," I said, in no hurry for my very first taste of the stuff. "Does the radio work?" I asked, twisting the knob.

"Nope," Rod said, roaring down Highway 27. All of a sudden a tan patch flashed in front of us, and Rod swerved, braked, and skidded to a halt on the soft shoulder. "Ha, you missed, Bucky!" he hooted at the young deer behind us, holding its twin spikes high and erect. The creature glared at us with big, glassy eyes and trotted back into the woods, my pulse pounding in my ears. Talk about a close call.

Before you know it, we had left the paved road and were bouncing and rocking down two ruts and tearing our way through branches clawing at our fenders and scraping bottom. Eastern Jackson County. The wrong side of the Black River. Not rich black-earth, homesteading land like what my great-grandparents settled west of town, but marshes and flowages and sand and jack pine and scrub oak. Worthless for farming, but pretty in its own way. And though all but empty of people, as crowded with white-tailed deer as anyplace in the state.

We came out onto a narrow gravel fire lane between two neat stands of scotch pine for harvesting eventually as Christmas trees. Rodney turned left and tooled along until we came to a crossroads. There he positioned his Chevy just this side of the junction, poised to barrel off right, left, or straight ahead, depending on which direction the fuzz might show up. We were positive nobody saw us leave the highway, but the cops patrolled this area regularly, hunting for kids out parking or drinking. Darkness was falling fast, like it always does early this late in the summer.

"Ready for a brew now, Onnie?" Rod asked with a wink.

"Okay," I said and swatted at my first mosquito. It didn't take the critters long to find me. The deer flies, whose bites hurt worse, weren't far behind. But the insects weren't bothering him. Or maybe they were, but it wasn't fazing him. Either way was pretty incredible.

Rodney opened me a cold one with his teeth, and I took a swig from it like I'd done this lots of times before. It tasted so bitter and awful I almost upchucked, but I kept at it. Meanwhile, he chugged his second brew like it was Kool-Aid, tossed the empty out the window, and opened himself a third. The skeeters and flies soon had me slapping at my arms and cheeks so often I hardly had the time to drink. It was a welcome excuse.

Rodney lit up a Lucky Strike and blew the smoke right on me. "That ought to keep the bugs off you for a while," he said and downed half his beer with a few loud glugs. "Come on, Onnie. Chug it." I tried to, but it caught on my throat and made me gag and I spit most of it out the window, making Rodney roar. But next try I did better and poured the beverage right down the hatch. With a loud belch, I likewise tossed the empty out the window, where it hit the ground with a shattering smash.

"Somebody's been here before!" Rodney crowed and began to sing, "I'm A Honky-Tonk Man" with a halfway decent voice. Suddenly he lunged forward, jerked on the ignition, gunned the engine, and tore off straight ahead, slamming me forearms first into the dashboard. "A car!" he shouted. "Behind us!"

There was one back there all right, bearing down hard. I grabbed the full six-pack and the two free bottles. "Where should I throw these out?"

"Nowhere!" Rodney yelled. "I paid good money for those! We'll drink them someplace else!"

That someplace else turned out to be just across the county line, safely out of Sheriff Jessup's jurisdiction. We pulled into the East Fork beach, opposite the cottages and boat dock on what folks call Lake Arbutus, though it's really just the dammed-up Black River.

There we sat, watching the full moon shimmer off the glassy water on a windless night, and my pulse gradually returned to normal. Meanwhile, Rodney slowed down with his drinking, like he was giving me a chance to catch up. The beer wasn't tasting half-bad anymore, and I was enjoying how it made me feel. Kind of silly and light-headed, like I didn't have a care in the world. Like if I flunked out at the "U," which I half-expected, it wouldn't matter. I stopped worrying about the mosquitoes and deer flies too. Let them suck my blood and get snockered along with us. There was plenty of joy-juice to go around.

"Rosie, Rosie, Rosie," Rod sang.

"You mean Rose Schermerhorn?" Only the cutest girl in our class, a living doll, and sweet to boot. And a member of my church. Next to knockout Rosie, my Marla was a plain Jane.

"Is there any other Rosie around these parts?"

There was a Rosemary Zielkowski, who'd graduated three classes ahead of us, but last I'd heard she'd married some guy in Stevens Point and had a kid already and another in the oven.

"Have you been dating Rose Schermerhorn too?" I asked with a chuckle. He hadn't mentioned her.

He didn't answer.

"Rodney," I said, "what's your secret? To all your dating, I mean."

He took a deep drag on his Lucky Strike. "My secret is that I don't date. And I don't spend money on women either, except for gas. Though I could get serious about a nice girl like Rosie and maybe even settle down."

I laughed. Rodney settle down? Come to think of it, describing what he did with women as dating was even funnier. Since he just picked them up, took them out parking someplace like the crossroads where we'd first stopped, had his fun, and took them home. If any of them were special, he was up for more of the same. But soon enough he always moved on to somebody different. The craziest thing about it all was that so many girls went for this routine. Why? Just because he was Rodney Smith, I guess. I mean, being with him was really a ball. Scary at times, but scads of fun.

"Rosie won't go out with me anymore," he said. "Not unless I take her to a show or out for supper. Like I'm supposed to be a big spender or something." I didn't have to ask why that was a problem.

"What's Rosie like?" I asked. I hardly even dared say hi to the girl myself.

"She'll say yes to riding around and parking and some kissy face, but no to cranking. And until I get serious about her, she won't even do that much again."

"I see," I said, feeling dumber than a stump. I could hardly believe he was talking about Rose Schermerhorn. It did sound like she had a crush on him.

"Am I ever sick of summer," Rod went on. "I wish it was November already so I could go deer hunting again. I love it when the ground freezes hard as stone and the whitetails leave tracks in the fresh snow. One of these years I'm going to land me a big twelve-point buck. You just wait and see."

I didn't want to talk about hunting, so I shut up.

Staring at the moon's shimmering reflection off the smooth water, he said, "The smallest buck I've ever shot had six points. Two had eight. The ten-pointer last year was the real beaut so far."

"You've bagged four deer?"

"Yup. One each season since I've been old enough to hunt. How about yourself?"

"Me? Oh, I just shot one."

"Well?" he said.

"I'd rather not talk about it."

"Suit yourself," he said with a sigh and hummed another tune. "You know, Onnie, sometimes I wish I had me a new Thunderbird. But then sometimes I wish I could fly like a hawk." He opened me another Hamm's with his teeth. "So how's your love life, Onnie? Stop being so darned quiet."

There was even less I wanted to say about that than my hunting.

"Onnie, beer making you deaf?"

"About the same," I finally answered. That was no lie.

"About the same as what? You mean, about the same as those big red boulders below the Black River dam? I hear they'll budge some day, but probably not before I've gone to the Happy Hunting Grounds."

"Yeah, kind of like that."

"Onnie, the moose juice is making you squirrelly. You ain't making no sense."

I could tell Rod wasn't really making fun of me, but still my inexperience with girls was making my face hot with shame.

"Say, Rodney," I said, eager to change the subject, "if bucks are so darn beautiful, how come guys want to kill them?"

"That's the squirreliest thing you've said yet."

"I mean, I just don't get it."

"Do you get cranking?" he snapped and gave me a look like President Kennedy in that creepy picture at the muffler plant. He chugged the rest of his beer and turned the ignition. "Okay, Onstad, it's high time to get you laid." That idea made my heart jump like a doe hearing a twig snap, but I was too far gone to climb out. Backing up hard, Rodney broke off a sapling and then smashed another jack pine in our path flat.

It didn't take long before his Chevy was crunching to a halt in the gravel parking lot outside the roller rink at Hatfield. Like Rodney, I climbed out, but unlike him I stepped on an empty beer bottle that rolled underfoot and landed me on my rear end. He grabbed my forearms with hands like vices, yanked me back onto my feet, and asked whether I was all right.

"You bet," I said, dusting off my pants. "I can hold my beer."

"Didn't say you couldn't." Rodney hustled on ahead, while I stayed put and massaged my throbbing ankle. Man, did that sucker hurt.

The lights were so bright inside the stuffy rink they made me squint. Halfway up the railing near the benches, Rodney was already talking to Anita Torgerson and—who else?—Rose Schermerhorn. Rosie kept her eyes glued on him like flypaper, while Anita stood off to the side with crossed arms.

"In Heaven There Is No Beer, That's Why We Drink It Here," a recorded voice sang through loudspeakers to accordion accompaniment, while skaters wove counterclockwise around the worn wooden floor. I took in the action from just inside the entrance, while rubbing my bad leg against my good one and trying to appear invisible—till Rodney shouted, "Hey, Onstad! Over here!"

"Hi, Eldon!" gorgeous Rosie greeted with a little wave. Of course she knew who I was, even though the two of us had never really talked, since around here everybody knows practically everybody else. Right then I wanted to be anywhere but in Hatfield, even back home, watching TV with my folks, but it was too late for wishing. I strolled over real slow and somehow didn't limp. Anita grinned at me, her sky-blue eyes sparkling.

"So do you want to come?" Rod asked the girls.

"Sure," Rosie said, her brown eyes darting. Anita nodded.

"Meet us at my Chevy in twenty minutes," Rod told them and headed toward the skating rink bar in the far corner. So to my amazement we just left the girls standing there, willing to do what we wanted and when. For Rodney it had all been about as easy as buying take-out beer underage. On my own I would never have gotten close enough to either one to say hello.

The rink bar looked a lot like the saloon my dad had taken me inside to use the restroom. High stools on scuffed wooden floors and a mechanical arm inside a big jukebox, picking up 45s and laying them down in turn. Guys at a pool table playing Eight-ball for quarters, while others slammed leather dice cups into the bartop to decide who'd pay for the next round.

We took the last two empty stools beside the cash register and faced a mounted buck with a thin, black smile. Rod ordered us a couple of seven-ounce Schlitz Shorties. What'd the poor deer ever do to deserve ending up like this? "Kind of dumb to take a six-pointer to the taxidermist I'd say," Rodney muttered. "Though a ten-pointer might be another story." Of course Rod had never had the dough to mount any of the bucks he'd bagged.

"How's that, son?" the bartender asked with a scowl.

"My friend was wondering," I butted in, "what kind of rifle you used to shoot that nice-looking deer."

The bald guy broke into a gap-toothed smile. "A thirty-ought-six. My first shot tore right through his gut, but he kept on moving. I just about had a heart attack before I finally ran that sucker down." The proud look on his oily face made me shudder.

"If you can't kill them outright, I say leave them alone!" Rod snapped. "It's cruel to wound them and let them run till they drop." The bartender squeezed the glass he was wiping like he wanted to bounce it off Rodney's skull.

I spun around to distract Rod, and, sure enough, he turned too. Who should stagger in right then but two other East Side boys. I couldn't recall ever being so glad to see Lefty Davis and Jack Woodford before. Both of them had bad reputations like Rodney, but then what do most folks know? They both shook my hand and patted me on the back like I was some kind of honored guest.

"So you was on the football team, huh, Eldon?" Lefty teased, feeling my puny biceps and squeezing till it hurt. He was six inches taller than Rodney but thinner and longer-limbed, while Jack was short and stocky and built like a fireplug. We sure could have used all three on our team, if only they hadn't all had to work after school.

"Uh-huh," I said and sipped some more of my brew. I didn't go into how I'd just been on the "B" team till my senior year, and then only got into games on kickoffs and punts. Or that I probably only lettered because my dad and Coach Iverson were friends on the Lion's Club.

"I think I can take you in arm-wrestling now, Smitty," Jack said, rolling up a sleeve. All the heavy lifting he was doing at the railroad yard showed.

"Smitty" bared his right arm too, giving us all a good look at the biggest pair of biceps around. Rod chugged the rest of his beer, ordered four more Shorties, and said, "Loser buys the round." Jack agreed and moved to the other side of the bar and braced his right elbow down against his left palm.

Bending over across from Jack, Rodney took hold of Woodford's hand. "Start on three," he said. "Onnie, you count off."

Jack screwed up his face like he was about to bulldog a bear, while I slowly counted, "One, two"—Rod smashed Jack's hand to the bar the very instant I said, "three."

"Thanks for the beers, Jackie," Rodney teased, grabbed a fresh cold one, and chugged it. Mine went down pretty easy too. "Hey, bartender!" he shouted. "How about a couple six-packs of Hamm's for the road?" The old guy gave him a nasty glare, but went ahead and sold them without a squawk. While Rod paid with the five bucks I slipped him, I grabbed the stubby bottles and hightailed it.

The two girls were waiting at Rod's Chevy as promised, looking pretty as ever and smelling even nicer. I started to climb in front next to Rodney like before, but he shoved me into the back along with Anita and let Rosie take my spot. He opened us four cold ones with his teeth and took off.

Back at the East Fork beach, we kicked off our shoes and ran barefoot across the sand till the girls plopped down side by side. Rodney seated himself flush with Rose, so I sat down on Anita's left, only not so near. There the four of us did some serious drinking, while Rod entertained us with funny stories about siphoning gas from our high school principal's Buick and kicking the chief of police's cabbage patch all over town. Rosie wasn't far into her second brew before she began giggling. Me, I was content to listen in silence. Eldon Onstad—Helmer and Mabel Onstad's boy—drinking beer outside of a bar. Eldon Onstad, sitting beside Anita Torgerson, who kept edging closer. Eldon Onstad, chatting with Rose Schermerhorn. None of this seemed real.

"You still with us, Eldon?" Rosie asked after while.

"His friends call him Onnie," Rod told her.

"Onnie!" Rose shouted.

"Onnie, Onnie, Onnie!" echoed back from across the lake.

I couldn't think of anything to reply. Actually, only Rodney called me Onnie, but coming from Rosie it sounded even better.

"Another beer and I'll be up for swimming," Rod said, slurring his words and raising his voice. Meaning he was finally feeling the juice too. Me, I wasn't feeling much of anything, except kind of sleepy and sad. Like it'd been a huge mistake for Rod and me to ever drive into Hatfield.

"Say something, Onnie!" Anita squealed and slapped my knee. Her touch so startled me I dropped my beer, but grabbed it before much spilled out. "Onnie, Onnie, Onnie!" echoed back again. I chugged the rest of my bottle.

"Attaboy, Onnie!" Rosie yelled, and Anita squeezed my arm. Marla never smelled half this good. Once again my nickname bounced off the other side.

"Hey, guys, feel that cool breeze?" Rodney said. "We'd better get in the water if we want to stay warm."

"Stay warm?" Rosie shrieked. "We'll freeze in there!"

Anita jumped up, giggling, and waded in to her ankles. "It does feel nice, Rosie! Come on and try it!" The idea sounded nutty, but I knew she was right. By this late in August, the lake had been warming up all summer and so after dark held the heat better than the air.

Rodney stripped down to his underpants on the spot, while the girls screamed and cheered. Against my better judgment, I stood up too, only I felt so woozy I plopped right back down.

"Come on, party pooper!" Rosie shouted. She took one arm and Anita the other and pulled me onto my feet. Did their soft hands ever feel nice, grabbing me like that.

Rodney yanked down his shorts to the girls' shrieks and whoops and dove into the water.

Anita bumped me hard with a hip, shouting, "Come on, Onnie!" and started unbuttoning her blouse. Rosie—yes, Rose

Schermerhorn!—was already down to her bra and panties. Me, I'd yet to take off a stitch.

A little ways out Rodney did a fast crawl back and forth, hardly splashing at all, plunged under like a duck, showing off his bare bottom, and bobbed right back up. "You chicken, Onstad!" he hollered.

"Onstad, Onstad, Onstad!" echoed from the other side. Me chicken? That did it. I unbuckled my belt, stepped out of my trousers, and tore off my shirt, popping a button.

"Don't stop there!" Anita teased.

That made me even madder, so I slipped off my boxer shorts, tossed them onto the pile, and to the girls' hoots dove into the lukewarm water that smelled like good farming dirt, and swam out to Rodney. Soon two figures with flared hips came wading towards us. I spun around and breast-stroked farther out and swallowed a mouthful of Lake Arbutus. Meanwhile, Rod aimed right for the girls underwater like a torpedo. Rosie's scream signaled a direct hit. The two dipped out of sight only to pop straight back up, wrestling. He mumbled something, to which she agreed. Before you know it, they were sloshing their way out of the water and trotting off down the beach into the bushes.

Meanwhile, Anita kept coming at me, so I swam farther out.

"Stop!" she yelled. A crazy impulse hit me to try swimming for the opposite shore. Who knew how far away that might be? I'm not sure what all happened next, but I definitely know what didn't. Anita and I kissed and hugged as best we could while treading water, her wet skin slippery to the touch like a bar of soap. Then we swam back to the beach and laid down on the sand. Pretty soon she was telling me, "You don't have to apologize," but that only made me feel worse.

Anita and I got dressed and sat down on a driftwood log a yard apart and watched the water riffling in the wind. Right then I wished more than anything in the world Rodney and

I'd just stayed here by ourselves instead of going into the rink and picking the girls up. From the bushes I made out muffled laughs followed by moans worse than a wounded deer's. The noise sent chills up and down my spine.

I hated that sound then, just like I've always hated hunting, ever since my first time out at fourteen. I never talk about what happened then, but to be honest I shot a doe right through the lungs. Good enough shot to kill it eventually, but not to do so outright. Dad and Uncle Oscar slapped me on the back anyhow and congratulated me like I'd really accomplished something, while we followed the poor creature's mile-long trail of blood. Of course it wasn't a buck, every hunter's dream, not even a young spike buck, but it was still a white-tailed deer. Dad said for a first-timer it was a good start. When we finally caught up to the miserable thing, it was lying on its side gasping for air through a twisted mouth. I had to shut my eyes and bite my tongue to keep from bawling, when my uncle reached for his knife and put it out of its misery.

Back home, Dad began calling me The Little Man of the House, and Mom beamed whenever she looked at me. But I felt so awful I went straight to bed after supper, and every hunting season since I've made sure all my shots have missed. Even though I've known all along the best thing for me would be to stop going altogether. But if I did, the men in my hometown would think I was peculiar. I suspected Uncle Oscar was on to me, but Dad would just scratch his head and mutter, "Better luck next time, son."

A big splash at our feet suddenly splattered Anita and me but good. Rosie popped up and shouted, "How about making a bonfire? I'm freezing!"

"Just get dressed!" Rodney snapped, strolling up the beach and kicking at the sand. He snatched his jeans and yanked them on.

"What's bugging you, Rodney?" Rosie slurred. "You got what you wanted."

"Come on, Onnie," he said. "Let's get lost."

The four of us climbed into the car front and back like before. In a jiffy Rodney was tearing into the roller rink parking lot and just missing a pickup, backing up. "You can get out anytime," he told the girls, staring straight ahead and squeezing the steering wheel like he wanted to rip it out.

"Don't I deserve at least a goodbye kiss?" Rosie cooed, nestling close. Rodney refused to budge.

"I had a really nice time, Eldon," Anita whispered into my ear, and I met her moist lips for a lingering kiss. "We can go out again, Eldon, if you want," she said. "Just give me a call."

"Uh-huh," I said. Though I already knew I wouldn't be phoning her or any other girl. Not anytime soon and maybe never.

Finally, Rod reached for Rosie and they started smooching. "I love you too," he whispered. That was quite a shock to hear.

After the girls hopped out, I moved up front, but Rodney just sat there, slouching with closed eyes like he wanted to nap. "The shortest route home is by way of County E," I piped up.

"Shorter ain't always quicker," he said with a bitter chuckle, sat up, and turned the ignition. "The back roads won't have any fuzz."

He handed me a lukewarm beer, which tasted even worse than the others had. Soon we were squealing around the curves of County K, and I was bouncing up and down and bracing myself against the dashboard. Once he'd swerved onto the straightaway of Highway 54, he really revved up his hot Chevy. I consoled myself that at least when I aimed for that doe my first time out I didn't completely miss, not like I'd just done with Anita. That's what I was thinking when a deer popped into our headlights, a huge buck with a monster rack. Rod hit the brakes and honked. But the brave creature stood its ground, its eyes shining our headlights back at us like two welder's arcs. Too bad a car was coming in the other lane because that left Rod only one other choice. He steered hard right and hit soft sand. We flipped onto our top and kept rolling till we smashed into a thick oak.

Right away I knew my left arm was broken, but it'd served me well in shielding my head. I scrambled out an open window and collapsed onto the ground, blinded by the hot blood streaming from my cut forehead. The ambulance driver claimed I kept asking him, "What about the buck?"

"You must have missed him," the guy told me.

That was one charmed animal, but Smitty's luck ran out.

I think passenger cars ought to have seat belts, just like the ones stock-car drivers wear during races. Anyway, we sure could have used a couple that night last August. The county coroner said the impact broke Rodney's neck and killed him instantly, so he never felt any pain, unlike that doe I tortured.

They say the place next to the driver is the death seat, but here I am still, while Rodney Smith's gone. As the weeks go by since his funeral, I regret that night more and more. I keep wondering if he'd had my folks and my advantages whether he'd be sitting here in a Madison dormitory like me, and whether he deserved it more. One thing for sure, no matter what my dad and uncle think, next week they're going deer hunting without me. Now what's this I hear on the radio about somebody shooting at the President in Dallas, Texas?

Flowage

I don't know why they call it a flowage because one thing it never does is flow. Creeks and springs and rain fill it up with water, which just sits there, getting darker and dirtier as time goes by. The same as it's been doing since long before I come along, and the same as it'll be doing long after I'm gone.

A flowage is a stream flooding its banks, a muddy marsh full of spruce, a shallow lake that stretches on and on so far you almost drop before you ever wade to shore. Trees die in a flowage, leaving black stumps behind to mark the spot until they rot and disappear. People die in flowages too just like they do in wars, but they don't leave them there to rot like they do trees. No, they dress them up in fancy clothes and lay them inside shiny boxes and lower them into deep holes and cover them up with dirt and put up stones to mark the spot for good.

They say a woman shouldn't be negative, because it only drags her down. The worst thing in my life happens because I need a ride, but now that I just sit here in my little apartment that problem is solved. I get by with my disability checks, but the farther along I go the farther behind I get. People say I'm retired, but they're wrong, because even though I'm fifty-five and have a grown-up son, I'm still waiting to start something to retire from. You know how people talk.

I spend my days watching Oprah and Sally Jessy and Phil and Geraldo, who I can always count on to gab and smile.

They don't ever say much of anything but I never complain. I appreciate their company while I sift through the boxes of things Mom left behind. Every day they have new guests. I keep sorting through all my choices, trying to decide what to keep and what to toss. Like me, Mom never throws out a thing so there's a lot to look over, before I ever make up my mind. I don't have room for much, but I'm afraid if I hurry I'll make another big mistake. Besides, I've got all the time I want and then some.

The cold, dark, dirty water climbs up my legs and soaks my new coat and makes me so heavy I'm afraid I might drown. My shoes get stuck in the muddy bottom, but I pull my feet right out of them and I keep wading on. I fall and swallow water and choke and cough. And I stand right back up and I spit out the slime. The stumps scratch my hands and tear my coat, but I don't complain because without something to grab onto I'm in danger of going under and never coming up again.

I wade right into Town Creek to save my brother, but Tom isn't there in the flowage when I need his help the most. Town Creek flows fast and clean on its way to the Black River, making a bubbling sound pretty as wedding bells. Chuck shouts and screams and splashes and thrashes behind me and then gets so quiet it scares me, so I turn the sound up on the TV. I pull out my cracked baby bottle, I pull out my faded high school graduation tassel, I pull out the unraveling quilt Mom sews from pieces of my torn new coat, I pull my feet right out of my shoes and I grab a rotting stump and I catch my breath.

I pull my thirteen-year-old brother Tom out of Town Creek, the cut on his forehead hardly bleeding, because of the icy water soaking his face. So because I'm there he lives just like because I'm not there he dies. My brother and I grow up together on a farm, and though he's a year older, we're close as twins. We cut off chunks of sod with old kitchen knives and dam the creek and splash and thrash until the dam bursts and our home-made pond is gone. My brother Tom looks out for his baby sister just like I look out for him. But when I'm not looking, Tom slips and falls and hits his head on a rock, but I come running and I pull him out in time.

Archie Engebretson is taking the back route home from Hatfield, when he swerves around me laying soaked and muddy and bleeding on the edge of the road. He slams on his brakes and spins around and gets me in his headlights and sticks his head out the window and shouts, "My God, Annie! Is that you?"

"Archie, help me!" I cry out. And I let him pick me up shivering and dripping and carry me in his big, strong arms. He takes off my torn, sopping coat and stuffs it in his trunk and lays me down in his back seat and covers me with a prickly army blanket and drives me home to Black River Falls. I can smell the beer he's been drinking, but it doesn't make him mean like it does Chuck. But then people say Chuck is the meanest drunk around.

It only takes one big mistake to mess up your life, and mine is not to have a ride that night. If I stay home that April Saturday and listen to the radio and iron clothes for school, nothing bad happens to me at all. But dumb me, I agree to go to Hatfield with Arlene Haugstad, and her mother drives us there. Then Arlene up and runs off with Donny Bills, leaving me on my own to get home.

Just before the roller rink closes, I run into Chuck Stenerud, who gives me a crooked smile. He's standing like he's maybe had one too many, but he offers to take me back to town. Chuck's the most popular boy in the senior class, and who am I to say no? He turns left out of the parking lot instead of right toward Highway 12, so I ask as nice as I can, "Where are we going?" Like I was just curious.

"You like chicken in the basket, don't you?" he says with that deep voice every gal I know adores.

"Who doesn't?" I answer, smiling to myself at his sweet offer to take me to Palms, since then like now I can't afford to go out to eat. He doesn't have to spell it out that he'll be treating because all the Steneruds have money, what with his dad owning the local Ford car dealership and his uncle the hardware store.

We race right by Palms.

"Wait," I say, laughing. "Wasn't that it back there?"

He presses harder on the accelerator.

"Chuck?" I say softly. "Are you drunk?"

He keeps tearing down County K toward 54, grinding his teeth like he's in pain.

"Chuck, stop," I say. "Let me out."

His big Oldsmobile engine keeps roaring, but he doesn't say a word.

"Chuck?"

His tires squeal around the last hairpin, and he fishtails onto 54, only he turns left instead of toward town.

"Chuck, where are we going?"

He floors it.

"Stop. Let me out." I'm doing my best to stay calm.

He doesn't slow down at all. He brakes and skids and swerves hard right and crunches down a narrow gravel road, and his high beams light up a flowage on both sides, the water black as tar all around. There's nothing living anywhere nearby except white-tailed deer, and they jump out of Chuck's way like I should have myself.

He slams to a halt and turns off the engine and sits there panting like he's been running instead of driving the car. Where we're parked is as close to nowhere as you can get and still be around.

"Annie," he says with that deep voice every gal I know adores. "You've teased me just about long enough." What in the world is he talking about? Chuck and I have never even gone out.

He slides over toward me and slips an arm around my shoulder. I sort through my choices, trying to make up my mind fast. When a rough hand reaches for a coat button, out the door I go and slam it hard and stumble back up the gravel road toward Highway 54. I don't get far before the Oldsmobile's red eyes are grinding after me, rolling along a lot faster than I can run.

I can't run at him, I can't run away from him, so I take the only choice that's left. I head for the flowage and the third step hit it with a splash. The cold, dark, dirty water climbs up my legs and soaks my new coat and weighs me down, but I keep my head up. My shoes get stuck in the muddy bottom, but I pull my feet right out and I keep wading on. I fall and swallow water and I choke and cough. But then I stand right back up and I spit out the slime.

"My God, Annie!" Chuck bellows from the road, but I keep sloshing toward the opposite shore.

"Annie!" he screams. "I'll take you straight home! I promise! Annie!"

I won't let the liar trick me again I tell myself, and I keep wading on. I feel bad about the shoes Mom scrubbed other people's floors to buy me, but I can't worry about that now. Chuck hits the water with a loud splash, and I speed up. The stumps scratch my arms and tear my coat, but I don't complain.

"Annie, help!" Chuck shrieks and splutters and then gets real quiet, but I'm not dumb enough to fall for that move. I cough and wheeze and pant and gasp and get so tired I'm afraid I'll drop. But I'd sooner die in the flowage than let him catch up.

At last I come upon an arm of land and grab a prickly pine and pull myself ashore. And though I'm weak and dizzy, I get up and wring my hair and my sleeves and stumble on. I don't know if I'm going toward the road, but one thing's for sure, I'm getting myself as far away from Chuck as I can. Then a car comes zooming not one hundred yards in front of my face and disappears before I can scream or shout. I wring my torn coat again and head straight for the road. And I shiver till it hurts, but I don't slow down till I reach the shoulder, where I collapse and pass out.

They find Chuck Stenerud floating facedown in the dirty flowage, while my brother Tom lies facedown in clean Town Creek. I pull Tom out and save him, but I leave Chuck where he is. Chuck is born to the bigshot Steneruds and Tom to just us lowly Dahlens, but it makes no difference in the end. It's too bad Tom is in Korea when I need him in the flowage, because I am there for him in Town Creek.

Archie acts so nice to me I say yes when he asks me out. It only takes one mistake to get pregnant, and mine is to leave precautions up to him. My son isn't expected, but he's still welcome, and I love Johnny every bit as much as my mom loves me. Archie does his duty and marries me before Labor Day and forgets about college and gets a job driving truck for the county and puts food on the table for the three of us to eat. My brother graduates a class ahead of me and does his duty and enlists in the Army to fight the communists in Korea.

Archie never really wants me or my son, so two years later he skips out on us both and is never heard from again. Daddy dies when I'm in the eighth grade and we move into town, and Mom dies when I'm fifty, and my aunts and uncles show up for that funeral too and then disappear again. My thirty-seven-year old son hardly ever writes or calls and when he does he never tells me a thing. So I don't know if he's married his last girlfriend or if he's found himself somebody else.

The newspaper says a stump scratches Chuck Stenerud's face, when it's really my fingernails, but since he can't say anything different neither do I. The Army says they don't know which side fires the bullet that kills my brother, but either way he's gone for good. Archie runs off somewhere, and fifteen years later my son takes off too. The law rules Chuck's death an accident, and people gossip about what he's doing in the flowage at night and don't come up with anything that makes much sense. No one ever finds out I'm even there, though Mom wonders about the scratches on my arms. Archie keeps his mouth shut, and I'll always love him for that. I never see Chuck or Tom again or for that matter Archie or Johnny. Some people say if you make a mistake big enough your life will be over right then, but here I am still, while everybody else is gone.

And the flowage keeps filling up with water, which just sits there, getting darker and dirtier as time goes by. The same as it's been doing since long before I come along, and the same as it'll be doing long after I'm gone. And I keep sorting through all my choices, trying to decide what to keep and what to toss. I don't have room for much, but I'm afraid if I hurry I'll make another big mistake. Besides, I've got all the time I want and then some. I don't notice when Mom's mantle clock stops ticking, but it still tells time close enough for me. And I still don't know why they call it a flowage because one thing it never does is flow.

Alma Mater

"Run! Run! Run!" Jeff Becker bellowed at the Badger tailback, streaking down the sideline past the Illini safety. "Come on, Nemec, you Polack! Faster! Faster!" The sellout crowd of seventy-seven thousand screaming fans at Camp Randall rose as one and swept Jeff along on their tidal wave of joy. "Touchdown! Touchdown!" he shrieked one sunny Saturday in late September. Could a person possibly be happier? Maybe if Big Red managed to pull this game out, won the Big Ten title, and went on to win the Rose Bowl. Ten years without another appearance there was way too long, not since Pat Richter's and Ron Vander Kelen's heroics on New Year's Day, 1963.

Jeff took a fiery swig from the hip flask he had sneaked into the stadium and thrust it at Ed Dombrowski, a fellow first-year medical student at the University of Wisconsin in Madison. "Actually, Nemec's a Czech name, not Polish," Eddie explained in accepting the liquor. "Or Bohemian as most folks say in this state." Jeff guffawed and gave his best buddy a quick shoulder hug. Such pedantry right after a Badger score? Only Ed could be so—well, so Ed.

A too hearty swallow of firewater left Dombrowski shuddering and blinking, and Becker again roared with laughter. "Eddie, my boy," he said, "excuse me while I hit the head during the extra point attempt."

Unfortunately, dozens of other guys with the same bright idea were stacked up eight deep behind every urinal. So Jeff doubled back toward the stalls just inside the restroom entrance. These lines were shorter, but the men using them, alas, slower too.

He was hopping on his toes to relieve the bladder pressure when the burly, bearded fellow ahead of him stormed into the just vacated stall, saying, "Don't worry, pal. I'll be quick." Jeff was still bouncing when what felt like a compact bruiser barged into the restroom and shouldered him against the latched door. "Just a second, pal!" the big guy out of sight behind it snapped. Jeff was shocked to turn and face a fetching coed who had collided with him.

"I'm really sorry," this pretty blonde in wire rims, black turtleneck, and blue jeans said, giving his tie-dyed T-shirt and bell bottoms an amused onceover. "Are you okay?"

Jeff nodded with an idiotic smile. Azure eyes, freckled cheeks, toothy smile, and gorgeous, long, blond hair. What wasn't there not to like?

"Would you mind if I used the facilities before you?" this beauty asked in a sweet soprano. "I don't think I can wait."

Mind? No, so long as he didn't wet his pants. With a sharp clack the stall door opened and the guy inside rushed out. Jeff graciously bowed, hiding his discomfort, and let this adorable stranger squeeze on ahead. A woman in the men's restroom? That was funny, but why not? Since women couldn't use urinals, the lines in their own johns had to be much worse.

Two aching minutes and a raucous, unseen Badger kickoff later Blondie emerged. "How can I ever repay you?" she said with a flirtatious grin. He found her so attractive all he could do was shrug. She sped off with a little wave, and he burst forward, slammed the door shut, and found merciful relief while the stadium crowd screamed and cheered.

When Jeff at last rejoined Ed in the stands, the Badgers were lining up to kick off again already. "What happened?" he asked, taking his flask back.

"We intercepted an Illini screen pass and ran it back," Ed said as earnestly as their gross anatomy instructor pointing out subcutaneous ganglia.

"I didn't even catch her name," Jeff mumbled and downed a slug of booze. Which was as dumb as a wide receiver letting a certain touchdown bounce off his chest. Pretty, sprightly, audacious, amusing—wasn't she everything he had been looking for but hadn't found? Not since breaking up with Betsy Rappaport his senior year of college at Marquette University in his hometown of Milwaukee.

He jumped up to hustle back and resume their john conversation only to freeze. Sure, she was in this stadium crowd somewhere, but what good was knowing that? Why, there had to be three times as many fans present than lived in Ed's entire northern Wisconsin home county. Jeff climbed up onto his seat, shaded his eyes with a hand against the bright sun and did a slow about-face. Even if scanning a horde this huge for one individual was as hopeless as searching for a football floating in Lake Michigan. He plopped back down in frustration.

Applause exploded like an artillery barrage on all sides, bringing the entire crowd to its feet. Except for Jeff, who remained seated and muttering. What if he placed a personal ad in *The Daily Cardinal* or *The Capital Times* and hoped she noticed it? But how would he identify her? Dear Coed-Who-Used-the-Men's-John-at-Camp-Randall? No, a better idea was to leave the game early, patrol the nearest exits, and maybe get lucky with seeing her coming out. Why in the devil hadn't he asked for her telephone number when he had the chance?

"Best play of the day," Ed said, sitting back down. "The Illini cornerback tipped the ball away from Killian right into Smitty's hands. Smith was way too fast for their secondary."

Jumping to his feet, Jeff blurted, "I'll meet you outside at our usual spot."

"What? But the score's tied with ten minutes to go!"

"I've got to meet somebody," Jeff said, handing Ed the flask.

A half hour later he was sullenly leaning against a pillar when Dombrowski filed out with the last stragglers. Grinning ear to ear, Ed said, "A forty-six-yard field goal won it for us on the very final play! Talk about a fantastic kick!"

Jeff could only scowl.

"So where's your friend?"

"I missed her."

As they slipped into a stream of fans flowing between the practice shell and Camp Randall toward Monroe Street, Jeffrey explained how he happened to meet the winsome blonde in wire rims.

"A Mifflin-Street type, eh?" Ed said. Meaning a hippie.

"No, she's very clean-cut." Jeff stepped over two youngsters laid out dead drunk on the grass. "And gorgeous and sweet. I'm not kidding—she's perfect."

Like swimmers riding a surf, the two med students let the crowd carry them across the street blocked to traffic toward Frank's Stadium Bar. Which already had a long line outside of would-be revelers like every other football Saturday. Ten minutes later they finally made it inside past the bouncer, checking IDs.

"There she is, Ed! The coed in that black turtleneck!" Jeff cried out, pointing across the crowd. "Standing beside that tall redhead! Hey, Blondie! Hey, you! Over here!" Dombrowski stood on his tiptoes and craned his neck but the duo had already disappeared from sight. "I swear it's that same coed I met in the stadium men's room!"

Ed rolled his bloodshot eyes.

"Eddie, this is deadly serious. You wait right here near the entrance and keep an eye out for a pretty blonde in wire rims and a black turtleneck. Meanwhile, I'll head toward the back and work my way toward you. If you spot her first, grab her until I get there." Like a halfback hitting a closing gap, Jeff charged into the mob of celebrants and sidled and wriggled his way forward.

Twenty minutes later he rejoined Ed, waiting where told. "No hippie came this way," Ed teased. "Maybe it was an angel you saw. Or an apparition."

Fans all around began to belt out a raucous, offkey rendition of the Badger alma mater, "Varsity." Droopy-eyed Ed sang along and swayed to its deliberate melody, while Jeff just stood there, stewing in sullen silence. The last thing he needed now was this melancholy piece of music he had never much liked. "Any brandy left?"

Ed shook his head and signaled the bald, sweaty bartender for two beers, which a hairy hand promptly thumped down on the bar and snatched up the waiting cash. Jeffrey grabbed a frosty can, took a deep swig, and winced at the unusually hoppy bitterness after brandy's sweetness.

"Okay," Ed said, furrowing his brow, "let's analyze the situation and adjust our game plan accordingly. Who knows how we missed her here, but if she stopped at one football bar, she's bound to hit another."

"Hogger's! She'll be at Johnny Hogger's!" Jeff shouted. After home games that place was even livelier than Frank's. Opening his throat like a drain, he poured his brew down the hatch and dashed for the door.

Unfortunately, the line outside Hogger's extended a good thirty yards up Regent Street and was barely budging. By the time they finally got past its pig-eyed bouncer, Jeff was so frustrated he was ready to punch somebody out. "Could that be your mystery blonde and her red-headed friend?" Ed said.

"Where?" Jeff shouted.

No sooner had his classmate pointed out two coeds in the beer garden toward the rear than Jeff took off like a halfback at the snap of the ball, Ed close upon his heels. "That's her all right, Eddie!" he yelled.

But no matter how hard the duo twisted and shoved against shoulders and torsos, they made no better headway than they would swimming upstream against a too powerful current. The throng finally forced them under an overhang and out of the sunlight. "Steady me," Jeff said, set a foot down on the unoccupied space at the end of a picnic table bench, and by pushing off Ed's head, raised himself high enough to look over the celebrants. "Oh, no," he moaned. "She's there all right. Only now with some schmuck."

Suddenly the crowd noise tripled in volume, womanly shrieks mixing with manly yowls. "What'd you say?" Ed yelled at his best buddy.

Jeff stuck his mouth in his pal's ear and shouted, "The knucklehead she's with just climbed up onto the low roof next door! And he's mooning the crowd!"

"You mean the guy dropped trou?" Ed screamed back.

Jeff nodded forlornly.

"I see him!" Ed cried out. "A guy in a Badger helmet!" Jeff gnashed his teeth. Screw Blondie if an asinine stunt like that impressed her. "Eddie!" he bellowed. "Let me buy us double brandies!"

* * *

"Run! Run! Run!" the jerk behind Dr. Jeffrey Becker screeched at the Badger tailback, sprinting down the sideline at Camp Randall an overcast Saturday in early October. Jeffrey turned and glared at the skinny student about thirty years his junior dressed in weirdly baggy garb instead of properly fitted khaki slacks and button-down dress shirt like his own. The twerp shrieked, "Touchdown! Touchdown!" as if relaying news to the blind and all but deaf. Jeffrey glanced past his wife, Helen, bedecked in a pleated skirt and dressy pumps. His old friend, Dr. Edward Dombrowski, had given up on watching the game and was glumly reading an alumni newsletter instead. His visible aging since their attending medical school together here in Madison a quarter century earlier was dismaying—no hair at all on top anymore, what was left on the sides gray, and wrinkles creasing his forehead and cheekbones. His once disarming grin had vanished too. But then Edward had mentioned a mysterious funk of late afflicting both him and his wife, Barbara. Not that Jeffrey himself was a stranger to gloom. Though he knew at least an okay remedy, namely, keeping himself busy all waking hours.

Jeffrey's own hairline wasn't what it used to be either, even if still only in retreat. Wrinkles had also chosen their lines on his face, poised to incise in time. All so unlike his wife, Helen's, persistent youth. Only three years younger than Jeffrey, and the mother of two teenage girls, she looked far younger. So much so, he was considering cosmetic surgery just to keep up. "Why bother?" Edward had advised over the phone. "You're already married for good, right?" Right. Or maybe not.

The crowd once more jumped to its feet, screaming, while Jeffrey sat there, watching Helen stretch to her full five foot ten inches. Retaking her seat, she asked with the merest hint of peevishness, "Would it be possible for us to leave this game early?"

Sure, it'd be possible. Just like it would be to take a suicidal dive hand in hand off the back of the stadium. But whether it'd also be a good idea, now that was another question. Echoes of his spouse's exaggerated politeness throughout their marriage buzzed in his ears like pesky gnats. Helen Schafer Becker, the paragon of propriety and tact. He was willing to bet the pricey mortgage on their home in swank Upper Arlington, Ohio that Edward hadn't noticed the trace of irritation in Helen's voice just now. But then hematologist Jeffrey had long since been able to read her every nuance like a detailed blood chart. Especially her multiple expressions of boredom, be it with football, basketball, hockey or baseball. Sure, she was willing to endure attending games on occasion at his side, but only as yet another conjugal duty. She was big on duty. Real big. Why had he so stupidly dragged her along to Madison anyway, when the whole point of this trip had been to frolic with Edward like the old days and cheer themselves up? Fat chance of that happening.

Jeffrey glanced away from Edward's polished wingtips and tailored trousers. "The Boilermakers ran an interception back," his old friend muttered.

Ho hum. Boilermakers—what he and Dombrowski used to drink at Madison bars like Mother's or the Brat and Brau back in the day. Namely, shots of whiskey chased down by beers. Going on three decades ago, though it seemed more like five lifetimes. It was depressing to witness Ed mirroring his own melancholiness, after he and his Barbara had come down from their hotel room for brunch that forenoon chuckling. Which was a grand improvement from their somber dinner together the night before when Helen had gotten them jabbering nonsense about the emptiness of life that lacked a higher purpose. "The great artists grant at least glimpses of the answer," Helen had declared, as if such gibberish actually meant something. It made Jeffrey long to ban graduate study in the humanities and put an end to such idle speculation forever. Thank goodness for the down-to-earth solidity of medicine.

Edward had been the only one of the four to order a before-dinner drink, and Helen hadn't been at all happy about that single Bloody Mary. Not that she voiced a word of disapproval, but Jeffrey read her forbidding, hypererect posture as a demand from others for a seemliness of bearing and behavior that she herself embodied. Just the opposite of Dombrowski's whatever-you-like-I'm-easy slouch.

Then on today's trek from their hotel on the Square to the game, Barbara had entertained them with droll anecdotes from her adolescence in Manitowoc along Lake Michigan—till they reached the old cream-brick university administration building that had served as UW-Hospitals way back when. At the sight Edward had dropped Barbara's hand and turned monosyllabic.

When they encountered security guards outside the stadium entrances frisking every fan for alcohol—underage students and middle-aged or even older alumni—Edward's sulking turned positively sour. As if a venial sin once tolerated had meanwhile become a gross offense. Jeffrey distracted the myrmidons long enough for grim Edward to slip his full hip flask into the trash.

In taking his stadium seat, Edward had commented with what for him was uncommon bitterness, "Excuse me, but this is a Badger football game and not a prison visitation? Frisking fans at a sporting event? Has Mad City gone puritanical?"

"Drinking in public has always been against the law where I grew up," Helen had dryly stated, meaning in Ohio, and Jeffrey had suppressed a groan. That one sentence summed his wife up perfectly. She was so unimaginative, so boring, so obedient. So what if they hadn't raised their voices with each other so much as ten times in their long years together? That didn't make their marriage good. Because it meant they had never experienced any exultation either, not on their wedding day, not on their honeymoon, not even when their daughters were born. No, their relationship had always remained as low-key and steady as a drive across an endless prairie with cruise control set precisely at the speed limit. Yet did he know anyone sweeter? Edward maybe—at least back then.

Jeffrey felt a twinge of guilt for thinking any ill of Helen, sentiments he would never voice, not even to Dombrowski. Still, he truly regretted not getting a chance to spend time alone here with his old buddy, but Helen had implied she'd just as soon not be stuck with Barbara.

Flashy, redheaded Barbara Nelson, at first glance an odd choice for dorky Edward, since she was half a head taller and outgoing. Yet somehow the two made a great couple. But then who could ever say what rendered any relationship a success? Jeffrey loved Barbara's good-natured needling and unexpected outrageousness, such as her quip over brunch, "Do you think I could trade these sesame buns in for the waiter's?" He stifled a chuckle to recall dear Helen's arched eyebrow at that remark.

Dear Helen, who never once in her entire life had voiced an improper word or showed any person, animal, or plant disrespect. But so what if her every act was commendable? He had never sought to marry a saint. Not that Helen wasn't accommodating in the bedroom, but still sex with her too often resembled making love to a warm, fleshy mannequin. Though if she had never once had an audible orgasm, she also had never once complained. Yet thinking about all her volunteer work with the Campfire Girls, United Way, and Red Cross and her disciplined reading and profound knowledge of both art and classical music—not to mention her persistent good looks—made her seem a prize catch. There was so much right about his life shared with Helen that it seemed shameful not to be content. So what was wrong?

Helen's spirit. Her energy. Her soul. Her spacey half-smile. Her quasi-tranquilized mellowness from her oh-so-quiet early morning alarm that went off unfailingly at six a.m. until lights out at exactly half past ten. Her never drinking coffee, tea or cola—or napping or taking any breaks. Worst of all, her never wanting to. She was so mindlessly happy it was driving him nuts. Even at a boring football game like today's, that faint smile that never left her face. Like Buddha himself reincarnated as a bright, well-preserved, middle-aged woman.

He couldn't remember when her constant grin had first struck him as obtuseness rather than mature obliviousness to unease, but now the oh-so-mellow togetherness it suggested never failed to make him ache for sin. Her normality in everything was worse than a lawn too perfectly manicured to dare pop a weed. Yet wasn't it this very self-possession that had initially drawn him to her? As if hinting at some profound secret that she would eventually share if only he stuck with her long enough. Over nineteen years now and counting and still waiting in vain.

Yet he knew he couldn't have found a better homemaker and mother if he had dated five hundred women before proposing. But there had to be more to adult life than this quiet, ungrudging performance of duty. Even months on end of despair would be better as long as there eventually occurred some ecstasy.

Though they did have Michelle and Jennifer, two marvelous daughters. Thank goodness, in looks they took after their mother, but unfortunately their souls were little Helens too. As musicians, if not as musicologists—not yet anyway—they actually surpassed their mother, especially Jenny on the viola. And at all their recitals Jeff had been as proud as any parent present. But classical music, no matter who played or composed it, still left him cold. His wife's favorite symphonies and concertos weren't at all like Bruce Springsteen, Howling Wolf or the Rolling Stones. They didn't spurt one drop of adrenaline into his blood and make him want to jump up and boogie in celebration of just being alive. Instead they left him so somber he almost despaired. Not that the pieces weren't beautiful—nobody could deny that—but, why would anybody want to be depressed? But Helen could sit motionlessly listening to them as if in a blessed trance. Of course one reason he had decided to marry her was to absorb some of this cultivation. But no matter how much he was exposed to her beloved Bach and Beethoven, it kept bouncing off like football passes hitting him square in the chest.

Still, his daughters' dream of one day forming their own string quartet was so classy he bragged about it to medical colleagues. But it also made him feel he had no genuine offspring. Not if he couldn't get the girls involved in tennis or another sport. But Helen had nixed these one and all because of their threat to the girls' delicate fingers. Would Jeff have loved to coach his own kids in something athletic. A son he would have taught how to toss a perfect spiral, shoot a basketball, and throw a curve and sinker.

"Do you guys want to leave?" Edward asked with two minutes left in the game.

Helen sat up even straighter, when Jeffrey nodded forlornly. Why ruin his personal shutout? So far fans jumping up in their seats had kept him from seeing a single score, not that he really gave a damn. So the two couples slipped out and moseyed between the practice shell and Camp Randall toward Frank's, just as he and Ed had planned. Not a single drunk in sight anywhere on the grass en route, sleeping a snootful off, not like it once had been.

"I thought this place was supposed to be packed," Barbara teased, peeking through the entrance into the sports bar. Not yet anyway, though twentyish and thirtyish men and women were rapidly converging, their poker-faced self-containment poised to burst into raucous jubilation once a critical mass of celebrants had assembled. Had Helen ever even imagined such fun? She certainly had never experienced it.

Glancing sheepishly at Helen, he ventured, "Should we bop on in and have ourselves a brew?" His spouse frowned in response. Without a word of explanation, Jeffrey marched onward toward Regent Street and Hogger's.

"Hey, I liked the vibes back there!" Barbara objected.

Vibes—great word, one Helen never used, probably because she was incapable of sensing them. Weren't vibes exactly what Jeffrey's life now so sorely lacked? Helen hurried on ahead as if anxious to escape, and he dutifully caught up. Not that he had the slightest concern she would cause a scene. Not when a statue would sooner step off its pedestal and do the tango.

"Slow down!" Edward shouted. "This isn't a race. I thought the whole point was to party hearty. You know, like we used to."

Fat chance Jeffrey thought, stopping. Those days are long gone. With an almost imperceptible toss of her head, Helen halted as well and faced the others with a spacey half-smile glued onto her chiseled face, that schizoid grin unrelated to anything happening. What exactly was she so blasted happy about? Sure, they had plenty of money, adorable kids, good health, a beautiful home, meaningful work, respect from the community—but was that enough? Where was the rapture, where was the resounding laughter, where were the thrills so intense goose bumps ran up and down your spine? Where was life at its ecstatic peak?

Moping along toward Hogger's, Jeffrey glanced away from the hint of patient weariness on Helen's face. Getting into the line behind Barbara, she pronounced in her dry, alto monotone, "This establishment also appears to be a dump." Four Perriers coming right up.

* * *

Med student Jeff chugged the rest of his double brandy up on the low-lying corrugated tin roof and unsnapped his jeans, and the crowd behind and below him in Hogger's beer garden howled its approval. All their energy focused on him so electrified him with excitement that his knees felt rubbery. He couldn't help chuckling at the outrageousness of what he was about to do. With a yank he unzipped his fly, and his fans hooted and hollered their encouragement. His bell bottoms weren't so easily dealt with. He had to tug and twist the tight fabric to pull them past his bulging thighs, the cheering growing even louder. He paused to relish the applause before lowering his shorts. Pandemonium all around in response. "Moon! Moon! Moon!" the mob screamed. He was about to oblige them by bending forward in the classic stance of a football center when it struck him—while he had everybody's, above all *her* attention, why not go for broke? Especially when he'd never be in this good a physical shape ever again. So he faced the crowd with arms akimbo, thereby flaunting everything he had.

And the world, at least this tiny corner of it, roared its approval. Trembling from the thrill and laughing along with his throng of admirers, Jeff scanned the toothy faces and red sweatshirts until he spotted the one person who counted. The long-haired blonde in the wire rims and black turtleneck was cheering along too! "Can I buy you a drink?" he mouthed. Her eager nod was an unmistakable, exultant yes. If he lived to be a hundred, could he ever surpass this personal triumph?

* * *

Dr. Jeffrey Becker loosened the snug belt of his dress slacks as he weaved back and forth among the crowd and led Helen, Edward, and Barbara toward an unoccupied picnic table out back in Hogger's patio. A waitress in a dirndl pounced upon the new customers as soon as they sat down. Jeffrey ordered tap beers for Edward and himself, while Barbara and Helen settled for Perriers. "You gals should have seen what this place was like in the old days," Jeffrey said, glancing up at the empty corrugated roof.

Barbara nodded without really understanding. Helen's delicate nose betrayed the tiniest note of disapproval, surely too subtle for either Dombrowski to notice. Jeffrey knew full well she detested slumming like this. Or disliked it rather. Helen didn't feel strongly enough about anything to detest it—or even hate it. But there was much that she disliked, in fact, everything that wasn't elegant, tasteful or decorous, which certainly included Quonset-hut bars and beer gardens. Why had they bothered to come here if they were merely going to demonstrate restraint? This homecoming was turning into a veritable wake.

While the tables around them gradually filled, the foursome sipped their beverages and quietly chatted about their respective lives in Ohio and Iowa. Edward didn't want to go into the details of his internist practice any more than Jeffrey did his own as a hematologist. Helen steered the conversation onto their kids, while the crowd around them stayed subdued—till four rowdy young revelers in blazing Badger cardinal staggered out onto the patio. A coed in a football helmet among them was so far gone she was reeling.

Had he and Edward ever gotten that plastered? You bet— on more than a few Friday nights thanks to boilermakers. The tipsy girl removed the helmet to reveal long, blonde hair and a toothy smile. Jeffrey laughed out loud.

"Would you please share the joke, Jeffrey?" Helen delicately inquired.

Jeffrey waved his wife off. From this distance the young drunk resembled the coed he had met in the Camp Randall restroom all those years ago. Namely Susie Dahl, the liveliest livewire old Jeffrey had ever known. Susie, a diploma-nurse at Madison General Hospital on Park Street and a native of Eau Claire, Wisconsin. Their first date the Saturday after their magical encounter in the Camp Randall john was still his single sweetest memory, closely followed by the next weekend when she slept over. Soon she was staying over every chance his studying permitted, and by herself turning that first year of med school into the most exciting of his life.

Though neither well-educated nor intellectual, Susie was nonetheless bright. And bursting with zany impulses, none of which were mean or selfish. No matter what Jeff brought up, she had a funny comeback. In retrospect that mother wit of hers seemed more comely than the most cultivated taste. Because her company had made him feel plugged into the wall. Her teasing had even brought dorky Dombrowski out of his shell. Best of all for Edward, Susie had been the person who introduced him to his future and forever wife.

"Is anybody else hungry?" Helen asked in that perfectly modulated alto that somehow could grate like a fingernail on a blackboard. Edward looked at Barbara and then his old med school pal. Blank stares signaled not yet.

Comfortable—that was Helen's greatest attribute. Right before steady, predictable, and controlled. Would she ever pose for nude photos and take them to the local drugstore for developing? Susie had. Would she ever plan a two-person orgy and carry it out till Jeffrey begged for mercy? Susie had. Neither hot nor cold, neither impatient nor dallying, Helen always moved right along the white median, bearing steadily toward the horizon, perfectly content that it never came.

His wife's face never lit up at the sight of anyone, not even their darling daughters. There wasn't anybody who could excite Helen out of her quiet restraint, although talking to lively people could energize Jeffrey better than a cup of espresso or a sellout crowd. Not that she was shy. But she was so indifferent in her happiness, so aloof in her mellowness, that he didn't know how much longer he could stand it.

Not that Jeffrey hadn't been thrilled to meet her. His and Susie's torrid affair was already burning itself out when his and Edward's fellow med student Beth Feinstein had invited them both to a dinner party. He was actually pleased Susie had to work that night because people that sophisticated would have made her uncomfortable. So he had gone with Edward, and Beth had seated him next to one Helen Marie Schafer. Since he had expected only physicians in training and their spouses or significant others, it was a pleasant surprise to find the unattached art history doctoral candidate Helen also present.

Over the shrimp cocktail Jeffrey warmed to Helen's reserved, articulate charm. By the chocolate mousse dessert, her regal froideur was actually turning him on. So unlike Susie's lusty bedazzlement, it bespoke a weightiness that could anchor a skiff in a tempest. It felt more like what he needed in a spouse, especially since he wanted children. Besides, there was a shallowness to Susie's zestiness that was already getting tiresome. There had to be more to life than fleeting pleasures, no matter how blissful. And the more Helen spoke, the more smitten he became. Her wide-ranging erudition, as at home with Bach and Beethoven or Proust and Pound as Rembrandt and Renoir, awed him, not that he understood all that much of what she said.

Soon he was having platonic lunches with Helen, while waiting for his once fiery fling with Susie to gutter out. Susie soon noticed his nights with her had become a chore that often left him drained and dejected. Then one day he hemmed and hawed on the phone about her next night over, and she hung up on him. And just like that it was over between them. He didn't wait longer than to sigh in relief before calling the stately Ms. Schafer and inviting her out to dinner. Her reply still rang in his ears—"Why, Jeffrey, that would be lovely." Her refined acceptance had amused him then, though now it made him cringe, whereas Susie's reply to his invitation for a first date —"How could I say no to a rooftop flasher?"—brought a smile to his face even now. As did recalling that November night when Susie had showed up at his door in a ratty woolen coat, and nothing on underneath. And what about that laughing gas party he and Susie had thrown, where Ed's pinched voice made Jeff guffaw so hard he could barely breathe?

"Barbara," Helen was saying when he tuned their conversation back in, "with all due respect, allow me to disagree. Bach's Third Orchestral Suite in D is his most sublime piece. Every time I hear it my soul quivers. It could convince a stone of divine grace."

With all due respect, with all due cultivation, with all due tedium. Such sensitivity was fine and dandy, but still it wasn't life. Because nothing was more boring than classical music—except perhaps Perrier with a twist. Susie had been a beer stein that never emptied, while Helen was Ming Dynasty bone china under glass. Next time he and Edward would leave their wives home, and do Mad City justice or perish in the attempt.

* * *

"When I lie awake early mornings waiting for the alarm," Edward muttered from the urinal to Jeffrey's immediate left, "longing for fun like we had back then seems really childish."

"Fun?" Jeffrey said. "Is that all you thought it was?"

Without another word Edward hurried off, while Jeffrey lingered at the sink, dwelling on that table of four rowdy party animals here. Okay, a pitcher of beer per person was excessive. Though in the old days he and Edward had knocked it back like that plenty of times. Not that they'd ever ended up making a pubic spectacle of themselves. Well, okay, that one time on the roof was an appalling exception. His gross immaturity then made him shudder now with mortification.

While exiting the john, he bumped into a fetching coed. "Susie?" he muttered, as if the woman he had known his first year of med school might not have aged a day during all the intervening years. Still, the resemblance was striking.

"I'm Kirsten," the young woman said with a voice not unlike Jennifer's and Michelle's. Only unlike his twins she was badly slurring her words. Like Susie used to whenever she drank more than a few beers. Which happened every time she imbibed back then. Which occurred multiple times per week.

"Today's my very special birthday!" Kirsten announced, grabbing Jeff's arm.

"Good for you," he said, removing her delicate fingers. He winced to see her pretty azure eyes this bloodshot. Just like Susie's used to get during those drinking binges. Afterwards her attractive face would always get puffy.

"You don't understand!" Kirsten shouted. "I'm finally twenty-one! Today's the first time it's legal for me to get hammered!" She cackled.

"I'm impressed," Jeff said, but this girl was too far gone to detect his sarcasm. Habitually getting snockered before attaining legal adulthood? What a horrible concept. In not too long his Jennifer and Michelle would be out on their own. And free to do what? Break his heart? Make him—and Helen—regret their kids had ever been born?

No indeed. Because their children would emulate their mother. Thank God. Or rather thank dear, capable Helen. Shaking his head and muttering, Jeff turned away from this pathetic coed. What this Kirsten and her pals were doing wasn't so much drinking as plain old abusing alcohol. At this rate she would end the evening on her knees, heaving her throat raw and leaving the acrid taste of bile lingering on her tongue. And what about her horrendous hangover to come? Odd that he routinely forgot about those when he fondly reminisced upon the good old days, all those mornings-after spent with a throbbing head and cottony mouth, accomplishing zilch. Because they were every bit a part of the partying as the jolly drinking, weren't they? Because ethanol was a poison so potent no antidote had ever been found. It was a wonder he and Edward hadn't flunked out of med school as badly and as often as they had indulged themselves.

Jeffrey plopped back down alongside Helen back at their table and glared at the bare corrugated roof. Once he had stood up there totally naked, and in response the world had awarded him triumph and joy. Or so he used to believe.

"You still with us, Jeffrey?" Edward asked, handing the waitress money for the two more beers she had just brought.

"Where else?" Jeff responded.

"Jeffrey," Helen said, "I don't believe you've had two beers in one day since we've been married."

True enough. Jeff took a sip and sloshed it around his mouth. Bitter and flat now no matter how good it might have tasted way back when. Leaning close to Helen's impassive face, Barbara asked in an earnest whisper, "Why Bach's Third Orchestral Suite?"

Grinning like a golden statue of Buddha, Helen replied, "Because it hints that we humans are nothing—except for our capacity to love. But for that we are saved."

Barbara smiled through tears and Edward wiped the corner of a misty eye, while Jeffrey stared at the empty adjacent rooftop and scowled. What in the devil had ever possessed him back then to climb up there and make an ass of himself? He grabbed his nearly full cup of beer and tossed it into the trash.

The four young drunken louts three tables over lurched to their feet and began to belt out, "Var-si-ty, Var-si-ty," the opening bars of the Badger alma mater anthem. Hogger's patrons by the score arose to the achingly slow and tender tune, including Edward, Barbara, and Helen—but not Jeffrey. "U-Rah-Rah-Wis-con-sin," they all intoned as one. Finally Jeffrey stood up too and grasped his wife's long, cool, slender hand—an appendage of flesh and bone that time and again had reached into the whitewater of his roiling emotions like a lifeline. Helen squeezed back. He shuddered to think where he would be today if the two had never met and married. And he joined in singing the deliberate, achingly poignant lyrics, "Hail to thee, our alma mater."

Vein

I was spending another July Saturday out back, taking a machete to the briars that crept onto my yard with every new spring and hustling to finish up before the cicadas' grating choruses resumed with the day's worst heat. Not that my hillside property includes much of a traditional yard. It's so far from level there's not a flat plot anywhere on it for a decent garden. Though I'll be darned if I ever give up trying to put one in.

I had just gulped two more aspirins to ease my regular weekend headache, when the cell phone up on the porch began buzzing. Now I can still move pretty good for an old fart, even uphill, so I got there before the caller hung up. Thank goodness, since it turned out to be my one and only child. Kevin! I gasped, breathless from the exertion.

My son said he and Tina had just returned from a marvelous week in the Cayman Islands.

Great, I replied and laughed. I was overjoyed to hear he had taken Tina along, and not just because her family is filthy rich. If Kevin had at last settled upon a career at the age of thirty-three, wasn't it high time he got married?

What's so funny? he snapped.

I don't know what got into me, but for some reason I simply told the truth. I don't know which makes me happier, I said, your hooking up with Tina or your landing this travel agency job.

Kevin's response was dead silence.

Honestly, being a travel agent sounds fabulous, I hastened to add. And not only on account of the free trips that come with this line of work.

More silence on the other end.

How was the fishing? I asked. Of course the question was a dumb joke, but I was hoping it would distract the boy out of his funk. While Kevin was still living at home, he and I had on occasion gone fishing together—as long as I let him bring along a book and leave his pole in a holder to free up his hands. This meant we could only fish for bottom-feeders like suckers and bullheads, but I figured the quality time with my son was always well spent.

Ha, ha, ha, Kevin replied with an irony others might have mistaken for bitter. Then he took a deep breath and dove into an eloquent account of his trip. If there's one thing he inherited from his old dad it's the gift of gab. The first two days the snorkeling had apparently been divine. That corner of the Caribbean had the clearest water he'd ever seen. And it was just teeming with snapper, grouper, grunts, and—most beautiful of all—barracudas with teeth like racks of little ivory knives.

I patiently let Kevin have his say, a tried-and-true salesman's trick I had already mastered by the age of fourteen.

The biggest highlight occurred on his second night. A sea urchin stew so upset Tina's stomach she hit the sack early. Well, Kevin told me, audibly smirking, he wasn't at all sleepy, so he moseyed down to the hotel desk and inquired about the local night life.

It didn't take him more than a glance around the liveliest lounge to spot a gorgeous local in a corner, humoring some pesky bald dork sunburned redder than the rump of a rhesus macaque. Kevin bided his time till Gramps traipsed off to the john, whereupon he lunged like a moray eel.

I giggled.

It was hard for my son to say which was more remarkable, the delicacy of Angelique's café-au-lait skin or the redolence of her wisteria breath.

I chortled.

When Kevin paused to blow his nose, I almost struck. But I decided to hold back a bit longer. Have you come down with a cold? I instead asked.

That he indeed had. In fact, he had picked it up right after he got back to Atlanta and still didn't know who to blame.

I guffawed.

Why the hell do you keep laughing at everything I say? he snapped.

As I had learned from countless knocks on strangers' doors, once a prospect's mood turns sour, you'd better get the conversation onto something funny fast. So I tried my old standby—my endless frustrations with my backyard garden. He knew all about my digging in the past only to hit clay, boulders or meandering tree roots. But he hadn't heard yet about my neighbor's black walnuts, the noxious limbs of which overhanging my property were withering my tomato plants.

When that elicited a barely audible chuckle, I pounced. You know, Kevin, I said, putting a well-practiced smile into my voice, would it ever be nice if you and Tina could come up for a visit. For the duration I promised to leave the fishing poles in the basement, not that I went out anymore anyway, since what fun is the pastime all by yourself?

The suggestion went exactly nowhere. So I quickly asked what he had meant a minute before by not knowing who to blame for his sniffles.

He let out a dramatic sigh.

I hastened to explain that each person is exposed to germs every single day, so warding them off was up to us. Thus nobody was ultimately to blame for our getting sick but ourselves.

Kevin announced that he had to go and hung up.

I didn't think too much of it at the time, but I guess I should have. That was the last time I ever heard my son's voice.

The next week I received a picture postcard of a man straining to hoist a trophy barracuda to its full length. On the back I read in Kevin's angular scrawl: Dear Dad, I don't see any reason why I can't make my home as peaceful as Little Cayman was. So the phone, TV, radio, and CD player have got to go. And please don't disturb me at work. From now on you and I will stay in touch via letters. Love, K.

That hit me like a slap across the teeth. I mulled it over and tried to put it in the best light, but failed. Finally, one particularly hungover Saturday I concluded he was only being wary of my renowned ability to talk anybody into just about anything. I mean, has there ever been a product I couldn't sell? Magazines, fruit baskets, vacuum cleaners, encyclopedias, TVs, used cars, new cars, advertising, and now real estate. You name it, I've sold it and earned good money doing so, ever since I was a kid. How? By first selling myself. Because that's one thing people have always been plenty willing to purchase. And why not? I've always made sure my customers got what exactly they deserved, since service is what sales is all about. And you can't serve anybody until you first figure out what makes them tick.

So why has Kevin always remained such a mystery to me? I mean, if he's practically my spitting image, how come he's so darned different? It's not that he's exactly aloof, but that he avoids people so. But me, before I even made it to kindergarten I was already popular, and that's one thing that'll never change. Whether it was choosing up sides for schoolyard kickball or buying the first round of cocktails, I've always been the one to get things going.

The girls never exactly ignored me either. From the first grade on, I had a different girlfriend every year—okay, they were merely special recess playmates at those young ages—even if it's been quite a while without one of late. From the seventh through the twelfth grades, classmates elected me to the Student Council. That's every year I was eligible to run. And my senior class at Milton picked me as its president. I'm talking about that nifty little business college south of Madison, Wisconsin that went defunct years ago. Don't let anybody tell you it was another rich kids' Flunk-Out U. I learned a lot there, even if hardly any of it came from books. The guys that ran that place were smart enough to make us stick to business, and not waste our time on stupid subjects like creative writing—unlike Kevin. Not that I didn't already know pretty much what's what before I showed up on campus.

That I basically had down before I was old enough to drive. When to use the soft sell and when the hard, when to back off and when to push for the name on the dotted line. Not that I ever took advantage of a soul. I never met a person I didn't like either, at least as long as necessary. I've never had the slightest problem getting people to listen to whatever I had to say either. They had better if you're in sales, believe you me. So that's why dear Kevin had so gotten under my skin. I not only couldn't talk sense into the kid, I couldn't talk to him period.

Still, nobody could ask for a finer son, the apple of this old man's eye, ever since the boy entered this world with a fuller head of coal-black hair than I've seen in the mirror since hitting thirty. He grew up to be tall and handsome and sharp as a tack. Three guesses why.

His mother and I didn't spoil him, we didn't neglect him, and we were always there. I never once regretted having to marry Jean either because I'd gotten her knocked up. Like my ex, I dearly loved Kevin as a baby, just as I did as a little boy and as teenager, just as I do now. I would have gladly sat there in the bleachers for him every single game, be it for Little League or varsity football, if my son had only been willing to play. But he never showed the slightest interest in any extracurricular activity, unless you count cross country. But heck, I encouraged that just like it was a genuine sport. I asked him about it over every dinner he was willing to eat with us until he graduated from high school and moved out on his own.

I can't say I haven't enjoyed corresponding with Kevin these past couple of years, no matter how strange his letters sometimes became. After an eloquent description of yet another exotic resort, often as not he would end up ranting about yet another jerk he had run into. Strange to admit, Kevin was seldom more articulate than when ticked off. Sort of like me. Except I'd only go on like that after one too many drinks, and then only with an old sales buddy. And I'd make sure it all came across as one big joke, regardless of how irate I really felt.

Usually Kevin and I each wrote about twice a month. I always answered his letters promptly, even if in a sense he never answered mine. Because no matter what I asked him—How was the hotel in Machu Pichu? Was the Extremadura food spicy?—he never truly replied. The Dear Dad he always began with might just as well have been Dear Diary, because he just used me as a sounding board.

Soon I began to feel like a subscriber to an eccentric magazine that mixed articulate travelogues to faraway places with raving editorials about all the assholes residing there. Customs officials, cab drivers, desk clerks, cleaning maids, waiters, maitre d's—he swore every last one of them was out to ruin his visit.

His letters always consisted of exactly three sheets handwritten on both sides, which came to six full pages of text. Still, he could have saved a lot of paper, if he hadn't insisted on writing so large or leaving so much space between the lines. But then I've always been one to cram my sentences so close together that the tails of my p's and q's overlapped the spikes of the t's and d's beneath—sort of nice and cozy, like my favorite bars. Not that I've done my drinking in such places for years, since the only guys frequenting the joints my age are derelicts.

Then one bleary-eyed Sunday morning I wrote what I thought was an innocent enough letter. I told Kevin about my most recent skirmish out back with the yellow jackets. I had annihilated a whole squadron of the winged varmints with a can of Raid that shot them out of the air from twenty feet. In closing, I happened to add: Kevin, you know I've never been picky, but do you realize you could save a whole sheet every letter, if you'd only stop leaving so much space between the lines? Believe you me, the pages add up. The trees you spare will thank you for it. Love, Dad.

Exactly four days later—two days for my letter to reach Atlanta, and two more for his immediate reply to make it back—I received the following: Dear Dad, your letters would be a lot more legible, if you only wouldn't cram everything so close together. What's the big difference between words and people anyway? K.

That last line shouldn't have given me such a twinge of pique, since it made no sense. Still, I read and reread it till it was echoing inside my head night and day. Finally, I resolved to ignore it and instead wrote back about the random patches of dead grass all over my lawn because of spraying so much of that potent pesticide. And I mentioned beginning a new flower bed just behind the garage and striking a vein of coal so thick it broke my shovel.

Three weeks later I got a picture postcard of the Grand Canyon. Kevin said he and Tina had just taken a rubber raft trip down the Colorado, a mighty river that kept cutting ever more deeply through the billion-year-old rock at the bottom.

And he asked whether there was enough coal in my backyard to warrant mining.

I snorted at that stupid remark. Or was it just a joke, since he knew full well all the local deposits are high in sulfur? Besides, why would I compromise the integrity of my own home's foundation just for more income, just because I was behind on all my bills? Love, K., he concluded as usual and added a brief P.S.: Dad, I just fulfilled the greatest fantasy of my life—I screwed a guy's wife in his very own bed.

Good God almighty! I bridled so hard at that remark I wrenched my neck. A good thing his mother had long since moved out, so she didn't have to read anything this awful. What in the world could the guy have done to deserve such a nasty revenge? I combed Kevin's card in a vain search for an explanation. Not that I hadn't enjoyed more affairs myself with married women than I'd care to recount, both before and since my divorce. But in my defense I at least suffered passing pangs of guilt.

I waited three weeks before writing back. I told my son about our drought so bad the copperheads nesting in my neighbor's brush pile had gone on the prowl. And then, as if only mildly curious, I added, What was it again that guy whose bed you recently warmed did to you?

Well, my phrasing seemed inoffensive, but, boy, was I ever wrong. Four days later, Kevin's reply hit my mailbox like a bomb. Inside a business envelope I found my own letter all crumpled, and across an index card he had scrawled in red ink: Thanks for ruining my day. K.

What? I almost gave Kevin's mother a call on the spot. But I held back, because Jean's new husband always answered their phone. So for two weeks I puzzled over that single weird sentence of my son's on my own and abandoned the yard to the vermin. Then I composed a highly diplomatic twelve-page reply, assuring him of my profound love and expressing my hopes that his life might be fulfilling in every imaginable sense. At long last, I got to the point: I admitted how offended I was by his curtness, verging on rudeness.

Four days later, a tiny envelope arrived with a brief note: Tina opened your last letter for me and decided your sniveling drivel might hurt my feelings, so she tore it up and flushed the pieces down the toilet. K.

Now that really straightened my back. The whole next week I tossed and turned in bed nights between dreams about tiptoeing among hissing and slithering vipers. Finally, I swallowed my pride and gave Jean a ring.

Yes? her hubby, Jack, answered in his rich baritone. I asked for Jean without identifying myself, but the audible gloat in his voice indicated he knew who was calling.

First thing my ex blurted, Dick, oh, I'm so glad you phoned! Kevin wouldn't answer any of her letters, she said, so she had called him at work. There they told her he'd quit his job.

I almost dropped the receiver on the floor.

Next Jean had immediately phoned Tina at the fitness center. Apparently, young Kevin had gotten it into his head that at heart he wasn't a travel agent, but rather a novelist. His trips had allegedly provided more than enough material for a dozen books, so now all he had to do was to write them out. For that he needed absolute freedom from any demands on his time, especially the burden of gainful employment.

Couldn't he write evenings and weekends? I shouted.

Jean had already suggested that, but Tina said he'd be too tired.

How about working halftime? Jean had tried that as well and was told that'd still be too distracting.

My God, how's he going to pay the bills? I hollered.

It seemed Tina was earning enough for the both of them, especially after the huge dollops of pre-inheritance her father was tossing their direction.

What are we going to do, Jean? I said in a panic.

Well, she wasn't going to do anything herself, since Kevin was long since old enough to make his own decisions and accept the consequences. Besides, as long as he refused to talk to her, whatever happened only served him right. Then Jean asked about me.

No, I wasn't dating or getting together with friends, I replied. My odd schedule with evening property showings and Sunday open houses simply made socializing too difficult. So whenever I wasn't working, I pretty much kept myself busy around the house.

Doing what?

I told her it was too long a story.

She excused herself to get going on the canapés for the dinner party she and Jack were hosting.

I hung up in a daze. Sure, our son was an adult, but what if his adult decisions were god-awful? I immediately sat down and wrote Kevin a long letter, begging him not to be hasty about giving up—my goodness!—a line of sales where the customers came looking for you. Couldn't he at first try writing in his spare time just to see how it went? Especially, since he had a better chance of flying by flapping his arms than ever seeing any books of his in print.

Exactly four days later, I got a picture postcard of Edvard Munch's "The Scream" with one short sentence: You always did want me to fail. K.

What? I had never ever wanted any such thing. That was as preposterous as saying I tried to ruin my marriage.

For two weeks I fretted and stewed over Kevin's nasty reproach till the taste of bile lingered in my mouth no matter how many times I brushed my teeth. Finally, one sleepless night I bolted out of bed at 3:00 a.m. and scribbled a hasty reply: Dear Kevin, your last note is so ridiculous I don't know whether to laugh or cry. Was that Munch postcard some sort of sick joke? In any case, it was cruel. And would you please call your mother once in a while—as a favor to her, to me, and yourself? Your loving father.

Four days later, I get another postcard, this time of Picasso's "Guernica." Dear Mr. Nortman, it read, I mean what I say and I say what I mean. You never did take me seriously. Kevin Vincent Van Gogh Nortman.

What in the hell was going on? This time I mulled my response over for a whole month. Then the morning after my black walnuts dropped all of their fronds with the leaves still intact, I stopped by the local Little Professor to check out the new employee a real estate prospect had casually mentioned. There was no denying Leslie was pretty, but for my taste too scrawny. My eyes came to rest upon a book entitled *The Craft of Fiction: a Handbook for New Writers*. I immediately bought a copy and shipped it off to Kevin.

Six evenings later, the UPS man dropped off a small package without a return address, but with an Atlanta postmark. My first happy thought was that my son was reciprocating my gift with a book on gardening. I slit the box open with four deft cuts and found the cover of the book I had sent him resting on a bed of confetti. Upon closer look I saw it was actually my present all ripped to shreds. And on the bottom lay a crumpled postcard of a Van Gogh self-portrait looking fierce enough to cut off his other ear. On the back was the brief typewritten message: I rest my case. It was unsigned.

Who knows how long I just stood there glaring at the damned mess? I recall picking it up and turning toward the garbage can. The next thing I knew I was flinging the scraps all over the kitchen and kicking the empty box off the walls. Then I grabbed a bottle of wine and charged outside.

I was still sprawled on my patio chaise lounge, when the twittering chimney swifts yielded the falling darkness and the flying insects to the nighthawks and bats. I still hadn't budged, when an unlucky lightning bug entangled itself in a spider web stretched across the rusty legs of Jean's favorite lawn chair. I watched the point of light flash on and off till it extinguished forever.

Despite all the wine, I couldn't fall asleep. At 2:30 I quit trying, got up, and wrote Kevin the heart-to-heart letter I should have sent ages ago. It took me an hour to get past the second paragraph, but once I did my feelings poured out like hornets from a hammered nest. As the night gave way to twilight, I kept scribbling away. In closing, I said I didn't know which upset me more, his wanton destruction of a perfectly good book or his callous rebuff of every attempt at reconciliation.

Just before I stuffed the letter in a large manila envelope, I proofread it and decided there was no way I could express myself any better. I was rising to my feet to put it in my briefcase by the door, when suddenly I found myself tearing the handwritten pages to ribbons. I snatched a fresh sheet, hopped over to the breakfast table, and scrawled, Kevin, you've turned out to be the most selfish son of a bitch I've ever met. You make me regret ever getting married. Sincerely, Dad. And I mailed it.

Four days later, a business envelope arrived from you-know-who. It felt empty to the touch. But when I opened it, a thin sheet slid out. Dearest Dad, it began. I'm out here in the backyard, taking a break from revising my novel. The cicadas up in the loblolly pines are serenading me like a chorus of hot whetstones, while the mosquitoes are whining in my ears for more blood. To replenish my creative juices, I'm quaffing ice tea. Your Loving Son, Kevin.

Fork

Inch by inch he nudged her from the hallway into his studio apartment, their lips never losing contact—

"—Stop."

Her fiery red hair tickling his cheeks, her cool fingers slipping beneath his tie-dyed shirt, he guided her toward the mattress, awaiting them on the floor.

"Gregory, stop."

"What?"

"That one's it." His wife was pointing at a residence across the street.

Gregory Melby blinked away the bittersweet memories and only then examined the ranch-style house with a big picture window, built-in garage, black eagle figurine, white picket fence, and putt-perfect lawn. Like every other home in this Madison neighborhood. Only this one belonged to their old University of Wisconsin friends, Dennis and Sandra Hecht.

"Hope they haven't given up on us," he muttered. "Since we're so late."

"Come on," Jane said. "We didn't get that lost at the fork."

Using the rear-view mirror, Greg combed a few stray strands of his Princeton-cut hair back into place. He frowned at its phony uniform brown. Not that Dennis and Sandy would mind whatever he'd done to further his business career. He shut his eyes and let out a weary sigh.

"Greg, what's the matter with you? If you're that light-headed, grab a snack, for Pete's sake!"

Sandy's invitation said to park their Volvo in the driveway, so that was what he now did. Meanwhile, Jane retrieved a half bagel with cream cheese from a shopping bag in the backseat and handed her husband the snack. Greg bit off an end from the ugly clump of bread and chewed away.

Five minutes later, he still hadn't eaten more than a morsel, while studying a yellow jacket futilely probing the windshield, as if the wasp just might find an opening. With a toss of her close-cropped, dark-haired head, Jane said, "Well, we can't sit here all day."

The front door of the ranch house swung open, and a gray-haired woman in a cardinal T-shirt, cutoff denims, and sandals emerged. "You made it!" she shouted and giggled like tinkling bells.

A grinning bald man, his hands awkwardly jammed into the front pockets of khaki slacks, joined her. "*Bienvenus, monsieur, madame!*" he greeted with a perfect Parisian accent. An entire decade having passed since they had last seen each another, his pencil moustache had gotten as grizzled as his temples.

Sandy and Dennis of course. Actually, neither looked bad for their later forties. Better than Gregory did himself anyway, though Jane was holding her age the best of all. The heads of a calico and a pure white cat popped through the curtains in the picture window and let out silent meows.

* * *

"So you decided against bringing the kids," Sandy piped up with an unmistakable wistfulness to her mellow alto, once their guests had carried their luggage into the spare bedroom and joined their hosts in the living room. Simone, the calico feline that her letter had warned shunned strangers, nestled into her lap. So he and Jane wouldn't take offense, she had meant.

"Ha!" Jane shouted. "You try telling two teenage boys where to go and when!"

Sandy's frown verged on a grimace. Good thing she let the issue drop, since neither Greg nor Jane was keen to discuss how their wayward sons were turning out.

"The usual, everybody?" Dennis asked. Gregory glanced away from his old grad school pal's bloodshot eyes and met kitty Jean-Paul's vertical slits. The white tomcat hopped up onto Greg's lap and scratched its snout against the stranger's stubbly chin. So their male feline at least was friendly.

"*Bien sur*," Jane replied in mediocre French. "*Un bon vin blanc pour moi.* But please make it a small serving."

Dennis's grin was still boyishly mischievous, though since last seen his once engaging gaze had become oddly disquieting. "How about you, Grégoire?"

"Sure," Greg replied, glancing away from what the air conditioner was doing to Sandy's chest under her Bucky Badger T-shirt. Why was the darned thing set at such a chilly temperature?

"Sure what? Would you like some wine, too?"

Greg met Sandy's eyes, the clear azure blue of a high Wisconsin sky, and shrugged. "I hardly drink anymore. But okay." On account of this special occasion.

"Gregory, wasn't your drink brandy back then?" Jane asked with a convivial chuckle. Sandy wrapped her slender fingers around the calico's flanks, and it purred in response.

"Yeah, that's right," Dennis said. "Brandy Manhattans at the 602 Club every Monday after Professor Jacomet's deadly seminars. Our first semester, wasn't it? Sandy, do we have any of that Korbel's left?"

She stood up with a distracted grin, and Greg looked away from her tight cutoffs. "Or was that during our second semester?" he asked. Even though he knew full well Dennis wasn't mistaken.

"*Flaubert et Maupassant, n'est-ce pas?*" Jane asked, her French accent as hopelessly American as ever.

"*Exactement, madame!*" Dennis pronounced like a debonair Parisian boulevardier. "*Le mot juste.* And all that other *merde.*"

"You know what, Denny," Greg muttered, sitting up straighter. "Maybe I'd best hold off on the alcohol for now. Do you have mineral water? And some sort of snack?"

Sandy halted in the doorway, a bottle of unopened brandy in hand, and retreated to the kitchen.

"Greg has hypoglycemia," Jane said, a familiar note of annoyance undercutting the blitheness. "It's not a problem so long as he avoids sugar like strychnine and snacks regularly."

Dennis stifled a chuckle. "Sort of like me with salt. Except I can eat a little."

Sandy returned with a platter of freshly baked chocolate chip cookies, visibly pleased with her handiwork. And why not? A shame such a natural nurturer never became a mom. Not that she and Denny hadn't sorely tried. An old letter implied the problem was his.

Gregory can't eat any sugar," Dennis told a visibly disappointed Sandy.

"I suppose one wouldn't hurt," Greg said, but their hostess knew better than to force a treat upon a guest.

"So how's the insurance business coming, Gregory?" Dennis asked.

Greg stared at him like a wary tomcat, sizing up a feline rival.

"Greg got promoted to Associate Director last month," Jane jumped in.

"My condolences," Dennis quipped.

A genuine smile flashed across Greg's face and as quickly vanished. Because the work was as bullshit as any other throughout his checkered career, but at least the salary was decent for a welcome change. Not that this made him feel any less discontented. He shut his eyes.

Clutching her curvaceous body flush against his and thrusting, her silky, long red hair tickling his cheek—

"—Greg?"

His eyes popped back open. "May I please use your bathroom?" he said.

"Come on, honey!" Jane shouted. "These guys are old friends! Just go!"

When he came back, sweetly grinning Sandy approached with a new food offering and bent forward deeply, saying, "Here, try some of these instead." Too deeply, in fact. Or was Greg imagining intent in mere accident? "Dennis eats these unsalted corn chips all the time," she added, her smile audible in her lilting alto. Amazing that after all these years she still had such a schoolgirl's innocent air, as if not even suspecting anything might ever go awry.

* * *

He hung his blue workshirt atop the bell-bottom jeans and tiptoed toward the mattress on the floor. If she was still asleep, he'd best not awaken her.

But the bed now lay empty, the sheets thrown back. "How can you read this?" she piped up from his desk chair. He spun around. There she sat, browsing through his thesis notes, goose bumps popping out all over her near naked, long-limbed, gangly body.

"Sartre's fiction's a lot simpler than his philosophy," he told her.

"I meant your handwriting," she said, widening her big, brown eyes.

"Oh, that's just my personal hieroglyphics."

She didn't laugh, not that he really expected her to, since she seldom found his quips amusing. She gave his near nudity an ironic double-take. "You mean we're finally going to do it?" she practically yelled.

He smoothed his shaggy hair back behind both ears and nodded.

"I'm in no mood for just fooling around," she teased, an edge to her soprano striking him exactly wrong. Even if at heart his fellow graduate student was anything but nasty or mean.

"Don't worry," he responded, his voice pinched with apprehension.

"Good-oh!" She dropped her bra and panties to the floor and bounced over to the mattress.

He turned his back toward her and lowered his jockey shorts and shyly faced her aggressive grin.

* * *

Greg perched sideways on the edge of the unforgiving mattress, his face only inches from the wallpaper with the seagull motif. His spent air whistled through nostrils strangely half-closed, his breathing twice as fast as Jane's, lying just behind him. Lucky girl to sleep so like a child. She had been his spouse now for twenty years, and his closest friend, and so of course also his best confidante. Who knew as much about him as any person on earth, including every family skeleton, faux pas, peccadillo, and embarrassment. Still, there were things she had never heard.

On paper it didn't make sense that he wasn't satisfied with his current life. Everybody who knew them insisted he and Jane made an ideal couple. Yet he was more frustrated with their marriage than he had once believed possible.

Images from their first day back in Madison, Wisconsin kept churning through his mind. Beaming Dennis showing off a labyrinth of musty, yellowing tomes in the used-book store he owned and ran. Embarrassed Sandy pointing out the tacky office building where she toiled as a legal secretary. State Street, once the laid-back, dinky downtown of a student ghetto, now a yuppie haven of tony shops selling Japanese imports, mountain bikes, and gourmet coffee—as if tasteful shopping were the long sought millennium at last attained. To think they had once risked their skulls against police billy clubs for this paltry a future.

But this was no time for dwelling on the past. No, somehow he had to get some rest, since the next day's schedule would permit no nap. Following an early morning tour of their alma mater and brunch at the Ovens of Brittany, they would head up to Devil's Lake State Park and spend the afternoon swimming and picnicking, before driving back for dinner at Paisan's, their favorite old haunt. Finally, they would take in a Gerard Depardieu French flick late at the Majestic Theater. As full as a typical day of graduate school, only this time it'd be sheer pleasure. At least that was the plan.

Not that it had ever been pure drudgery back then. Yet the prospect of so much relentless relaxation on so little rest made him tense with dread. But how was he supposed to doze off, if he just wasn't sleepy? Exhausted sure, after the long drive from St. Louis, but not drowsy.

A half hour later Greg still lay there, his thoughts roiling as before. Why, if he hadn't drunk more than two swallows of brandy and a fourth of the St. Pauli Girl beer that Dennis had foisted upon him. Just before going to bed, he had made a point of eating cheese and crackers to ward off low blood sugar. So if he wasn't hungry, then why was his stomach growling? Hadn't he slept well in plenty of worse beds, for instance just last month at that Kansas City conference?

The thing to do was to concentrate on a pleasant memory till it drowned everything else out. Perhaps one from junior high. It didn't take long before he was focused on swimming as a thirteen-year-old in his hometown public pool under the lifeguards' watchful gaze. A flick of his thumb would send a dime knifing into the water twenty feet ahead. He would plunge after it, surging forward with long, smooth leg kicks and arm strokes, and catch the coin just before it touched bottom. The silvery face tumbled brow over neck, slowing with every rotation instead of accelerating. Why was this such a favorite pastime? Because no one else could swim underwater so ably? Because to people above the surface he moved in a wobbly blur? The dime would land in his palm as softly as an eyelash tickling a cheek.

* * *

He stood in his bare feet, his toes sinking into the shag carpet, dropped his jockey shorts to the floor, grabbed the trunks from the chair, and tugged them on. "Man, I hope the pool's warmer than your apartment," he quipped, the fit of the borrowed swimsuit so snug it gave his crotch a dull ache. She giggled behind his back like tinkling bells.

"Come on in!" she teased with that adorable alto voice and dipped out of sight, moments later to rocket out, shaking her long red hair like a sopping dog. A freezing plume of water hit him square in the face.

* * *

She stood, holding the refrigerator door open, its light illuminating her flowing, diaphanous nightgown and silhouetting what he shouldn't notice, not on such a dear, old friend. "There's yogurt," she said with a lilting giggle. "And brie and crackers. And cantaloupe, strawberries, and bagels. How about a croissant?" As starved as he felt, it all looked tempting, especially the dark patch between her legs.

Afterwards, back in bed his thickening felt so uncomfortable squished against the mattress he shifted his buttocks till he found relief. As the snack crept into his blood, he finally began to relax.

* * *

"Just lie down and go limp," Denny instructed, stroking his bearded chin. "Make yourself heavy as possible, like a sack of potatoes. Whatever you do, don't resist."

Sandy's bright, cherubic smile dimmed a few watts. Jane nodded with a gulp, as Greg grabbed her clammy hand.

"They're here," Dennis said and took a deep breath. Three paddy wagons pulled up in quick succession. The back doors flew open and out spilled helmeted city cops, billy clubs in hand. The grim officers stepped silently among the hippies, blocking a main campus intersection, their spit-polished shoes just missing the sprawling bodies.

"They're coming this way!" Jane squealed.

A coed nearby let out a yelp. A friendly hand clasped her mouth and hugged her close.

"I hope I don't wet my pants!" Jane said, snuggling against Greg.

"Remember, like a sack of potatoes," Denny whispered.

"French fries good enough?" Greg joked, his pulse pounding in his ears, and Sandy giggled. The zigzagging columns of navy blue converged without comment or curse upon Dennis, the man on the megaphone throughout the last three days of campus unrest. After commandeering a spontaneous library mall rally, he had persuaded the protesters to occupy the Administration building and that day to block Park Street at University Avenue.

Madison's finest at last reached their target, and two beefy cops calmly thrust their hands into Denny's Caucasian Afro and hoisted him off the ground by his hair.

* * *

"How's the moussaka?" Jane asked their guests.

"Fine," Greg told her and lifted his Manhattan high to drain the last few drops into his gaping mouth. His wife wrinkled her brow in disgust.

"Are you okay, Greg?" Sandy said from across the table, wanly grinning. Had anyone in his entire life expressed concern more sincerely?

Greg ogled her chiseled upper lip and shrugged. Just what about that particular feature was so compelling? But then what was attractive about anything on anybody? Or what made one relationship effortless and another teeth-gnashingly difficult? "Hey, guys, how about another round?" he called out. "Waiter, you call this place a bar? It's more like a funeral parlor without the gladiolas."

When the refills arrived, Dennis said, "Greg, you still haven't said a word about your work."

"What do you want to hear?" he replied and swiped a swig of his wife's brandy. "How I spend my days? Read the emails and wastebasket them. Back up important memos and delete the other ninety-nine percent. Surf the Web till I'm close to drowning. If it gets really bad, conjugate new verbs. Such as byte, bit, bought. Or better yet baud, bode, can't abide? Neither has a perfective, because the action is never completed. Ditto for the conditional, because nobody has any choice. Do you think this flood of information will ever dry out?"

"Greg," Jane pleaded.

"Stop the war!" Greg shouted. "Off the pigs! Don't trust anybody under thirty! Or was it over thirty? I forget."

"Whatever you're up to, it doesn't sound like Flaubert," Dennis said.

"I'll drink to that," Greg said. "And a vulture isn't a warbler. But it goes to bed well-fed."

Jane slipped a hand into her spouse's. "Remember that Mifflin Street party we all went to?" she piped up. "Drinking brandy straight from the bottle and passing joints around the size of cigars. Was that right before or right after we got engaged, Greg?"

"Shhh, don't say that word so loud," he teased.

"Engaged?"

"No, the j-word," Greg said with a guffaw, and Dennis scowled.

"No, wait," Jane went on. "Denny, by then you were already over in Paris, researching that thesis you never finished. But Sandy—"

"—Sandy joined me in France the following summer," Dennis blurted, his tone suddenly metallic.

"You mean the summer Greg and I got engaged?"

"And then the following year Jane got pregnant," Greg added with a chortle. "And we both bagged grad school for good. Or was it for bad?"

"Yeah, I was at that block party," Sandy muttered, slowly rotating her empty wine glass between both palms.

"Of course!" Jane said. "That was the weekend my Mount Holyoke professor came to town, and I met him for dinner. Man, did I get wrecked. But old Fabrice never let on that he noticed. Greg, didn't you and Sandy go see some obscure New Wave French flick then?"

Dennis sat up straight, gnashed his teeth, and grasped his fork like a dagger. Sandy blinked, while Greg stared dumbly straight ahead.

Nobody said a word, while Sandy crossed her arms and slumped.

"Greg," Jane said, "you and Sandy went to several movies together back then. Whenever I had a paper due or something."

Greg grabbed his wife's drink and chugged the rest of it.

* * *

He opened the door just enough for her to sidle inside. With one hand he secured the deadbolt, while the other pulled her curvaceous body close, and their lips locked on, her teeth raking his tongue and her hands grasping his belt. The instant they hit the mattress on the floor, the phone began ringing and wouldn't stop while they writhed and groaned.

Afterwards, they lay intertwined in dreamy exhaustion. When the telephone again jangled, he snatched it and mumbled, "Uh-huh."

"Where have you been?" his girlfriend whined into his ear.

"At the library," he said, lying with ease. Too bad it took him so long to recognize this valuable management skill. When his surprise guest tried to stand up, he grabbed her wrist. She yanked it free and got dressed.

"Are we going to get engaged then?" his girlfriend whimpered over the phone.

"Oh, honey," he replied. Cupping his hand tightly over the receiver, he whispered, "Don't go."

His guest paused at the door to mutter, "I'm dropping out of school and flying to Paris as soon as I can."

"Greg, are you still there?" the tinny voice said in his hand.

The apartment door clicked shut. "Of course we'll be getting engaged, honey," he told her.

* * *

"Hey, waiter, did you lose one earring or what?" Greg yelled at their twenty-something waiter. "And isn't it high time to mow your unruly mop again?"

The pony-tailed youngster rolled his eyes.

"Seriously, young man," Greg said, "how about another round while we're deciding upon dessert?"

"Greg," Jane pleaded, laying a hand upon his.

"Do you have anything without sugar?" Sandy asked.

"Since she's sweet enough as it is!" Greg blurted.

"Ma'am," the waiter replied, "I assure you there's not one grain of sucrose on the premises. Least of all not in any dessert."

"Right on!" Greg hollered, his fist shooting into the air. "Power to the people! The personal is political!"

"Please don't bring us any more drinks," Jane said.

"I'll drink to that!" Greg shouted. "Denny, you still with us? Hey, somebody take his pulse."

Dennis's bloodshot eyes glanced up from his empty stein. "Get the damn bill," he snapped at the server.

Sandy's azure eyes glistened with tears.

* * *

She shuffled off her blue workshirt and bell bottoms and stepped into his naked embrace. No, he shouldn't have taken her hand during the movie. Nor should he have put his arm around her, walking back to campus. Just as he shouldn't have kissed her in the stairwell. Because she was not just a good friend, but a good friend's girlfriend. He hadn't planned on any of it. But yet it had happened. Whatever sense that made.

"Just this once," he promised.

"Just this once," she echoed.

Hope Chest

Have a little more, Lisa, Mom says. You're much too thin. And listen to the rest of the French tape. Finish what you start. Only take something out to use. Follow through to the end. Anything worth doing at all is worth doing well. Put things back when you're done. Change to a blouse that's been pressed. Dear, aren't those jeans dirty?

Sort of.

Sort of is not a choice, Dear. Exactly, invariably, evidently, absolutely, of course, of course not—now those are choices. But not sort of.

Whatever.

Whatever is not a choice either, Dear. Dirty clothes go in the hamper, not back on your body. Why don't you hurry and take another shower before we go do our shopping? If there's a sale, you might want to try something on. A person can never be too clean.

Mom, do I have to?

Absolutely, Dad pipes up.

Can't I go out like this?

Dear, you could if we were going out to sweep the sidewalk or to wash the windows, but not to the mall. Besides, it's not a question of can, but of may. Everything has its place. Have you found the key to your hope chest yet?

Not yet, I say.

Don't forget to scrub the stall when you're done, Dear. And if you use the toilet, scrub that too. Put the Ajax back under the sink. And don't forget to wash your hands.

Whatever, I mumble.

I beg your pardon, Dear.

Yes, Ma'am.

I'm the only girl I know who likes school better than Saturdays. Sure, the teachers are like guards and the principal a warden, but nobody tells me what to do there half as much as at home, where it's just Mom and Dad and me. Me, I'm Lisa Blunt. I'm a junior in high school, and Dad teaches French at the college and smokes a pipe, but only outside of course, even when it's freezing. A house is no place to smoke a pipe. Everything has its place.

As for Mom, well, where should I start? Mom's as smart as Dad, or probably smarter. And she's a professor too, but of library science. A library is made up of Public and Technical Services. Public Services is divided into Reference, Circulation, Reserve, and Interlibrary Loan. Technical Services is divided into Acquisitions and Cataloging. Cataloging consists of description and access. Access consists of main and added entries. The Anglo-American Cataloging Rules are rules, not recommendations or guidelines. And a rule is a rule. A period is never to be confused with a colon, or a semicolon with a comma, or a bracket with a parenthesis, or a dash with an ellipsis. Absolutely. Mom never tires of teaching me things.

Mom is what you might call organized. So is Dad for that matter. Finish what you start. Only take something out to use. Follow through to the end. Anything worth doing at all is worth doing well. Put things back when you're done. No ifs, ands, or buts. Exactly, invariably, evidently, absolutely, of course, of course not—now those are choices. But not sort of. And not whatever.

Saturdays begin when our two alarms go off at seven a.m. On the dot. We get up, we brush our teeth, we take our showers, we turn on a Mozart CD, we fix yolkless omelets and wholewheat toast and squeeze fresh orange juice. Invariably. And we make cafe au lait for Mom and Dad and pour milk for me. I'm not old enough yet for coffee. Of course not. Me, I'm in charge of the bread and fruit, Mom the eggs and coffee, and Dad the morning paper.

Has the key turned up yet, Dear?

Not yet, I say.

We finish eating at eight on the dot and I turn off the Mozart CD. Music is out of place when Mom needs to think clearly. She gets out a fresh sheet of paper and rewrites the shopping list in columns like the supermarket's aisles. Exactly. I get going on the dishes. Dad finishes up the paper and heads off to his college office to word-process more of his latest monograph. Which is like a book, only a lot shorter. Pretty soon he'll be done with his fourth, about some playwright named Molly Eyre. Only it's a guy.

Once I finish up the washing, I move on to drying. The spoons all go in the spoon drawer. The serving spoons go on the left, the soup spoons in the middle, the dessert spoons on the right. The scuffed combat boots go on the hope chest bottom.

The forks all go in the fork drawer. The serving forks go on the left, the entree forks in the middle, the salad forks on the right. The torn plaid shirt goes on top of the combat boots.

The knives all go in the knife drawer. The cutting knives go on the left, the entree knives in the middle, the butter knives on the right. The striped miniskirt goes on top of the plaid shirt.

I excuse myself to clean up. I take another shower in the downstairs bathroom. Where I comb my hair. Where I'd put on my face, if I was allowed to have a face. I put on a pressed Madras blouse, white cardigan, pleated khakis, and penny loafers. Without socks. And I wash my hands. Again. A person can never be too clean.

Can I drive this time, Mom? I say.

That's not funny, Dear, she says.

What else is new? Nothing I ever say is funny. I got my license now, but Mom and Dad don't let me drive either of our cars, though hers is only a Toyota Celica and Dad's a Mitsubishi. A person can never be too careful.

When you're out on your own and paying your own insurance, Mom says, will be plenty soon enough for you to be driving. Has the key turned up yet, Dear?

Not yet, I say.

It'd be easier to go just down the road to Easttowne because the other mall is clear across town. But Mom figures Westtowne is on the average one per cent cheaper. Not that we have to pinch pennies. But a penny saved is a penny earned. A stitch in time saves nine. The early bird catches the worm. Put things back when you're done. Everything has its place.

My job at Kroger's is to push the cart and check off the list and listen to Mom's instruction. On sniffing cantaloupe. On squeezing tomatoes. On hefting head lettuce. On comparing prices per ounce. On counting sodium milligrams. Mom never tires of teaching me things.

When I go to college, if I ever go to college, I have no idea what I'll major in. Shopping, cooking, and cleaning are what I'm best at, but they're not choices. Of course not.

By eleven-twenty I wheel our heaping cart out to the car, which is parked in the lot's far left corner. Invariably. Because that way there's less chance of scratching a door. Absolutely.

Mom always takes the shortest route home through the residential Near West Side despite all the stops and turns. Three tenths of a mile times two per trip times fifty-two Saturdays per year adds up to a lot of gas. Of course.

Mom backs up our driveway and into our double garage. Invariably. We carry the bags into the kitchen, where Mom takes charge of the perishables and me the rest. Everything has its place.

At noon on the dot I put the Mozart CD back on and start warming up the soup. Mom gets out the Gruyere and whole wheat bread for the toasted cheese sandwiches. Since it's Saturday.

The moment we're done with lunch, I turn off the Mozart CD and get going on the dishes. Music is out of place when Mom needs to think clearly. She begins writing out the new grocery list. The earlier the start, the better the result. Work fast and steady. Never hurry. Check your work. A person can never be too careful.

The small water tumblers go along the left front of the cupboard. The big tumblers go behind them. The tea cups go on the right front. The coffee cups go behind them. The saucers go in the middle. The black nylons go on top of the miniskirt.

The tumblers go upside down so the dust collects on the outside. The cups and saucers go upside down too. Dust them off before using them anyway. A person can never be too clean.

You know, Mom, I say, this wouldn't be necessary if the dust only stayed in its place.

That's not funny, Dear.

What else is new? Nothing I ever say is funny. Dad is sometimes funny though. If he's had enough wine. Mom doesn't want to be funny. It doesn't matter what I want.

Don't let a wet plate slip out of your grip, Dear. A person can never be too careful.

The Chinese china goes on the bottom shelf of the buffet. The Finnish china goes in the middle. The Wedgwood goes on top. The floppy-eared hunting cap goes alongside the black nylons.

At one thirty on the dot Mom shoves in the first load of laundry, the colors. Invariably. I get down on my hands and knees and scrub the kitchen floor, starting with tile number one in the back left corner. Ninety-five tiles to go. You can never see germs. You can sometimes see dirt. You can always see grunge. None are welcome in our house.

Change the water after tile number forty-eight, Dear. Wring out the mop. The Ajax goes back under the sink when you're done. The broom goes on the basement landing. The mop goes in the plastic pail.

As soon as I finish the kitchen, I get going on the two bathrooms. Fifty-six and forty-eight tiles. Between the loads of laundry, Mom picks up and vacuums. Not that there ever is anything to pick up or vacuum.

Did you lose the key at school, Dear?

Mom, I never took it to school.

The scuffed combat boots go on the hope chest bottom. The torn plaid shirt goes on top of the combat boots. The striped miniskirt goes on top of the plaid shirt. The black nylons go on top of the miniskirt. The floppy-eared hunting cap goes right next to the black nylons. The shiny little key goes inside the left Nike sneaker.

If I hurry, I can finish my chores by four, so by all means I hurry. Because from whenever I finish till five on the dot I'm free. That's when Mom and I start dinner. Invariably. My room I leave till last because I never let it get dirty. Which makes cleaning it easy. I never wear any shoes or comb my hair in there and I always shut the door to keep out dust. I only go in my room to change clothes or to pretend to study or to stuff more things into my hope chest. It's getting way too full.

The sweaters go in the bottom dresser drawer. The socks go in the top drawer. The blouses go on hangers. The Raggedy Ann doll goes on my bed propped against the two fluffed pillows.

The Nikes go against the back wall of the closet. The bag of marshmallows goes in the hope chest on top of the hunting cap.

When was the last time you saw your key, Dear?

Whenever. It's around here someplace.

Whenever is not a choice, Dear. You need to look harder. If at first you don't succeed, try, try again.

Hope chest is what Mom calls it anyway, because girls don't have hope chests anymore. They haven't for about a zillion years. It's just this old varnished wooden trunk that used to belong to my grandmother and then Mom when she was my age and now me.

Where could the key be then, Dear?

Mom, why do you keep asking? It feels like you're prying.

I never pry, Dear. I show concern.

Whatever.

Whatever is not a choice, Dear.

Yes, Ma'am.

Mom is real big on showing concern. Like on the phone with her best friend. Now wait a minute, Anita, she shouts, not that either is hard of hearing. Are you saying Bill McMichael's latest is the Joan Davis who was married to Tony Paniglia or do you mean the Joan Davis in the Development Office? Neither? You mean there's a third Joan Davis? By all means fill me in. Now you're talking about Tony Paniglia's ex, aren't you? The one who used to run the sewing shop on Court Street with her sister. No, not that sister. Angie is Joan's younger sister. That's right. It was Debby, her older sister that Joan went into business with. Yes, Debby Entwhistle! She's a Davis too. The woman whose husband had an affair with Judge Lawton's wife. Exactly.

Not that Mom actually knows anybody named Joan Davis or Debby Entwhistle or Bill McMichael or Tony Paniglia. Of course not. She's never met a one of them. But given enough time, she'll have every important detail of their lives in its place.

I finish my chores by four because from whenever I finish till five on the dot I'm free. Free to make phone calls. Only at that hour my girlfriends are still at the mall. Who else can I call?

The first time nobody answers.

The second time no answer either.

Crabtree residence, an older woman says the third try. Oh, my goodness, his mother! I slam down the phone. The marshmallows go in the hope chest. The empty marshmallow bags go in the bottom of my purse. My purse goes to school, where I dig out the wrappers and throw them in the trash.

It's almost five before I get up enough courage to try again.

Yeah, Rocky answers.

Awesome! He's at home!

Rocky, this is Lisa Blunt.

What?

Lisa Blunt. We're in the same American Problems class.

Sure. What's up, Lisa?

Well, I was just wondering what you were doing. You know, tonight. Later.

Whatever.

Right. Well, anyway, Rocky, I was just thinking that it might be fun if you and I got together.

Is this the Lisa whose dad teaches at the college?

Yeah, that's right. But Dad's okay. Honestly. Like, he doesn't mean anything by the way he is. Mom neither.

Uh-huh. Well, I'm going to a party tonight, but what if I come by and pick you up at ten? Would that work out?

Work out? Would it ever! Rocky, I gotta go now. See you later. I mean, tonight. I'll be there. I mean, here. Bye!

I hang up and pogo around the room.

What's going on in there, Dear?

Oh, nothing, Mom. I'll be right out.

I reach inside the Nike shoe and stop midway and pull my hand back out. I'm coming, Mom, I say.

At five on the dot Mom and I begin preparing dinner, which is vegetarian pasta. Since it's Saturday. Mom begins by telling me again that it'd taste better if we made it from scratch, but we don't have the time to do that every week. Or actually any week that I remember.

* * *

Have a little more, Dear. You're much too thin.

Have a little more pasta, Dear.

Absolutely, Dad pipes up.

But, Mom, if I have seconds, I'll have to skip dessert.

Dear, we never skip dessert and we never have seconds. We just have a little more.

Absolutely, Dad pipes up.

Whatever.

How do you like the pasta, Dear?

The same as ever.

Does that mean it's good, Dear? The same as ever is not a choice.

Absolutely, Dad pipes up.

Don't interrupt, James. It sets a bad example. Does the same as ever mean it's good, Dear?

Absolutely, I say.

Mom smiles.

Mom. Ah, Dad, like, you both work full time and we're not hurting for money, so I was just wondering if maybe we could afford a cleaning service.

We don't need a cleaning service, Dear. What brings on this strange question?

Oh, I don't know. Just sometimes I'd like to join the other kids at the mall. You know, like on Saturdays.

No, I don't know. And do what?

Whatever. Hang out.

I beg your pardon, Dear.

I shrug. I blush. I get hot. How can I explain hanging out to Mom? She's never wasted a minute in her life.

Did you say hang out, Dear?

Yeah.

Don't slur your words, Dear. Say yes if you mean yes, and no if you mean no. But yeah is not a choice, and nah isn't either.

Absolutely, Dad pipes up.

I'm still waiting to hear what hanging out means, Dear.

I get hotter. I guess I don't know, I say.

But you do know, Dear, or you wouldn't have said it. I'm still waiting for you to explain yourself.

Hanging out means, ah, like, to just stand or sit around with your friends, and, well, I don't know.

With what eventual goal, Dear?

I stammer.

Don't just make noises, Dear. And please refrain from using like except as a preposition or verb. If you need time to think, then think, but to yourself of course. And then after you've decided what you want to say, say it.

Absolutely, Dad pipes up.

Well, like, there is no goal, I guess.

You mean hanging out is pointless?

No.

If there's no goal, then hanging out is definitely pointless.

Well, I guess the point is to have fun.

Doing what?

Hanging out.

You're being redundant, Dear. It sounds like a waste of time.

Absolutely, Dad pipes up.

I nod. I give up. Nodding is the same as giving up. Hanging out is like hiring a cleaning service, which is like trying to get a cat. Which would be fine if we lived out in the country, but not in a house like ours in the city. Here a cat would be out of place.

Dear, is it merely my imagination or are your teeth getting discolored?

I nod. I give up. Nodding is the same as giving up.

As soon as we're done eating, I brush them again. And again. They're still the same color as before, a dirty white, a dull gray. I guess I'm losing enamel. Like Mom did a long time ago.

I help Mom do dishes. She washes, I dry. Dad attacks *The New York Times*.

When Mom and I are done, we join Dad in the living room, where he's sitting in his easy chair. I take my place against the left arm of the couch and Mom hers against the right arm. Everything has its place. It's time to watch a videotape. A French movie with English subtitles of course. The subtitles are for my benefit. Mom and Dad don't need them.

French movies are always awful and not because I can't understand them. They just don't have any plot or anything else interesting. This one is even worse. This mother and father and their two little boys go on an endless family vacation to a sunny pile of rocks. Nothing bad ever happens, nothing good ever happens, nothing much happens at all. But they're all really happy anyway.

The Hershey bars go in the hope chest alongside the marshmallows. The empty wrappers go in the bottom of my purse. My purse goes to school where I dig out the wrappers and throw them in the trash.

This French film is even too much for Dad. Once he even yawns, but with his mouth shut. Of course. Because visible yawning is rude. I yawn with my mouth shut, too. Over and over. We watch the film all the way to the end anyway. Of course. Don't start a book you don't finish. The same goes for films. Follow through to the end. Anything worth doing at all is worth doing well. Put it back when you're done. Everything has its place. Exactly, invariably, evidently, absolutely, of course, of course not. It's enough to make me want to throw up.

The Milky Ways go in the hope chest alongside the Hershey bars. The empty wrappers go in the bottom of my purse. My purse goes to school where I dig out the wrappers and throw them in the trash.

The movie mercifully comes to an end, and Dad yawns again with his mouth shut. I keep my fingers crossed. Maybe I'm going to get my chance. Finally.

But first Mom has to discuss one tiny scene that doesn't make any sense. She doesn't allow anything not to make any sense. Dad offers some explanation I don't follow, but it makes Mom happy. Mom and Dad get up, while I stay put on the couch.

Aren't you going to bed, Dear? Mom says.

Absolutely, Dad pipes up.

It's still early, Mom.

Early for what?

It's Saturday night. I don't have school tomorrow. Kids in my class stay up later Saturday nights. And they go out.

Dear, who says they go out?

I do, Mom.

What?

Mom. Ah, Dad, I talked to a classmate on the phone and I'm getting picked up tonight at ten. We won't be out long.

Out?

Yeah, out. We watched all of the movie so the evening is over. I mean, it's over for us together as a family.

When did your classmate call, Dear? I don't recall the phone ringing today.

Well, actually I called him.

Him?

Yeah. It's a new boy. New to our school this year anyway.

Young woman, don't you think such behavior on your part is out of place? First of all, we haven't met this boy. Second, we don't know his parents. Third, we haven't decided whether he's suitable for you. Fourth, he didn't call you—

—Mom, I didn't see what harm it'd do for me to call him first.

Please don't interrupt, Dear. Call him back and tell him you're not going.

Absolutely, Dad pipes up.

It's too late. He's already out somewhere.

This story gets worse as it goes along. Young woman, go directly to your room and get ready for bed. Your evening is over as of this very minute.

Absolutely, Dad pipes up.

I stand up.

Good night, Dear.

Good night, Dear, Dad pipes up.

I nod. Nodding is the same as giving up. But not always.

Good night, Mom, Dad, I say. I go to my room. I take off my penny loafers, pleated khakis, white cardigan, and pressed Madras blouse. No need to take off any socks. I get down on my knees and crawl to the back of the closet and reach deep inside my left Nike sneaker and grab the shiny little key. I unlock my hope chest. I eat the bag of marshmallows. I eat the bag of Hershey bars. I eat the bag of Milky Ways. I smile.

I fold the marshmallow wrappers into one pile. I fold the Milky Way wrappers into a second pile. I fold the Hershey bar wrappers into a third pile. I neatly tie the piles with rubber bands and stuff them into the bottom of my purse. I lock my hope chest. I put the key back in the sneaker. Put things back when you're done.

I tiptoe into the bathroom. I kneel in front of the bowl. I stick a finger down my throat. I throw up. Vomit goes in the toilet. Everything has its place. I smile. I brush my teeth. They're still gray. I smile anyway.

I flush the toilet. I get the Ajax out. I scrub the bowl. The Ajax goes back under the sink. Put things back when you're done. Finish what you start. Follow through to the end. Anything worth doing at all is worth doing well. A person can never be too careful. A person can never be too clean. Exactly, invariably, evidently, absolutely, of course, of course not.

I return to my bedroom. I climb into bed. I chuckle. I wait.

I hear Mom and Dad going to bed.

I chuckle. I wait some more.

The house gets quiet.

I get back out of bed.

I reach my hand deep inside my Nike sneaker. I grab the shiny little key. I unlock my hope chest. I put on the black nylons. I put on the striped miniskirt. I put on the torn plaid shirt. I put on the scuffed combat boots. I pull the floppy-eared cap over my head. I listen. Mom and Dad are asleep. I put a hand over my mouth to keep from laughing out loud.

I sneak out the front door. I climb into the front seat of the waiting Chevy beater. Rocky looks me over good and shakes his head and laughs and says, Do you ever look grungy!

Thanks, I say and laugh, too.

How's Cleveland sound? he says.

Whatever, I say. Actually, I've never been there. Or anywhere else in Ohio.

I got a friend we can stay with, he says.

Whatever.

We take off.

Tonic Harmony

A turkey was baking in the kitchen of an American Foursquare in the Midwest, just as the holiday treat also was in millions of other homes coast to coast. Inside this one, retired plumber Elmer White stood in his dining room, admiring the vintage photos on the mantelpiece above the fireplace. To the left, a naive, eighteen-year-old, smooth-cheeked Marine, fresh out of Boot Camp, about to experience combat in the South Pacific. On the right, a proud, thirtyish couple seated beside four grinning youngsters, ages five to thirteen. Between these precious pictures rested a prized family heirloom, namely, a vintage wooden mantel clock, ticking at its deliberate, reassuring pace. Like a voice forever repeating all was well—even if things were anything but.

"Wind up the mantel clock, Elmer," his spouse of forty-odd years ordered from the kitchen, where Florence White perched atop a stool at the sink, scrubbing pots and pans. "The darned thing's been losing time."

Really? He removed a pocket watch from his olive drab workpants and compared the timepieces. Both read precisely eleven fifty-eight. Still, to avoid an argument he opened the round glass face, slid the key out from underneath, and tightened the spring an unnecessary notch. Had it ever been a memorable day, when his father gave him this antique as a wedding gift with the stipulation that he pass it along in turn to his own first-born son when the boy got married. But was that day ever going to come?

Bracing a hand against his arthritic right hip, Elmer faced the mahogany dining room table set for six. Nothing not in its proper place, nothing on display that wouldn't see good use that Thanksgiving Day. "The old Soviet Union continues to break apart," a newscaster proclaimed from the television in the adjacent living room. "Even six months ago who would have ever predicted—"

"—Turn that junk off!" Florence yelled. Elmer obeyed without protest or, for that matter, a response. Once accomplished, he limped into the kitchen to help his spouse.

"Where's that daughter of yours, Elmer?" Florence snapped.

"You mean Megan?"

"Who the heck else?"

He grabbed the largest washed beet from a bowl on the granite countertop and shoved it through the slicer. "Well," he said, taking care not to let his reply sound like a rebuttal, "Joan's our daughter, too."

"Come on! Joan can't cook a lick. Or smell or taste. It's like the big schnoz she inherited from you is permanently plugged."

The mantel clock in the living room whirred, paused, and struck at sweet intervals, till it reached the count of twelve and ceased. Of course it was keeping perfect time. As it had been ever since he had taken the intricate machine apart last summer and thoroughly cleaned the parts.

He picked up two smaller beets and pushed these through side by side, juicy bluish-red pieces plopping out the back. "Joan probably has allergies," he said hoarsely and cleared his throat.

"Elmer, will you speak up? You're the one with the hearing aids, remember?"

"I said Joan most likely has allergies." As he himself also did in old age, along with back pains, iffy balance, dry eyes, creaky knees, nagging heartburn, and frequent insomnia. None of which had afflicted him till he passed the age of seventy.

"Well, who doesn't, with all the mold, pollen, and soot in the air around here?"

He blinked back tears. Cheer up, he told himself. His family deserved nothing less on that special day.

"Elmer, hurry up with those beets!" Florence shouted. "We've still got to prepare the spuds. Johnny *loves* scalloped potatoes."

"I could call John and ask him and Barbara to come over early to help."

"No, this is Meg's chore! And, by God, she's going to do it or I'll know the reason why!"

"John wouldn't mind. And he is a good cook."

"He'd better be! As helpless as his Barb is around the kitchen!"

Elmer's stomach growled, but then he had only eaten a light breakfast on account of the day's feast. "I believe Barbara will make him a good wife," he said. "They treat each other so well."

"My goodness, Elmer, look at the time!" Florence yelled. "And we don't even have all of the vegetables sliced!"

"Honey, does it really matter if we're a bit behind schedule? We're not exactly bringing off an amphibious invasion."

"Now don't start up again with your war stories. They're so depressing. Today my family's going to be happy, so help me God."

Clenching his teeth from the sciatic pain shooting down a leg, Elmer brought the beet slices to the salad serving bowl and dumped them onto the mixed greens. He licked his lips at the sight of both apple and blueberry pies fresh out of the oven cooling on the breakfast nook table. If he only weren't so determined to control his weight, he would devour a wedge of each.

The two frosted fifths of gin alongside the desserts, along with six tumblers, five wine glasses, and four bottles of tonic water were a different story. He would only touch the latter from among that day's beverages. Unlike how he once had abused alcohol, though by no means whatsoever in many years. In fact, over the past decade he had demonstrated time and again an immunity to the intoxicant's onetime irresistible appeal. But then he prided himself on his self-discipline.

He got to work on the potatoes.

"Elmer, give Meg a call. I told her to be here at eleven-thirty on the dot."

He just stood there, concentrating on the spuds.

"Elmer!"

"Honey, I'll be finished with these in a jiffy."

"Elmer White, get your daughter over here this minute!"

Two dozen more shoves and the potatoes were done. The last pieces turned out thicker than the rest, but he didn't see what difference that should make. He had no sooner hobbled his way to the landline phone in the foyer than Florence screamed, "Elmer, you've sliced them too wide!"

"Not all of them, honey. Check out those on the bottom."

"Lord, have mercy! The thin pieces will be cooked to mush while the thick ones are still raw. Hurry up and call your daughter while I try to salvage this mess." She snatched a paring knife and, muttering curses under her breath, assaulted the butchered potatoes.

"Hello?" a soft, womanly voice answered on the other end of the line.

"Megan?"

"Hi, Daddy! What's up?"

"Your mother thought you'd be here at eleven-thirty."

"She did? But we're not eating till two."

"She needs your help now with preparing the meal."

"Oh, Daddy, I had such a good time last night I didn't want it to ever end. Okay, I'll hurry and shower and get over there as fast as I can."

"Would you, Meg? But whatever you do, please don't speed."

"Daddy, remember I passed Driver's Education, what, twenty years ago."

"Just drive carefully, babe."

Back in the kitchen, Elmer was pleasantly surprised to find Joan at her mother's side, painstakingly layering the potatoes and onions in a glass cooking pan. "Hi, Dad," his older daughter greeted and gave him a little wave.

"You're filling it too full!" Florence snapped.

"But otherwise there'll be this little bit left over," Joan said.

"Who cares? Toss it down the garbage disposal, for heaven's sake! But don't ruin the dish!"

"Waste not, want not," Joan replied.

Her mother rolled her eyes. "Please spare us the sermon."

Her perky smile never relenting, their older daughter added crumbled blue cheese to the salad and tossed it. "What else can I do to help?"

"Everything's done now, no thanks to my good-for-nothing children," her mother muttered despite Joan's contribution. Which meant the trio could move into the living room and relax for the time being.

Noticing Joan's recent weight gain of late with dismay, Elmer longed to ask whether there was finally some man in her life. But if she wasn't going to be forthcoming, he certainly wouldn't pry. Though he was willing to bet their paid-off mortgage there hadn't been one in ages. He sneaked a wary glance at Florence. He longed to sit beside his elder daughter, but instead carefully lowered himself next to his wife on the closer love-seat.

The three of them listened in silence together to the mantel clock's patient ticking while awaiting the rest of their family. When a sleek, red Toyota pulled into the driveway alongside Joan's blue Honda, Elmer slyly grinned. Bracing a hand against his aching lower back, he bent forward with a wince and straightened the cribbage board and deck of cards on the near corner of the glass coffee table.

"Who in the Sam Hill does that daughter of yours think she is, showing up this late?" Florence said.

"I'm here!" Megan said, bursting into the kitchen, the tips of her dishwater blond hair still damp. "What is it you wanted me to do?"

"It's too late!" her mother snapped. "What I wanted you to do was exactly what you agreed to last Sunday on the phone. How quickly they forget."

"Don't worry, Meg, honey," Elmer said, accepting his baby girl's brief kiss on the lips. "Your sister helped take up the slack."

"She did not!" Florence said, tolerating Meg's perfunctory peck on a cheek.

"Sorry, Mom," Megan told her, bounced across the room, and gave her big sister a lingering hug.

"I smell smoke on somebody," Florence intoned like a drill sergeant spotting a gig.

"Not I," Meg replied. "Haven't touched the demon weed in years." Joan jumped up, ran into the kitchen, grabbed a scouring pad, and attacked the sink. "Oh, I know," Meg added. "I bet it's from this sweater I wore to a bar yesterday."

"You mean to tell your mother you're still going to bars at your age?"

"Of course," Meg said with a shrug. "They're a great place to find Mr. Wonderful. Which is exactly what I did last night."

"Plea-s-s-se," her mother replied, rolling her eyes. "Why can't you meet people in church like everybody else?"

"None of us belong to a church anymore, Mom. Or did you and Daddy start going again?"

"That's not what I said! Don't twist my words!"

"Are you all right, Dad?" Joan asked, resting a hand on his shoulder.

Elmer quit rubbing his throbbing temples and forced a thin smile. "I'm fine," he said, lying. He certainly hoped Megan had finally found Mr. Right, since he knew only too well where all her nights spent in bars would lead. With closed eyes, he envisioned the two imported fifths on the breakfast nook that had awakened long dormant memories of gin's deliciousness.

Meg plopped down on the easy chair between her sister and father. "How about you and I playing a little cribbage till my brothers arrive, Daddy?" she suggested and moved the board and cards on the glass-top table closer.

"You don't have the time!" Florence snapped.

"Yes, we do, honey," Elmer dared to rebut. "No problem if we need to quit wherever we are."

"How can you stand that stupid game?" Florence said. "All you do is march those little pegs around in circles."

"That's why we love it, Mom. It's just like life. Except somebody wins."

"Plea-s-s-se."

"It's just a pastime, honey," Elmer said. As Megan riffled the deck as expertly as a Las Vegas croupier, his face brightened for the first time in weeks. She dealt out six cards apiece, two of which each discarded into a so-called crib beside the board.

"He's here!" Florence shouted.

"Richard?" Joan jumped up and straightened a slightly misaligned knife on the dining table.

"No, John!" her mother snapped, but peered out the window to make sure. The front door just barely clicked, and then again, as if a cat burglar had sneaked inside.

"Hi, Richard," Florence greeted glumly, realizing her mistake. She glared at her thirty-four-year-old boy's shaggy beard and hair.

"How's it goin', Richie?" Elmer asked as he marched his rear peg a half dozen holes ahead of the first. He glanced away from his son's darting, bloodshot gaze.

"I'm not late, am I?" Richard all but whispered. He coughed, cleared his throat, poured himself a glass of water in the kitchen, and audibly chugged it.

"Not at all," Meg said, keeping her eyes glued to her cards.

Rich cautiously lowered himself into the far living room easy chair, as if his scrawny body just might be heavier than the piece could bear. Joan rushed over and gave her younger brother a warm hug, which he didn't reciprocate. "How's the job hunting going?" she asked him.

"I've been working," he replied hoarsely.

"Doing what?" his mother snapped.

"This and that. Whatever comes up."

"Please?"

"I'm doing whatever gigs I can get."

"What kind of answer is that?" Florence shrieked, and Elmer lost track of his count. "Richard, who exactly are you working for?"

"You don't know him."

Elmer put down his cards with a sigh. "You okay, Daddy?" Meg asked, as her father struggled to fight back the tears and somehow succeeded.

"He's here!" Florence shouted, straining to stand up. "Elmer! No, somebody else pour the gin and tonics!"

"Let me do it, Dad!" Joan said, jumping to her feet. "Once I get the scalloped potatoes into the oven." Meg finished counting off her cribbage points, while Richard and Elmer stayed put like landing craft run aground. "Does anybody want a soda or fruit juice instead?" Joan asked. "Or coffee?"

Tall, slender, gray-templed, beaming John emerged from the foyer and stepped into his mother's hearty embrace. "*He has come*," Meg declared. "Let the festivities begin." Holding Florence's hand and grinning beneath his well-trimmed moustache, her older son wished everyone a Happy Thanksgiving and took a seat on the easy chair alongside his mother.

The first drink Joan delivered directly to her father, explaining that it was pure quinine water on the rocks with a twist.

What else? Since Elmer hadn't touched a drop of alcohol in ages. Not that his drinking was ever as bad as his family made out. Sure, he was arrested twice for driving under the influence, but he never passed out in public or missed a day of work. Of course, all the boozing had taken a toll on his liver and led to that extramarital affair. But nothing but perfect abstinence for him since. So why that particular day was he daydreaming about gin's divine flavor—and especially its sweet relief?

He scowled as his family members received their drinks in turn. And bridled when Joan left an open gin bottle on the coffee table right in front of him. Once glum Richard was handed his cocktail, Florence declared, "A toast!"

"To the Whites," John replied.

"To the Whites," his mother added more softly, followed by half-hearted echoes from the daughters. But nary a peep from glum Elmer. Everybody but Rich drank deeply, his G and T remaining right where Joan had placed it.

"You forgot the gin, Sis," Meg teased, making her father wince.

"No, I didn't," Joan said. "It was a level shot."

Meg grabbed the fifth and glugged in a healthy dollop of the quality British liquor. "I really like to taste the gin."

Just as I always used to, Elmer thought. Warily eyeing his baby girl's big swallows, he took a deep draft from his own glass and frowned at the bitter sweetness of nothing but tonic. Meg was keen to play more cribbage, but his heart was no longer in the card game. Why hadn't John brought along his fiancée, Barbara, he wondered.

When the phone rang, Joan hustled to answer it. "The White residence," she said into the receiver. "Meg, it's for you. Some guy with a sexy baritone."

"I bet it's Skip!" Meg replied and jumped up, leaving her freshened drink on the coffee table beside the cribbage board.

"Barb woke up with a sick headache," John explained with a strained grin. "Which just wouldn't go away." Elmer didn't buy that story, but who could blame the woman for not coming?

"Well, Johnny," Florence said, "you can bring Barbara over any time. Who knows, someday she may become part of our family, too."

"You never can tell," John told her, feigning a smile. The last time Barbara had visited, she had brought a side dish, which her mother-in-law-to-be had criticized, and Barb had stalked off without eating dessert. Caught in the middle, John had drowned his sorrows in G and Ts till he turned maudlin. Not that he was visibly tipsy when he left for home, but his old man hated seeing him get behind the wheel in that condition.

Elmer glanced away from Richard's brimming glass sitting untouched on the coffee table and eyed Meg's within easier reach. Pine-scented memories of white-tail deer bounding through evergreen trees left him licking his lips.

"You dirty old man!" Meg squealed into the receiver.

If Elmer cared to, he could probably get away with switching their drinks. Not that he truly wanted to. Still, whatever he drank, Meg couldn't, so wouldn't that make the swap a good deed? Its two or three shots of booze would have been a cinch for a guy like him to handle in the old days. Maybe now it'd even lift him out of his doldrums. Or, better yet, turn him into the merry host his kids deserved that holiday.

"Elmer!" his wife hollered. "Come over here and greet your son!"

But *was* John truly his son? Elmer nonchalantly grabbed Meg's tumbler and gulped half of it. What a thrill to be gripping a genuine drink again. He moved his own tonic water toward his daughter's end of the cribbage board, stood up, and limped over to John, still seated, and dutifully shook the boy's hand.

"How you doin', Richie?" he said to his youngest child, busy studying the mantel clock's face as if it were a conundrum in want of a solution.

Feeling more chipper with every passing moment, Elmer sat down with a groan beside his wife on her love-seat. Diet Pepsi in hand, Joan perched herself atop the arm of her baby brother's easy chair, facing them. "Richie," she teased, "you haven't even touched your drinkie-pooh. Would you like a soda instead?" Stiffly twisting his head, he viewed her like she just might be an alien species from outer space. "Are your eyes ever bloodshot," she told him.

"You should see how they look from this side," he replied and smiled, revealing gray, neglected teeth.

"If you don't want your G and T, don't feel obligated to drink it."

"Don't worry. I wouldn't touch such poison. And not because of the ethyl alcohol, but all that sugary tonic." Elmer quaffed the rest of his divine highball and began pondering how to finagle himself another.

The instant Meg hung up, Florence shouted, "Is this guy single?"

"Mother, please."

"If he's divorced, don't count on my liking him any better than the others. Once a loser, always a loser in my book."

Elmer chortled at nothing in particular, and then again when he got a gander at John's sour puss. His present girlfriend, Barbara, had been divorced twice. Sweet gal though. No doubt about that. In fact, he wished John would hang on to this one and finally settle down. And maybe even give them—or at least Florence, strictly speaking—a grandchild. Grandson or granddaughter, nobody would be fussy.

Meg retook the easy chair next to her father, drank from what she mistook as her own glass, made a face, and muttered, "I still can't taste the gin." So again she grabbed the open fifth and poured in more.

Elmer let out a big sigh. No need to bother asking what kind of guy Megan had gotten herself mixed up with this time. Since every last one was the same—handsome, flashy, fun-loving, and, in the end, a lout. Married he bet too. She seemed incapable of falling in love with anybody actually available.

Meg took several deep swallows from what had been her father's pure tonic and pensively watched the ravenous dark-eyed juncos outside the window at the bird feeder. The sight of his dearest, sweetest, prettiest child sitting so forlornly made Elmer pine for more booze.

"Seven per cent?" his wife suddenly screamed, making Elmer flinch. "Don't let them feed you that hogwash! A realtor's fee is always negotiable!" John nodded meekly. The kid sure had a thick mat of dark hair on his head, so unlike any other White, including all of the aunts and uncles and cousins, even much darker than Florence's. He was also the only White with brown eyes. "Don't let the buyers dicker you down either," his mother added.

"If Barb's leaving you, why bother moving?" Meg blurted. Her brother grimaced, as if bullwhipped across the face, and then slumped. Elmer felt a twinge of affection toward his wife for not pressing John about this unwelcome news, not that he doubted it for an instant.

The oven alarm dinged.

Meg slammed down her empty glass, announced, "Come and get it!" and rushed into the kitchen to help Joan. They hauled out sizzling pans of turkey and scalloped potatoes and set them down on the dining room table beside the tossed salad, dressed with vinaigrette.

Florence ceremoniously took her place at the head of the dining table, and glum Richard slid in against the wall two chairs away. "That's Meg's seat!" his mother hollered. "You sit here." She thumped the empty spot on her immediate left. Rich grimly scooted over as commanded.

Elmer stood up, lingered in place till everyone's attention was elsewhere, grasped Rich's untouched G and T, and gulped it all.

"Come on and carve the bird, Daddy!" Meg said.

"Pumpkin, maybe I'll just carve you," he told her with a guffaw. Florence's head shot around, and her eyes grew wide as Elmer brandished the cutlery like a jolly pirate. "Just like cutting butter with a hot knife. Man, it's one beautiful bird, if I do say so myself. Since I was the genius who picked it out. Ha!" He playfully hip-bumped Joan, who stood there dumbfounded, but didn't take offense.

Ensconced at the table upon his mother's right hand, John mumbled, "Should I get the wine?"

"Do you honestly think we need any?" Joan said. "There's plenty of fruit juice and soda to go around."

Pinching her mouth and furrowing her brow, as if bracing for an incoming artillery salvo, Florence muttered, "Wine for me."

John retrieved the bottle of pinot noir from the kitchen. "Wow, a whole magnum," he commented upon his return and poured out servings for everyone except Elmer.

Once they had all taken their seats, Florence said, "John, please say grace."

"Just a minute, honeybee," Elmer replied, spryly jumping up. "Just because I can't have wine doesn't mean I can't have more quinine water." He limped into the kitchen with Richard's empty glass and soon returned. Nobody noticed his would-be pure tonic wasn't fizzy. "Okay, Johnno, give that Big Guy in the Sky our thanks."

John's downcast glance sneaked up to meet his mother's. "Do I have time to get a refill, too?" Meg asked. "Mine's already half gone."

"No!" Florence shouted. "John, would you say that damned prayer?"

John reciprocated Joan's wink, folded his hands, and rattled off, "Come-Lord-Jesus-be-our-guest-and-let-these-gifts-to-us-be-blest-amen."

"You can say that again!" Elmer shouted. "And cheers, everybody!" He stretched his tumbler toward Joan for a toast, but she just sat there as if paralyzed. "To the Whites! To one big, happy family!"

"To us," John added morosely.

"To us," his sisters echoed, while Richard remained mum. At first, only John joined his dad in imbibing, till Meg grabbed her wine and guzzled it.

With a gleeful grin, Elmer leaned forward to get a better whiff of the sumptuous cuisine. "So what'll it be, Johnno, white or dark meat?"

John drank half of his wine all at once. "A little of everything would be fine. As long as I save room for dessert." He scrutinized his father, as if sizing up a suspicious stranger.

"Sure thing," Elmer replied merrily. "A little white meat and a little dark meat coming right up for John Boy. With all the trimmings." He handed him a plate heaped with gargantuan portions, which John accepted without complaint.

"Joan?" Elmer asked next.

"Just a little of everything. Only skip the dark meat. It's got way too much fat in it."

"Fat gives it flavor, dear," her mother told her. "That's why dark meat tastes the best. Elmer, give her that big hunk in the corner. And also a big helping of potatoes. One reason I made so many is that you always liked them so much."

"Used to, Mom, used to," Joan protested. Her serving was three-fourths of John's, and so three times what she wanted. "I'm on a diet, I'm on a diet."

"Now listen here, young woman," Florence snapped. "After all the time I spent slaving away on this feast, you'll eat what's served and you'll like it!"

"Honeybee," Elmer said with a giggle, "everything's simply scrumptious." He hoisted his tumbler upside down to shake the last few drops into his gaping mouth. Meg handed her empty glass to her older brother in charge of the wine. He filled hers, his mother's, and his own.

"Make Meg's serving smaller," Florence said. "This time we'll make sure she has room for dessert."

"Mother!" Megan begged. "I can't eat any sweets. I'm hypoglycemic."

"Nonsense, child. You're no more hypoglycemic than I am. You just get weak when you're hungry. Eat more! You're much too thin."

"Maybe you're hypoglycemic, too, Mom, if hunger makes you irritable."

"I resent that insinuation!"

Elmer guffawed at such a comical exchange and dished Richard a heaping plate just like he had John.

"I'm a vegetarian," Richard feebly protested. "Vegan even."

"Richard," his mother shot back. "Don't give us that mumbo-jumbo crap. When you're at your parents, you'll eat meat like everybody else. It's one of the house rules. Like nobody is allowed to smoke on the premises, no matter how stupid they want to behave other places."

"Dad," Meg told him, "give me a little more meat. But take it easy with the potatoes. And I do absolutely refuse to eat any dessert."

"Hy-po-gly-ce-mi-a," Florence mouthed. "What'll those quacks think of next to rip a person off? There wasn't any of that going around when I was a girl."

"Yes, there was, Mother. It's not an infection."

"There wasn't any AIDS then either. Because none of us were leading filthy lives that God needed to punish."

"Come on, mother," Meg said. "Don't give me that crap. People slept around then the same as now. Only then instead of AIDS, the problem was unwanted pregnancy."

At that remark Elmer's smile collapsed, and his eyelids drooped. His bleary gaze first sought out Richard, the spitting image of his dad, and then John, the dark, handsome stranger.

Florence gripped her empty wine glass like she wanted to fling it off her daughter's head. "One thing we never did was murder babies in the womb!" she shouted.

"Forced marriages were better? Give me a break!"

Florence covered her face with her pudgy fingers, while Elmer rubbed his misty eyes. The buzz from the alcohol in his blood was fast ebbing.

Joan spoke up hesitantly. "I heard there were abortions back then too. Only they were illegal and dangerous."

Florence shrieked, "There were not! Not around here!"

Meg opened her mouth as if to rebut, but thought better of it. In the ensuing silence the family all concentrated on eating.

After while John piped up with his salesman's workaday cheeriness, "Mom, are your scalloped potatoes ever delicious! Could you please give me some more, Dad?"

"Sure thing!" Elmer said, echoing this forced tone. "How about you, Ricky?" His son didn't reply, his bloodshot gaze glued to his clean plate. Grabbing Rich's full glass of wine, Elmer jumped up. "I forgot you don't like wine. Here let me get you some fruit juice instead." The instant he rounded the corner into the kitchen, he tossed his son's wine down his throat, hoisted the gin, and chugged a few ounces of booze straight from the bottle.

Returning with a rakish smile, he said, "Here you go, Dickie Boy. Apple juice from the finest fruit grown in the great state of Oregon."

"The apples are from Washington, for Pete's sake!" Florence told him.

"Well," Elmer said, "let's just say they're from the beautiful Pacific Northwest. One gorgeous corner of our great and glorious nation, if I do say so myself."

John glared at his clean plate, while Joan picked around the edges of her serving. Meg rapped her empty glass against the table, as Rich slumped in his chair like a propped-up carcass.

"How come everybody looks so glum?" Elmer said with a chortle. Nobody moved a muscle.

"Will you all please excuse me?" Richard whispered and stood up gingerly, as if the merest brush against any object might send it toppling.

"We certainly shall excuse you, kind Sir," Elmer said with a laugh and started rapping his own empty glass in imitation of Megan.

"Elmer!" Florence suddenly yelled.

"Yes, honeybee."

"Elmer, what have you been doing?"

"Why, I've been partaking of your heavenly vittles, which have delighted my nose and palate with all the subtleties of your celebrated cooking. Even as we await yet another of your mouth-watering desserts."

"Elmer White, you lowdown, sneaky, gutless rat!"

"Florence, honey, I don't believe I deserve such aspersions cast upon my character. Certainly not in front of our dear children, who we see so seldom of late."

Florence gnashed her teeth and balled her fists.

"Calm down, honeybun," Elmer said. "Getting mad doesn't do your blood pressure one bit of good."

Upon Richard's return, John got up without a word and marched off to the bathroom.

"I'm splitting," Meg mumbled, standing up.

"Sit back down, woman!" Florence bellowed. "Show some manners."

"Honeybee," Elmer butted in, "our kids have lives of their own and places they need to be."

Meg plopped back down. "Remember I'm hypoglycemic. My body honestly cannot tolerate sweets."

"Don't give your mother orders, child."

John came back, looking like he had just survived a head-on car collision. "Dad, you'd better check out the toilet. There's a problem with the electrical wiring or something. It stinks like burning rope in there. Rich, was it you who left the bathroom fan running?"

When Elmer arose, he lurched into the table, spilling Rich's juice. John grabbed his father's arm to steady him, as Richard slouched even more deeply into his chair. Five minutes later, Elmer hobbled back, his eyes pink and watery.

"Well?" John asked.

Richard was sitting so low he looked practically melted.

"It's not the wiring," their father mumbled.

Meg rested her head back against the wall and closed her eyes.

"What in the devil is it then?" Florence said.

"Nothing new," Elmer replied, as Richard began to fidget.

"What the hell is going on?" Florence snapped.

Now Meg had slumped against her big brother's shoulder was gently snoring.

"Let me take care of dessert!" Joan squealed, springing to her feet.

"I'm never going to have any grandchildren, am I?" Florence wailed.

With John's help Elmer lowered himself into an easy chair in the living room, his jaw trembling and tears flowing down his cheeks. It was his fault that Florence was so miserable and the kids so lost. But then everything was his fault. After ten years of remaining dry—ten whole years!—he had blown it all. The mantel clock whirred, paused, and struck at those familiar intervals. At least it was running perfectly, but then it was a simple device easy to fix.

"Daddy," a voice said tenderly, using Meg's term of endearment, only this time it wasn't his younger daughter speaking. Elmer looked up into eyes as bloodshot as his own. "Daddy," Richard repeated, resting a gentle hand on his father's forearm. "You and I need help."

Joan handed her father a wedge of blueberry pie and caressed his cheek.

"We could go together," Richard said.

Recalling the comforting firmness of Marine Corps buddies pressed against his shoulders inside the jam-packed landing craft racing toward the slaughter on Tarawa, Elmer wiped away his tears.

Still Waters

It all depends, it all depends. Frank, is that all you can ever say?

It all depends, Vicky, he says again. And he doesn't mean it as a joke. Because the older Frank gets, the less he speaks, so I suppose I shouldn't complain as long as he says anything.

But I guess I am complaining. Because this Route 66 Festival is only about the nicest thing to happen in Flagstaff since we moved out here from Wisconsin. But if Frank doesn't want to take me and the kids, what can I do, go alone?

The phone rings, I grab for it, but I'm way too slow. Frank practically jumps out of his skin, before I make it stop. Sudden noises really get to him lately, even though we've got the bell turned way down. Oh, hi, Sherry, I say. Sherry and Dennis are our best friends. Sure, we're going, I say, only we're not sure when. Well, okay, the Jack Daniels tent sounds fine. See you there.

I hang up and look at Frank, sitting on the couch all sweaty and bug-eyed. What'd you tell her that for, Vicky? he says. He's not exactly accusing me of anything, but I hear what he's saying.

Oh, the tent's just where they're going to be. We don't have to hang around there long.

Frank wipes his brow. Me, I'm not sweating at all, even though the air-conditioning is hardly running to save us money. I can guess what's on his mind. Nobody can knock the booze back better than Dennis. I'm not exactly happy about meeting them there myself, but I figure we can zip in and zip right back out.

The festival's already started, I say softly. I don't want to nag, but I don't want to miss out on the fun either.

Frank looks at me like I'm speaking Vietnamese or something. And just keeps staring. Sometimes, I wish he would tell me what's eating him, but that wasn't his way when I met him and it's not his way now.

I say, I mean, we don't have to get there early, just so we get there eventually.

Frank Junior barges in right then and says, Dad, can Terry ride along with us?

Frank looks our son over like he's never seen the kid before and just barely nods. Francis runs back outside all excited.

Are you feeling okay, Frank? I say. He shrugs. Only it's more like a flinch. Beads of sweat are popping out on his forehead and trickling down into his eyebrows. Honey, I'm fine, he says. Just kind of tired is all.

Tired? I say. From what? As early as we went to bed last night? Not that that was how I wanted to spend Friday night, but what else am I supposed to do?

Frank keeps slumping deeper into the couch. Me, I feel like smashing windows. Holler, Frank! I shout. Get mad! Do something! Anything's better than just sitting here like a bump on a log.

Frank scratches an ear and keeps staring at the TV. Some interview with a politician is on, the kind of show he just hates.

Frank, I say as sweetly as I can. Would you take me and the kids to the festival as a favor? We don't have to stay long.

He scratches the other ear.

Our daughter, Amy, hits the front door like a bomb and stomps upstairs.

Would you pretty please? I say.

Frank rises to his feet with a groan and says, Okay. But first I'd better mow the lawn.

I throw up my hands. He just mowed the darned thing last Sunday, and it hasn't grown any since that a person could notice. He gives me that crooked smile of his that makes him look drunk and heads outside.

The funny thing is Frank being so quiet was the first thing I liked about him. When we were both in high school back in Wisconsin, he used to sit the same way in study hall. At sixteen he was already such a man that one look at him and I just about swooned. He was just about everything I thought a guy should be. He wasn't just handsome, but big and strong and not skinny at all like he is now. And dependable and good at fixing just about anything. And co-captain of the football team and all-conference both his junior and senior years. But still so shy he wouldn't give a girl the time of day.

Between classes I'd go out of my way to run into him in the halls and give him a great big smile. After while, he'd grin back a little, even though he kept walking on. Then one day he moseys over to my locker and says, Vicky, I was just wondering if you might be willing to go to a show. With me, I mean.

Might? I just about had a conniption on the spot.

Our first date went well and so did the second. Before you know it we were going steady. I felt so happy I thought I had died and gone to heaven. We've been together ever since.

As a high school yearbook editor, I was the one who came up with the motto to go under his senior picture. It says, Frank slips all his troubles into a box, sits on the lid, and grins. That's him to a T. You know what Norwegians are like. Nice, wholesome, and, above all, quiet. Not at all like my people, the Irish.

Right after graduation, Frank gets his draft notice and does his duty and goes to fight in Vietnam. Meanwhile, I'm living with my folks and earning my keep by working checkout at the

Piggly Wiggly. Frank writes me almost every day from over there, but his brief letters never say a word about the war. Instead he writes about the Friday night fish fries we always loved and the Hatfield beach where we first went all the way. And going hunting and fishing with his dad and brother, and helping his mom out around the house. Then one day there comes a letter asking me what kind of a house I'd like.

A ranch house, I write back. He doesn't have to spell it out. We're as good as engaged!

Thank God, Frank makes it back home all in one piece, though he does have scars on both legs. Whenever I ask him about it, he makes a face and says it's nothing, just some flesh wounds. That fall he takes his veteran's benefits and goes to college in Eau Claire and earns himself a business degree. The week after he graduates there, we finally tie the knot.

Frank lands himself a good job right off the bat in our hometown bank, handling loans, and we start saving for a down payment on a house and decide to put off having kids. Then his dad up and dies of a heart attack, and his brother moves to Texas. Frank takes both losses in stride.

Every year the bank gives him a nice raise, and we keep squirreling more money away. Then Frank's put in charge of the entire Loan Department, and we make a down payment on a new three-bedroom ranch house. Which means it's high time to get going on a family.

Before too long, the doctor announces I'm pregnant with Amanda, our daughter, who's already a freshman in high school. And three years later, Francis Junior comes along, giving us the boy and girl we'd planned on. So what with Frank's job, our ranch house, and two kids, it seems like we've got it made.

So that's why it doesn't figure, when Frank starts hitting the bottle. I don't mean a drink or two now and then. I mean, getting really plastered. And what's really strange about it is even when he was sowing wild oats in his younger days he never drank all that much. Sure, we'd go to bars once in a while and have a good time, but it was no big deal. But now every night he gets smashed at home and doesn't care whether I join him or not.

At first, the whiskey never fails to make him jolly, but after while it only turns him blue. Even so, he keeps that stupid grin glued to his face, but he can't fool me. Then the tantrums start. Which consist of stomping around the house and kicking things and once in a while breaking a piece of furniture or something. But he never loses control so bad he lays a finger on me or the kids.

I try asking Frank what's wrong, but it's no use.

Nothing, he says. Everything's fine.

Now I'm not saying he's a bad husband or father or that I love him any less than ever, but I do worry about what all this drinking is doing to his health.

Then one day I come home from work after two like usual, and there's Frank already sitting on the couch. In one hand he's got a half-empty fifth and no glass in sight. He gives me a crooked smile and says, I lost my job.

What?

They fired me.

Fired? Employee of the year fired? But the people at the bank love him. They even said they were going to make him Vice President some day. I have to grill him, before he finally owns up to putting some loan applications in a drawer and forgetting about them. Which means some couples are going to lose their dream homes.

Forget? I say. What do you mean forget?

He shrugs and takes another swig.

It doesn't take long before Frank's name is mud around town, and the best job he can get is pumping gas. My dad advises us to pull up stakes and start over from scratch in Texas. Frank's uncle agrees. But Frank doesn't want to be anywhere near his brother, so we make it Arizona instead.

So we rent a big U-Haul and move ourselves and the kids out here. We have to live off our equity for a while, but pretty soon Frank gets himself a job keeping books for a computer parts company, where he's been ever since. He doesn't make as much money as he used to, and there's no chance of a promotion but we get along okay, especially what with my income from clerking part-time in a women's ready-to-wear store.

The scenery around Flagstaff has got to be about the best in the country. The San Francisco Peaks in plain sight, and close by Oak Creek Canyon and Sunset Crater and Meteor Crater and the Grand Canyon, and what have you. Not that we get to these places much, but we can anytime we might want to.

So I guess I don't have much right to complain, but here I am doing it just the same. And it's not because Frank's gone back to drinking. No, we straightened that problem out the night he came home after landing this new job and hauled out a fifth to celebrate. That's when I put my foot down. Frank Iverson, you'd better not lose this job too, I said right to his face.

He didn't get mad at me or nothing. He just said, You're right, honey, and handed me the whiskey. And there wasn't a peep out of him, when I got rid of his other bottles either. Some nights now we might have a beer or two, but that's not a problem.

Nowadays Frank's never happy like he once was, so that's why I'm wondering if the Route 66 Festival might cheer him up. It won't just be Dennis and Sherry there, but everybody else we know. I mean, it'll be practically everybody in town. So I say, trying to sound real upbeat, Hey, come on, Frank. Let's drive into town.

He keeps staring at the pointy-heads on TV like for once he gives a darn.

Well, I say, you might as well be at work today, if this is how you're going to spend your time off.

I can't, he mumbles.

What?

I can't go back to work, he says a bit louder.

Frank, I don't want you to go to work. It's Saturday. That's just an expression. Come on, let's go to the festival.

They fired me, he says.

What?

I lost my job, he says.

I sit down before I faint. I have to give him a couple beers, before I pry out of him what went wrong. It seems he did the store's taxes this spring like always and got his boss Jim to sign and date all the forms and everything. And then what's Frank up and do? He puts the papers in a drawer and just leaves them sitting there.

What'd you do that for, Frank? I scream.

Amy comes stomping down the stairs to see what's wrong.

Frank shrugs and says, I forgot.

I collapse on the couch. And I say, Frank, what are we going to do now?

Move, I guess, he says.

Bosom Buddies

I, Thomas Judd, never was a breast man or, for that matter, a breast boy. Not when I was in high school adolescing, not when I was a Little Man On Campus first genuinely dating, not when I finally got married at the ripe age of thirty, and, most certainly, not last year after my divorce. So while Deborah Walker's antics were shocking, my reaction to them shocked me more.

Deb and I had arrived early for a Steering Committee meeting and were passing the time exchanging office scuttlebutt. Naturally, she also wasn't displeased with the turmoil within a competitor's management, though neither of us had ever been one to gloat. Then innocently enough, she asked, "Are you sleeping enough of late, Tom?"

I shook my head. To judge from the dark circles under my eyes I obviously wasn't, not that I hadn't been sorely trying. Actually, I hadn't slept all the way till my alarm even once in weeks—or gotten myself to work on time. Somehow my newly single state was making me both too sluggish and too antsy. And so without having changed, the accounting job I had always enjoyed had become a chore.

"You dating any?" Deb said.

I responded with stricken silence.

"Do I know her? Or should I say them?"

I blushed and loosened my tie.

Her pretty azure eyes narrowing, she reached over and patted my wrist. "Hey, Tom, don't date till you're ready. No matter how long that takes."

It was a relief when our Chairperson finally joined us.

How many hours had I already spent at home beside my phone unable to pick it up? What prospect was there to call, I kept asking myself. What would I say? Wasn't I too old to be phoning near strangers and inviting them out on dates? The whole idea struck me as weirder than auditioning as a male exotic dancer. Once having dated was a vague recollection from a distant past during the LBJ Presidency, back when all of us registered for college courses on IBM punch cards and majored in either History or English to get off to a fast start in the business world.

The instant our meeting ended, I raced for the door and hid out inside my office till four. Then I dutifully showed up at the farewell party in the Director's Conference Room for Joan Covington, a Division Head who had accepted a position as head of sales in Denver. There I hovered over the punchless punch, in no hurry to give Joan my personal regards in front of an audience and, above all, anxious to avoid Deb. Not that I wasn't going to miss sweet Joanie, since she was the rare administrator who always dealt with me fairly, though our relations remained more cordial than close.

After partaking of the pineapple juice till my stomach was sloshing, I bellied up to the carrot and celery sticks and squared my back toward the brownies. Since my divorce I had developed an insatiable sweet tooth that resisted little temptation. Right there beside the sliced vegetables was where I was standing, when the first incident, shall we say, occurred. What felt like a paunch brushed against my elbow. I turned sideways to let the portly fellow past.

"Hi there, handsome," Deborah greeted, flashing that toothy grin of hers. No one else was anywhere close. Suddenly it struck me what the paunch had in fact been. I crossed my arms in chagrin.

"Did you know Leslie Pratt got divorced?" Deb said, leaning against me to let a colleague sidle by behind her. Leslie had left us for a rival company across town two years before.

"Really?" I said, flushing at the light pressure against my ribs and holding my breath until Deb mercifully withdrew. What in the devil was going on? Up until then our greatest intimacy had been one stiff shoulder hug upon her return from maternity leave. Our Director ambled through, and Deb made way by bouncing herself into the back of my hand, and I dropped a carrot slice inside a pants cuff. Though Deborah had always struck me as the type to wear a bra even to bed, she felt soft enough not to be wearing one at all. Not that I gladly entertained such thoughts about such a classic mom, close colleague, and good friend.

"You could give her a call," Deb said, stretching her smile an extra notch.

"That I could," I mumbled, stepping back. My pulse felt close to fibrillation.

When Deb leaned too close again a moment later, I excused myself, took hasty leave of Joan, and bolted. That evening I got as far as punching all seven digits of Leslie's number and letting it ring twice before cutting the line.

The following morning, Deborah stopped by my office and asked whether I had given Ms. Pratt a buzz.

"Not yet," I said, half-lying. Deb nodded thoughtfully. Then she gave me a quizzical grin and asked whether I might critique a draft of the Evaluation Committee report she was writing up. Of course I agreed. So that night I took her printout home and red-pencilled the document in bed. All I really found wrong were a couple of typos a spell checker couldn't have missed. The intro might have been clearer, but it was good enough as it stood.

On the next morning's break, I popped into Deborah's office and bridled. Instead of her customary smart but functional outfit, there she sat in a sheer turquoise blouse. I cleared my throat and pointed out those two errors. "You know, Deb," I said, "the intro's fine as it is, but what if you inserted the next-to-last section right after the first paragraph? Wouldn't that make it all—well, more transparent—from the very start?" It meant moving a block of text, a trifle now that we all have new dual-floppy-drive computers

"Hmmm, let's see how that would look," Deb said with a wink, rose up, removed the staple from the upper left corner, and spread the twelve pages across her clear desk. As I stood across from her, she bent down close enough to smell the ink. Did she forget her contacts, was my first thought, followed by, oh, my goodness—her blouse was drooping. I glanced out the window at the steel girders going up for yet another high-rise, but my eyes didn't linger there long.

"That's very interesting," she said, her lingering lowered gaze like an invitation to feast my eyes. I let them pig out.

"Which section did you want me to move again?" she asked.

Bracing my thighs against her desk, I leaned forward and tapped the relevant text. "These four paragraphs."

"And move them where?"

My trembling finger touched a sheet mere inches from her dangling silk.

"Hmmm," she said.

"Did you lose a contact?" I stepped back and loosened my tie.

She neither replied nor budged.

There was no way I could look anywhere in her direction and not see what I ought not, so I faced the window, as though fascinated by the construction outside. Finally, she stood up straight. "Thanks a lot, Tom."

"It looks great," I said. "I mean, much better than I thought—I mean, Deb, I gotta go. Bye." I sped out the door.

My concentration was shot for the rest of the day, so instead of analyzing accounts I straightened my desk, backed up all of my computer files twice, and watched the crane outside lift plate glass with the delicacy of a mother hawk, grooming her chicks. That evening at home, I tossed all the leftovers together, zapped them in the microwave, and wolfed down the motley stew. I watched CNN Headline News five times without hearing a word, before it hit me I was missing the showdown between the New York Knicks and my beloved Milwaukee Bucks. I managed to catch the final shot bouncing off the rim at the buzzer to end a rally that just fell short. "What a basketball game!" the announcer enthused.

What in the world had gotten into Deborah wasn't the only puzzle. What in the devil had gotten into me? Because now wherever I looked, eyes open or shut, I saw Deb half-spilling out of her clothes. Which certainly shouldn't be occurring. Because Deb and I were friends. Because Deb was happily married. Because I had never done or said anything to her remotely resembling flirting, and in my post-divorce paralysis wasn't about to begin. Not with another man's wife, not with a colleague, and, above all, not with a dear friend.

Now like I said, I had taken my time learning the ropes before I had ever gotten around to tying the knot. Finally, after years of playing the field, I decided upon one Janet McNab, a fine, bright woman, and probably finer and brighter than I deserved. She had the tall, leggy look I had always found sexy, along with the rather boyish torso of all my other serious girlfriends. If you can call three all. What I'm saying is that Cupid's bow never twanged in my ear around chests all that different from mine, so when I claim I never was a breast man and I'm not one now, I'm being sincere.

Now Deborah's body is shorter and thicker than my ideal, not that I ever truly noticed or cared. And not that anyone would ever confuse her with a man. No indeed. For a woman in her forties, her teeth are still remarkably white, her full head of chestnut hair only now gradually streaking with gray, and her deepening laugh lines well-earned. To wit, she's an attractive, mature woman in the prime of life.

The next morning Deb phoned me in my department and asked me to stop by her office before lunch if I had the time. I made the time. There she spread the dozen freshly printed pages of her report across her desk and once again bent low. She had changed her intro exactly as I had recommended, but that wasn't all that she brought to my acute attention.

From then on about twice a week, Deb scrounged up documents for us to examine together as a pretext for our—how shall I put it?—silly game. Its tacit rules were that she kept on her side of the desk and I on mine, as if so guaranteeing these displays never led to anything further and thus making them their own reward. And were they indeed rewarding. And energizing. So much so, in fact, that soon I was popping awake mornings bright-eyed at the first ring of the alarm and getting to work early and gladly staying late.

Now don't get me wrong. The last thing in the world anybody could ever call Deborah Walker is a tease. Not when she's been a conspicuously contented spouse for some seventeen years and a devoted mother of two darling girls and a capable manager and a supportive colleague universally esteemed by superiors and subordinates alike, regardless of gender or sexual persuasion. Why is no mystery, since Deb's so obviously kind, generous, even-tempered, conscientious, and loyal, not to mention talented. And, to boot, a master at juggling the demands of both work and home. In sum, a great employee, a fine woman, and an admirable human being. And of all her good points, everybody would agree the most outstanding is her wholesomeness, and not from any apparent effort, but as if the trait were innate. So what had gotten into her? Not that I wasn't relishing it, not that it wasn't reawakening desires that hadn't been dead after all, but merely dormant. But if I never had been a breast man, then why was I acting like one? After a lifetime of presumably knowing exactly who I was, I had become a stranger unto myself.

I was six years old, when my older brother first told me about our mother having breast-fed us. I didn't believe him for a minute. Later when I learned he was telling the truth, I still was skeptical. Because my mother was my mother and hence not really a woman. And no matter how her squat appearance changed with the years, to me she always looked exactly the same—like the embodiment of unconditional love.

I was about ten, when I first became aware of breasts. They belonged to a young actress regularly featured in my older sister's favorite magazine, *Modern Screen*. Her name was Elizabeth Taylor. Miss Taylor's were so big she couldn't find a dress to properly contain them, and they always snuggled together like newborn puppies, as if to keep each other warm.

I never could understand the kick my mom got out of her *True Confessions* or my dad his *Field and Stream* or my brother his *Hot Rod*. But my sister wanting to read about movie stars and Hollywood glamour made perfect sense, though mostly I just looked at the pictures. Whenever I actually wanted to read something as a little tyke, I turned to comic books like *Blackhawk* and *Uncle Scrooge*.

At the end of the eighth grade, this all changed for good. My sister graduated from high school and moved out on her own, after which I never glimpsed another frozen smile or technicolor face. Soon peach fuzz showed up on my cheeks and inside my boxer shorts, and I began pondering ways to get close to real live girls in my class.

Still, I kept my distance. Because once I reached this age girls made me shy, or should I say, shyer. Though I was good at reading, writing, and arithmetic and other school subjects, I was backward at what my brother called life. His sniggering with pals about wet dreams and Kotex machines never failed to send me scurrying from the room.

Finally, during my junior year, at the overdue age of sixteen and a half, I somehow got myself out on a date. Joan Reichenbach was the girl's name. Now I'm not going to say she was lucky, not as lucky as I was anyway. By the time I graduated from high school she turned out to be the first girl I ever kissed and—well, no matter how you fill in the sentence, you won't be far off. Her breasts turned out to be a nicer handful than they looked, but of course I had to wait quite some time before I ever got to so-called first base. I guess it was quite a thrill. But what I remember better was how they felt. Well, strange. Not at all like the firm limbs and torsos familiar from football tackling, but more like water balloons. So what was all the fuss about? I still don't really know. I mean, can anybody make sense of American men's obsession with mammary glands? After all, unlike genitalia, they aren't even sex organs.

If you check out old movies and magazines, you can see it was in the Fifties when our national fascination became a bona fide obsession—all those camera angles calculated to accentuate already exaggerated profiles, all those pushup bras. Then Hugh Hefner launched *Playboy* magazine, which quickly turned this fixation into an institution. But where else in esthetics are proportion and balance so completely ignored? Would even the most gorgeous mouth be anything but ugly, if it stretched from ear to ear?

My whole life the most attractive women to me have been the willowy Audrey Hepburns, Mia Farrows, and Julie Christies. You have to grant their appeal. Maybe they're not so overtly sexual as the zaftig Liz Taylors and Kim Novaks, but then what do newborn puppies have to do with sex? Yet if I've never been a breast man, then why has the slightest protrusion of a woman's chest, even if from obvious padding, never failed to grab my attention?

Now nobody who knows Deborah would believe that she, well, flirted with me. But I swear she did, because I saw it, or rather them, with my own two bug-eyes. Afterwards, I kept trying to fathom her motives, not that I ever got very far. She certainly wasn't trying to win my affection. That she already had as a friend, and without a doubt that was enough for us both. My best guess was that she was having trouble dealing with aging. Turning forty is hardly a cause for anyone to celebrate, especially not in a culture like ours that glorifies youth. So maybe she was saying in deed, if not in word, I think you're attractive, so what do you think about me? I presume my bug-eyes were sufficiently eloquent. So perhaps we were both getting from a friend exactly what we needed. And isn't that what friends are for?

Then came our annual national conference. In past years, Janet and I had gone together and made a mini-vacation of it, but newly single I drove to Chicago alone. And I checked into the Hilton on Michigan Avenue alone and went to bed alone and got up alone and ate breakfast alone too. Early the second evening, I was sitting alone in my room dreading another dinner out by myself, when the phone rang. It was dear Deborah, one floor up, wondering whether I might want to tag along with her and two networking buddies to a nearby Thai restaurant. I definitely wanted.

I have to admit I was disappointed to find Deborah in the lounge still wearing a proper business suit, de rigueur conference attire for her, as a jacket and tie were for me. The whole pungent meal Deb regaled us with tales about her beloved daughters, Heather and Jennifer, the twin suns around which her world revolved. As always her wit didn't throw off any sparks, but its lambent charm also never dimmed. Her husband, whom I knew casually from our holiday parties, came across as more problematical. Not because of what she said about him, but because of what she didn't. She scarcely mentioned Matthew.

Afterwards, Deb and I strolled back to our hotel together in the comfortable silence of old friends. At the elevator she announced she wasn't sleepy yet and asked whether I would mind escorting her to the hotel bar.

Mind? Well, actually, no.

At a corner table she gently persisted until she got me to open up about my dating.

"I haven't really been up to dating yet," I said. "And I fear I'll never be."

"Nonsense, Thomas," she teased, flashing that toothy grin. "Just cool it for a while longer until it does feel natural. Meanwhile, rest assured there are women who want your bod."

Women wanted my bod? Such language from Deborah's lips was startling, to say the least. "Really?"

She nodded deeply and reached over and rested a cool, dry hand on mine, and our fingers intertwined and didn't let go. Peering deeply into her unstinting gaze, I was soon convinced. Later, we took the elevator to our respective rooms without so much as a goodbye handshake. For the rest of the conference our paths didn't cross once.

The same evening I got back here, I impulsively called Leslie Pratt, who was thrilled to hear it was me. I was about to ask her out for dinner at L'Etoile for the coming weekend, when I blurted, "Leslie, are you doing anything right now? I mean, how about coming over to watch a movie on videotape? I could phone for a pizza."

"Great idea!" Leslie said. And so just like that, after a hiatus of nearly two decades, my dating resumed.

First thing the next morning, I stopped by Deb's office to relay the great news. She jumped up and gave me a heartfelt hug, and her eyes got misty above a gleeful grin. That week she didn't suggest laying anything out across her desk for us to examine together. Or ever again.

Kathy, the third woman I dated, turned out to be a competent CPA—like me—as well as a sweet and thoughtful human being. And she had a leggy, rather boyish figure like my ex's, and following a subdued and seemly courtship, we got married.

One morning about two months after our wedding, I ran into Deborah on the elevator looking horridly hungover, though I had never seen her drink more than a single glass of white wine at a sitting. "Are the girls okay?" I asked.

"They're fine," she snapped and darted off at her floor.

Deborah Walker peevish? Not in my experience. Within the hour I was in her office, asking whether she had heard about the impending budget cut. Which she couldn't have, since I had made the rumor up whole cloth. Her wrinkled ankle-length brown dress was so unbecoming it would have even struck my down-home mother as dowdy. Grim-faced Deb sat frozen, refusing to meet my gaze, her arms tightly folded across her chest.

"Is something wrong?" I said.

She bit a lip and shook her head. Later that day, I asked our Division Head whether Deborah wasn't feeling well.

"Haven't you heard?" he said.

"Did Matt get a transfer?" I asked, my heart sinking.

His face as grave as the day his mother died, Mr. Bathrick said, "Deborah's going into the hospital Friday for exploratory surgery. If the biopsy confirms the suspected malignancy, I'm afraid she's facing a mastectomy."

I thanked him breathlessly for keeping me posted and slipped into the privacy of a bathroom stall, where I silently sobbed over poor Deborah's plight. Once I regained my composure, I debated how best to express my concern, the memory of our dumb desktop game making my head hot with shame. I decided to wait until she was willing to share a matter this delicate with me, and then offer to help her and Matt as best I could, whether that meant hauling their daughters to their lessons, buying groceries, or even cooking or cleaning house.

The rest of that week I worked poorly and slept even worse. I've always been one to grant people as much space around me as they required. Like a stray cat, I've kept my distance until their posture and tone invited approach. So now I kept expecting Deb to give me the cue, since I didn't feel I had the right to bring up the issue without her permission.

But she didn't call. She didn't send a note. She didn't ask Matt or anyone else to phone. The two times we ran into each other outside the elevator, she just averted her eyes, muttered a perfunctory, "Hello," and hurried on. So I'm sorry to say Deb was admitted to the hospital without our having exchanged more than the briefest of greetings—as if I were a mere passing acquaintance and not a dear friend.

When the biopsy turned out badly, the surgeon proceeded with a bilateral mastectomy. The next day I stopped by the hospital for a visit, but Matt intercepted me in the corridor and said Deb wasn't up to seeing any co-workers. I sent her a get-well card, but under the circumstances that was embarrassingly paltry. And so against my intent, my honorable aim of respecting her feelings was turning into abject disloyalty. Even if Deb had been unable to broach this matter with me, that was no excuse for my virtually abandoning our friendship. If as good a male friend had developed some equally ticklish affliction like testicular cancer, I wouldn't have remained aloof. But it was too late to undo my mistake, and so now I could only do my best to make amends once Deb finally returned to work.

During her absence, Mr. Bathrick relayed scanty progress reports. My imagination filled in the omitted details, and soon lurid nightmares about scalpels and sutures were rousing me before dawn in a clammy sweat to listen to Kathy's measured breathing and wait for the night's blackness to fade.

The Monday Deb was scheduled to return I awoke so alert I skipped my morning coffee. My plan was to stop by her office early, but I kept putting it off. Finally, just before lunch, I popped in. One quick glance and my stomach sank. Deb's cheeks were thinner, her hair much grayer, and fresh wrinkles creased her brow. But worst of all was the vulnerability in her bloodshot eyes. "I really missed you, Deborah," I muttered.

"Thanks, Thomas," she half-whispered, cleared her throat, and added more strongly, "I missed you too."

Locking my gaze on her darting eyes to keep it from drifting lower, I said lamely, "I'm so sorry that"—her grimace made me stop. "Deb," I began again, "I know I should have ..." My voice trailed off, unable to complete the sentence.

Her eyes teared over, but she kept smiling gamely. "It's okay," she told me.

"If there's anything I can do," I said. "Anything."

She blinked hard. "The THC helps against the nausea, but it gives me such crazy thoughts."

THC as in marijuana? Straight-arrow Deborah Walker and pot went together like nuns and Frederick's of Hollywood. Not even twenty years ago and certainly not now. But of course the drug was an antidote to the side effects of chemotherapy. I didn't have to ask whether these were her first pot highs.

"Really, if there's anything I can do to help," I said again. "Driving the girls places, shopping, or whatever else you might need."

Deb nodded gravely. And slowly clasped her hands behind her head and stretched back against her chair and stared outside across the street at the busy offices of the completed high-rise. It was then I noticed she was wearing the turquoise blouse she had worn the day she first spread out that committee report across her desk. My scalp prickled.

Their shape was different. Higher. A tad larger. Less pointed. Not exactly how they had been before. But of course still feminine, still a womanly bosom. And even in my discomfiture, against my will, they still turned me on.

My glance jerked back up and met Deb's stare, and she broke into her familiar, toothy grin. "You know, Thomas," she said, "there is one thing you could do. Could you take me out for lunch?"

"My pleasure."

Lair of Lazarus

Once upon a time in a big city not all that far away a couple had lived alone so long they began to feel lonesome, even though they of course had each other as well as their shaggy dog, Hank. Then, wonder of wonders, one day despite their graying hair the two were blessed with the birth of a darling daughter. Amanda they named the welcome child. No one could say exactly why, just like no one could imagine another name that fit the girl better. The proud parents thought she was the prettiest baby they had ever seen, but then what new parents think anything different and are any of them mistaken? Not only her mother and father, but both sets of grandparents and all the aunts and uncles adored the newborn too. That's one thing that will never change so long as the earth shall endure.

The baby Amanda was bathed and scrubbed in sweet love and powdered and dressed with tender care. Such a cheerful child was a sheer joy for all to hug and behold. Old Hank so adored the girl he sneaked in licks to the baby's delight whenever nobody was looking.

It didn't take that many months before the little girl was crawling across the carpet. Once that starts, walking soon follows, and then talking comes too. Nobody around could recall a child who learned new words quicker or who talked more grownup. Whenever she and Hank played fetch out on the well-manicured lawn, the little girl even talked to the dog, who barked back just like he understood the words.

Then one warm June night the year Amanda turned six, Hank fell asleep on his favorite living room chair and never woke up. For the dear dog had lived to the end of his life as everything alive one day must. By the time Amanda arose that morning, her beloved Hank was gone. Try as her parents might, they couldn't explain to their daughter why their pet was no longer around to wag his tail or lick her face. But what puzzled her the most was where he could be if he was nowhere in sight.

After such a hard loss Amanda turned quiet and gloomy, and she refused to sleep alone in her room nights or nap anywhere at all afternoons. When asked what was wrong, the little girl said she was afraid that while she was asleep she might vanish just like old Hank.

"But Hank's gone to heaven," her mother said.

"Where's that?" Amanda asked.

Her mother looked at her father and he looked at his spouse, but neither could explain it in a way that made any sense to the child. Talking together that night, her parents decided their daughter was just going through a phase that would soon pass. But as surely as July became August, Amanda remained glum. So her dad called his sister clear across the state. Auntie Ann wondered whether a change of scenery might help her little niece. The suggestion struck both parents as an excellent idea.

So early one late summer morning they strapped their daughter into the back seat of their car and took off driving toward the rising sun. And they drove on till they were passing barns and cornfields, which gave way to rivers and steep hills blanketed with trees.

"Where are we going?" Amanda piped up from the back seat.

"Somewhere you're never been before," her dad said.

"Why?" the little girl wanted to know next.

"You'll find out," he told her with a chuckle.

"Is it far?" Amanda asked through a big yawn.

"Farther than you've ever gone," her mom replied with a wink.

"Mandy," her dad said, using a favorite nickname, "why don't you just close your eyes and have a little snooze."

"But I don't want to miss anything along the way," Amanda replied, looking every which direction. If the tall, shaggy-barked trees on one side didn't fascinate her, then the big, jagged rocks on the other side did.

"Mandy, what'd your father tell you about taking a nap?" her mother gently coaxed.

"Can't I look just a little bit longer?" the little girl asked.

Her mom and her dad's gazes met and they agreed to give in. So Amanda feasted her eyes to their utmost delight. Still, the farther along they went, the more she yawned till try as she might she could barely keep her eyes open. But she simply wouldn't let herself doze off.

Before you know it, the car was stopping and her mom and dad were climbing out and people were hollering from a big front porch. There came Auntie Ann and Uncle Dave thumping down the steps. Both looked grayer than the last time she had seen them, although neither had really changed. "Auntie Ann! Uncle Dave!" Amanda shouted. "What are you doing here?" The little girl unsnapped her seatbelt and scrambled out too.

"This is our home," Auntie Ann replied. She and Uncle Dave both looked at their little niece like she was all the Christmas presents in the world wrapped into a single precious package. Auntie Ann scooped her up and spun her around. "Oof, you're getting so big," she said. Her aunt's hands always felt so nice and cool.

Soon Mandy was flying into her uncle's arms without once grazing the ground. When he hoisted her onto his shoulders, she snatched his thinning hair like reins and hollered, "Giddyup!" His strong hands grasped her ankles like stirrups, and together they galloped down the driveway. "Kitties!" the little girl shouted at the sight of three felines, lounging on the lawn.

"Mandy, I'd like you to meet Mortimer, Raven, and Lazarus," Uncle Dave said and lowered his niece to the ground.

A big orange tabby greeted the little girl with a friendly meow. Amanda knelt and petted the pudgy tom. "That one's Mortimer," Uncle Dave explained as she felt firm muscle beneath some furry flab. A black kitty rose onto delicate paws and wrapped a flank around the little girl's bare legs. "Raven wants you to pet her too," Uncle Dave told her.

Happy to oblige, Amanda stroked Raven's sleek, silky fur so unlike Mortimer's rougher, oilier coat. All of a sudden she stuck both arms under the dark female's stomach and hefted her. Raven's entire body stiffened and her yellow eyes grew big till she wriggled free and hopped onto the grass.

Lazarus, gray-colored like a rabbit except for a long, black-striped tail, took one look at Raven's plight and bolted down the bushy hill. "Here, kitty, kitty," Amanda coaxed, stepping right out of her shoes in pursuit, but the cat stayed hidden in the thick brush.

"Lazarus is pretty shy," Uncle Dave told his niece. "He's got himself a good place to hide somewhere down in the hollow, but nobody can figure out where."

Amanda's bright chestnut eyes danced to hear that fact. Then she burst out laughing—Mortimer's pink sandpaper-tongue was tickling her feet. The back porch screen swung open, and her mom shouted, "Mandy, where are your shoes?"

Her priceless daughter shrugged.

"You really ought to put on something on your feet," her dad said. "You never know what might be hidden in the tall grass. Who knows, maybe even a snake."

"Poison ivy is more like it," her mom added. "And bees and all kinds of other icky creatures."

"What's a 'creature'?" Amanda asked, stepping into her teensy shoes and letting Uncle Dave tie them for her.

Her dad was stumped, but her mom wasn't. "Any animal that's ever been created," she said.

Now Mandy wanted to know what "created" meant.

Her mother glanced at her husband for help, but he didn't know how else to explain. With a good-natured chuckle he pointed at his brother-in-law's shaggy grass and teased, "Say, Dave, did your lawn mower die?"

Uncle Dave stood motionless as a tree.

"You mean 'die' like old Hank?" Mandy asked, her eyes turning sad as the day their dear doggy passed on. "I still don't understand what 'die' means?"

"It's like when you go to sleep," Auntie Ann told her.

"Only your dreams are all sweet," Uncle Dave hastened to add.

"And they last forever," Auntie Ann said. She led her sister-in-law into the house, leaving the two men alone out back to watch over her darling niece.

A bird hidden in nearby leaves sang out like a flute. One good look at the dandelions ablaze in the shaggy grass and Mandy's wrinkled brow unfurrowed. Suddenly the girl let out a chortle—sneaky Lazarus was trying to squirt between her ankles. She reached down and grabbed the kitty's flanks, but the little tom slithered out of her grasp like a slippery fish and disappeared beneath the back porch. What were those prickly lumps she had just felt on him? Like something entangled in the feline's fur.

Uncle Dave rattled a loose board till Lazarus darted out and sped off. Soon his green eyes were glowing out of the tall grass partway down the hillside. Giggling with glee, Amanda took off in pursuit as the cat ducked out of sight. "Wait for me, Lazarus!" the girl shouted, plunging straight into a sea of stalks and stems tall enough to tickle her cheeks.

Toward the bottom of the hollow the little girl heard a thudding and a crackling. But how could tiny Lazarus be making that much racket? "Mandy, get out of there!" her dad hollered. Ever the obedient child, Amanda stumbled out of the high weeds and tumbled onto the overgrown grass. "Don't worry about Lazarus," her dad said, helping her back onto her feet. "That rapscallion can take care of himself."

"What's a rapscallion?" Amanda asked as Mortimer and Raven wrapped their flanks around her calves.

"Like a rascal," her dad said, kissing her cheek. "Only smaller." He picked his beloved daughter up and held her tight.

"Sort of like you," Uncle Dave piped up with an adoring grin.

As her dad carried his little girl inside, Amanda glanced downhill and spotted a creature bigger than a cat with huge eyes, poking its head above the weeds. "Hank?" she muttered. The instant her dad lowered her to the floor, she raced to the back door, but the mystery creature had already vanished.

Before you know it, Amanda was walking hand in hand with her mother on a tour of the oddest house she had ever seen. In the center of the living room sat a big glass table covered with rocks of every color and shape. On the walls hung drawings of mountains and plants and animals. And books, books, and more books. In fact, there wasn't a room without a bookshelf, including the kitchen and the bedrooms upstairs. There were even bookshelves in the basement. And shoes scattered across the foyer like large, legless ants. Speaking of ants, big black ones were skittering here and there. Cats and adults alike paid them no heed—like these insects were welcome here too.

Soon everybody was sitting around the dining room table, set for lunch. The more the grownups talked, the more excited they got till all four were speaking at once. Leaning so close her kind, brown eyes looked big as the lemur's at the zoo, Auntie Ann asked, "You've gotten so quiet, Mandy? Is anything wrong?"

The little girl's mother said, "She's gets like this a lot lately."

"Ever since H-A-N-K D-I-E-D," her dad explained, spelling out what he didn't dare pronounce.

"You mean your old retriever?" Uncle Dave said, stabbing another juicy slice of tomato with his fork. Auntie Ann shushed him.

"Hank went to heaven," Amanda said, staring out a window with wide eyes as a patch of golden fur flashed by. "Wherever that place is," she mumbled through a yawn.

"It's up there," Auntie Ann said, pointing at the ceiling.

Mandy raised her gaze, but all she saw was a rusty spider walking upside down. Another of Auntie Ann and Uncle Dave's pets most likely. "Does Mandy ever need a nap," her father whispered. Everybody stopped talking to concentrate on cleaning off their plates that much sooner. All of a sudden Amanda let out a squeal. A cat had landed on her lap and its furry black tail was tickling her chin.

"Be careful now, Raven," Auntie Ann said. "Amanda isn't a big girl yet like you." The little girl's parents braced for disaster while the feline kneaded the little girl's thighs with its tiny paws.

"Don't worry," Uncle Dave said. "The kitty wouldn't dream of hurting her."

"Maybe somehow it'll even help," Auntie Ann added. She stood up, gathered a stack of dirty dishes, and carried them into the kitchen.

Meanwhile without so much as a peep—or for that matter a meow—Mortimer thumped smack dab in the middle of the dining room table, and Mandy burst out laughing. The big orange tomcat moseyed over and rubbed his stiff whiskers against the cackling girl's cheeks. "Now where's Lazarus?" she wanted to know. She slid off her chair, sending Raven bounding to the floor.

"Mandy, wait for dessert!" Auntie Ann cried out as she came with bowls of rainbow arrays of fruit. Amanda sat back down. Uncle Dave helped his wife serve up the colorful chunks. Soon all four grownups were chattering away again like so many birds at a busy feeder. By the time Amanda had eaten every last piece of her watermelon and cantaloupe and peaches and pears and oranges and bananas and apples, the adults had again grown silent. Like her mom and dad, her aunt and uncle were muffling yawns.

"I bet the long drive tired you all out," Uncle Dave piped up.

"Feel free to take a nap," Auntie Ann said. "We're not on any schedule."

Without further ado, the four grownups retreated upstairs with little Amanda in tow. Auntie Ann and Uncle Dave headed straight for the master bedroom, while Mandy's parents led her into the bright guest room. The little girl ran to the window overlooking the street and stuck her snub nose against the screen. Alas, not one car was driving by. Her dad drew the shades. "But now I can't see anything," Amanda said.

"You're not supposed to, Skeeters," her mom said. "Because we're all going to nap." Her parents stretched out on the guest bed, and Amanda climbed in between them like she'd been sleeping at home of late. Her parents shut their eyes and grew still while Mandy just lay there staring at the ceiling. Her eyes scanned back and forth, but no matter how hard she tried she couldn't spot another spider.

It wasn't long before her mom was breathing like a whistle and her dad snoring like a saw. But as tired as her folks obviously were, Mandy herself didn't feel drowsy. Still, she laid a cheek against the soft pillow, closed her eyes, and did her best to doze off to memories of playing fetch with Hank. She sure wished she could figure out where her doggie had disappeared.

The next thing Amanda knew she was sitting up and staring at the shelves stuffed with books. So many of them standing side by side on end. How much longer before she would be able to read what all those squiggly lines in them meant?

Since her mom and dad were still asleep, Mandy carefully crawled to the foot of the bed and lowered herself to the floor. In a jiffy she was out on the landing and walking toward an open door into who knew what room. Among the shadows inside she made out a desk and boxes and cabinets, jammed close together. So this was where Uncle Dave worked at home. She stuck her head inside for a better look at a shiny box like a TV, attached to a contraption fed by a big roll of paper.

Amanda peered through the study's least smudged window pane down into the tall grass of her aunt and uncle's marvelous backyard. There she spotted a rabbit-gray kitty with a raccoon tail scampering along. "Lazarus!" the little girl squealed and slapped a hand over her mouth—mustn't wake the adults. She tiptoed downstairs, holding onto the railing as her parents had taught.

She opened and closed the porch screen door as quietly as a butterfly landing on a flower. Before Amanda had even turned around on the porch, big orange Mortimer came running up with skinny, black Raven close behind. The two cats rubbed their cheeks on the little girl's ankles and meowed.

"What's wrong?" Mandy asked the kitties. Raven pressed her little black nose against the screen door. "You want to go inside?" The two kitties meowed even louder till she let them into the kitchen.

But where now was Lazarus, the rapscallion no one could keep track of? Amanda was dying to learn that cat's secret hideout. The little girl worked her way down the porch steps, calling out the wily kitty's name again and again, only not so loud as to awaken the napping adults. But no matter how many times she repeated it, he didn't reply. Gradually Mandy became aware of a sound she had been hearing all along without really noticing it. Like a high-pitched motor, only this was coming from the trees. Actually it was more like a shrill song, sung not by just one voice, but a whole chorus singing in weird harmony.

She marched down the hillside that grew wilder with every new step till stems of high grasses and weeds were tickling her cheeks. She walked on right into a patch of wildflowers in glorious bloom. There she stopped to admire the orange and black butterflies flitting among the blossoms. Ants were clambering up and down plant stalks too and fuzzy bumblebees buzzed just inches off her nose without frightening her at all. The little girl's lips stretched into a gigantic grin. To think that the yards back home had grass cut short as a brush when they could look like this. And it all had such a wonderful aroma. She took another deep whiff. Like her Grandma's rising bread dough, only sweeter. Actually this wasn't so much a yard, but a dreamy paradise.

Not twenty feet off Amanda spotted two big, pointy ears jutting above a long, narrow snout, and a pair of big, black eyes staring right at her. The rays of the sun, no longer so high in the sky, made this creature's coat look as if golden threads were sewn into the fur. "Are you a horsie?" Mandy asked the animal, standing perfectly still.

One of its large ears twitched.

"Where do you live?" Amanda asked next.

The creature's other ear jerked.

"I know—you're a deer! Just like at the zoo!" No sooner had the little girl said that than the doe disappeared, as though Mandy had only imagined seeing the animal. She snatched a handful of grass and held on. No, there was no denying this yard and everything in it was as real as what she now grasped.

Something tickled Amanda's ankle. She glanced down to see a gray cat between her legs. "Lazarus!" she shouted. "Where have you been?" The kitty's fur glowed in the setting sunlight.

Lazarus shoved his fuzzy head into the little girl's hand with a meow, the better to relish her caresses. She stroked the little tyke's flanks and again felt odd little lumps. One, two, three of them, she counted. What in the world might they be? No better time than right now to find out. So while one hand tickled the tom's neck, the other dug into his coat till she got a good grip. With tugs and twists she worked the prickly things free one by one. "They're seeds!" she said. She put them all into her pocket, while the feline darted off deeper into the hollow.

Mandy rose onto her tiptoes to see where, but towering plants blocked her view. Should she take off in pursuit? She glanced up the hill toward her aunt and uncle's house, but from down here beneath the hump in the backyard all she could make out was its slate roof. She was just about to head back when Lazarus meowed from not ten feet away. "I'm coming!" Mandy shouted.

It didn't take long for the little girl to emerge into a patch of low-lying purple flowers surrounded by yellow blossoms so heavy they wobbled atop their skinny stalks. While butterflies fluttered before her eyes and bees hummed beside her ears, she heard rustling a short distance away. The prospect of finding the kitty's hideout so excited the little girl she marched into a thick patch of weeds that needled her shins. She paused and gingerly picked a prickly seed off her shoe—exactly like the three she had pried from Lazarus's fur! She pocketed this one as well. "Lazarus!" she called out, but the only reply was the wind whispering through the leaves like grownups sharing secrets. Mandy poked this way and that for a route around the prickly patch. Farther down the hill it only got worse, so she doubled back, stooping to pass beneath low branches that patted her neck like loving hands.

She found herself upon a narrow path goodness only knew what had worn so flat. But there was neither sight nor sound of Lazarus. Could she have made a wrong turn? There was only this one trail through the thick briars no matter how much it wound this way and that. So she followed it till the path ended in bushy grass soft as her mother's fine hair. The little girl glanced down—at her feet the gentle rapscallion lay asleep, his puny chest rising and falling with every kitty breath. In a flash she realized he was sleeping on a patch of grass flattened in the perfect outline of a deer resting upon its side. A deer bed! And Lazarus was resting inside it! Mandy dropped to her knees and stroked the cat's silky flank, free of all prickly lumps thanks to his new friend. The little fellow purred, but didn't wake up.

Letting out a big yawn, the little girl lowered herself to the pillowy grass and curled up flush against Lazarus's golden fur and shut her eyes. She took a deep breath of the earthy air as the insects hidden in the trees above sang out their shrill chorus. After while a wet tongue began to lick her cheek—just like Hank always used to. Through barely parted lids Amanda looked up at their beloved old doggy, only now he had long erect pointy ears and huge black eyes that glistened with all the kindness in the entire world. To the caress of this warm and tender tongue, the little girl dozed off into pure bliss. ...

"Mandy?" a voice called out just like her father's.

Amanda opened her eyes and found everybody standing around the bed—Mommy and Daddy and Auntie Ann and Uncle Dave, all looking worried. "What's wrong?" Mandy asked and they all burst out laughing.

"That's what we were just saying about you," her dad said. "No matter how hard we tried, we couldn't wake you up."

The little girl wiped the sleep from her eyes.

"I guess you really needed that nap," her Mommy added with a big smile.

Grinning just as wide, Amanda stuck a hand into her pocket. One, two, three, four prickly seeds, she counted. So none were missing. As soon as they got home, she would plant them in their own backyard and make it grow so wild and lush the lair of Lazarus would never be far off.

Falls

"Ain't it something, Jake?" my Bonnie tells me.

"It'd better be," I say. "After driving all day clear across Ohio, Pennsylvania, and New York." Never in my entire life have I seen a swifter river. Like you couldn't even set both feet in it without getting swept away. Next to this, the Ohio's just a pokey Sunday stroll, like those my family used to take after church back when I was a boy.

All around us people are yukking it up like a bunch of monkeys. The thunder coming from out of sight just won't let up. At least it's somewhat drowning out the awful gabbing. I stare at the ripples rocks hidden beneath the surface are making in the current. Water this swift has got to be eating away at the banks something fierce, no matter how firm Goat Island here feels underfoot.

"Too bad we ain't got a camera," Bonnie says.

No need to bring that up. Too bad we ain't got lots of things. Still, that don't mean we can't get the heck out of here. Or better yet take a little swim on the spot.

"Jake, I didn't mean nothing by mentioning a camera," Bonnie tells me like she truly means it. But these days being sincere and a buck will get you a cup of coffee. "Are you okay?" she says real sweet like.

"Uh-huh," I say and begin limping back toward our old beater. No matter how fast I walk, the water races on by like we're standing still. The way it's running, it's a wonder it ain't already worn those boulders in its bed down to bits.

"Come on, Jake," Bonnie says. "This is our vacation."

"Did I say it wasn't?" I snap.

"What's the matter, Jacob?" she says.

"I hate this place," I say. "I mean, so here we are alongside this weird river that's moving along faster than Interstate traffic. Before you know it, it's going to flow straight off a cliff. So what?"

"But waterfalls are beautiful," Bonnie says. "Just look at the great big smiles on everybody."

No need to tell me about those. In fact, I might feel a whole lot more like smiling myself, if I didn't have to look at all their pukey grins.

"Why don't we stroll across to the other side?" she says, pointing at a huge tower sticking up from the opposite bank.

How much is it going to cost, is my first question. Because even if this place is a genuine wonder of the world, that's no excuse for blowing dough hand over fist. Because ever since we checked into a local Motel 6, it's been, Jake, can we buy this, can we buy that? Oh, how about a souvenir? Or a couple caramel apples? Or better yet, some cotton candy? It's like there ain't a thought in that woman's pretty head but figuring out new ways to empty our pockets. Which lately ain't exactly hard.

Still, it's not like Bonnie ain't always earned every dime she's ever touched and then some. That goes for her and me both. And it ain't like we don't deserve this trip in the worst way, on account of how poorly things have been going. And it sure as heck ain't like Bonnie's not the best thing in my life.

"Okay," I say.

"Honest?" Bonnie practically squeals.

"So how do we get across?"

"With the bridge!" she shouts, hurrying on ahead. Before you know it, we're walking through a woods, and then down a shaggy path behind a dingy building that looks abandoned. It's enough to make a person wonder how a town this rundown could be a famous resort.

"Bonnie, this can't be right," I say. But she just keeps marching along like she's been here before. Though I know full well she's hardly been out of Ohio. Despite my gimpy hip I keep up.

Pretty soon we come to a huge sign announcing, "Rainbow Bridge, Pedestrians to Canada." We go through a gate and along a raised plank walkway behind barbed wire and then past a little hut with a handwritten sign that reads "U.S. Customs." Like some government piker just stuck it up.

I follow Bonnie up onto the bridge, keeping my eyes glued to her feet. I figure I ought to do fine as long as I don't look around. Still, this ain't no place for lollygagging, not as dizzy as heights make me. Or worse, the crazy thoughts they give me.

"Jake," Bonnie says, "don't forget we've got to buy Larry a souvenir. The same goes for Mom and Dad. And Dolores of course too." She's talking about her son and her folks and the dear daughter I lost through my divorce.

I trudge along, never letting go of the railing. The thunder on the left just keeps getting louder. Like a thousand trucks revving up at once. Or an artillery barrage zeroing in. Or a tornado coming straight for our trailer court.

Midway across, I can't help but glance between the supports at a small boat below packed with folks in yellow raincoats. "Maid of the Mist II" it reads across the bow. Which is an even dumber name than Rainbow, and a stupider thing to do than this here stroll. Though I have to admire how the boat's fighting the current with everything's it got. It don't take long before that awful sinking I always felt, whenever the coal mine shaft lights used to flicker, hits my stomach. Too bad it's a lot longer bridge than I was counting on.

"Ain't it beautiful?" Bonnie says, stopping and facing the falls. She grins just like Lawrence, her twelve-year-old son by her first marriage. I hope the bashful boy's doing okay with her folks back in Dayton.

"I'll have to take your word for it, honey," I say.

"Come on, Jake. Just take a quick peek." She's grinning like she's having the time of her life. Too bad I ain't, not how my head's aching. Like there's a big bomb inside and nobody knows how much fuse is left. At least we get to see young Larry plenty, since he stays with us, unlike my daughter, who lives with my ex in Texas. Of course I can't afford to phone anyplace that far all too often.

Keeping my eyes fixed on my sneakers, I grab the sturdy iron bars behind me. Holes worn clear through the shoes at both little toes, and two more working their way there alongside. Between the supports I can't help seeing pools of foam, swirling out of sight faster than my paychecks. Back when they were still coming in every two weeks. The pressure inside my head feels close to exploding. I try hard to tune out the roar behind my tingling back, but simply can't.

"Come on, Jake," Bonnie says. "A sight like this is how come we drove all this way."

"That's not why I came," I say. But if it ain't, then what the heck else is? A couple in Bermuda shorts hurries past, their skins both tanner than leather. The guy's jabbering about playing blackjack.

"Hey, Jake, guess what?" Bonnie shouts. "That tall building yonder across the bridge is a casino!"

"Good," I say. "Because now the both of us know exactly where not to go."

It ain't like I've ever been to Canada before or anyplace else outside the good old US of A. Except for Vietnam of course. Not that I wasn't anxious to get away from the American side here just now. I mean, if we wanted to stick around some rundown rat hole, we could just as soon have stayed home. Down river I see some blame fool hovering up in the air thanks to a crazy kite contraption. Good way to get yourself killed, if you ask me.

"Jake, I'm sorry I ever brought up that camera," Bonnie says.

"Forget about it," I tell her.

"Jacob, what's the matter with you today?" she says. "This was supposed to be our honeymoon, remember? The one we never got to take."

She grabs for my hand, but I yank it away.

"What do you want to do instead then?" Bonnie says, again real sweet like.

"First of all, get the heck off this bridge." She don't disagree. So we march straight toward the casino. Like maybe we're going to stroll right in and blow all our dough on one roll of the dice.

"Where is everybody?" Bonnie asks, when we finally reach the Canadian side. I glance back, struck by how few folks are on the bridge heading in either direction. My stomach starts sinking again, so I slip through a door quick and march down a glass corridor.

"Customs," a woman around forty pipes up from behind a counter. She's got on a dark blue uniform, just like the older fellow at her elbow. "Where are you from?" the woman asks me.

I shrug. What business is that of hers anyway?

Bonnie throws me an anxious glance. "Dayton, Ohio," she tells the official.

"Here on vacation, eh?" the woman says next.

"Yes, Ma'am," Bonnie answers.

"Can he talk too?" the guy asks.

I've seen his type around plenty. I glare back.

"Could we please see some identification?" the woman says.

"Sure," I say, reaching for my ratty billfold. "How about a driver's license? Or better yet, my union card? In fact, you can keep that worthless piece of crap, if you like."

"It's our honeymoon," Bonnie pipes up. "We just want to visit for a few hours."

"Do you have anything to declare?" the woman says.

"Like what?" I say. Like any blame fool can't see all we've got is what's in my pockets or Bonnie's purse. She starts to fork that over, when the guy waves us through with a smirk, and we hustle the heck out of there.

"Wherever we're going, it sure ain't inside that casino," I tell Bonnie once we've made it outside. Now it's like the roaring's moved inside my head, which hurts so bad I almost feel cross-eyed.

"So I guess there's no sense even bothering to go to Clifton Hill," Bonnie says. "Since everything there costs money."

"You got that straight." No need for me to ask what the heck Clifton Hill is. Nothing I bet but honkytonks, dumps, and dives, each one a bigger rip-off than the last. Me, I'm doing my best not to dwell on how so far this honeymoon's mostly been a bust. Heck, it ain't like Bonnie and I are strangers in bed. We've both been around the block and then some. The main difference is her spouse passed away, while mine filed for divorce on account of what her hifalutin lawyer called irreconcilable differences. Kind of a fancy way of saying I was broke more often than I wasn't. That sure ain't changed.

"Can we get a close-up look at the falls?" Bonnie asks me.

Her tone's so sweet I can't hardly say no. So we head upriver, the opposite of what we just did on the American side. The closer we get to the point of all this fuss, the source of the endless thundering, the more I tense up. Though we're still out of sight from it. We wind our way among the packs of tourists, milling around with stupid grins, like somebody just hit them between the eyes with a ball-peen hammer. What's worse a good half of them are foreigners. Actually, I've never seen more swarthy people at one place in my whole life, and I don't mean dark like my cousin Andy's wife. A lot of them are speaking English, only with peculiar accents.

We shove our way onto the concrete overlook, but it's so crowded all I see is the backs of people's heads. But we sure can hear the water crashing. It sure ain't like nothing I've ever heard before. Sort of like a TV station used to after it's signed off, only about a thousand times louder. And there ain't no switch to turn it off. "Haven't we seen plenty already?" I say, itching to scram.

Bonnie grabs for my hand again, but I make a fist, so she can't grasp it. "Come on, Jake," she teases. "These folks are strangers. Just like you and I are to them."

A snazzy pair butts in front of us, both of them dressed head to toe in white, with sweaters tied around their necks, and sunglasses perched in their hair, like they've got eyes on top of their heads. "The falls were definitely more gorgeous down at the bottom," this jerk says.

"Did you hear that, Jake?" Bonnie says.

"I thought the only way down there was over the top inside a barrel," I say.

Bonnie gives me such a sad stare that my heart just aches. I look down at my toes sticking out of my worn-out sneakers. It's hard to believe a gal sweet as Bonnie Crabtree was willing to marry old Jake McTavish. Just thinking about it makes me feel like buying a big bucket and taking it for a ride.

"Okay, let's go," I say. At least it'll get us away from this here mob.

Bonnie's face lights up, and she races toward the souvenir shop like she knows that's exactly where to go. But then her gabby sister's honeymooned here twice. She drags me past enough knickknacks to stuff a landfill, and down two flights of stairs, where a great big sign reads "Journey Beneath the Falls."

"No way," I say. The end of the line is already poking out the door.

"Come on, Jake," Bonnie begs, hopping into line. Before you know it, another couple crowds behind her. So I step alongside my wife, hanging my head. It ain't long before a whole passel of foreigners is jabbering behind us. Why couldn't they just stay wherever they're from and not come over here and steal a poor workingman's job?

Every little while we edge another step closer to the door, while I do my darnedest not to squirm. One quick peek inside wipes the grin off Bonnie's face. "No big deal," she says with that pinched voice she gets whenever she's stretching the truth.

Somehow I manage to put up with all the yammering till we finally push through the door. "You've got to be kidding!" I shout. A line is snaking all around the room inside, just like a burger joint Saturday noon. Worse, plain as day a sign says, "Adults $6." "Twelve bucks for what?" I snap, eager to scram.

Bonnie gives me such a hurt look I stay put. Every so often we move forward a few feet more. The roar's gotten so loud now I can hardly stand it. It's like I'm back inside that coal mine shaft everybody knew was trouble. I grab the railing in a mood to rip it from the floor. My head throbs so bad I shut my eyes.

When I finally open them, we're at a cashier window, manned by a woman my age. I hand her five brass two-dollar coins and two smaller silver dollars. What's a gray-hair like her trying to pull, sporting a ponytail?

"Thank you kindly," the woman tells me. "I need all the toonies and loonies I can get today."

"I wish we used dollar coins back home," Bonnie says to her. Like they're cousins or something.

The woman hands us two folded wedges of soft, yellow plastic. "So you won't get wet!" she says with a horsey laugh.

I jerk around and meet a little Asian girl's chestnut-eyed stare. The child drops her delicate grip on her Mama's hand just as a squinty-eyed man slips a square of yellow over her head. So the plastic wedges are raincoats.

"Bonnie," I say, "I ain't going no place where I'll get wet." I glance back as the father pulls the girl's hood into place. God, I hope my Dolores' stepdad treats her half this good.

"We'll dry off soon enough," Bonnie tells me.

Now the mother's straightening the raincoat across her daughter's narrow shoulders. My eyes blur over.

"I hate being down here," I say and turn my back on the family, so I don't break down bawling.

"Gosh, you're strong, Jacob," Bonnie whispers, leaning close and grabbing hold of my biceps. "Your arms feel like granite."

Even inside like this we can hear the water crashing and smashing outside, like a cyclone wrecking everything in its path. That sinking feeling creeps back into my gut. "Didn't you also think that job was going to last me till retirement?" I ask. "Mr. Doughty was even talking about a promotion. And then that pink slip hit like a bomb."

The way the job before last ended was even worse. Downsized, they told us. What a piece of crap. Why couldn't the cowards call a spade a spade? Worst of all, the high muckety-mucks in the office didn't have the guts to drop the ax themselves. Instead the gutless wonders brought in hired guns to do the dirty work, when any fool with half a brain knew they were just going to dump every guy over forty.

"It's not your fault, Jacob," Bonnie tells me.

"Has getting fired ever been?"

"I know, Jacob. What I'm saying is that this time it was the out-of-state owners that decided to close the mine down."

"But what am I going to do now?"

My dear wife manages a thin smile. "You know, Jake, it's not what *you're* going to do. It's what *we're* going to do. And one thing we're going to do is make it. Because folks like us are tough."

I give my beloved Bonnie a little hug. And in my heart I thank God for giving me such a good woman. Because sometimes the hard knocks can really batter a guy down.

"Jake, think of it this way," Bonnie says, nudging my elbow. "At least you got yourself out of those mines for good."

"A lot of choice I had," I say. "Since nobody wants high-sulfur coal these days anyhow."

The little girl with the chestnut eyes gives me a tender look. Why couldn't Dolores end up with us? But then my ex and her new husband have got tons of money.

"At least this line ain't like the unemployment office," Bonnie says. "I mean, it moves right along." Just like that, it jerks forward another good twelve feet, and then another ten. I close my eyes and try not to think about the constant thunder right outside. Finally, just as we're about to enter a tunnel I slip on the plastic raincoat, and Bonnie pulls the hood up over my hair.

"Sir, would you please take our picture?" a little, high-pitched voice asks from behind. It's the cute Asian girl, grinning right at me, just like her folks. I take the camera from her tiny hands and motion the family closer together.

I line the shot up just right. "Smile," I say. When they do, I click the shutter.

"Where you all from?" Bonnie asks as I hand the camera back. My throat is all tightened up.

"Hong Kong," the father says with a toothy grin. The way he says it almost sounds like music. No matter how many times I try I just can't swallow.

"Mister, how about taking one of us too?" a young black boy asks next. Turns out he and his parents and little sister are from some islands in the Atlantic called Bermuda. To my ears their accent sounds British.

This time I'm even more careful. "Hope the photo turns out okay," I tell the friendly family. They all thank me kindly, and I choke up even worse.

"These are all fine people, ain't they, Jacob?" Bonnie whispers in my ear. "Even if they're colored."

I nod. Actually, their skin is a whole range of yellow and browns. But then us whites ain't all that white either. Me, I'm pinker than a piglet, at least whenever I get a little sun. I have to chuckle. If you only go back far enough, every last one of our ancestors was a foreigner once too.

I follow Bonnie down a low corridor straight for an elevator, manned by a youngster in a uniform. I wipe my watery eyes as the floor inside plunges.

"That's it!" Bonnie shouts, pointing down a long, narrow tunnel straighter than a breechloader barrel. A weird wall of slushy white is blocking the other end.

"That's it," Bonnie says again, only this time real soft. She grabs my hand, and we march down the tunnel together. The closer we get to the end, the louder it roars. Up close, I see the wall is actually water shooting past from above.

A nudge from Bonnie and we move on to a low fence, where side tunnels fan out in both directions. "Which way?" I say, leaning on the iron.

Tightening her grip, Bonnie steers me to the left. There we come out onto a platform of cement that's wet from ton after ton of water, crashing and splashing at our feet from up on high. My mouth gapes to witness such awesome power. So this is Niagara Falls.

"This is really something," I say, squeezing Bonnie's hand. The rolling mist the falls throws up feels soothing against my prickly skin. Like earth parched far too long getting a good soaking. People are so excited all around they're shouting. And it's like we're all wearing gowns, only they're made from flimsy plastic.

A ways out from where the falls is landing I spot a huge boulder getting battered. I can't exactly make out this big rock, but I can see its outline under the splashing. It's taking everything the falls has to dish out and then some. I hug Bonnie close and rub my cheek against her sopping hair, and we both chuckle. And I lick the sweet water off her soft skin and pull her close and kiss her forehead over and over.

The water keeps thundering and thundering, as it works to smash the rocks in its path to bits. A river this strong really can grind away over time. Still, the only reason there's a falls here at all is because the rock that makes up its bed is so darned tough. And I know no matter how hard the boulder out there gets pounded, it'll stand its ground today and tomorrow and on and on till kingdom come.

I hang on to Bonnie tight and close my eyes. Soon it don't feel like we're touching the concrete at all. And my stomach's sinking again, but somehow now I don't mind. Because this time it's not like we're falling. It's more like we're floating, like the lighter we become, the higher we can climb.

Snitch

"Martha Administrator of the Year? No way!" Kathy practically shouts in my ear. Kathy and I chat whenever we run into each other, which we make sure happens several times per day. "Who told you such a preposterous story, Tammy?"

"I overheard Martha herself talking about it with Ethel," I say.

Kathy laughs out loud. "I bet Sharpshooter will do the nominating!" she tells me. That's what Kathy calls Ethel on account of how she walks around the department with her head tilted back like she's using her nose as a gun sight. I'm giggling so hard myself I've got goose bumps, but then I'm always freezing.

Too late I spot Ethel at the copier not thirty feet away, listening to our every word. "Shhh," I whisper, but Kathy keeps cackling like a little kid. Like she's still waiting to experience any of life's hard knocks. That's one thing Matt and I know only too well, especially since he got downsized. His new job pays so much less.

Kathy's still chuckling, when Ethel stalks off toward Martha's office in the far corner of our cube farm. Me, I'm dying inside, since we all know she's our boss's snitch. Why Martha needs one I'll never comprehend, but then what I understand about management could fit inside a thimble. I hope Ethel's extra pay is worth her dreadful reputation.

I shush Kathy the instant I detect the approach of those familiar, sharp clicks. Nobody's walk is more distinctive than Martha's, especially when she's ticked off. "I'd better get back to my desk," I whisper, but it's too late.

"You two out of work?" our boss snaps behind my tingling back.

Without a word I scurry off to my cube. Where I make so many dumb mistakes inputting workforms into my computer I have to keep starting over. When I'm happy and relaxed, my fingers just fly, but when I'm tense it's the reverse. My most productive days are always when Martha's home sick or away at a conference. But now all I can think about is her latest tongue-lashing. If only I could fathom our boss's moods. I mean, one minute she's sunshine, the next thunder and lightning. And nobody can tell which is going to come—or, worse, why the abrupt switches. Some days it's like Martha's not happy till she's made herself and everybody else miserable.

Me, I've always tried to make the best out of a bad situation. Though it's certainly been a struggle, since Matt got laid off from that good job. Still, the way I see it, every day spent being glum is like a day I got cheated out of living.

I've finally gotten one workform input perfectly, when Martha's grim face pops up above my cubicle divider. "What was that all about, Tammy?" she asks, her voice sweet as honey.

"What was what about?" I say.

"That conversation over at Kathy's desk." No need to ask how Martha knows about it, not when you have such a reliable snitch as Ethel.

My thoughts scatter like a flock of sparrows at the sight of my boss's German-shepherd smile. I take a deep breath. If my folks taught me anything, it was never to lie—God rest their sweet, sincere souls. "Oh, I just heard you're interested in being nominated Administrator of the Year," I finally say. "And why not? Since you're the best boss I've ever had." Which is true because she's also my one and only boss ever, since during my past summer and part-time jobs I always worked on my own. I was a homemaker till my youngest made it to junior high.

Martha's smile relaxes a notch. "What's so funny about that?"

I shrug and I hem and haw. At that moment I feel so flustered I couldn't have told her the names of my own brother and sister.

My boss's back straightens. "Okay, that's it! A meeting everybody!" she screams. "Right now!" She continues to shriek commands till every underling of hers has dropped whatever they're doing and rushed to our conference room.

I hurry to grab the last empty chair in back, right beside Kathy. There the entire department staff sits in sullen silence a good ten minutes before Martha finally shows up, her posture so erect she's almost bending backwards. "This unit had better shape up fast," she begins, glaring around the room. "From now on nobody had better waste *any* time."

Kathy mutters under her breath, "This meeting is already the most time I've wasted in a month." I slap a hand over my mouth so as not to laugh out loud.

"So if you aren't on break or at lunch," Martha goes on, "I expect you to be hard at work. And don't forget breaks are twenty minutes desk to desk and not one second more."

Kathy whispers so that only I can hear, "Also don't forget to bring a little rug for nappy time." I bite my tongue and hold my breath till I almost choke.

"A problem over there, Tammy?" Martha hollers.

I cough and blink. "No, Ma'am."

"Okay," our boss continues, "let's move on to equipment requests. Any complaints about what you've got now?"

Ethel just barely raises her hand. "The photocopier keeps jamming."

"Then unjam it!" Martha yells, her mouth narrowing to the width of a paper cut. "Anybody else feel like whining?"

Nobody in the room says a word. Or barely dares to breathe.

"Come on, speak up!" Martha snaps like she hates our guts. "Does anybody need anything?"

"How about a lobotomy?" Kathy mutters. By now the hair is standing on the back of my neck. I can hardly wait to get the heck out of the room. Just hearing Martha's voice, just sitting this close to the woman, makes my stomach hurt. Ethel herself is looking awful pale.

"I don't want anybody bitching about not having the right equipment!" Martha shouts. "If there's one thing I believe in, it's empowering my staff." Kathy's eyes roll back and her head lolls to one side, like she's just kicked the bucket. It's so quiet in the room I can hear the whirring of the wall clock. And the whistling of my breathing.

All of a sudden our boss breaks into a jolly grin. "Come on, everybody, lighten up. You all look so tense." A few co-workers shift their chairs, but still nobody speaks up. "Gee, why doesn't anybody ever talk at our meetings?"

Nobody is going to now, not after Ethel tried and miserably failed. And so without any word of encouragement the meeting ends. Whenever our boss dishes out praise anyway, it's so begrudging and insincere it only makes the person feel worse.

On the way back to our cubes, Kathy tells me, "I've had about enough of this crap. If I don't get a promotion soon, I'm bugging out of here." My stomach sinks to hear that. Because Kathy and I have always been so close.

Afterwards, it takes me a whole half hour to calm down enough to do another workform without any mistakes, me a top typist ever since high school. By skipping my morning break, I manage to input twenty-four workforms before lunch, twelve below my personal morning quota. Not bad considering how much time I lost on account of that stupid meeting. I pride myself on being the second-best inputter in the department. After Kathy of course.

On the way to the staff lounge to eat lunch, I notice Ethel exiting the building elbow to elbow with Martha. Going out to a fancy restaurant no doubt. How could she enjoy even the most scrumptious meal in her company?

Over sandwiches we brought from home, Kathy laughs her head off at Martha's expense. Especially to think that as of last spring our boss is eligible to retire, but refuses to. "Ordering people around just gives her too darn much pleasure," Kathy jokes.

Eleven workforms into the afternoon, I sense somebody behind my back. I turn and see Ethel's pale, round face. "Martha wants to see you at her desk," she tells me. I just sit there, my pulse all of a sudden pounding in my ears. "Right now," Ethel adds with a spiteful grin. If it only wasn't a sin to hate, I could work up a real grudge against that woman. One thing I've never comprehended is the joy a person could take in another's misery. Though I strive not to be too hard on her, since she's got the worst job in the whole department, her cube located right beside Martha's, at the mercy of all those hollers and shouts.

I save the workform I just began and hightail it to the corner foxhole. That's what Kathy calls Martha's cubicle, what with all the boxes and dividers blocking the path to her desk. You can't reach it without edging your way back and forth.

"Hi, Tammy," Martha greets, her tone sweet enough to make my molars ache. "Have a seat." I sit down as she slips a glossy women's clothing catalog inside a manila folder. Must be nice to afford fancy duds or to shop on company time. "Quite a close call this morning," she goes on.

"I beg your pardon." I brace for terrible news.

"I almost hit a turtle on the way to work. After my front wheel just missed it, I pulled over and carried the poor creature to safety on the shoulder."

I let out a sigh. Too bad Martha doesn't have that soft a spot for people.

"You and Matt wouldn't be looking for another kitty, would you?" she asks.

"Matt already thinks our tomcat is one too many," I say.

Martha's grin vanishes faster than I can blink, and she gives me a dirty glare. Like I made a pass at her husband or worse. Which would be tough since he works clear across the country. "So what's that snake Kathy been saying about me this time?" she asks.

"Kathy Hayden?"

"Do you know another Kathy in this department?" Martha snaps.

I clasp my hands to conceal their trembling.

"Come on, spit it out!" she shouts.

I throw up my palms and take several deep breaths. "I don't know," I say. Which isn't false because at that very moment I'd have trouble telling her my home address.

"I've never been able to figure out where that arrogant Kathy gets off," Martha goes on.

"Kathy arrogant?" I say. Since nobody's nicer to fellow employees, including the custodians. Which is another reason why she's my dearest friend.

"Kathy Hayden is the most arrogant person in the building," Martha declares.

Huh? Not the Kathy who volunteered to come over and clean and cook and babysit during my horrible bout of flu, while Matt was working two jobs for the extra income we sorely needed. "She never struck me that way," I mumble. My mouth feels so parched I can barely talk. And I'm perspiring so bad my blouse sticks to my skin.

"It's nasty people like Kathy who make my job so tough."

Kathy nasty? Not in my experience. And what about her excellent productivity?

"She's two-faced to boot," Martha says.

"Well, Kathy can be a sweet space cadet—"

"—Kathy is not sweet!" she screams so loud her cheeks turn splotchy. Like my youngest child did when he came down with the measles. The longer this conversation goes on the more my temples hurt.

"I've never seen that other face I guess," I mutter.

"Exactly! Kathy *never* shows that other face!"

I think that remark over hard, but still can't make sense of it. The pain shifts to right behind my eyeballs. "I see," I whisper to say something. I stare out the picture window at the sickly sycamore.

"Nothing would make me happier than to hear Kathy has resigned," Martha says, slipping the glossy catalog out from the manila folder for another peek.

Maybe so, though no news would devastate me worse.

"Did I tell you I'm looking for somebody to head up my new digitization unit?" Martha asks, her tone again sunny.

"Really?"

"It'd be a lot of responsibility. With pay to match," she tells me.

My eyes grow big. I sit up straighter.

"I'm looking for somebody who's got integrity. Somebody who is steady and energetic."

Kathy's name pops into my head, but I bite my tongue.

"I hear you and Matt could use some more income."

"I'll say!"

"And this department could use a little reorganization," she adds, stroking her chin. What a flabbergasting, twist this conversation is taking.

Over dishes that evening, I discuss the prospect with Matt. During the night we kick the idea around some more. "Go for it," he urges, but I still have trouble making up my mind.

The first thing the next morning, I stop by Kathy's desk to ask her advice. "Watch out. Sharpshooter's coming," she says with a wink. I hustle off to my own cube before I get a chance to mention the possible new job.

I've no sooner begun the day's first workform than Ethel is standing at my cube. "Okay, here's the deal," she tells me. "Martha would like to be named Administrator of the Year. But somebody's got to nominate her first. That somebody can't be me."

"Why not?"

Ethel makes a face like I'm dumber than a stump. "I hear you're interested in a promotion," she says.

I nod.

"One hand washes the other, like my Daddy always used to say." She hands me a form that reads "Administrator of the Year" across the top.

When I stop by Kathy's desk at break time, a cube neighbor informs me Kathy's son got sick at school, so she left to take him to the doctor.

Over dishes that night Matt asks if it'll be announced who made the nominations.

"They never have before," I say.

"Can you honestly say she's a good boss?"

"The best I've ever had." We both have a good chuckle over that.

"Our fridge is about worn out," he tells me. Like all we need is another big bill. That settles it. I get up early and carefully type out the nomination form on our old Underwood and hand it in at the office the next morning.

Over lunch I'm just about to tell Kathy what I've done when she starts chattering about her wanting to head up the new digitization unit that's the latest hot gossip topic. She's so excited I can't bring myself to tell her it's already decided.

That Friday afternoon Kathy drags me off on a break I don't want. "Some moron actually nominated Martha for Administrator of the Year!" she shouts in my face. "Shirley wouldn't tell me who, but she swears it wasn't Ethel." I feel so embarrassed I break out in a sweat. If Kathy had asked me point blank, I would have confessed, but something that crazy never occurred to her. Of course not.

The following Monday a memo appears on the bulletin board declaring Martha the Administrator of the Year. Who knows what must have gone on upstairs, what wheeling and dealing, what promises and threats, for that to occur. The more boxes of digitizing equipment the movers unload in the near corner, the antsier I get, especially anywhere around Kathy.

That afternoon on our way back from break Martha's voice screeches from out of sight, "Tammy!"

"Your presence is desired in the corner foxhole," Kathy teases.

"I'm coming," I say as loud as I can without shouting. In my family while I was growing up, raising one's voice, except to prevent an accident, was considered almost as bad as lying.

"Where were you?" Martha demands, when I finally make it to her guest chair.

"On break," I say. I thought everybody knew that if I take a break at all I always go at the exact same time. Since I love sticking to a schedule. Just the opposite of Martha's spontaneous style. Because nothing bugs me more than not knowing what I'll be doing and when all day long.

Then I notice the commotion on the other side of the divider in Ethel's cube. Like things are getting slammed into boxes there. "Last night my neighbor came by with two puppies," my boss says, breaking into smile that's a lot closer to a scowl. Somehow I manage not to squirm, but try as I might I never could relax in her presence. "You wouldn't be interested in an addition to the family now, would you, Tammy?"

"I'll have to ask Matt," I say. Which is true. I mean, I just can't say no, not when Martha's dangling a big promotion right in front of my nose. Besides, I always ask him before making changes to our household. Though I know he'd never go for a new pet. Walking on eggshells like this makes my head hurt.

Martha flashes a scowl. "So have you thought any about a promotion?"

"Plenty," I say. Suddenly my mouth is dry.

My boss's eyes zero in on me.

"I've decided to take it," I whisper.

"Outstanding," Martha says and clasps her hands behind her neck. "Now, Tammy, people tell me you refuse to tell a lie." When I nod, she breaks into a smile bright enough to dry spilled blood. "Ethel!" she hollers.

"Yeah?" Ethel yells back from behind the divider.

"Ethel, after you get all your stuff over to Digitization, would you please help Tammy move into your old cubicle here?"

"Okay," she lamely replies. I slump in the chair, my heart thumping like it wants to escape from my chest.

"Now, Tammy, once you've taken over here for Ethel," Martha goes on, "just keep your eyes and ears open, and report everything you see or hear directly to me. And then there'll be the odd little chores off and on all day."

"I see," I say and wipe the sweat off my brow. I mope back to my old desk and start clearing it off. No sooner have I filled the first cardboard box than Kathy marches past, her jaw bitterly set, without giving me so much as a sidelong glance.

Ice Time

The winter when Iran toppled its Shah and the world mistook that for good news, John Ripp's funk turned scary. For a quarter hour straight he had been pacing the tattered carpet past the bathroom and cursing in German under his breath. Fifteen whole minutes of precious dissertation time already wasted and no end in sight. If he had only known Nancy was going to take this long getting ready, he would have never interrupted his research. With effort he merely tapped on the restroom door because he felt like hammering it.

No response yet again. In fact, the only sound inside their shabby rental was the furnace rumbling underfoot. That nearly constant racket threatened to drive John batty if this cold snap didn't break soon, and not just from the noise. Their December heating bill had already been whopping enough. "Nancy?" he repeated.

Still no reply. A gust of wind rattled the windows, sending a shiver down John's back. He and Alan would definitely have to dress warmly for that night's ice hockey game in weather this Siberian. Outside, that foxy-snouted gray kitty was clawing at the neighbors' garbage bags again. He and Nancy had both been trying to pet the wary scavenger since moving into this apartment last July without ever managing to touch it.

The neighbors' door swung open and stout Mrs. Schmidt charged out, brandishing a broom, and the wily feline darted under the engineless old Dodge her husband had put up on blocks. The temperature, already below zero, was plunging toward a predicted minus thirty, so how was the pathetic stray going to survive?

The instant John heard retching inside the bathroom, he shouted, "Nancy, are you okay?" The toilet flushed, the door unlatched, and his wife emerged, dressed white as a blizzard from head to toe in her nursing uniform. "Are you all right?" he asked more softly.

"I'm fine!" she snapped, marching straight for the kitchen.

There he joined his wife at the Formica table there and gobbled down his tuna salad sandwich, while she nibbled at the corners of hers. "How's the dissertation going today?" she asked.

"Poorly," he said.

"What? But you've been driving yourself like a slave! I can't wait for your thesis to be over with, so our life can resume!"

John took a deep breath. "You used to be in grad school, too. This dissertation is a thousand times harder than a seminar paper."

"You'd get more done if you didn't go to ice hockey games with Alan."

His temper flashed but didn't ignite. Though his shoulders did slump and his temples did throb. Since he had been pushing himself hard twelve hours per day for three straight weeks, didn't he deserve at least an evening off? Especially one spent with his closest friend from their small hometown in northern Wisconsin.

"I'm sorry," Nancy said, her eyes misting over. "Of course you need some fun in your life."

John swirled the few drops of milk around in his glass.

She glanced at her watch and blurted, "I'm late." She slipped on her snorkel parka and reached for a goodbye hug. "You'll finish," she whispered, her tears wetting his cheek. "I'm sorry for what I said about you and Alan. I just feel so crappy lately."

"I'm sorry too, Nancy," he said, clutching his dear wife. "Especially for you having to support us by working as a nurse. I can't help feeling I dragged you down. Because when we first met, you showed every bit as much academic promise as me."

"No, I didn't," she replied, gamely smiling. "Besides, you and I couldn't have both stayed in German. No way could we have gotten teaching jobs in the same city. Not as hard as it is nowadays for just one person to land a professorship."

A final kiss and a promise to drive carefully and Nancy left for work at the University of Wisconsin Hospitals. John trudged back to his desk in the guest bedroom he was using as his study. So far they hadn't been able to afford even a mattress to throw across the worn-out linoleum there, much less a cot, but then they had yet to entertain a single overnight guest.

He resumed taking notes where he had left off in a scholarly tome analyzing Wilhelm Raabe's narrative technique, but concern over his wife's nausea soon left him staring with unseeing eyes at the text. It tore him up inside that a woman as bright as his wife had dropped out of the doctoral program in German that they had begun together and switched to nursing. Not that anybody could deny the degree was practical—because with it you could land a grueling, unprestigious, modest-paying job almost anywhere.

Stomping on the front porch signaled the mailman's arrival. John restrained himself a full minute before checking to see what had come. The storm door spring groaned open, and he stretched his bare hands and head out into the bone-chilling air. The gray neighborhood stray, shivering on the edge of their porch, gave a plaintive meow before hopping into the deep, powdery snow and plowing a path toward the street. What a gutsy kitty to be living in cold so brutal every inch of John's exposed skin already felt both burned and benumbed. He cursed to find no reply yet again today to his many teaching applications. Not that he truly expected anything but further rejections without a finished thesis. He darted back inside with a piece of junk mail from a Madison bank.

Standing over the forced-air vent grating to warm his shivering legs, he tore off the end of the business envelope, and two rectangular pieces of plastic clattered to the floor. Credit cards. Master Card and Visa to be precise. What Nancy had badgered him into acquiring. Never having handled the weird objects before, despite his thirty years of life, he scrutinized the magnetic strips on the back and fingered the embossed numbers and letters. He still didn't understand why the thingamajigs were necessary, but Nancy had insisted. Weren't they already in enough debt from school loans? The way he figured it if they didn't have the money to buy something major now, they should wait until they did. He tossed the credit cards into the telephone table drawer, his grab bag for stuff he wanted to keep but would hardly use.

Books—those were the big exception. He had always bought too many of them, generally paperback editions when available and hardbound titles if on sale. Oh, yes, also his manual typewriter, which he had paid for by tutoring a slow-witted, rich Milwaukee kid. He also had to count his desk, which because of its deep scratches and big crack he had picked up for a measly fifty bucks. Their car was still the old Chevy clunker that Nancy had been driving since nursing school. Sure, it was rusting out, but still ran okay. To help ends meet, their apartment was the cheapest they could find. Who cared if it wasn't fashionable to lease the downstairs of a shabby, small wooden house in northeast Madison far from campus near the smelly Oscar Mayer plant? Not that the rent wasn't bound to jump next summer, but for now they were getting by. So why was she complaining?

John knew the answer full well. For one thing, her rotating shifts at UW-Hospitals weren't just ruining her sleep and their married life, but now apparently also her health. But wouldn't her other choice—straight mids—be even worse? If only he could finish this dissertation and land a tenure-track assistant professorship. Where didn't much matter.

When he couldn't quit shivering, he slipped on a second sweater, the one with holes in the elbows. Their apartment was bone-chilling with the thermostat set at fifty-eight, but their strapped budget simply couldn't afford to keep it warmer. He took his leather gloves out of his parka, removed the linings, slipped those on, and returned to his desk. Ten scrawled note cards later, the phone's jarring ring startled him.

"How's it goin', Ace?" Alan Schwarmer greeted.

"About the same."

"Ree-searching, I suppose," Alan said, accenting the first syllable. "Good excuse for loafing I'd say."

"Very funny." John normally didn't mind Alan's jibes, but not today.

"Did you hear about the Shah of Iran?"

"You know I hate set jokes." Unlike spontaneous wit.

"I'm serious. The Shah got overthrown, and some guy named Ayatollah is gonna replace him."

John didn't comment. Since the start of graduate school, he had shut his eyes and ears to all things political. As little as he kept up with the news, maybe Jimmy Carter was no longer President.

"Say, Ace, is six too early to pick you up tonight?"

"It's fine."

"I'll bring you a little present. Got good reason to celebrate. I just sold Auto Glass Mart four thousand bucks worth of advertising. And our mortgage on the house got approved."

"Congratulations," John muttered.

"Say, I didn't mean any offense back there, Cowboy."

"None taken." John wanted to show more enthusiasm for his friend's good fortune, but just couldn't muster it.

"About time I'd say. Since I hadn't made a new sale since Lake Mendota froze over. The sales manager here at WSIN was pressuring me to find new sponsors or else. Last night I was even talking with Sally about maybe having to resign from the radio station."

"Sales must be rough," John said. In fact, he couldn't imagine a job that involved not only thinking about windshields and windows and jingles and pitches and commissions, but actually talking about all that crap. Such mundane materialism was beneath discussion—just like credit cards.

"A guy's gotta earn a living," Alan said, muffling a chuckle. "But then what would you know about that?"

"What's that supposed to mean?"

"Just a little joke. That reminds me. Bill Bleicher at Auto Glass Mart can get me a couple tickets for tomorrow night's Badger hockey game. Wanna go to that one too?"

"Sure, I want to go. But I can't. I'm taking too much time away from my thesis tonight as it is. I'll never finish it if I don't keep grinding away."

"Think you ever will?"

John gasped.

"Another joke, John Boy. Come on, calm down. Save your energy for cheering against the Gophers. You and I both know full well you'll finish that darned thing the way you've been slaving at it. See you then at six."

John set the receiver down like a ticking bomb and glared out the window at the Schmidts' stranded Dodge. This time Alan's sarcasm had gone too far. It was no excuse to claim he had just been teasing, because as everybody knew much truth was said in jest. No, what John needed now was sympathy, not more needling, because writing this dissertation was without question the low point of his entire life. Three years of work on it already behind him and still no end in sight. What the hell did Alan know about it anyway? He'd abandoned grad school for good the instant he earned his Master's in English Lit.

Feeling overheated, John yanked off his extra sweater and the glove shells, plopped down on the threadbare sofa with dirty stuffing sticking out, and massaged the weird pain, building beneath his forehead. Just because Alan had sold out didn't mean he himself ever would. Because when he had declared he'd feel more self-respect as a bank robber than as a salesman or computer programmer he had meant every word. The materialistic mediocrity of people who slaved away at jobs they didn't believe in just for the money was disgusting. So why did he keep hanging around with Schwarmer?

That was no great mystery. Because John had cut himself off from all of his local grad school chums. Once he had finished his doctoral courses, passed the comprehensive exam, and received his last teaching assistantship, there had been no more need to stop by campus other than to use the library—except for infrequent, unavoidable progress reports to his advisor, Professor Heym. Besides, he no longer felt part of what was happening in the German Department, and the interrogations from all sides there when he visited felt like running a gauntlet.

John slipped into the bathroom, soaked his head with a piping hot washcloth till it stopped throbbing. He scarcely recognized himself in the mirror despite the familiar bushy, reddish-brown beard and long hair. Not with the polar pallor of his skin and dark spots beneath gray-blue eyes. He returned with teeth-gnashing determination to the monograph written in convoluted German. All along he had agreed with critics that *Stopfkuchen* was Wilhelm Raabe's masterpiece, so why this compulsion to compile endless evidence? Because a comparison of that novel with Joseph Conrad's *Lord Jim* was to be the key chapter of his dissertation, culminating in proof that the former had influenced the writing of the latter. Chills went up and down his spine for fear he wouldn't in fact establish such a connection.

Yet he knew full well from teaching the German language to undergraduates that he was an inspiring teacher, even if no natural scholar. Explaining *der, die, das* and the strong and weak adjective endings or the two kinds of subjunctives was apparently beneath his own professors' dignity and intellect, but John excelled at such elementary instruction. And his love for the classic literature was infectious too, even if he could hardly articulate what made any of it great. It was just that he didn't want to analyze why the best of Raabe or Goethe or any other writer was that good any more than he wanted to know why water was wet. Did it matter as long as you could swim in it like a fish?

Still, he would never secure a professorship if he didn't first establish a scholarly reputation. Though deep down did he truly want to emulate Heym, a professor who so preferred criticism to actual literature that he gave entire courses without assigning a single creative work? Like a man who would rather debate the Kinsey report than enjoy genuine sex. But to succeed in academia isn't that exactly how John would also have to think?

Such ruminations, already so chewed over that they sloshed inside his mind like so much pig slop, only aggravated John's funk. He set aside the critique of Raabe and instead grabbed Part One of Goethe's tragic play *Faust*, which fell open to his favorite scene. Soon he became so thrilled by the lively cadence, brilliant wording, and sumptuous imagery that he began declaiming the text aloud. Yes! This was why he had majored in German! This was why he had wanted to make a career out of literature. Because no matter how much he had come to detest abstract analysis, he adored the great writers' actual works. And he was a master at making bright, but unsophisticated, Wisconsin youngsters relish them too.

He hadn't read aloud more than two pages before a sense of panic welled up from his guts that despite having worked so hard and long to become so much he was in danger of ending up nothing. His nearly perfect grade point average of 3.94 was threatening to flip from a stupendous achievement that promised future success to a silly stunt worthy of the Guinness Book of Records—alongside the most hot dogs consumed within ten minutes.

He stared out the window at a pair of starlings, pecking at the flecks spilling from the Schmidts' ripped garbage bag. He flinched when a sizable chunk of snow slid off the roof with a clatter and scared the birds away. He couldn't help regretting the precious eighteen months lost on a false start before admitting his first thesis topic was unfeasible. Professor Heym should have known it would have taken him an entire lifetime to trace the development of the German social novel from the Baroque all the way to the present. A year and a half hadn't sufficed to plow through even half of the major examples, much less poke at the mountain of their interpretations. But was his new topic, a comparison of Conrad and Raabe—two prolific authors—that much easier?

Such thoughts swirled like a maelstrom around his mind till they settled upon Badger ice hockey. Nothing in his current life was more consistently calming than envisioning the college team's precision power play, which last season had taken Wisconsin all the way to the national title. Greg Norden, the All-American defenseman, ignited the action, though freshman phenom, Matt Jenkins, was fast becoming another sparkplug. The coach's son had been around the sport so long that his every feint, pass, and shot flowed from instinct—just like John's spoken German.

The starlings were back to pecking forlornly at the snow when a furry gray blur dove into their midst, scattering the birds pell-mell. "Good try, Grayling," John said. How in the devil was that poor kitty finding enough to eat?

Squelching the crazy impulse to tear all his rejection letters to shreds, he put *Faust* down and returned to the tome of criticism. He had no sooner begun reading the latter aloud to force concentration than the front door slammed and heavy footsteps stomped up the hallway stairs. So the nineteen-year-old living above them with his parents had returned. Moments later radio station WSIN flipped on overhead and through the thin ceiling John made out Alan's recorded voice peddling televisions for Crazy TV Eddie. The instant the ad ended, what sounded like castrati began wailing in shrill harmony about "staying alive."

"Shut up!" John screamed. The radio racket above momentarily went silent before coming back on half as loud. He glared at the torn chunk of linoleum lying over bare boards beneath his feet. Didn't Nancy realize he hated living in this crappy rental as much as she did? But what choice did they have? It wasn't his fault that his impoverished family couldn't help him pay for college, much less graduate school. The instant the phone rang again he pounced upon it.

"Johnny," Nancy said on the other end, "I've got important news."

He braced for the worst.

"I've had some tests run on me," Nan went on. "The results are what I suspected."

"Is the news good or bad?" His tone was grim.

"That all depends."

"Is it related to your nausea?"

"Uh-huh."

The wind howled, the windows rattled, and a vehicle crunched its way past out front. "Well, I guess that means we have to do something about it."

Nancy was silent a long time before speaking up. "How come we always have to do what you want? Don't I get a vote?"

"Nan," he pleaded, "you know our situation full well."

"I guess I do. I'd better get back to work."

John gently put the receiver down and stood staring at the snow whirling in gusts around the motorless Dodge. He knew what he ought to do, but how could he simply abandon his lifelong dream of becoming a college teacher? He shuffled back to his study and laid his aching head down across the notes on his desk. The pressure in his sinuses was verging on unbearable.

Above the wind's whining and the branches' scraping against the clapboards he made out what sounded like a baby crying. Ed Schmidt emerged next door and began sweeping away the snowflakes that had drifted onto their clothesline walk. John marveled at how many opportunities the old geezer—who was actually only about fifty-five—found for working in the yard since Oscar Mayer had laid him off.

With a start John jumped up, ran to the phone, and dialed Nancy's unit. The head nurse who answered said Nan was occupied with a Code Blue, but she'd have her call him back as soon as she became free.

He hung up, plopped down on the ratty couch, and poked at the stuffing sticking out. All of a sudden he gave the sofa a peevish slap. Why was he giving a rat's behind about their furniture? Like he was becoming a fricking materialist. If he didn't watch out, next he'd be combing ads for new carpets and chairs. How was Joseph Conrad's home adorned? Or Wilhelm Raabe's? Who the hell cared? All that mattered was their artistic achievement, not their interior decoration.

Again, toward the rear of the house, above the howling gale he made out a noise like a child in pain. Pressing a cheek against an icy window, he spotted the forlorn gray cat trudging through the drifts, its tiny legs sinking in all the way. Finally, the kitty reached the opening beneath their side porch steps, shook the snow from its fur, and disappeared from view.

"So that's where it's been sleeping," John mumbled, fighting back tears. Such a plucky little fellow. But then what choice did it have? Either it would win its fight for survival or it would perish. Sheltered now on three sides, at least it was out of the wind. Still, how awful for it to be sleeping on frozen ground.

Why not check out the animal's makeshift lair from a cellar window? Or basement, as Nancy insisted upon calling it, even though it was dusty and unfinished. Flashlight in hand, he clambered down the rickety stairs and braced an empty wooden crate the long way against the wall. Perching unsteadily atop it, he wiped the inside dust from the window with a sweater sleeve. Sure enough, there lay the darling feline on a dirty rag, its legs curled under its belly, its intense green eyes fixed on him. It meowed as if in greeting. Through the pane and against the howling wind, John could barely hear it.

He returned to his desk and read aloud to concentrate. But no matter what sounds his mouth made, all he heard was the rumbling furnace, the howling wind, the rattling windows, and the memory of those muffled meows. God, that feline must be suffering, when even inside this heated home he was shivering.

John jumped up, slipped on his parka and gloves, and marched out into the drifts towards the shed. Despite a forehead smarting from the brutal cold, he fumbled through the clutter till he uncovered a flattened cardboard box. That he jammed across the lone opening along the side porch steps, piled snow against this barrier, thus effectively trapping the stray. Two minutes later he was back in the cellar atop the tottering crate.

He jimmied the window with a screwdriver while the shy creature kept itself curled and uttered muffled meows. When the frame finally gave way, he yanked the glass loose and carefully lowered it to the floor, the cat's plaintive cries now easily piercing the wind's howl.

"Here, kitty, kitty," John coaxed, but the creature wouldn't budge. So he stretched onto his tiptoes until a begloved hand touched a furry flank. In response, the cat retreated into the far corner.

"I'm just trying to help you, Grayling," John pleaded. In response it yowled. He tried leaning forward farther to reach the kitty, but it was no use. So he gripped a board, shoved off with a little jump, sending the crate underfoot smashing to the floor, and scrambled under the side porch. The frozen mud felt like sharp rocks against his knees. "Nothing to worry about," he cooed, stuffing his gloves into his pockets, as the cat cowered in a trembling ball. "I wouldn't dream of hurting you." Bit by bit he inched his bare fingers forward till he grasped the cat's slender torso. Hardly more than a bag of fur, the animal let itself be lifted into John's lap. And didn't let out a peep when he unzipped his coat and nestled it against his own warm stomach. "Is that better, you fluffy icicle?"

The feline purred in reply.

"Got any bright ideas about how we're going to get back down? My ladder fell over."

Grayling's response was even louder.

To get off his aching knees, John sat back on his haunches, his buttocks pushing hard against the makeshift snow-and-cardboard barrier. "But of course!" he shouted. Keeping the grip on his precious cargo firm yet gentle, he painstakingly turned around, shoved the blockade free with his feet, and scooted out into the blustery wind.

Minutes later, the cat lay safely stretched across the outline arrayed across John's desk. A quick inspection beneath the tail revealed that it was a neutered tom, meaning it had once belonged to somebody. John fetched the spare plastic dish pan from beneath the kitchen sink, tore his rejection letters into scraps, and covered the bottom of his homemade cat box with them.

He had no sooner prepared a feast of milk and tuna in the kitchen than Grayling came running and didn't stop chomping until every last bite of nourishment was devoured. John opened another can and forked out a few more chunks. These the scrawny cat readily consumed as well.

The feast finally at an end, John carried the adorable critter into his study and laid it upon a folded woolen Army blanket right beside a vent. Before nestling down there, the purring cat stood up and kneaded the new bed like a kitten. "Our very first house guest," John muttered with a chuckle.

Once the basement window was replaced, he resumed taking notes, only now with a smile, while the rescued stray dozed behind him with a gentle snore. The more cards he scribbled full, the more he dwelt on the animal's effortless acknowledgement of its own neediness, and a lump formed in his throat. Such blind trust in an imposing stranger it had always run from before. But why not, since his entire life he had always wished everyone and everything well? One glance at Grayling's tiny paw with finger-like toes shading its eyes to shut out the desk-lamp light, and an overwhelming feeling of gratitude toward the cosmos rose up deep inside John. Finally—finally!—he had gotten the chance to do another living being outside himself some good again. In that moment he realized why he so detested researching. It was such a selfish, self-contained, useless activity, one that brought the absolute worst possible out of him, and he didn't want to continue living like this any more than Nancy did. Yet how could he abandon his lifelong dream of becoming a professor? Whatever his shortcomings during his three decades of life, no one had ever accused John Fischer of lacking resolve. When this ballpoint ran dry, he snatched another from his desk drawer and attacked more blank cards.

Soon after dark he straightened the stacks of notes and quietly closed the door on the sleeping kitty. High time to fix himself supper. They of course wouldn't be able to keep the kitty, not after her big news, but they still could find the sweet creature a worthy home.

Promptly at six o'clock a car crunched to a halt outside on the packed snow just as John was gulping down the last of a bologna sandwich. Alan entered without knocking and with a deft sweep whipped out a bottle of Southern Comfort from a brown-paper bag. "Some spirits to lift your spirits, Ace!" he said.

"Thanks," John replied, taking the bottle and hefting it. "Gee, a whole quart."

"Got a couple clean glasses?"

John retrieved two tumblers from the cupboard. "How about some ice?"

"In January? Hey, we need to warm up!"

John led his best friend since junior high to the Formica table in the kitchen, broke the seal, and poured them each an ounce. Alan took a sip, sighed dramatically, and smacked his lips. "So how did the ree-searching go today?"

John shrugged. He considered showing Grayling to Alan, but decided against letting on he had wasted research time doing anything else. No, for now it was better to keep that a secret—just like Nancy's pregnancy.

"No, seriously, how is the thesis going, Ace?"

"Could be worse."

"Do you ever consider just dropping this horseshit and getting into something less frustrating? And, shall we say, more financially rewarding?"

John gulped the booze, which burned all the way down. "What do you mean?"

"I mean, if you don't stop this crap now, you'll be doing this the rest of your life. Just let go and get out into the real world."

He felt that awful ache gripping his sinuses again. "Is that what you've done? Gone out into the real world?"

"Yeah. It wasn't the easiest switch, but what the heck. A guy's gotta make a living."

John tried in vain to swirl the viscous drops remaining in his glass.

"I'm not saying I didn't love that Joseph Conrad seminar we took together way back when," Alan went on. "But it's been a lot of sales calls since I last cared about 'My task is before all to make you *see*.'"

"You're saying you like your job?" John wasn't trying to speak with an unpleasant edge, but that's how his words kept coming out.

Alan stared at his tumbler. "No, but I had to do something different. A Ph.D. in English lit and two bits will get you a cup of coffee. So it was smart of me to quit before I fell further behind."

"But what about your short stories?"

Alan poured himself a good three more ounces and John the same. "I don't have time for that now. With Sally working too, I have to babysit while she does housework. Besides, at home I write a lot of the commercials that I sell during the day."

"You can drop your life's dream just like that?"

"What are you trying to say, John Boy?"

"I'm talking about ideals. I'm talking about doing the work you want to do and nothing but. I'm talking about doing work for the satisfaction it brings and not the money. Or if it does earn a lot, then that's incidental."

"Are you implying there's something wrong with being a salesman?"

"Not per se. But, Alan, I know full well you're capable of better things."

"Like what? I got a mortgage to pay now, you know, and a kid to support. I need a good, steady income."

"But what a comedown for you."

"Comedown, hell! I've finally grown up. I've finally accepted responsibility."

"Growing up? Accepting responsibility? Those are just philistine euphemisms for surrendering your integrity. You gave up. You sold out."

"The hell I have! If I don't write, I still read!"

"What do you still read?"

Alan gripped the glass like he wanted to crush it. "Both Madison newspapers, *Sports Illustrated*, what have you. Do you think because you're holed up here all day poring over scholarly gobbledygook that you're better than other people? Than me?"

"Better on what grounds?"

"That you're a more worthwhile person? More valuable to mankind? Well, if you think that, you're just like those elitist bastards in the English Department here who believe that just because they know what every fourth-rate critic said about every third-rate author, they're better than Christ's disciples. Bullshit! As far as I'm concerned, they're just bums in tweed suits!"

"Alan, I can't believe you're saying this! Don't you respect knowledge? Or literary scholarship?"

"What good is it doing anybody?"

John felt so insulted he couldn't speak. Yet deep down did he truly disagree? "I think it'd be better if I didn't go to the game," he muttered.

"Come on, Ace. Don't be ridiculous. Get your parka."

John sat there a full minute in silence before donning the stiff, padded garment and following his friend out the front door.

As Alan's car crunched down the streets, frigid air attacked John's forehead, exposed even with the snorkel hood up. Every couple of blocks they hit another icy patch, but the spinning wheels never failed to whine their way to firmer traction. He welcomed the alcoholic haze beclouding the image of the countless note cards he kept accumulating without making significant progress.

"I'm sorry," Alan said. "I'd give anything to be an English prof at some small college. I'd love to teach Fitzgerald or Hemingway, and maybe write a little fiction on the side. And of course, John, the last thing in the world I want to do is hurt your feelings. Because you're the best friend I've ever had."

They joined a half-mile line of cars backed up in front of the Dane County Coliseum. Alan tuned the radio to the pre-game show. "Good evening, hockey fans!" the announcer intoned, and the crowd already inside roared. The two old friends, as close as brothers, moved and halted, moved and halted, a car-length closer to the action with every lurch.

John asked with a pinched voice, "What kind of work do you think I might find in Madison?"

"Part-time, you mean?"

"No, full-time."

The announcer proclaimed, "Tonight will be the long awaited showdown between the first-place Minnesota Gophers and the second-place Badgers. Over the years whenever these two bitter college hockey rivals have stepped onto the rink, the excitement has been electric. Wisconsin will be skating sophomore Erickson at center on the number two line to replace the injured veteran Meeker. The St. Paul native was highly recruited by every school in the conference, but up till now hasn't gotten enough ice time to show what he can really do."

The vehicle kept crunching and waiting, crunching and waiting. Alan said, his voice breaking, "You could try sales."

Resurrection

Kneeling on the squishy ground inside a grove of moonlit pines, Thomas clawed at a pile of clay with his bare hands and flung the clumps into the pit. No one must even suspect a corpse was buried here. Though if someone did, how would they ever connect it to so respected a citizen as Thomas Hendricks? At the thought of the many neighbors living close-by, nervous sweat trickled beneath his pajama top. "Tommy?" a familiar woman's voice whispered.

Paying the interruption no heed, Thomas jumped up and tamped down the refilled hole with his feet. Thank goodness for their outlandish width at a time like this. Once the dirt was stomped level, he tossed on sticks, stones, leaves—anything to conceal all trace of his digging. But wouldn't somebody be bound to chance upon this disturbance sooner or later? Futile to fret about that now. Still, he regretted not having dug the grave deeper? Too little time was the explanation, the story of his life, ever since meeting and marrying Kay James. He threw one last sprig and took off running—only for whatever odd reason he failed to budge.

"Tommy?" his wife whispered again, and her warm hand cradled his neck. Thomas opened his eyes but only saw pitch blackness—thanks to the opaque shades they had purchased to combat his troubled sleep. "Bad dream again?" Kay asked more loudly.

"Uh-huh." He sighed with audible relief to feel no trace of clay on his clammy palms. So he truly was safe now inside their home. He glanced at the alarm clock for the reassurance of its dim red digits. Three hours to go before another begrudged day of work would begin.

"Do you want to tell me about it?"

"Just another dumb dream, honey." In fact, the very same ridiculous nightmare that had been torturing him for months. Yet it felt more real than this bedroom inside their elegant Victorian home. Or than Kay herself, the beloved woman at his side that he shared a comfortable life with. Or than Aaron, the son they were rearing. How could the dear boy already be fifteen years old?

"Remember when about everything struck you as hilarious?" his wife asked, audibly yawning. "Back when you slept like a baby."

"Things change."

"You're telling me. Still, anything would be better than your thrashing around in bed like you're fighting for your life."

But that's exactly how it felt, as crazy as that sounded.

A half hour later, long after Kay had dozed off, Thomas still lay there, dwelling on the burial of that mysterious stranger in total panic. Odd that he knew nothing about the deceased, not even how the person had died. Not even whether it was male or female, though somehow he sensed it had to be a man to require so lengthy a grave. A suspicion of foul play sent adrenaline spurting into his blood.

After twenty more minutes of fruitless struggling to fall back asleep, Thomas climbed out of bed and tiptoed downstairs. There he flipped on the lights and poured himself a glass of milk. Grasping the chilled liquid between both palms to warm it a little, he strolled into the living room and paused in front of the Albrecht Dürer print. The famous self-portrait depicted the artist ensconced inside a veritable tent of glorious, shoulder-length hair. Thomas turned away from the proud resolve captured in the painter's pursed lips toward a wall cluttered with his own honors and awards—from Phi Beta Kappa and Phi Kappa Phi to Rotary Club President and Employee of the Year. Then this past winter the promotion to Associate Director, overnight making him the company's heir apparent.

Alas, none of these achievements impressed him in the least. Because the name "Thomas Hendricks" he answered the phone with sounded more like a phrase from a memorized play than an honest response.

He moved over to the antique sideboard, displaying pictures from his and Kay's blissful wedding day. If he had ever been happier in his entire life, it could only have been the morning their son was born. The photos of Aaron maturing from infancy into adolescence brought at least a passing smile to his father's face. His proudest accomplishment as a parent was instilling his own love of reading in the sweet youngster, especially since none of Aaron's friends ever cracked a book except under duress. And what about their fancy summer vacations? Last year they had spent ten days in a picturesque Tuscan villa near Florence and Siena, two of the most beautiful cities on earth.

So if there was no doubt he was a good husband, a caring father, and a business success, why then these harrowing nightmares about concealing a stranger's death so dubious it suggested murder? Especially since throughout his four decades of life thus far he had never intentionally harmed a single creature, not counting the unfortunate insects and spiders that invaded the premises. Was there anything from his past that could make him feel even passing regret?

Well, yes. Namely, those embarrassing fifteen months he had wasted as a ne'er-do-well upon completing his Bachelor of Arts degree. But what sort of a decent occupation was he supposed to find with a major as impractical as English? As if that were a defense for that profligate spell as a latter-day hippie. The back of Thomas's neck prickled with chagrin to recall the wild partying and general goofing off while he held down intermittent jobs like bartending and roofing.

Then one clear August day a mutual friend introduced him to Kay Overby, and overnight everything changed. Within the month he was shaving off his beard and trimming his hair and talking his way into an MBA program despite lacking prerequisites. Once he had earned that Master's, he had stepped onto the straight and narrow path and never again strayed.

Down close to the new Persian rug, a furry flank rubbed against his ankles. "I love you too, Odin," he cooed at their all-black feline and crouched to scratch the kitty behind the ears till he brought it to full-throttle purring.

Before long, Thomas was climbing carefully back into bed so as not to awaken his wife. But there he lay wide awake, contemplating his obvious discontent. Though inspiring others at the office to do their best did gratify, it also never truly satisfied. Still, how could he complain, considering his affluent lifestyle and solid marriage?

By nestling Odin close and concentrating on the pet's silky feel, Thomas eventually dozed off. And again found himself kneeling on squishy ground, only this time in a thick fog. Once more he clawed at a heap of clay and flung it by the clump into an open grave. But this time no matter how much he piled on, the corpse's oversized feet stuck out. More gobs of earth flew till only the cadaver's big toe protruded.

"Tommy?" a woman whispered. In a panic Thomas jumped up to flee but made no headway on account of the slick mud. Or actually because he was sitting cross-legged on the waxed floorboards.

The bedroom light snapped on. "Do you have a cramp in your foot, honey?" Kay asked. He was indeed clutching his toes. "You simply must see a doctor."

"I swear I never hurt anybody," he pleaded, peeling off his sweat-soaked pajama top.

"Who ever claimed you did?"

Long after Kay was again softly snoring, he still lay awake, staring into the night's blackness. A dream was just a dream, he kept telling himself without conviction. Because he recalled this particular nightmare in such detail, from the slipperiness underfoot to the thudding clay better than anything accomplished at the office in months. But then so little happened there worth remembering. Most likely because countless other people could perform these tasks equally well.

An hour before the alarm, Thomas finally gave up on getting more rest and tiptoed downstairs to shower, shave, and arrive at the office early. That way he could at least finish the new action plan before the day's interruptions began.

While the coffee took its time percolating, he wandered into the living room, this time keeping his back toward Dürer's reproachful stare. A paperback copy of *The Great Gatsby* shelved among Aaron's kung fu videotapes caught his eye. It was a decades-old classic he had relished back in junior high. Actually, it was this novel and others like it that had inspired him to major in English. He had just immersed himself in a favorite passage when Kay appeared in bathrobe and slippers. "What are you doing up already, Tom?" she asked.

He shrugged.

After another uneventful, efficient day at work, he spent a pleasant enough evening at home rereading the Fitzgerald masterpiece on the couch while Kay attended her Habitat for Humanity meeting and Aaron studied upstairs in his room. But when bedtime came, Thomas couldn't fall asleep at all. Three hours later he still lay there, pondering why this nightmare should be tormenting him at the age of forty. Then from the murky depths of his mind a startling thought welled up—could the murder he kept dreaming about be a genuine memory? And might the woods he saw himself digging in be the arboretum just off his old college campus instead of the local suburban grove?

The possibility electrified Thomas with terror. Because nobody could say what hare-brained stunts he had pulled during that hippie-dippie phase before meeting Kay and straightening himself out. What about those drunken parties when he had gotten too blasted to remember much of anything the following day? Or that appalling beer blast that had lasted an entire weekend? That Monday morning he had awakened miles across town from his shared apartment on the damp concrete floor of a stranger's garage without a clue as to how he had gotten there. Thank goodness, antics that outrageous had never led to an arrest. Not that such excess didn't deserve a citation or worse. Still, wasn't that as bad as his behavior got?

Maybe not. And so now no matter how he reasoned and rationalized he couldn't dispel the fear that he had actually done something truly reprehensible—no matter how unlike the respectable Thomas Hendricks of today that sounded. But if he was indeed guilty of manslaughter, if not actual murder, why did he lack even an inkling of the victim's identity? Certainly it couldn't have been a friend or acquaintance. But if not, how could he have become violently enraged at a person he didn't even know? That he recalled no anger in these dreams provided little comfort, not so hot as his temper could flare when provoked, even if this rarely occurred. But then was there anything that he didn't do with the utmost zeal?

When the alarm finally buzzed after an hour of shallow sleep, Thomas stumbled to his feet, feeling more exhausted than upon retiring. Under a hot shower he concentrated on his wastrel stretch but failed to jog any memory of violence. Next he strove to recall who might have wronged him enough to incite rage, again without success. At least he no longer was doubting the cadaver was male. Could he possibly have done the guy a favor by putting him out of his misery? Then wrath wouldn't have played a role. Who was he trying to kid? Somehow he had to get a look at the corpse's face. But would the dream permit a peek as late in the burial as it always began?

Thomas was drying himself after a hot shower when he froze in place. He hadn't only indulged himself as a latter-day hippie, had he? Not as hard as he had tried to create a novel. And he had written not one, not two, but three complete drafts before setting the book aside—right around the time he and Kay had met. An apprenticeship novel he had called this work then to friends, though where was the apprenticeship that didn't result in eventual mastery? Whatever had become of that manuscript anyway? Odd that he didn't recollect giving this worthy effort a second thought since.

That afternoon he left the office early and hurried home while Kay was shopping at Lazarus and Aaron was receiving another piano lesson. On the upstairs landing Thomas unlocked a door seldom opened and climbed the steep stairs to the attic, where he rummaged among the many dusty boxes. What all didn't turn up? A baseball glove still gripping the ball from his playoff-winning Little League home run. An old basketball from junior high, now deflated. Even a pair of ratty bell-bottom jeans and a plaid polyester shirt. Kay apparently had thrown nothing out—bless her nostalgic heart.

The door down at the landing creaked open. "What're you doing up there, Tommy?" his wife shouted.

"Looking for something," he replied.

"That I assumed."

"Just a couple more minutes, honey." He was removing his old desert boots from a duffel bag when he froze. Toward the bottom he felt a thick wad of legal-size yellow sheets, folded double.

That evening over chocolate mousse dessert Kay asked, "What in the devil has gotten into you lately?"

He shrugged, suppressing a smirk.

Later after a few hours of fitful sleep, he again found himself kneeling on squishy mud, only this time he was clawing the clay away from the corpse instead of covering it up. Because if he had killed someone, it was high time he found out exactly who. He exposed a toenail attached to a warm foot. Warm?

A light flipped on, and its brightness made him blink. "What are you doing down there on the floor, Tom?" Kay was saying. He let go of his toe and scrutinized both hands—not a trace of clay on either one.

Without another word he stood up and marched across the varnished wooden floor and out the bedroom. But instead of continuing on downstairs, he slipped into his study, locked its door, turned on a lamp, and booted up his computer. As the processor groaned and whirred, he untied the string that had held the legal-size sheets together all these past years and dusted off the old manuscript. Strange how neat his handwriting looked back then compared to today's hasty scrawl. He flattened these artifacts from his second adolescence that had come between the bachelor's and master's degrees. Because he hadn't only partied and indulged himself those days, had he, not if he had created this book? And if it wasn't well enough written for publication, at least it was completely unique and personal work.

A quick perusal sufficed to separate the pages into their three different drafts in chronological order. Good, better, best. If practice doesn't make perfect, it at least promotes steady improvement. The two clearly inferior versions he set aside, spread out the best version alongside the monitor, and studied the text. It was already worded surprisingly well, so why not input that now and then improve it as needed? Of course it wouldn't be easy to rekindle his long dormant inspiration. But was there any doubt it could flame again as persistently as his passion to do totally original work had been smoldering deep inside him?

He typed an entire page before pausing. Something was amiss, but what? He stared at the pulsing cursor, uncertain how to proceed. In a flash he saw the solution. It all started too late, didn't it, without a proper introduction, whatever that might be. Without any plan or deliberation, his fingers clattered away. "He clawed at the clay in a frenzy to uncover the prematurely buried body before the spark of life in it extinguished for good," he wrote. "As soon as he exposed a foot, he spun around and flung off more earth till a nose emerged. He cleared its nostrils of debris and slapped both cheeks. The cadaver took a deep breath and sneezed. The rescuer chuckled through tears to see the man's surprisingly familiar features." But whose? Thomas was wiping his own moist eyes when Odin meowed out on the landing. Of course! A simple click and the monitor's vibrant black and white went dark. The resurrected author moved this way and that till his own reflection was staring back at him from the darkened screen's glassy shadows. "A strong, long-bridged nose above a full mouth pursed with newfound resolve," he keyed, describing what was mirrored.

A tap on the study door, and a gentle voice asked, "You okay in there, Tommy?"

"Couldn't be better, honey," he told Kay. And he resolved to ignore this interruption, as he would have to many another from now on during his free evenings and weekends—if he was to become what deep down he had always dreamt he might be—a writer.

Black River Falls

They weren't kidding when they named this river Black. It's blacker than my uncle's fresh-plowed dirt. They say it's white pine that makes the water so dark. It's blacker than a white pine woods on a cloudy night. It's almost as black as Dick Larkin's heart. It's funny how a wood that light can make water black. Just like it's funny how enough cold can leave water high and dry. A lot of funny things ain't funny to nobody. Me, I'm Grace Jenson. Though most folks call me just plain old Gracie.

Sometimes the river'll go up, just like sometimes it'll go down. Rivers ain't much different that way than anything else. I've been living alongside this one now for pretty near sixty years. Jobs may come and go, but the water just keeps flowing on.

If it gets too high, they'll open up a gate. If it gets worse, they'll open up two or three. But no matter how many get raised, they never stay up for long. That's when I hurry down to the great big red rocks below the dam. Because water ain't the only thing that gets stranded. If I'm lucky, I'll find a fish in a pool that ain't yet dead. It's funny how the slippery things can breathe underwater. Just like it's funny how they'll drown out in the air. It ain't ever easy but I catch them with both hands and toss them back in. I've saved more fish than a person could count. I'm counting on the fish someday paying me back. You don't need arms to lend a helping hand.

Ever since I screwed my life up but good, I've been combing these banks. They cradle the river just like a mother does a darling baby. Just because something gets lost once don't mean it won't never turn up. Mostly I turn up old bottles and rusty cans. Once I dig up a winter coat my size, but there ain't nothing inside but stinky mud. Finding chunks of driftwood gets my hopes up. If you soak a stick a while in water, it gets so heavy it sinks. But if you keep at it, it'll get so light it'll float. It gets lighter than white pine ever dreamt of being. White pines grow so tall and pretty. Way back when that's about all that's growing around here. Though now there's about none of them here except above the dam around the Larkins' cabin.

Today the ice is again melting, just like it was way back when. That means the suckers'll be fighting their way upstream before too long, even though there ain't no way they'll ever get past the dam. When they spawn, they swim so thick together their backs look like stepping stones across. I ain't never yet seen a fish jump for joy.

"Gracie!" Dick keeps calling inside my head. There ain't a gal who don't think he's the dreamiest dreamboat around. A voice will really carry over water glassy like that. Up here above the gates, it'll get smooth like a mirror. There ain't no big rocks here like there is splashing down below the dam.

Today the river's white as a wedding dress, but underneath the ice it's still black as pitch. And I still can hear those kids laughing up on the pier though it's been over forty years. I guess the idea of a big-shot Larkin going after Gracie really is a gas.

As kids, Ethel and I know how to have a ball. We have all the fun we want and then some. Till one night our fun goes too far and I mess my life up but good. Now I know better, but knowing better now's too late. What's done is water under the bridge and out of sight for good.

The Black River ain't all that big for a river, but without little rivers like it the Mississippi wouldn't amount to much. Just like if it wasn't for the falls, there wouldn't be my home town. Folks call them both Black River Falls. And if it wasn't for the river, there wouldn't be that pier up above the dam. That's what everybody calls what's left of the old railroad bridge that got washed out during the big flood before I was born. It's really just a boxy stack of stones sticking out of the water. The pier ain't all that far from the Larkins' cabin. Their cabin in the white pine woods ain't as fancy as you might expect either. Even though Dick's dad's a doctor and his mom's a Greeley, so they can blow money hand over fist and not think about it twice.

Too bad I don't know enough to stay home that night. But then it's too bad about lots of things. Too bad Daddy's older brother gets all of Grandpa's land, but that's the way Norwegians did it around here. Too bad Daddy's so worried about what folks say behind his back. Just like it's too bad he can't make a go of it on the puny farm where I was born. Too bad he has to sell out and move us into town. Too bad he has to get a job sweeping floors. Too bad he starts having those awful spells. The way he rants and raves about scares me and Mom half to death.

There are three things Daddy keeps blabbering about—stallions, saloons, and coffin nails. Coffin nails is what he's got against Ethel. He don't give a hoot that she's my best friend. Jimmy Waarvik is a nice boy who's sweet on me, but he'll drink a beer now and then too. When Daddy gets wind of that, he chews Jim out so bad he never comes back. Ray Gutknecht is an even nicer boy. Raymond wouldn't dream of lighting up or setting foot in a saloon. But one night Daddy catches us smooching on the porch and really blows his stack. He calls Ray a stallion right to his face, and I never see my dreamboat again. After that, word gets around school fast and pretty soon no boy will look at me twice. So that's why the invite to Dick Larkin's cabin sounds so swell.

My whole life I've lived in this town with the same name as the falls. The falls are here long before folks show up. Before the Civil War that's about all this place is, along with all those white pines. Then old Jacob Greeley takes off from old New England and heads out west. One look at the water splashing down the great big red rocks and he builds himself a sawmill on the spot and dams the river up but good. It don't take long before old Greeley's mowing the white pines down like hay. The river gets so jam-packed with logs you can walk across and not even get wet. The more boards he saws up, the more trains keep hauling them every which way. That's how the falls turns into a town. And that's how the Greeleys get filthy rich to stay.

Before long, settlers from the old country start showing up too. Over in Norway there ain't enough decent land to go around I guess. My grandparents come with that bunch and stake out homesteads west of town. Farmers always need a place to trade, so Saturdays they drive their buggies into town and shop. Pretty soon they've got themselves a county seat in Black River Falls, and here's where it's been sitting ever since.

My dad's folks do okay for themselves, but a hundred and sixty acres ain't much when it comes time to divvying up. So my uncle gets it all and rents Daddy a sandy quarter to work as best he can. It don't take long before Daddy's selling out and moving us into town. He finds us a place to live over in Hardscrabble. That's what folks around here call the Eastside. That's where I grow up and where I still call home.

"Don't you dare go in that river," Daddy keeps telling me. "If the drop-offs and rocks don't get you, the snakes and snapping turtles will." Daddy ain't one to be telling no lies. So I always do my best to listen. Too bad I don't try nearly so hard to obey.

When I'm growing up, I never once set foot in the river. The closest poor kids like Ethel and me get is playing along the banks below the dam. But we hear stories about rich kids going swimming up above the gates where the water's deep. Dick and the Bailey twins are too stuck-up to go in the free city pool like rest of us.

Somehow I manage to make it all the way through high school. That means it's time for me to get a full-time job. I apply at the clinic, but they already got all the nurse's aides they want. It's the same story at the telephone company and the five and dime. I try loads of places before I come up with anything. Gjerseth's Cafe out on Highway 12 needs somebody to wash dishes. G's ain't all that far from our place. It's where truckers like to stop for coffee and a bite to eat. I have to work weekends, but then I get Mondays and Tuesdays off. It ain't exactly what I'm looking for, but I'll have to make do.

June flows by pretty fast and so does July. But then comes August and things slow down. It gets so hot it hardly cools off even after dark. One Sunday Ethel stops by G's, and Mrs. Gjerseth gives me a break.

"Wanna go to a beer party tomorrow night?" she says. Just like she's talking about stopping at the A and W for a frosty mug.

"Are you nuts?" I say. I ain't ever tasted the stuff, and I ain't in no hurry to start. But Ethel ain't pulling my leg. And she ain't talking about just any old beer party out in the Eastside sticks. No, it's Dick Larkin throwing this party. And it's at his parents' cabin in that stand of white pines up above the dam.

"But what if Daddy finds out?" I say. Just the thought of that's so scary it makes my scalp prickle.

"Who says you have to tell him?" Ethel tells me.

I think about that a while but still shake my head no.

"Sally Jensen and Tommy Dahl can give us a ride," she says.

I think that over good. My classmate Sally's always been nice to me and so has her boyfriend, Tommy. "Still I'd better not," I say.

Then Ethel says, "Dick told me personally to invite you."

That settles it. I agree to go.

So the next night I put on my A & W uniform at home like I'm getting ready for work and hide a pair of clean jeans and a blouse in a paper bag. I head out the front door like always, but at the corner I turn left instead of right. Tommy's Studebaker is waiting at Ethel's.

I hurry up and change clothes behind some bushes, and just like that we're on our way. Tommy tears across the bridge and up Water Street onto German Hill. He turns onto Cemetery Road and guns it like we're going to be late. Pretty soon he tools along so fast the white pine woods passes by in a blur. All of a sudden he hits the brakes and swerves to a stop. "THE LARKINS" a great big sign says plain as day.

From the outside the cabin looks kind of teensy and not fancy at all like I expect. But what do I know about fancy? I follow Tommy and Sally and Ethel on inside, just like I've been here oodles of times before. The icebox and cupboards look brand-spanking new, and the walls are so white they shine. Dick and the Bailey twins say hi just like we're all old pals. The guys are galloping along on a pony of beer and raring for us to catch up.

The first cup of Old Style tastes awful bitter, but the next one goes down better. I take a ciggy-butt from Ethel and inhale just like I've seen her do plenty. By the third brew I'm feeling no pain and laughing along like one of the gang.

That's when Dick pipes up, "Let's all go swimming."

"The pool's already closed," I say.

The guys all roar. "I meant in the Black River," Dick says. Just the thought of going in that dark water makes me shiver.

"Up here above the dam it's just like a lake," Tommy says. "There ain't no current or rocks or nothing."

"What about snapping turtles and snakes?" I say.

They roar even louder.

"But I didn't bring along a suit," I say next.

"We won't look," Dick says. The guys just about split a gut.

Dick hands me another beer. By the time that one's down, I'm game to go in too. So we all head on outside. The sky's clouded all up, and the night's turned black as pitch. Dick takes a flashlight and leads us through about the only white pine woods still around. The needles prick my arms and legs, but I keep up okay.

We get to the boat dock, and the guys strip down to their shorts. I don't know if it's the beer or the pine pitch or what, but my head's spinning so bad it ain't even funny. And I ain't in no mood for taking off much of anything, leastways not in front of three guys. Sally and Ethel ain't exactly in no hurry neither I see.

"Come on, girls," Dick teases. "What you waiting for, Christmas?"

Maybe Ethel's put away more suds than me because she whips off her blouse and her pedal pushers, just like she's in the girls locker room and it's time for gym. The next thing Sally's down to her bra and panties, leaving me standing there all dressed like a fool.

"Come on, Gracie," Dick says. "Who do you think you are?"

That's a pretty tough question, way too tough for me. I don't see no other choice but to play along. So I take my blouse and blue jeans off too, and I wade on in just like everybody else. At first, it ain't all that different from the city pool except for the slime oozing between my toes. Though the water sure does feel sticky, and it smells like my uncle's fresh-plowed dirt. All of a sudden I hit a drop-off and my head slips under and I swallow water and I cough and I choke. For a while there I'm panting and paddling like a puppy. What I want to know, if there ain't no current how come I'm drifting downstream?

I catch my breath and make it out to the pier like everyone else. It's just a boxy stack of stones sticking out of the river. I try hard to grab hold, but it's too smooth to get a good grip. Dick shouts from on high, "Come on up!" Who knows what he does to get up there, but that's where he is. Then Dick lets out a grunt and Ethel a squeal, and just like that she's up there too. Ned and Ted and Sally and Tommy follow close behind. But me, I'm still treading water and getting so tired it ain't even funny. I don't see no other choice but to take off swimming for Hardscrabble and home. But, dumb me, I left my clothes on the other bank.

So I turn around and I side-stroke and dog-paddle and about everything else except drown. Finally it gets shallow enough to touch bottom. I pant and pant and I crawl up onto the shore and collapse on the ground.

"Gracie!" Dick keeps calling out. There ain't a gal who don't think he's the dreamiest dreamboat around. The pine needles I'm laying on poke and prickle, but I'm too tuckered to budge.

"She made it to shore!" Tommy shouts. A voice will really carry over water glassy like that. Out by the pier there's a loud kerplunk, and somebody comes splashing up a storm.

Soon whoever it is plops down right beside me. "Where you going so fast, Gracie?" Dick says real soft like. He's leaning so close he's dripping on my face. I still can hear the kids laughing up on the pier though it's been over forty years. Well, now I'm older and wiser, but then I not only don't know better I don't even know good. Dick puts his arm around me and whispers sweet nothings into my ear. At first it's kind of scary, but it don't take long before it gets dreamy. Pretty soon one thing leads to another and before you know it I've gone so far it's all the way. That's still the only night of my life that's ever been too short.

Back home I tiptoe inside. Lucky me, Daddy don't wake up or nothing. Mom asks me if I'm okay. "Uh-huh," I tell her. What else can I say? The next day my stomach's queasy and my head's achy, but I'm so happy about me and Dick I hum and sing while I iron and sew.

Every night at G's I keep looking for Dick, but he never shows his face. Labor Day comes and goes and he's off to college up in Eau Claire. Where he stays every week and all weekend to boot.

The leaves are already laying on the ground and curling up, when mornings I begin waking up sick. I do my best to hide it from Mom, but she's been around too long not to know the score. From the look on her face, I can tell she's really scared. What Daddy'll do when he finds out scares me so bad too my hands shake.

No matter how little I eat my stomach starts swelling up and won't stop. And there ain't no gates you can raise to help it back down. When I ask Mom about seeing a doctor, she lays down on the couch and cries. I write Dick a letter, but I can't bring myself to mail it. I think about phoning his folks, but who am I be calling up big shots? I think about running away, but there ain't no place to go.

Thank God, Dick makes it home for Thanksgiving. I spot his big Buick tooling along Main Street and wave like crazy, but he zips right on by like I'm a white pine stump. I walk on over to the Larkin house way up on Price Hill. His mom stands in their great big picture window and makes faces at me, but Dick won't come outside. He's back in Eau Claire before we ever get a chance to talk.

For Christmas Dick makes it home again. This time I spot his Buick outside a downtown saloon. I slip in through the back door and lean over the jukebox, like I've got a dime to waste and can't make up my mind on what tune. Dick sits there on a stool with the Bailey twins, drinking beer and smoking cigarettes and playing poker dice for quarters.

"Hold it, guys!" Dick hollers. "Gotta shake the grapes!" He strolls right on by me like I'm clothesline post and slips inside the john.

When he comes back out, I step right into his path. I'm shaking all over, but still I get the words out. "Dick, I'm in trouble," I say.

"So?" he says and laughs right in my face.

"I mean it," I say and pull my coat tight so he can see how big my belly's gotten.

"It happens every day," he says with a shrug and starts to stroll off.

I grab his arm and I say, "But, Dick, you're the father."

"Oh, no, you don't!" he says and yanks my grip free. "No broad's going to pull that old trick on Dick Larkin."

"Richard, I swear to God there's never been anybody else."

"Your turn, Dickie!" Ned Bailey shouts from the bar. Richard rolls his eyes and moseys off. I'm lucky to make it outside before I break down bawling.

January comes and the river freezes hard as stone. Powdery snow soon covers the ice like a blanket. The ice starts off thin but it don't take long to get thick. Before you know it, it's February. One day I'm sitting knitting, when Daddy stomps by with a pail of ashes from our stove in the front room. He gives me a dirty look and growls, "You look like hell." What else what with how little I eat?

In April things warm up and begin to thaw out. Once that starts, there's no way you can make it stop. Just like once a chunk of ice breaks off, it floats clean out of sight. The more the ice breaks up, the blacker the river gets. Then along comes an awful Friday. It's got to be the worst Friday of my life. I hike on over to the West bank and up into the Larkins' white pine woods. That's got to be the best hiding place around. I've no sooner set foot in there than a trickle runs down my leg. Before you know it, it's streaming onto the dirty snow. First, out comes a little head and then the rest. Because it's a boy I name him Eugene. His little mouth looks just like Dick's, and he's making tiny fists. He's got hair black like his dad's, but his skin's white as Christmas. Eugene don't cry. He don't make a sound. There ain't never been a boy born so still.

I take my coat off and wrap it around my baby boy and hug him against me tight as I can. I hum a lullaby into his tiny ears cold as ice. Me, I can't stop shivering, but Gene's too nice a boy to make a fuss. He's got to be about the nicest boy a mother ever had.

By the time it gets dark, I'm shivering so bad my back cramps. That's when I walk on out onto the ice. And I kneel down and ladle out a handful of icy water with my hand and baptize my baby Eugene Leroy Larkin. He don't whimper or cry or nothing. Eugene's way too nice a boy for anything like that.

I don't know what to do next. I can't take Gene home to Daddy and Mom. I can't leave him where he is, and there ain't no place for dropping him off. That's when I remember baby Moses in the Bible and what his folks do for him. So I zip my coat around my darling and lay him down on the ice near the edge. I step back and stomp with all my might till the great big chunk he's on breaks off. I take my foot and shove it away from the bank. Before you know it, Eugene's floating away free as a white pine log. First, he drifts toward the pier, but then he turns and floats straight for the falls. Soon he's hurrying for the only open gate. The closer he gets, the faster he goes. Till Gene rushes clean through and down the falls and out of sight I fear for good. I tell myself it's all for the best, but still the sight does make a mother sad.

Now it's forty years later and the ice is thawing again, just like it was that awful Friday, just like it always does this time of year. Daddy and Mom have long since passed away. Nothing ever stays the same, just like white pine ain't used for lumber wood like it used to be. I hear Ethel's on her third husband now down by Whitewater, and Dick's a big-shot doctor up in Eau Claire and a grandpa six times over.

It's been such a long, long winter I was afraid April was never going to come. But here it is, and things are again melting. The river is getting blacker than my cousin's fresh-plowed dirt. Big chunks of ice break off and race for the only open gate. I can hear them crashing on the great big red rocks down below. That means the suckers'll be fighting their way back upstream before too long to spawn. Even though there ain't no way they can get past the dam. They say it's white pine that makes the water this dark. That's funny because there ain't hardly no white pine left.

I'm praying the river ain't too black to wash me clean. They say a handful of water's enough to wash away a baby's sins. A whole riverful ought to do it for me.

Upper Kensington

This past June I got a life-changing phone call. When I picked up, a familiar voice said, "Hey, troop, wanna party?"

"I beg your pardon?"

"Bakken, this is Dave Mueller! Your old Army buddy over in Deutschland! You know, Umlaut! Remember?"

How could I forget? Umlaut told me he was organizing a Det Q reunion at Chicago's Beacon Hotel over the upcoming Labor Day weekend. Everybody stationed over there between 1968 and 1973 would be welcome. "We won't get *too* drunk!" he said with a chortle. "I was wondering if you could help me make a few arrangements."

I asked how he had gotten my address.

"From your mother," he said, laughing.

I pleaded a lack of free time.

"How about at least contacting Scott Dickinson? Since you guys live so close."

We did? It turned out Scotty had moved back to his home town of Columbus, Ohio, after working several years in New York City. Umlaut couldn't remember what Scotty was doing for a living, but the dude wasn't hurting for money. "Why're you asking me?" he teased. "You knew him better than I did, troop. Anyway, I'd sure appreciate it if you could call a few guys for me. As a personal favor to an old Army buddy."

I truly was busy, I insisted. But did I truly want to write that Nietzsche article? How could contacting old Army buddies not be more important than dissecting the scribblings of a long-dead German philosopher? It wouldn't to my chairman, of course, but then the only place he had ever experienced friendship was in novels. Of course I wanted to see those guys again. Especially when for years I'd been meeting people I had a lot in common with, yet never connecting. But back then just being thrown into the same boat sufficed to make us buddies, but middle age, alas, for me was boatless. And of all the buddies I had, I felt closest to the Monks. You bet, I knew Scotty better than Umlaut did. Sure, I'd make those calls.

"Outstanding!" Umlaut said and gave me Dickinson's phone number and address. "I'll have to get back to you on Hoffman and Burke. Somebody must know how to get messages to them. You're on your own with locating Peter Zielsdorf. Nobody seems to know where that dude's at."

"I certainly don't," I blurted.

"Do you think he's someplace back in Wisconsin?"

"I haven't heard that he isn't."

"Or maybe he married that Fräulein he was dating and settled down in Germany."

"You never know." I hated lying. His marriage to Katja should have been the epitome of conjugal bliss. A woman like her—so unlike Karen—would have made me happy, too. I only laid eyes on Katja twice, but that was enough to know she was as every bit as remarkable as Peter insisted.

Umlaut didn't get back to me until mid-July. This time he asked me not only to get the other Monks to come but to persuade them to help him organize as well. "If I don't find some more assistants, my old lady's moving out. See as many of our buddies as you can in person. Because you can really count on a person's word when they give it to you face to face."

Dickinson I could see on the drive to my parents in Madison, Wisconsin the next month, Columbus being on the way.

I thought about phoning Scotty, but it was easier to send a note. He wrote right back: "Thomas, stop by anytime and stay as long as you like. Scott."

Two weeks later, I still hadn't responded. Three days before my departure, I finally forced myself to call. A soft female voice purred, "Scotty's right here," and a man came on the line. It was Dickinson all right, his voice lower-pitched, less excited, more controlled than I recalled, but the whinnying giggle was the same. I agreed to arrive in time for lunch on Saturday, August 2nd, though that meant moving my departure back a day.

The next day a note arrived from Will Burke, postmarked Austin, Texas, saying he would be in Milwaukee the following weekend. If convenient, I should drive over from Madison, and we could have dinner together. So Umlaut had gotten in touch with him, too. I made another photocopy of Peter's diary for Burke.

It annoyed me that my yard badly "needed mowed," as the locals phrased it, but did a lawn honestly require a fresh military buzz cut? In unshaded patches the grass had even gone to seed, but I didn't see the harm in having it thicker in spots next year. I wasn't going to worry about the weeds either, since many of them were in fact wildflowers. What was the point of beheading blooming dandelions for no better reason than to prove I was the boss and not the plants? There was earth and water and sunshine to spare for whatever wanted to flourish. As for my cluttered rain gutters, the leaves, twigs, and black walnuts would just have to sit and rot a while longer.

I packed light and dropped my orange tabby tom, Nebuchadnezzar, off at Mrs. Gardiner's, a widowed neighbor with five felines of her own. Finally, I set out for the fresher, nippier air of the North, happy to escape the stifling heat and humidity of southern Ohio my body had never adjusted to. In Columbus I veered off Highway 33 into a neighborhood of mansions surrounded by perfect putting greens, as though the owners couldn't get in enough strokes at the country clubs. The fiercely trimmed lawns were a dismal display of nature controlled and tamed, like teary-eyed elephants compelled to perform circus tricks.

This was Upper Kensington, the other Ohio, the one still prospering in the 1980s. Unlike the southeastern mining towns, already depressed now for decades, or the more recently impoverished smokestack belt in the state's northeast corner. I quickly got lost in this strange suburb without sidewalks, as if people were helpless to get around without vehicles. By sheer dumb luck, I chanced upon Walnut Creek Crescent, where house numbers led me to a white brick palace with rounded upstairs windows cut into a high, steep roof. The Dickinson mansion.

I couldn't deny its grandeur, but it still looked as out of place in the Midwest I knew as a diamond tiara on a dairy farmer. Four or five of my parents' ticky-tacky tract Cape Cods near the Oscar Mayer plant in Madison would have easily fit inside this palace, which probably cost ten or twenty times as much. And we hadn't been poor, living at least on the lower fringes of the middle class. Compared to Peter's hardscrabble family, we had been downright affluent.

I parked my Toyota in the spacious driveway between a boxy, black BMW and a sportier, burgundy two-seater Porsche. I supposed I would have taken either in trade for my Corolla, but only if they were as maintenance-free. All I ever asked of a car was that it got me where I needed to be with the least possible fuss. It didn't matter what it looked like, and the cheaper the better.

The polished brass doorbell chimed, and a puffy-faced man with thinning hair, a deep tan, and estuaries of wrinkles fanning out from both eyes emerged. His jaw dropped, as if in happy recognition, and he burst forward and gave me a muscular hug. "Hey, Bakken!" he greeted. This old geezer was Dickinson? I wouldn't have recognized him in a crowd. Contact lenses now instead of wire rims, and hair so uniformly blond it had to be dyed. A canary yellow polo shirt with a green reptile sown above its pocket and sleeves pinching biceps bigger than they had been in Monterey. There was no visible membership tag on his immaculate white slacks. But why the lurid splotch on his left cheek?

"Get your stuff, Bakken. No, hell, I'll carry it for you." I beat Scotty to the backpack with the diary photocopies, leaving him the suitcase. What in the devil had happened to his face?

On second glance, his body was slim as ever or even slimmer, so the puffy cheeks were deceptive. His smile was still wide and bright, but his eyes no longer joined in the mirth. And why were they so bloodshot? The minty, medicinal smell he exuded hinted at an explanation.

I followed him into a kitchen so wall-to-wall white I had to squint. A pretty brunette, standing over the sink, said, "Hi, Tommy," as if we already were acquainted. Five-seven. About thirty-five, or if older, well-preserved. Long, thin, angular features. Skin too fair to tan—like mine. Jet-black hair pulled back into a bun and the rest hanging airily to her waist like Spanish moss. No makeup that I could detect. Nervous eyes.

Scott introduced his wife, Elizabeth Brown Dickinson, with ironic formality. In a husky voice, she asked me to call her "Beth."

"Give me your rucksack, too, Tommy," Scott said. "I'll carry everything up to your bedroom."

"No-no," I stammered, "I need that close-by."

"Whatever." He zipped off with my suitcase.

"I've heard a lot about you, Tommy," Beth droned, as if reading from a script.

I scanned the kitchen for a safe place to put the backpack down. Finding none, I slung it around a shoulder.

"Scott said you were quiet, but this is ridiculous," Beth muttered.

Dickinson popped back in. "So what have you been up to, Thomas?"

The only other thing I could think of were the Soviet misinterpretations of Nietzsche I had been scouring and synthesizing, but I was too polite to mention those. So I said, "Not much."

Scotty chuckled nervously and picked up an opaque blue tumbler from the counter. "Beth has already begun lunch," he announced with forced good cheer. "You can set another place, right, honey?"

She glared darts at him.

"Thomas, let me give you a tour of my humble abode, while Liz finishes up. Could I get you a G and T?"

Before lunch? I made it a coke.

Scotty snatched the backpack out of my grasp. "Let me at least put this in the hallway closet. You can get your pills or whatever you need from it any time." I carefully watched him hang it on a hook and close the door. Beth grimly thrust a frosted tumbler into my hand, and I pursued Dickinson into a monstrous living room. I slowly turned full circle to take in the Persian rug, American colonial furniture, and an indoor jungle of exotic ferns and vines. Mirror-lined walls reflected the two of us like a kaleidoscope, our image shrinking inside of images till the two of us disappeared into a point. By no means was this room small, but its enormity was an optical illusion.

"It has class, doesn't it?" Scotty said, beaming with pride.

I nodded, though that depended on which class you meant. The freezing soft drink hit my queasy stomach exactly wrong. Dickinson pointed out objets d'art scattered oh-so meaningfully about the house, but my mind kept drifting back to what was hanging in his closet. Did I ever long to hand him a diary copy and scram.

"So what are the other Monks up to?" Scott said, patting his reddened cheek.

"I have no idea. I'll be seeing Will next weekend, when he visits Milwaukee for a chess tournament. Rich I'll contact as soon as Umlaut gets his address. He lives someplace without a phone."

"Not having one sounds about Rich's speed."

I grimaced to hear Scott slurring his "s's."

"Oh, I like Hoffman all right," he went on, "but we never really got over a tiff in Knittelstedt when he called me 'a bourgeois asshole.' So he was at least half-right. Seriously, I'm not that bourgeois compared to everyone else here in UK. But I can't abide people proud of being hippie-dippie either."

He led me upstairs to his study overlooking an immense backyard. I recognized a television, two VCRs, and a stereo system with speakers the Rolling Stones could have used at Altamont, all the equipment more overwhelming than impressive. Perhaps because I never could cozy up to any man-made object with moving parts or electrical wiring, as much as I depended on some of them.

We stomped downstairs and headed out back, where I stepped gingerly across the putt-perfect lawn. "How are your parents doing?" he asked, a sweet question.

"Fine for their age," I said, glancing away from his discolored cheek.

New, cooler air blowing in from the west began to condense the stifling humidity into a fine mist. Ignoring the precipitation, Scott and I circled the house. "Remember how I used to whip everyone's ass running?" he said. "Hell, I was even faster than Zielsdorf. But now I'm too pokey for slow-pitch softball. Without legs, my tennis is a joke. And you know the latest? No matter how skinny I get I can't flatten my stomach."

I said nothing, debating the best way to bring up Peter's diary.

"Don't you hate getting old, Thomas? I mean, aging's a bitch. My back hurts a lot these days. Not that I can't manage the pain with exercise and pills. The tea helps of course, too." He hoisted his tumbler, wrinkling his facial splotch with a grin. "The other day I glanced down, and it looked like I was riding a chicken."

Maybe he should eat more and worry less, I thought but didn't voice. Had he somehow hit his cheek falling?

"Now don't get me wrong," he went on, guiding me back into the living room. "I love Beth and the house and the kids. I love being a family man. But little things are driving me crazy. Like Beth's refusal to cut her damned hair. I mean, I don't really care, but her billowing tresses make her look like an adolescent getting wrinkles. She'll turn forty in October, for Christ's sake. And why won't she gain some weight? That way her curves would come back."

I didn't respond. It wasn't exactly accurate that she had no curves, not from behind anyway, though I did my best not to notice.

Scott fidgeted with his empty tumbler. "It bugs me how I always play things safe now. I'm a coward compared to the old days, when everything didn't depend on the bottom line. I used to accept people for whatever they had to offer personally no matter who they were or what they earned, but that's not how UK works."

A lump formed in my throat. I missed Company D, Det Q, and, above all, Peter.

"Not that I want a different job," he added, "or to move somewhere else. You can't go backwards in lifestyle and ever be happy. But I wish I wasn't such a clone. Ring the doorbell of any house around here and somebody like me will answer. Sure, I liked settling down, but I never expected it to be a life sentence. Right now I can tell you exactly how I'm going to spend the next twenty-five years, and that scares the crap out of me. So I'm a nice professional with a nice house and a nice wife and nice kids in a nice suburb. What's missing? Everything. I'm winning a game I don't even want to play."

"You seem really good at it though," I said.

"For that, I have to thank my father. He showed me the ropes. And to beat the tax man, he's been giving me some of my inheritance in advance every year. Which has made a big difference. But where is all this heading? It can't be just so the next generation can do more of the same, can it?"

"Why are we here?"

"Exactly. Where's Zielsdorf when we really need him? He could really contribute to this discussion." Scotty tried to take a swig from his empty glass. "But then maybe we're not supposed to ask the questions Peter always did. It struck me one day that my cat can live without knowing why, so why can't I? Since I'm supposed to be superior to the dumb animal. So now when negative thoughts arise, I drive them out by dwelling on positive things like sexy broads. That black despair just below the surface with Peter was such a waste of energy. What was bugging him so much anyway? Remember how he acted in Germany? He was in such bad shape when I flew home to ETS I felt guilty leaving the poor bastard behind."

This was the perfect time to fetch the diary and fork it over. Still, I just sat there.

Scotty swirled the sliver of ice left in his tumbler. "Where'd you say Peter was living?"

"I didn't." A hot flush suffused my face. "I mean, I don't know."

"You haven't heard from Peter? Good grief, I'm surprised. You guys were really close. Wasn't he a character though? I bet he's got tenure at some place like Yale."

"I don't think he's a professor."

"Come on. Who would be, if Peter isn't? No, I'd bet my house he's teaching at an outstanding university. Why makes you say he isn't?"

"I don't think anyone knows what happened to him. Umlaut thinks he might be in Germany, since nobody he's called knows anything about him. That theory is plausible." Yet obviously false. Why was I lying? Because if I had said Peter was dead, I would have to explain how I knew it, and that would open the floodgates to everything I was holding back and wasn't ready to confess. Not yet. But I had to very soon. Before I left, in fact. Why not right now? I felt close to bawling.

"Hey, you don't know much, huh, Tommy," Scotty said with a smarmy chuckle. "I miss old Zielsdorf. Wasn't he a great linguist? Don't laugh, but when I arrived in Monterey, I expected to be the best student. I had been pretty good at Stanford, you realize. The best thing about Peter is that he refused to accept himself as he was. He just never stopped growing."

"No!" I snapped. "Not accepting himself was his worst fault! At some point enough should have been enough! He didn't have to keep on proving himself over and over!"

Too late, I regretted my vehemence. "But he always managed to pull it off," Scotty rebutted, staring at me with alarm. "I think we should all be more like Zielsdorf. Tom, the way you talk about him makes it sound—"

"—I fear he's dead." There I had said it.

Dickinson's jaw dropped.

"I mean, why else wouldn't anybody have heard from him? He would never have settled in Germany."

I was on the brink of revealing it all, yet face to face with Scotty I still held back. Had I waited too long to come forward? Once the story got out, the FBI couldn't help but suspect complicity on my part. But I couldn't bottle this story up forever either. Still, wouldn't it be better to wait until breakfast the next day just before departing? Dickinson was in no condition now for what I had to say anyway.

"So how are you paying the bills?" Scotty asked, again rubbing his cheek.

"I'm a professor at a little college down in Brownsville."

He looked dumbfounded. "But of course. Got tenure?"

"Yup." Not that I would ever advance to full professor.

"Hey, congratulations, Bakken. I knew you could do it." He didn't sound convinced. "So what do you teach?"

"Comp Lit. Russian. German. Linguistics. Whatever they want me to do."

"Do you publish?"

"I revised my dissertation and published that. I get a book review in print every year. And so far a grand total of two journal articles."

Scotty insisted I tell him everything that had happened since Det Q, so I obliged, keeping it brief. I had earned a doctorate in Comp Lit at UW-Madison in 1979, passing prelims without distinction after four years of course work, and then researched and wrote my thesis for three more. I compared Wilhelm Raabe to Joseph Conrad and proved the German hadn't influenced the Anglicized Pole, despite similarities. At best it was journeyman research, and my career reflects its mediocrity. My achievements, modest though they were, I owed to a good memory, because I wasn't that smart. I just keep plugging away.

"Who the hell is Wilhelm Raabe?"

"A nineteenth-century German Realist. Fairly well-known within Germany, unknown outside of it."

Scott nodded vacantly. "Do you still buy books faster than you can read?"

"My walls are double shelved."

He guffawed. "My, you ended up off the beaten track! How in the world did you choose Brownsville, Ohio?"

"It chose me. I sent out fifty résumés and got exactly one interview. I took that job at Northern Appalachian State, and I'm grateful for it. Thousands of better scholars than I am don't have tenure and never will. Some of my colleagues see NAU as a life sentence, but I don't. I haven't even bothered to apply anyplace else. Brownsville is an island of the Sixties in the wash of the Eighties. The quaint, laid-back college town was laid out among thickly wooded hills long before the invention of the automobile and so has many narrow, brick-paved streets. I can't complain."

"Outstanding," he said with a frown. "And you're married to Karen, right?"

I shrugged, my temples tightening.

"How come you didn't bring the little woman along?"

"Karen lives in Grand Forks, North Dakota, where she's been teaching linguistics for three years. We got a dissolution last year. "

Scott eyed me with grave sympathy.

"I'm still adjusting to being divorced."

"Well, at least you're no longer getting screwed on taxes, Bakken. That damned marriage penalty."

"I don't give a shit about money."

That unexpected bile startled us both. I tried to explain what had gone wrong between my undergraduate sweetheart and me, but it was obvious I didn't really know. It seemed Karen's and my emotions were too similar, too Norwegian, for us to get along. We both had abandoned the marriage years before we separated, after while becoming mere roommates, always in each other's way. And she had become a more serious scholar, but then she had more aptitude. It was a relief for us both when she took the assistant professorship at UND. Our split was just a legal technicality, recognizing what had long since occurred.

"My God, Brownsville, Ohio and Grand Forks, North Dakota," Scotty said like they were Timbuktu and Machu Picchu. Probably because they were.

"Karen won't be stuck there long. At the rate she's publishing she'll land a job at some major university."

"You know," Scotty told me, "Beth and I are heading apart, too. Right before you got here, I almost punched the bitch out. Would you be dumb enough to slug somebody bigger than you? Well, she is. I was so dumbfounded by her punch that I didn't hit her back. It's kind of funny actually."

About as funny as a hit-and-run accident.

He quickly freshened his "ice tea" and returned. "I want more of everything and Beth wants less. I want to speed up. She wants to slow down. Hell, the way I figure it, after we're dead we'll have all of eternity for mellowing out, but for now I resent the day's measly twenty-four hours. In fact, I hate to relax. The only time I try is when I'm asleep." He paused, swirling the ice in his glass. "Maybe we'll stick it out though for the kids' sake. You didn't mention any kids of yours. Got two myself."

"None for me. Just as well, considering how things turned out." What if I just handed him a copy of Peter's diary and scrammed?

"You wanted some, right?"

"Yup. Still do."

"It's not too late. Find yourself a younger wife. Or one who already has children. So do you date?"

I shook my head.

Scotty giggled at that preposterous notion and began chewing on a chunk of ice. "Hey, you really are still a secular monk. So what do you do for sex?"

I said nothing, my forehead prickling with chagrin. Noticing my discomfort, he kindly launched into a practiced spiel about his work. Investments in commercial real estate earned him the real money, but he spent most of his time handling dissolutions, divorces, and pre-nuptial agreements, for which he was a local legend. "For really big bucks I ought to move into tort law, but, believe you me, Bakken, there still are some things I won't do for money. So I use the law to protect my clients' wealth? Excuse me! That's what lawyers do."

No doubt. Maybe he'd sober up after lunch, and then I'd give him what Peter had written. No way could I stand to wait till tomorrow.

"Graduate school was my biggest mistake. I got my Master's at Stanford in English history and worked two semesters toward a doctorate before calling time out. My father took me aside and advised a more practical tack. A couple of phone calls from him got me into the Ohio State University Law School, and here I am practicing in my home town. Sure, I feel sheepish living where I was born and bred, but I am good at what I do. Still, I wonder whether I should have stayed in New York. I was good enough to make it there, but really miserable, and so was Beth. Hell, she thinks Columbus is too urban."

"Do you keep up on English history?"

"Hell, no. I have trouble keeping up on the Buckeyes. Though while in New York I did read a slew of history articles and monographs in my spare time."

Whether he was drunk or not, I simply couldn't wait. I walked over to the hallway closet and grabbed the photocopy from the backpack.

Scotty chortled.

No, I decided, he was too far gone. Right after lunch would be better. I put the diary back and handed him Umlaut's list of names to call for the Chicago reunion.

"Outstanding," he said, skimming the sheet. "This reunion really sounds like fun. You know, it's weird, Thomas, but I can't talk to anybody I know in town the way I can to you. My UK friends here are like clothes in a closet. Every so often new ones get added, worn out, and replaced. The turnover is so slow you don't even notice there's almost nobody left you were seeing five years ago. I always used to think friendship was easy, but it sure hasn't been. But we Monks were different. So you want me to phone these guys?"

"Exactly."

To my relief, lunch was ready at last. Beth had spread the table with a rainbow of ceramic ware, each piece a single color and none of them matching. I could have sworn they were the same style as my mother's during my youth on the wrong side of Madison, but how could that be? For the rare occasion of my visit, Scotty opened a bottle of genuine Champagne from the actual French province. So to a CD of *Don Giovanni*, I finally experienced the real thing, not that I noticed any difference.

My small glass of bubbly lasted the whole meal, while Scott and Beth quaffed the rest. I didn't catch what they called the little rolls of raw fish and rice wrapped in weird vegetation, but it sounded Russian. If you could get past the consistency and texture, which to me had always been the most salient features of any dish, it did have an interesting taste. If one was "into" interesting tastes. To me, analyzing food has always seemed like rating brothels, a gross abuse of intellect in pursuit of sensuality.

Scotty babbled on about their delightfully remote cottage beside a tiny Minnesota lake with the deepest, cleanest water. From the pier you could watch muskies lurking in the weeds and perhaps even witness the sudden vanishing of an unlucky duckling. Ha ha. I did my best to listen, but my thoughts kept drifting back to the Baltic Sea.

Though once a favorite piece—before classical music began to aggravate my depression—this Mozart opera now struck me as torture. Such poignant sublimity made me feel like Peter's waterlogged corpse had been hauled ashore and left dripping at my feet.

Beth made it till the chocolate mousse dessert before she began slurring her words. "Lasht" year she had persuaded Scott to let Jennifer and Jason be exposed to Christianity. So Saturdays the kids took special classes at the local Congregational church and Sundays attended the actual services. Later they'd move on to the Episcopalians, so the kids could be exposed to "a range" of religious beliefs.

Scotty glowered at her.

"So you belong to a church?" I asked. I personally didn't.

"Beth does," Scotty said with a sneer. The mark on his cheek had almost faded.

"I only went there twice," she rebutted.

"We don't mention it around here, Thomas. It's one of those off-the-wall outfits that crawled out of the woodwork in the Seventies."

Beth's eyes flashed pique. "It's the New Age Church."

"Never heard of it," I replied. "Is it Protestant?"

"Protestant? Shit, it isn't even Christian. Sure, you went only twice, honey, but you really wanted us to join, remember? Thomas, it's a bunch of hippies finally dressing like normal people and worshipping only God knows what."

Since when had Dickinson ever cared about religion?

"The members work on getting in touch with Light-Fire, the Godhead principle of the Cosmos," Beth explained. "And learn to beam that energy toward benevolent ends."

Scotty tossed back his head. "Needless to say, it's not in Upper Kensington."

"It's near Yellow Springs, this side of Dayton," Beth added, hopping up to fetch a carafe of white wine. In her absence, Scott whispered that it was good for business occasionally to attend the Congregational services downtown, and he was considering becoming a Mason for the same reason. Besides, it was hard to make their Jennifer go, if they never set an example, not that he wanted his children to believe in any mumbo-jumbo.

Upon her return, Beth asked about my own denomination.

"Like most Norwegian-Americans, I was brought up Lutheran," I said. "But I haven't gone since—well, since meeting Peter Zielsdorf." I cleared my throat. "Brownsville has untraditional churches, too."

"Untraditional?" Scotty blurted. "You mean hippie-dippie?"

"Counterculture they prefer to call it. If I were a joiner, I'd join, too."

"Whatever," Scotty said. "It must be tough for aging longhairs to build an entire life out of not accepting responsibility."

"Actually, it's easy. And you miss the whole idea. They absolutely refuse to accept responsibility for the wrong turn America has taken since Jimmy Carter, and they try to point a better way with their own lives." To my dismay, lunch wasn't sobering Dickinson whatsoever.

The phone rang, and Scott excused himself to answer it.

After an awkward silence, I asked Beth, "Where did you grow up?"

"Worthington, just north of UK. Say, did you drive through Lower Kensington getting here?"

"I must have." I glanced away from the goose bumps plainly visible on her chest.

She chortled bitterly. "There is no Lower Kensington. There is no Kensington. There is only *Upper* Kensington." I contemplated that long and hard, but it still made no sense.

Beth leaned forward, tears oozing from her eyes. "You know what bugs me the most? I do want children and I do want to be a mother, but I also want to live out in the country and be self-sufficient. Not live like this. Who's impressed by all the crap we own? If anybody is, I don't want them around. UK is a terrible place for kids because the families are all so isolated. It's enough to make a person puke."

What could I say? Scotty stumbled back into the room, and I started worrying about their staying on their feet till sundown. Was he ever going to sober up?

"Who was it?" Beth asked.

"The FBI."

I flinched. For fifteen years I had dreaded nothing so much as their knock.

"You mean Robert?" Beth said.

"Yeah, Bob Blair. His wife screwed up royally by accepting a second bid on their house. So he's going to pick me up and we'll straighten things out. Sorry, Tommy, but it shouldn't take long."

The meal resumed in sullen silence. A creature rubbed on my shins. I glanced down at a jet-black, golden-eyed tomcat, whining at me like a child. Beth bent toward me to offer the kitty a morsel of raw tuna, cooing, "Here, Henry." Before I could look away, I had glimpsed her entire exposed breasts.

Henry meowed approval as I muttered, "Holy moly," under my breath. I scratched the backs of his ears and stemmed the shove of the muscular beastie's head. I longed for Nebuchadnezzar's gentler touch. Or even better, getting the hell out of there.

Beth's triumphant grin showed she was fully aware of what she had done and its effect on me. I noticed makeup wasn't the reason her cheeks looked sunken. They were genuinely hollow. Other fine bones on her head also stuck out, rendering her otherwise pretty face a virtual skull with skin on it. Add a little dust and dirt and she could have gotten work as a Holocaust film extra.

A cup of espresso got Beth chattering about her jogging, and Scott's mood turned edgy. Most Saturdays she "carbed up" before the week's biggest run Sunday mornings, but today she needed protein because it would slow the absorption of alcohol during the party.

"What party?" I blurted.

"Just a little summer soirée," Scott said. "We've been planning it for two months. My birthday's next Tuesday, but we're celebrating it tonight. The big four-oh. You'll love it."

I nodded gravely. The thought of two dozen Prince Charmings drunk as Dickinson within four walls was alarming. And we still hadn't discussed Zielsdorf's diary.

"Are wives coming to this Army reunion?" droopy-lidded Beth asked.

"They're certainly welcome," I muttered. "As are kids."

"No way am I leaving you here alone, Liz!" Dickinson snapped. "Forget about taking the rug rats." At that, Beth jumped up and stalked off.

My stomach churned at the prospect of consuming even one more spoonful of mousse.

"Give up on it, Bakken," Dickinson muttered.

Grateful words. I excused myself to use the john. The bathroom door was ajar, so I nudged it open and immediately yanked it back shut. What had I just seen? Beth kneeling over the toilet bowl and retching. Could she be that drunk?

"You forgot to knock," she teased, when she emerged. She looked embarrassed.

Once I rejoined them at the table, Beth stuck the tip of a little finger provocatively into the corner of her mouth and winked. "So how's the single life in Brownsville, Tommy?"

Dickinson glared at her. "Don't ask."

"Don't answer for him, Scott," she snapped.

"I didn't answer for him, *dear*."

I ducked the question by describing instead the uneasy truce between town and gown and the whole gamut of American lifestyles living elbow to elbow. The fundamentalist natives didn't exactly hanker to outsiders, but all of us got along reasonably well. Everybody was somebody, everybody worth an hello.

Bob Blair's arrival rescued me from this interrogation. The square-jawed six-footer, five years my junior, was wearing a navy blue suit and had a ROTC haircut. Beth's long, welcoming hug wiped the scowl off his face, especially when she rubbed her pert chest against his arm.

Scotty slipped on a camel's hair blazer, and the two men departed. Unfortunately, that left me alone with Beth. "Why did Scott say Bob was an FBI agent?" I asked her.

"Because he is. Last month Bobby nailed some schmuck at Wright-Paterson Air Force Base for selling the Soviets photocopied blueprints of a new airplane prototype. A co-worker caught the guy sneaking them back to work and called the Bureau. For this, Robert's getting a promotion and a transfer to DC."

My first impulse was to sprint for the closet, snatch the backpack, and flee. But I controlled myself and despite throbbing temples politely sauntered after Beth into the living room, where we sat down together on the couch. For the next hour I endured the Dickinson photo albums, beginning with a page from Scotty's Army days, taken at Umlaut's ETS party. In one, young, robust, handsome Zielsdorf sat exactly how I remembered him. Another showed Peter in profile with Karl-Heinz, obviously speaking

German, his jaw, lips and posture so altered he no longer looked like the same person. It tore me up inside to contemplate my best buddy's wretched demise.

The next page was worse. In one picture I was drunkenly hugging a column at Club 69. Another captured me dancing with Dagmar. I flipped ahead, but mischievous Beth turned right back to the shots of me. "This one of you dancing is my favorite," she said. "The others make you look like some sort of bewildered tourist."

I blushed, feeling stripped naked.

"Why are you guys so fond of Peter? He sounds selfish. Cute though."

"Too bad you never met him. He didn't—I mean, doesn't—come across as selfish. He likes most people, and they liked him."

Beth put a cassette in the tape deck and sat back down so close I retreated flush against the sofa arm. To Bob Dylan's adenoidal twang, we paged through her college-era photos of pickets and policemen blocking High Street and flower children hanging out on the Ohio State campus.

The next volume documented their son and daughter's growth from infancy a season at a time to their current ages of seven and thirteen. Both blond like Scott, Jason had his father's sky-blue eyes, while Jennifer's were chestnut like her mother's. Beth assured me she truly loved them both, even Jenny. What in the devil was holding Dickinson up, I wondered.

Next came pages of Beth and Scott in sportswear over the years. Dickinson had indeed regressed from the imposing mini-brute of Monterey to a well-biceped scarecrow. "This is Wolfgang," Beth said, fondly fingering the photo of a beefy, bronzed athlete in tennis whites, standing close behind her to guide her serve. "He's the secret to my ground strokes. And the best instructor in Columbus. Scott hates his guts. He's a teetotaler and a vegetarian. So what if he doesn't earn that much? Wolfie's a real man."

The next section consisted of a too trim Beth in various revealing swimsuits. She needed to gain at least twenty pounds. "It isn't hard for me to keep my weight down," she said, flipping forward to a buxom blonde in a low-cut knit top. "Take a gander at Linda. Would you leave me for a slut like her?"

I shrugged. Come on, Dickinson, hurry up.

"What does Scott see in such a whore? Sure, she's a looker if you're into sleaze, but dumb as tits. All that money of his and he's still got zero taste. The bastard truly disgusts me sometimes. And he's getting blitzed today again, but what else is new?"

"What about his kindness, charm, and good cheer?" I said, feeling obliged to defend a fellow Monk.

"Constant buzz you mean. Would you want to live with a drunken comedian? Sure, he's a terrific host and guest, but one shitty husband. If I had only a fraction of his dough, I would have moved out ages ago. But I can't live alone without money. Not with two kids. But I'm sick of talking about myself. How come you and Karen split?"

I sat there with my mouth agape. Discussing Karen threatened almost as much pain as would talking about Peter. I could have betrayed my ex by confessing that if she hadn't learned about sex from books and movies, it would never have occurred to her, since she had no instinct for it, her every desire actually a should. But we had not parted bitterly and were still friends, even if we had lost contact, and so I kept her secrets. Just as I always had Peter's.

"You're lucky you don't have kids," Beth told me. "My Jenny's a budding fascist. Openly racist and elitist and doesn't feel there's anything wrong with it. She knows product labels better than a retailer. UK to the core."

A car door thumped outside, and two skinny, blond youngsters scampered into the house and gave their mother a perfunctory embrace. Scotty soon followed, looking upset.

Jason lugged a thick book over from an end table and with a high-pitched, angelic voice asked, "Will you read to me, Uncle Tommy?"

"The babysitter will read to you tonight," Scotty told him an octave lower.

Jason stood at our knees, examining us each in turn. His flawless skin and perfect hair made our adulthood look like physical corruption.

"I'd be happy to read to him," I muttered.

"We wouldn't hear of it!" Scotty snapped.

"Calm down, asshole," Beth said.

"I'd enjoy doing it," I insisted. "Really."

"Read me 'Rumpelstilzchen,' Uncle Tommy. Please, please."

"Stop pestering company, Jason. And go to your room," Scott said.

Jennifer grabbed her brother's wrist and told him, "You should be able to read fairy tales yourself at your age, Dummy." Chuckling triumphantly, she tugged the boy toward the stairwell.

"Leave me alone," he cried, struggling to twist free.

"Sit on it," she jeered, tugging him along.

"Stop it, you two!" Scotty yelled. "Don't go anywhere, son. You can't run away from your problems."

"But you told him to go his room!" Beth shouted.

"Shut up, Liz. Jennifer, why can't you two behave in front of company? You guys could have done a lot worse job of choosing your parents, so show some appreciation."

"Give me a break, Dad," Jennifer whined.

"Let the boy go to his room!" Beth screamed.

"Daddy," Jason pleaded, wiping his eyes.

"Jenny, what's the matter with you two?" Beth snapped.

"I've got a nerd for a brother. You can't expect me to get along with *him*."

"My God, Jenny," Beth said, "he's only seven years old! We're taking you kids to Dorothy's right now—for the night. We don't want to carry you both home asleep again."

"Good excuse," Jennifer said, setting her jaw. "Maybe I should carry you to bed, Mom. I weigh more. And I won't be drunk."

"Jennifer Dickinson!" Beth shouted. "Go to your room! Both of you. Go on, Jason. Change clothes this instant."

Smirking Jennifer stalked off, her head held proudly erect, while hangdog Jason whimpered after her. Minutes later, they returned in new outfits, carrying little overnight bags, and tolerated a hug from each parent. "Can we stay there overnight tomorrow, too, Mom?" Jennifer asked. "I can't stand the stink of our house the day after your parties. You'd ground me for a month if my room looked as filthy as our living room will."

"I'll ground you for the rest of your life if you don't watch your tongue."

"Come on, Mom, you're not that out of it. My room is perfect, while yours is a pigsty, and I still get all the criticism around here."

"That's because," Scotty said, butting in, "you're the kids and we're the parents. Guess who makes the rules?"

"It's not fair," Jennifer said.

"Whoever said life is fair?" Scotty snapped.

Letting her father have the last word, she led her brother out the door. Such a hellish exchange left my body shaking. "How about we all take a nap before the party?" Beth asked.

"Excellent idea," I agreed, figuring the Dickinsons couldn't drink while they slept.

"I hope you brought a tie and jacket," Scotty said.

"Sure. For attending church with my mother in Madison."

"I thought you said you quit going?"

"I did. I only go when I'm home to make her happy. Otherwise she worries about my immortal soul. As do I."

"Whatever gets you off. Anyway, people dress up for parties here in UK."

While they napped, I lay in my canopy bed and struggled further with the Constance Garnett translation of *The Possessed*. Tolstoy's clear, Frenchified prose I always read in the original, but not Dostoevsky's more genuine, idiomatic Russian. Twenty pages later I dozed off with my glasses on. Before long a dreamy voice gently commanded in my slumber, "Rise and shine, Tommy." It was Peter, somehow still alive and well. I opened my eyes, and there he stood in our DLI barracks room, dressed in a preppy pink shirt, navy blue blazer, and red tie with little indigo polka dots, and grinning just like Scott Dickinson. No, wait, it really was Scotty, and I was in Upper Kensington—and Peter had been dead fifteen years.

"Thirty minutes till blast off," Scotty announced. "All systems go. Name your poison, and I'll fix it for you, buddy. To help you get totally geared to party hearty by the time the door bell rings." He was slurring his words worse than ever, and his flushed skin nearly matched the pink of his shirt.

"A gin and tonic," I said. How I was ever going to endure this soirée?

"Excellent summer choice, Specialist Bakken. Get dressed ASAP and I'll bring you the cocktail. How about a cup of coffee, too, for an extra boost? Tonight I'll be sure to introduce you to some foxy chicks."

I cringed.

"Now to hustle, Bakken, you have to be totally on. Like a standup comedian finally getting his big chance on the Johnny Carson show. I've discovered the surefire way to impress. In the Sixties, people called it good vibes, but it's really pheromones, which people smell subconsciously. So flood yourself with these miraculous biochemicals by lusting. That'll be easy with tonight's crowd. Thomas, if I may be so bold, you did well to divorce Karen, because you need an earthier woman. Some gal like Linda Atkins."

Somehow I didn't groan.

"Hey, get fired up, troop. Parties make the world go around. If I see an attractive woman, I'm always attracted to her. And I never apologize for it. Often as not they enjoy my attention, even if we're only friends. And we are only friends—mostly." He chortled. "If anyone disapproves of my flirting, I tell them my parents blew it, when bringing me up, and I ended up heterosexual."

"But aren't you married? Is this why Beth hit you?"

Bitter anger I never saw in the Army flashed across his eyes. "Yeah, I'm married, but so what? I wear this gold band around my finger, not my penis. There's nothing wrong with flirting. Beth flirts, too, as I think you've noticed. It's just a way of saying I think you're attractive, and I hope you think I am, too."

Was I ever regretting this stop in Upper Kensington.

Scotty took a deep drink from his opaque tumbler and bounced out of the room like an adolescent following his very first kiss.

I got dressed and moped my way downstairs. Beth, stunning in thick makeup and a short, diaphanous aquamarine dress, her waist-length hair now pinned atop her head, was anxiously rearranging objets d'art.

"Liz," Scott said, "give Wolfgang a call. It'd be a shame to let the jerk pass up a chance at mooching. Maybe he can take you upstairs and show you a few new strokes."

"Sure, darling. We'll try not to walk in on you and Linda."

"Bob Blair's coming, too," Scott told me. "You'll enjoy meeting him. His work reminds me of our old days at Det Q."

"Great," I said, suppressing panic.

The telephone's abrupt jangle startled me. Scotty picked it up, listened a moment, mumbled something, laughed, and murmured some more before motioning me over. My mother no doubt, since nobody else knew I was here.

"Hello, Mom," I said into the receiver. The response was a sharp click. "They hung up," I added.

"You'll never guess who it was," Dickinson said, his grin closer to a grimace. "It was Peter, Tommy! Peter Zielsdorf! I swear it! He was affecting an odd drawl, but I'm positive it was him. I don't forget voices."

Suddenly I felt so unsteady on my feet I plopped down on the nearest chair.

"The guy claimed to be an old Army buddy of Thomas Bakken's," Scott went on, "eager to get back in touch. He said years ago he had given you a manuscript for safekeeping. Now he wanted it back and thought I could maybe help find you. I said, 'Is this Peter?' Instead of answering, the guy asked for your address, so I told him, 'Why don't you just talk to Tom right now?' And handed you the phone."

Why was Dickinson playing such a mean prank on me? My pulse thumped in my ears.

"I sure hope he calls back," Scotty slurred.

God help me if Scotty wasn't joking.

"Not used to the demon rum, huh, Bakken? Or were you always a short hitter? I forget."

Could it really have been Peter who called? Dickinson had no reason to deceive me. But if it truly had been Zielsdorf, then he had played me for a pathetic fool all these years. But why? If he hadn't drowned himself in the Baltic, like the diary claimed, it made me question how Katja and Breitenbach had really died? Could the lying bastard have killed them both himself and not the GRU? Might he have thrown in his lot with the Soviets after all?

Which would make him not only a cold-blooded murderer, but also a traitor? And me guilty of aiding and abetting espionage.

"Man, I miss old Zielsdorf," Scott said. "We'll get that guy to the reunion yet, and it'll be the time of our lives. What else with every Monk present along with so many other guys? Peter must have gotten my phone number from a Det Q buddy, and that person knows where he's living. Probably Umlaut. Out-fucking-standing, Bakken!" Giggling with boozy effervescence he slapped me on the back and glugged more gin into his glass. "By the way, what's this manuscript Peter was asking about?"

"Some weird confession. It's hard to know what to make of it." Peter alive? If true, what in the world could I say when we met again? I felt like such an idiot that my body trembled. Zielsdorf couldn't have possibly deceived me worse than this.

"Beth, you brought out the wrong dishes," Scott said. "Fiestaware's too dorky for this crowd."

"What else? Your mother's fucking china?"

"Exactly."

The second G and T Scotty handed me reeked of juniper berries it contained so little tonic mix. I handed the drink back and muttered that no matter how much they might be offended I couldn't possibly stay. The divorce was getting to me, I said, lying, and so wasn't up to a party.

Scowling, he opened the cupboard and began reshelving Beth's cherished dinnerware. "Don't be silly, Thomas."

"Stop it, you asshole!" Beth screamed.

"You and your beloved Fiestaware. You practically have orgasms over the damned things."

"At least they stay hard."

At that, Scott stretched his arms high overhead, threatening to fling the ceramic collectibles onto the floor.

"I dare you," Beth taunted.

With a jump, Dickinson heaved his handful of dishes against the kitchen tiles, smashing them to bits.

She flailed her puny fists against his chest, and he didn't resist, while protecting his face with open hands. I squeezed my way between them, her weak punches hammering my shoulder and aching head, before she collapsed onto the broken pieces in a sobbing heap.

"Don't cut yourself," he snapped and added more softly, "I'm sorry, Elizabeth. I'll replace them all." Close to tears himself, he bent over to caress her neck, and she didn't object.

"I'm splitting," I announced.

Morose Scott didn't argue with me.

Colorado

The farther the driver of a beat-up, decade-old Ford Escort sped along Highway 160 across northern Arizona, the more his eyelids drooped. What else after another sleepless night and skipping morning coffee? An oncoming truck's blaring horn jolted him back right of center not a second too soon. Talk about a close call.

"It's okay to be Bobby Daniels," he said for the umpteenth time since fleeing Phoenix. Even if there was nobody else inside his vehicle that April Sunday. Yet no matter how often he repeated the words he never felt convinced. But then what was there to like about Robert Richard Daniels? Hardly his awful appearance. Skin way too wrinkled for him being only fifty-six. Missing front teeth. Scarred chin. Discolored cheek. Faded T-shirt. Tattered blue jeans. Worn-out sneakers. Soiled Stetson.

His work record was no better. Nothing but odd jobs, few lasting all that long. Dishwasher, yard mower, tree trimmer, exterminator, snow shoveler, house painter, garage cleaner, ditch digger—you name it, he'd done it. The last one arguably the best as handyman-janitor for three run-down apartment buildings on the outskirts of town. Leaky sinks, wonky locks, flaking paint, broken screws, running toilets, worn-out sockets—whatever needed fixing, he'd repaired. Plus a whole lot of cleaning up messes. Any hour of the day or night too. Which he didn't mind, since he never went places anymore. Wages weren't all that great, but still okay, so long as he and Jackie were sharing expenses, a nifty partnership ending that very day. Which was a genuine shame considering all the good things they'd gotten going together, even if their rental home was cramped and located in an iffy neighborhood.

He cringed at the thought of the pathetic farewell note he'd written the love of his life before sneaking off that morning. "I saw no other choice" was all he'd scribbled and then not signing it. "Sorry, Jackie," he muttered. Jackie Begay being Angie's mother, but not a mudwump unlike her daughter. If there was one thing he'd done his darnedest to stay away from throughout his life it'd been mudwumps. Look at the mess making one measly exception had created.

So much for his resolution to turn over a new leaf and stick to it upon his release from Waupun prison in Wisconsin three years ago, where he'd been sent on a bullshit charge. Sure, he'd been drinking the night of his arrest by a state trooper, but that didn't mean his driving'd been erratic. But then nobody ever cut Bobby Daniels a break.

With his uninjured arm he lifted the Stetson off his head and fanned his overheated face with it. Cursed auto A/C to go on the fritz when he most needed it. Not that he was actually sweating, not in air so dry as here in the desert Southwest. The blasted car's radio wasn't working either. He really could use the company of another person's voice. He eyed the unopened pint of tequila, laying beside him on the passenger seat and licked his lips. For now he made do with cold water from the canteen he'd also brought along.

He dozed off again, only for his eyes to pop back open and the Ford to lurch back into its proper lane. If he didn't watch out, his life would end before he even made the state line. Which was pretty much what he deserved.

Staring at the empty road up ahead, he pictured Angie's face. Broad forehead. High cheekbones. Deep-set, dark eyes. Strong nose. Full lips. Straight, black hair. Skin the color of coffee with cream. Not the darkest shade of brown, but still there was no mistaking the kid's mudwump features—so unlike her fair-skinned, blue-eyed mother's.

In the rearview mirror he spotted that pesky black Chevy Suburban back on his tail. If it was an unmarked cop car like he suspected, why didn't the jerks simply pull him over? Probably because the knuckleheads were expecting him to lead them to Angela. Still, if that truly was the fuzz, so much for the fib he'd fed their Phoenix landlord about heading to Las Vegas that morning instead of toward the Four Corners like he was doing.

His empty stomach growled. If only there was a place around here to stop for a cup of coffee and a bite to eat. But no such luck along this empty stretch. Better of course would be another helping of Jackie's delicious corn, beans, and squash. Even if it bugged him how she always served whatever she cooked to Angie first. But then the kid was her own flesh and blood, and who was he but some deadbeat who'd wormed himself into their household?

Did he ever regret not burning the bloodied underwear. But then he'd been too riled three nights ago to think straight. Still, the place he'd buried them would be hard to notice. The fear of the cops doing it anyway made him feel like the bastards were fastening those pads, belts, and cuff on him again. Like they meant to execute him before even getting around to a trial.

* * *

"Bobby, this is Mr. Chastain, a polygraph-criminologist," Detective Gonzalez had explained the day before. Another mudwump to judge from the cop's swarthy complexion.

"Pleased to meet you, Mr. Daniels," the pig-eyed guy greeted.

Bobby's stomach sank. Because even if he wasn't guilty like they claimed, he sure wasn't blameless.

"To establish your innocence or lack thereof, Mr. Daniels," the expert said, "we'll be giving you an impartial scientific test."

Impartial? Bobby snorted.

"Let me say a few words about how the polygraph works," Mr. Chastain went on. "Attachments to your body will measure emotional reactions to questions. First, I'll strap these rubber belts around your abdomen to measure your breathing. Then I'll fasten pads to the ends of two fingers to detect sweating. Finally, I'll wrap this blood pressure cuff around your upper arm. Whatever they all register, this graph paper will record."

Bobby glared at that infernal scroll. Squiggly lines scrawled across a sheet were able to reveal the secrets of a soul? What a crock.

"Now this equipment is perfectly safe," the expert added. "And none of it will hurt one bit. Is everything clear?"

Sure, clear as mud.

"Okay. Just sign this consent form, and we'll get going."

* * *

They'd gotten going all right and so now he was hightailing it farther and farther from Phoenix. All because he'd screwed up the worst in his whole life, and that was really saying something. He kept tooling past the Hopi mesas. Weird for the tribe to live so high up in the sky. Which had little actual blue in it. Like the sun'd bleached away much of the color.

He came to the town of Kayenta with its rundown shacks, rickety mobile homes, abandoned cars, and electrical appliances, rusting in dirt yards. When he spotted a Burger King, he pulled in, but then just sat there, waiting for that Chevy Suburban to overtake him. Sure enough it did, only to cruise right on past, even though his Escort was parked in plain sight. Which didn't mean the bastards wouldn't stop up ahead and wait for him. What if he crossed them up and doubled back? But no way was he willing to return to Phoenix. Maybe there was a different route for reaching the Four Corners. But first he'd buy himself that food and coffee.

Inside the fast-food joint he passed a display about so-called Navajo Code Talkers who'd served in the Marines. Talk about gobbledygook. Like Navajos didn't talk in code with their strange, singsong lingo every time they spoke.

He'd just gotten into line to order when he bridled. Mudwumps had him surrounded. In fact, he'd never seen so many of them in one place since a Ho-Chunk gathering in Wisconsin Dells ages ago.

"Sir, could I give you this?" a gray-haired Navajo fellow asked, offering him a brochure. Bobby snatched the pamphlet from the mudwump's hand and hustled for the exit.

Once safely inside his Escort with every door secured, he just sat there, panting and massaging his throbbing shoulder. He missed the snub-nosed revolver he'd always used to own, but not of course since prison, firearms being forbidden to felons. Besides, Jackie would never've tolerated a weapon on the premises. Just as well considering how things'd turned out. Would he've even made it this far if he'd been packing?

He grabbed the pint bottle and sniffed it. Like a person could smell through glass. No matter how much he longed for a taste, he put the tequila back down unopened. At least the fright inside the Burger King had chased his drowsiness.

He got out the map of Arizona from the glove compartment. Huh? Kayenta was situated inside the so-called Navajo Nation? Like this country was anything but the United States coast to coast. No wonder that Burger King'd been crawling with mudwumps. One good thing though he saw—if he turned left onto 163 a short distance up ahead, he'd reach Utah even quicker.

Where Bobby'd grown up in Eau Claire, Wisconsin, everybody'd been white and most blue-eyed and many also blond. About as white as people get, in other words. Like he'd been himself, before his hair turned gray at forty, what little was left of it atop his head. No surprise about his fair coloring what with the Norwegian ancestry on his mom's side and English on his dad's. One uncle even claimed that branch of the family could be traced back to the Pilgrims. Or was it the Puritans? He'd never been able to keep the two straight.

In any case, this country was meant for whites like him, because they'd been the ones who'd settled it. Besides, it was wrong to mix things that didn't belong together. For instance, no Wisconsin dairy farmer would dream of crossing his Guernsey cows with Holsteins, not if he wanted his farm to prosper. Otherwise you'd end up with mongrels and mutts to milk and less income.

Bobby forced himself to concentrate on the passing terrain. To judge from the scattered hogans, the Navajos liked some distance between their homes. Unlike what he'd heard about the Hopis, huddling together in villages. As he approached Utah, he recognized the familiar burnt-red buttes and broad mesas of Monument Valley. Just like the pictures in magazines. Okay, the site was truly scenic. Whoever said it wasn't? Still, he'd never considered paying the place a visit, not on a mudwump reservation.

Cruising along highway 163, he sang a country western tune with a croaking-frog voice. Navajo Code Talkers? Talk about an idiotic term. Though not nearly so dumb as him entering a burger joint without checking the place out first. He fondled the pint of booze beside him yet again. The temptation irked him, so much so in fact that he'd no sooner crossed into Utah than he pulled over and poured the liquor out. Even if somebody'd paid good money for it. Which couldn't have been underage Angie. So who else? Certainly not her mother.

"Chill out, Bob," the girl'd teased the night he'd moved in with them, back when the kid was only fourteen and he and her mother barely ever squabbled. "Just 'cause I said your TV show is lame," Angie'd gone on, "doesn't mean it isn't cool to watch it." He'd chuckled at that remark, at once friendly and fresh. Bob was what the girl always called him—instead of Bobby like everybody else. Though Jackie'd been calling him Robert recently, whenever she got ticked off, which'd been happening more and more often.

"Chill out, Bob," he echoed, mimicking Angie's high-pitched voice. He'd been a smart-ass kid like her once too. Like that one time he'd wisecracked to his father, "I am listening. I'm just not obeying." Man, did he get his hide tanned for that comeback.

His first night in the Begay household just to please Angie he'd changed the TV station to a music video channel for her sake, but she'd switched it right back to the crime-solver show he liked. Why he couldn't rightly say. It sure wasn't because he could abide the sight of police in person. Not how the bastards sniffed around for trouble till they found it.

He checked his bulging wallet in the right back pocket. Had his billfold ever held this much cash before? But then all those fifties and twenties were his life savings, which he'd never dared entrust to a bank. As thick as the wad felt, he knew it still wouldn't last all that long, not as pricy as stuff'd gotten. Which meant he'd have to land himself a job pretty quick wherever he ended up. Though even if he did find himself a decent place for starting over, wouldn't his name still be on their wanted lists?

People forgot all the good things he'd done for Angie. Okay, maybe not so much during the first year of them living together. Eventually though he'd started driving the kid places and buying her regular treats. Then came the biggest favor of all, teaching Angela to drive. He'd been real patient with his instruction too. Which was why he'd bet she'd pass her driving test first try. Or she could've anyhow, today being the very day she would've turned sixteen.

He was surprised to find a swift, narrow stream flowing right through the middle of Mexican Hat, the first town inside Utah. A bad feeling about the place, maybe just on account of its name, kept him from stopping. Not long after Highway 163 turned into 191, he came to a village named Bluff, where he spotted a roadside café and pulled in. Not one mudwump on the premises, but then the place was all but deserted mid-Sunday afternoon. Did he ever relish the hamburger, fries, and coffee he bought.

A half hour later he was back on the road, heading farther north. The terrain kept changing, while still staying barren. The Canyonlands National Park didn't look any less desolate than anyplace else, only it took longer to pass. Odd that he still wasn't noticeably sweating despite how overheated he felt. Not like he'd done so often during Wisconsin's sweltering summers. Though he'd sure perspired plenty yesterday inside that Phoenix police station.

* * *

"Try to relax, Mr. Daniels," Mr. Chastain had said, while wrapping a pair of rubber tubes around Bobby's chest. Next the mudwump fixed a cuff to his arm and fastened pads on a couple of fingers. "Just answer yes or no to the questions." he added. "This'll all be over before you know it."

Bobby glanced back at the pens already making lines on a moving paper scroll.

"Is your full name Robert Richard Daniels?" was the first question.

"Yes," Bobby said.

"Do you live in Phoenix?"

"Yes." This grilling sure was unnerving.

"Mr. Daniels," Gonzalez butted in, "please try to sit still."

Bobby took a deep breath and closed his eyes.

"Do you know where Angela Begay is?"

"No."

"Have you ever stolen anything?"

Bobby hesitated. "Sure." Hadn't everybody at some point?

"Yes."

"Did you see Angela Begay after 8:00 p.m. last Thursday?"

"No." The blasted device beeped.

"Did you argue with Angela Begay that evening?"

Bobby paused again before answering, "No." Another beep.

Mr. Chastain jotted something down on the scroll. "Did you serve time in Waupun prison for an assault on a Wisconsin law officer?"

"Yes." Okay, a huge blemish on his record.

"Do you live on Trabajo Street, Phoenix, Arizona?"

"Yes." Why'd they keep asking him such dumb questions?

"Did you serve in the U.S. military?"

"Y-Yes."

Another cursed beep. Bobby glared at the do-hickeys attached to a pair of his fingers. "What's that got to do with Angela's disappearance?"

"Just answer my questions," Mr. Chastain chided. "No other comments please."

"Did you kill Angela Begay?" There they'd finally said it.

"No." Yet another maddening beep. And once more the examiner scribbled on the endless sheet of paper. Before you know it, Mr. Chastain was saying, "That's it," and thanking him for his cooperation. He removed the attachments in quick order, and Gonzalez led him into an adjoining room to await the interrogation.

* * *

As he drove on, Bobby's thoughts drifted back to the day things began going to hell. If only he hadn't gotten tired of sitting around the house, watching TV, and instead decided to do something useful, namely, to clean up the house, starting with sweeping and vacuuming. He left Angie's bedroom inside their cozy bungalow till last. He'd just slid her cot away from the wall to get at the dust underneath, when Angie burst in. "Get the hell out of my room!" she yelled, planted her hands on his chest, and shoved him toward the door. Not that she was actually big or strong enough to push a man his size anywhere, but he'd let her do it.

"I was just tidying up in here, honey," he said. "You know, doing you a little favor."

"How about you never setting foot in here again?"

After that blowup, he'd waited a whole week before sticking his nose back where it didn't belong. He could tell the girl was hiding something in there or she wouldn't be so uptight about him trespassing. Drugs was his biggest fear, a problem that didn't exist when he was growing up in Wisconsin.

More recently, while Angie was visiting a girlfriend and Jackie waiting table, he'd rummaged through the girl's closet without turning up anything but jeans, jumpers, blouses, and T-shirts and other stuff anybody'd expect a girl her age to own. He was closing a dresser drawer, when he spotted something beneath her cot. With a groan he lowered himself to the floor, reached under the bed, and pulled out a Victoria's Secret package. It sure was lightweight, whatever the contents. He could well imagine what it might be, but still put it back, when his hand nudged glassware. A pint of rotgut tequila it turned out and still sealed. The same cheap brand he'd knocked back a lot during his boozing days.

The next thing he knew the bedroom door was flying open and Angie storming in, screaming, "I said leave my stuff alone! Get the hell out of here, you creep!"

"Okay, okay, honey," he told her, fending off her attempts to grab the liquor from him. "We're just concerned about you."

"Where do you get this 'we'? It's just Mom and me here! And you're this loser who showed up and has been mooching off us ever since!"

Jackie's Chevy Blazer rumbled up outside.

"If you mention one word of this to Mom, I'll tell her what you did."

"What I did?"

"To me, asshole." Angie flashed a bitter grin. "You dirty old man."

"I've never touched you, girl," Bobby said, doubling up his fists. "Not even so much as a single hug."

"Who's she going to believe, her precious daughter or a drunken ex-con?"

That insult so stung he wisely stepped back. He'd learned the hard way you couldn't lay a hand on a person out of your reach. "I haven't had even a drop in ages," he muttered. He limped out of Angie's room just as Jackie entered the kitchen.

Angie stuck her head out and yelled, "I don't want him in here ever again!"

"What's going on, Bobby?" Jackie asked.

"I'll explain it later." While she chewed her daughter out for skipping school, Bobby slipped outside.

Somehow things'd blown over that day. Only for Angie to disappear for good the next night.

* * *

Bobby wasn't at all happy about abandoning Phoenix like this, even if the big city lacked the four distinct seasons he'd grown up with and taken for granted back in Wisconsin. Plenty of other poor folks at least living near where he and Jackie did, so he'd never felt out of place. And he'd mostly enjoyed the job of handyman-janitor for three apartment buildings, especially how many tenants respected him and his service.

Moab, Utah turned out to be larger than expected and prosperous to boot. He passed a shoe store, burger joint, coffee shop, hair salon, and what have you, but no place selling booze, not on Sundays He'd decided there was no good reason not to buy a whole fifth, if the fuzz were going to lock him up, which was sure how things looked. Even if he'd given Jackie his word about giving up drinking. He passed a Slick Rock Mountain Bike Shop and then a gas station, where he pulled in, filled up, and set off again. At least he'd gotten that Suburban off his tail. Exiting town, he passed an abandoned plant for processing uranium ore. Talk about one treacherous mineral.

When the highway forked outside Moab, for no particular reason he turned right to follow the swift river, flowing against his direction about fifty feet off to the left. Colorado was a good name for a stream this dirty, transporting mud by the countless ton. Because the word meant colored, didn't it? Not that he knew much Spanish except for *loco* and a few other choice insults. *El Diablo* one drunk'd called him, right before he'd gone up the side of the guy's head. Still, he wasn't all bad, even if he'd boozed and brawled way too often. Not that he'd done any of either since Jackie took him in. Not the way she'd laid down the law. Because the woman truly cared for him.

He felt a sudden urge to head back to Phoenix and face the music. But the more he thought about doing that, the more he pictured Angie's blood-stained bedroom. No, he'd rather be dead than rot in prison again.

He pulled over onto the shoulder here in the middle of nowhere and sat there, staring at the churning current. It sure was no river for taking a dip, not like about every one back in Wisconsin. He climbed out to stretch. The wind whistled across one ear and the other and then made a sound like a woman moaning nearby. Like she was maybe laying in the princess plume at the river's edge a bit upstream. Only there wasn't another soul in sight. Rock-strewn sand stretched to the horizon in every direction between buttes interrupting the flat terrain.

A semi approached with a rising whine and sped past with a falling zoom. He did a double take upon noticing two navy blue clumps a hundred feet ahead, just off the shoulder of the road. If he didn't know better, he'd swear they were backpacks. Which was impossible, since his was the only vehicle in sight. Again, he heard a sound like a woman moaning. The desert wind sure could play tricks on a person.

He crossed the highway to get closer to the river. So much water rushing by and so fast. He'd never seen a stream even close to this swift in the Midwest. Certainly not the Mississippi or its tributaries. No surprise then that this one'd cut the Grand Canyon out of solid rock over time.

* * *

"You said you served in the military," Detective Gonzalez asked Bobby to begin the interrogation. "Which military branch?"

He hesitated before answering, "The Army."

Gonzalez snorted. "You never served in the military, Mr. Daniels. The Defense Department keeps meticulous records."

Bobby stared at the floor.

Gonzalez's Anglo partner, Sgt. Jenkins, sat back with crossed arms, while the mudwump cop went on. "How would you describe your relationship with Angela?"

Bobby chose his words carefully. "In some ways she's like a daughter to me. Even if her mother and I never did marry." Oh, man, was that a lot less than what he could've said.

"So Angie's not a blood relative?" Jenkins asked.

Bobby shook his head. What a dumb question.

"Mr. Daniels," Gonzalez went on, "when was the last time you saw the girl?"

"Thursday night."

"Did you ever argue with her?"

"Doesn't every person living in the same household at one time or another?"

"Did you have an argument with Angie that night?"

"Un-huh."

"About what?"

"I don't remember." His biggest lie so far.

"Would you call Angela Begay a pretty girl?" Gonzalez asked.

"Yeah, I guess she was."

"Was"? Jenkins blurted.

"Was. Is. Same difference."

"Did you molest Angela Joseph?" Jenkins said.

"No." Bobby cringed at the pinched sound of his voice.

"Did you hurt Angela Joseph?" Gonzales asked.

"No."

Gonzalez glared at him. "So where is she?"

"I-I have no idea."

"How come you ended up at a diner Thursday night, if you were so worried about what had become of her?"

"I got hungry."

"Did you kill Angela Begay?"

Fighting back tears, Bobby shook his head.

* * *

Jenkins and Gonzales didn't much like his answers, yet they'd still let him go. And here he found himself outside Moab, Utah on a bank of the Colorado. He moved nearer to the water so muddy a person couldn't see a thing even just beneath the surface. Though you sure could tell a lot was happening. He tossed his Stetson onto the bank behind him and then his belt.

Yesterday Gonzalez'd advised him to stick around town, if he knew what was good for him, the stupid cop. So not what Bobby'd done, four hundred miles and then some from Phoenix and fearing he'd come to the end of the line for him. The mudwump-brown current never quit swirling and carrying some of where it'd been. Called the Colorado on account of all the mud in it. Mud being a good thing since it was made of water and soil. Without either the earth would be dead as barren grit.

Where'd he come up with that weird term mudwump anyway? It seemed like he'd heard it in a history class way back when, only there it'd meant something quite different. Not a name Angie deserved in any case, not such a lively, cheerful, sweet child. Even if she'd turned sullen of late while blossoming into a young woman. From the neck up a wiseass street tough, but at heart still a kid.

With open eyes, he saw Angie's non-white features. What he wouldn't give to see the girl in the flesh, standing right in front of him again with her black hair, strong nose, and swarthy skin, alive and well. If only this was possible. Which it wasn't of course. He scanned the arid, rocky, sandy landscape, so unlike Wisconsin's wooded bluffs, rolling coulees, wetlands, cornfields, and pastures. A spiraling dust devil lifted and dropped one tumbleweed and then another and pumped the pair like gigantic pistons.

If only he hadn't kept messing up last Thursday. Jackie'd been working a swing shift, leaving him home alone while Angie was visiting a girlfriend. Or so she'd said. He suspected the kid was secretly seeing a boyfriend, something her mother'd strictly forbidden. That evening Bobby barely budged off the living room couch in front of the television. He was still laying there, when Angie came home late, wearing sunglasses. Odd for after dark. She had makeup on too, including smudged lipstick. Three guesses how it got that way. Something he'd never seen on the teenager before, but then Jackie didn't allow it. "Did you have a nice time, Angie?" he asked, while the girl rattled around in the kitchen. Without a word in reply, she hustled off into her bedroom with a heaping bowl of ice cream, slammed the door shut, and snapped the latch. More bizarre behavior.

While pretend cops on TV chased make-believe robbers, Bobby thought back to how Angie'd never acted like this when he'd first moved in. The harder he tried to concentrate on the police show, the more he pictured that pint of tequila, hidden in his Ford Escort trunk.

He turned the TV volume down and limped up to Angie's door. Not a peep inside. "Angie, could you and I have a little talk?"

The door flung open, and Angie screamed into his face, "Isn't there some bar where you could go and drink yourself shit-faced? After you've guzzled the booze you stole from me!"

"You mudwump whore!" he snapped back. "Painting your face like that!"

Angie stood stunned and then hissed through gnashed teeth, "You have no right." Bobby's rage was already relenting, when she slammed her door shut and locked it. Drawers banged and thumped.

"I didn't mean those words, Angie, honey," he said. "Somehow they just came out."

Inside he heard a loud bang, glass shattering, cursing in Spanish, fabric tearing, and then silence. "Angie?" he said. No response. "What's going on in there, honey?" More chilling stillness. Bobby feared what all the smart-ass twerp was capable of. Just think of his own dumb stunts at that age. He slammed a shoulder into the bedroom door, but it wouldn't budge. He backed up for a running start, charged as fast as he could move, and rammed it. Pain shot from his right shoulder down that arm to the elbow, but the door sprung open.

He found the window that'd always been stuck smashed, blood spattered beneath it along the wall and among the glass shards scattered on the floor. Meaning she'd cut herself really bad. He ran over to the broken window and yelled, "Angie!" A coyote yipped off in the darkness. What should he do? Call Jackie at the diner? And tell her what?

He stood there, massaging his throbbing shoulder, his thoughts swirling like dust devils. The scuffed suitcase was gone. So was the Victoria's Secret package, except for two pair of silky panties. He snatched those to dab up the blood. Why he did this, he couldn't rightly say.

Leaving his Escort where he'd parked it alongside the house, he set off on foot with a flashlight, stopping every so often to wipe up more scattered drops on the sidewalk. Which kept getting farther apart, like her bleeding was maybe slowing down. Or was it because she'd begun to run? On the outskirts of the development, he lost track of the trail, but still headed cross country. A quarter mile into the barrens, he began stepping from stone to stone so as not to leave footprints. When he reached firmer sand, he buried the soiled underwear and smoothed over the disturbed ground.

"What do you mean you don't remember when you last saw her?" Jackie screamed at him, when he finally got back after two a.m.

"She'll come home before long," he said in a pitiful attempt to console her. Words he didn't believe for a second.

"I seen how you been looking at Angie lately."

"You yourself said she was practically a grown woman," Bobby dared to respond.

"A high school sophomore? Who's not quite sixteen?"

"That's not why I was looking at her."

"Why the hell were you then?"

Bobby was wary of putting it into words, but he still did. "Because of her dark eyes. And dark hair. And dark skin. Because of her features so different from yours. Or mine."

"She takes after her Navajo father, you stupid bastard!" Jackie hollered.

That he knew full well, and that was the problem. "That's what I can't stop thinking about."

"Why the devil do you care so much about my ex? You never met the man. And now you never will."

"You mean he's dead?"

Jackie nodded. Bobby'd never asked because he couldn't stand to talk about the guy. Did he ever hate seeing the love of his life this miserable. "So where was your ex living?"

"Back where he grew up. On the Navajo reservation. Where folks accepted him for who he was. A mugwump, mudwump or whatever you call it, you bigot." Jackie bared her graying teeth. "Martin was one of the finest men I've ever met. But the two of us simply couldn't make a marriage work. Because I didn't fit in there. And he didn't fit in here. And poor Angie doesn't seem to fit in anywhere."

Bobby's shoulders slumped.

"You know why, Bobby? Because Angela's mixed race. You know, a half-breed. What people called it back when they were even more ignorant than now."

He bowed his head.

"If anything's happened to my darling daughter, I'd rather be dead." He reached for Jackie's hand to comfort his true love, but she slapped it away. "You damned lowlife! I should have known you was trouble when I first laid eyes on you! The way you was checking out other women."

Okay, Angie'd cut herself something terrible, but she still could've survived. But that wasn't what his gut was telling him. "I'm so sorry."

"Get the hell out of her, you bastard!"

So that was what he'd done for that night at least, sleeping inside his Ford Escort. First thing Friday morning, Jackie'd finally called the cops and reported her child missing. Meanwhile, he'd kept looking for the girl everywhere around their part of Phoenix without turning up a trace. Then yesterday afternoon the cops'd hauled his butt down to the station for that lie detector test and a grilling. And today he'd gotten out of bed at dawn, slipped out of the house, and driven till now he found himself on the very edge of a dangerous river. Though not for too much longer.

He cringed to think of all that blood spattered across Angie's bedroom. Could there be any doubt she was gone from this earth and her body laying someplace hidden? Why else hadn't she phoned Jackie by the time he'd left that morning? Just not how the kid treated her mother. And who was to blame? Robert Richard Daniels. Because he'd driven the girl into breaking that window and cutting herself so bad she bled out. And for this he could never forgive himself.

He set one foot and then the other into the stream. Which felt surprisingly cold, probably because some of it was snowmelt. He tossed his bulging wallet onto the bank beside the Stetson and then his coins. From another jeans pocket he removed the brochure that mudwump'd given him in the Kayenta Burger King. He browsed among its pages. Okay, some mudwumps'd served Uncle Sam honorably during World War Two. Okay, some'd helped the US defeat the Japanese. Okay, some'd been genuine patriots and even heroes.

Unlike Bobby Daniels, who'd never served Uncle Sam for one minute despite the lies about military service he'd told the Phoenix cops and others. He'd never graduated from high school either. Because he'd been no good at studying he'd always told himself. When the real problem was him never honestly trying. And he'd deserved that prison sentence back in Wisconsin too. What else after punching the state trooper who'd arrested him for drunken driving? Which he was also guilty of, as soused as he'd been getting behind the wheel. But then just about everything that'd gone wrong in his life'd been his own fault. No Native American, in any case, was to blame for even one bad thing that'd happened to him.

A few more steps and he was standing mid-calf in the Colorado and trembling from head to toe. It wasn't Angie's fault who her father'd been, was it? Since no person can choose their parents. He stared at the water and then his untanned upper arms. His skin wasn't really white, was it? More of a sickly pale pink. But then no white people were truly white except for albinos and a few other exceptions. And it didn't make a whole lot of sense for so many Americans to claim so-called whites'd settled this country first four centuries ago when Native Americans'd already been living here for many thousands of years.

So why'd he care so much that Angie was part Native American? Because it'd meant Jackie'd had sex with a Navajo, wasn't it? But what else when Martin'd been her husband? In other words, he'd been blaming the girl for something her mother'd done. Which Jackie'd had every right to do. His prejudice against Native Americans was like blaming the Colorado River for being a muddy brown. Here when that was a good thing because it meant the stream was carrying soil by the ton. Soil which plants use to grow and feed people.

Wobbling yet somehow not falling, Bobby moved farther out till the current came to his knees.

"Mister!" a young man cried out from up on the highway.

"Please don't!" a girlish voice shouted from even closer. "Take my hand!"

Bobby staggered in turning around, yet somehow kept his balance.

"Take it!" the girl screamed, whoever she might be.

Curious who on earth might care whether Bobby Daniels lived or died, he soon found himself staring into eyes black as coal and matching hair, high cheekbones, and skin the color of this river. A hand just as brown reached out toward him, while the other one grasped the outstretched arm of a stocky, blue-eyed, blond boy, standing behind her.

"Please, mister," the girl begged. Her Native American features were dark like poor Angie's and just as attractive. Yes, young Angela Begay was good looking Bobby finally admitted. He grasped this Navajo angel's warm, sinewy hand, and the Anglo boy, clutching her other hand, pulled all three to safety upon the bank.

There Bobby stood sopping wet and dripping. If these two youngsters were to marry, they'd sure have nice-looking kids. So what if she or anybody else in the world was colored? Pretty was pretty, just like a river was a river.

He gathered his Stetson hat, belt, wallet, coins, and brochure from the ground and followed the couple up to the road, where the boy dug a cell phone out of a navy blue backpack.

"Are you drunk, Bobby?" was the first thing Jackie said when he called her in Phoenix.

"Nope," he told her. "But I sure am thirsty."

"Where are you?"

"Outside Moab, Utah. Any news about Angie?" His voice cracked as he asked the question.

"She's ticked at you, Bobby," Jackie replied.

"Angie's ticked at me?" he whispered, as tears oozed from his eyes. Who cared if the girl hated him or even wanted him dead as long as she was alive and okay? Which he now was himself. Or at least was beginning to be. Thanks to these hitchhikers and the Colorado.

Jackie explained how the boy Angie'd run off with to Las Vegas had dumped her yesterday while leaving her enough money to catch a bus back to Phoenix this morning. She'd showed up at the house with a big bandage on a forearm but was otherwise fine.

Bobby both laughed and wept at this wonderful news.

"Are you okay, Mister?" the Navajo girl asked him.

Bobby cackled.

"Hello, Bob," a younger voice spoke over the phone.

"Hi, Angie," Bobby said, his heart thumping at the sound of the precious child's voice. Despite all the miles separating them, he saw her strong nose, high cheekbones, coal-black hair, sable eyes, angular mouth, and coffee-brown skin plain as day. Thanks to her Navajo father, bless the man's departed soul.

"I'm sorry, Angie," he said.

"I am too."

"Tell your mother I love her. Just like I do you, honey."

Silence on the other end till Angie replied, "I love you too, Bobby. And thank you for all the things you've done for me, like taking me places. And especially the driving lessons."

"Happy birthday!" he crowed, recalling today was her very special day. "Happy sweet sixteen!"

Bobby handed the cell back to the hitchhikers and marched toward his pickup in a joyous, teary trance. "Where you heading, Mister?" the young Navajo asked.

"To Phoenix."

"Could you give us a lift?"

"You betcha."

Communion

Pastor Eric Thorstad pulled up at the red light and stared across the river at the brick eyesore, towering over this rustic small town in the Coulee Region of west central Wisconsin. Six more long years before he'd be assigned a new congregation and then without any guarantee it'd lie anywhere near his hometown Minneapolis, so that he and Anna might enjoy a gourmet dinner out upon occasion. How was he ever going to endure the interim?

The Lutheran clergyman yawned. Why so tired since he had gotten his usual seven hours of sleep. But then he had felt out of sorts ever since the week's long run Saturday, when mid-course his legs had turned to lead and he'd had to finish the last three miles on sheer guts. But then his stamina often lagged recently, as if at only twenty-nine he had already gotten old, which of course was preposterous.

A gentle honk to his rear snapped Thorstad out of his reverie. Okay, okay, the traffic light had turned green. He gave the driver behind him a wave, edged his late-model Buick forward, and turned down the bridge. The dork back there in the John Deere cap had certainly been patient. A lot politer than he would have been himself if the roles had been reversed. At least of late.

Once across the river, he cruised up Main Street through the town's little shopping district toward that morning's destination.

Actually, his wife was the one who ought to be exhausted as much as she fussed over their four-year-old twins, Mary and Martha. But Anna had yet to admit feeling fatigue before bedtime.

He soon steered onto the blacktop beside the aging, three-story, red-brick structure he had eyed from the opposite bank. From the outside it looked like a vintage grade school, which is exactly what it once had been, just as this parking lot had served as its playground. The inscription beneath the eaves read 1871, which by Wisconsin standards made the building practically ancient.

He had to admire its high windows. Behind those, generations of the town's youngsters had sat and learned their three R's along with the virtues of diligence and citizenship. So in that sense it hadn't just been a cornerstone of the community, but its very foundation. But like everything else, over time the edifice had deteriorated, and a modern elementary school had taken its place toward the town outskirts.

Two years ago City Councilman Lars Ingeseth had proposed tearing this decrepit building down. At first Thorstad had backed the reasonable enough plan—till he learned that Ted Anderson, the town's Methodist minister and hence a major rival, coveted the resulting vacant lot as adjunct parking space just across the street from his own church. "Fat chance, bub," Thorstad had reacted. Not when Anderson's congregation was fast overtaking his own in numbers.

His other chief competitor, Father George Kozlowski, had suggested leaving the town's most prominent landmark in place and converting it into apartments for the local elderly. Instantly changing his mind, Thorstad had seconded the priest's better idea. "The Lord works in mysterious ways," as his grandfather, a Lutheran minister too, often said. He grinned at the memory of the dear ancestor's naiveté, since as a rational being he knew full well no higher power directly influenced human endeavors on earth. Not that religion, if correctly interpreted, was a sham. When going into the ministry, Thorstad had no inkling of the role politics would play. But after a clumsy beginning, he had learned to relish its subtleties as much as those of golf or tennis. Still, he somehow had to stanch the slow hemorrhaging of his congregation before the local Lutherans found themselves trailing both the Catholics and Methodists in size, potentially not only a public humiliation but also a blow to his career.

It was hard to believe he had already spent four years in this Wisconsin backwater, not near anything more interesting than sleepy La Crosse and Eau Claire, cities of around fifty thousand an hour's drive away. Why, his parishioners here actually took all the superstitions and rituals of antiquated Christianity literally. Many honestly believed the sacrament of the altar wasn't a mere symbolic act reenacted out of respect for church tradition, but only God knew what? No pun intended.

Thorstad suspected some of these Norskies, especially the old biddies, loved communion because it was their only chance in life for a little nip, even if it was merely Mogen David, arguably the worst wine in the world. As for the wafers, Thorstad had never put anything in his mouth closer in texture and taste to Styrofoam, and if he could avoid it, never would do so again.

Just because he had dithered and stewed over possible career choices before settling upon becoming a Lutheran minister didn't mean he deserved to end up in this hick town. Not that its residents weren't sweet and friendly. That had never been the problem. Not at all. Still, he wanted out of this place so badly, he would have even prayed for it, if only he had believed doing so might help. Not that he didn't believe a Supreme Being observed and judged our every word and deed. But this didn't mean that this deity intervened in earthly affairs. And without that, prayer served little purpose other than to comfort a person. But what about the claim Jesus Christ was God's Son?

Thorstad had never been convinced, not that he dismissed the possibility out of hand. Such doubts of course left him with no better than a partial Christian faith, an embarrassing state he shared with nobody, not even his beloved wife, and least of all his congregation.

Not that he didn't know much of the Bible by heart. In fact, no seminarian in his class could match his knowledge of scriptural text, especially the King James Version, which he considered the most beautiful book ever written in English. But then memorizing had always come easily to him.

Okay, enough stalling. Time to get these shut-in visitations over with. If he hustled through all thirteen of them here and bolted lunch, he just might make that two p.m. tee time at the golf course. The pastor grabbed his briefcase and climbed out. No need to lock his Buick, one nice advantage to living in so rural a location.

Upon opening the building's outside door, he hit a wall of stale, overheated air, reeking of ammonia and floor wax. Holding his breath, he scanned the directory on the wall for a name he recognized.

"Arndt, Leonard" wasn't in his congregation, but "Bergdahl, Gladys" was. He rang her number. No response, so he tried again. Why couldn't it be Wednesday, his day for visiting the local hospital? Hardly a picnic either, but still a cakewalk compared to all the stops here, since a number of patients there were bound to be too ill to speak for long or even at all.

The fifth time he pressed the button it finally buzzed back, and the inner door unlatched with a clack. Once all the way inside he marched straight to Mrs. Bergdahl's and gave the door several sharp raps.

Two minutes later a white-haired lady, leaning on a walker, opened it. "Oh, Pastor, it's you," Lydia Lundstrom greeted. "Gladys, Reverend Thorstad's here!"

"Oh, my, already?" a high-pitched voice responded from the opposite end of the studio apartment.

"And how are you today, Mrs. Lundstrom?" Thorstad asked.

"Lydia!" she snapped. "I told you to call me Lydia!"

"Yes, of course—Lydia," he said. Though it felt improper to be addressing a person half a century his senior by her first name.

It frustrated him to inch along behind her, while she worked her way one pokey step at a time, until he finally reached the eighty-four-year-old widow he had come to see. She tried to get up from the couch but couldn't, so she offered him a warm hand from where she lay on the couch. He shook it, saying, "And how are you feeling today, Mrs. Bergdahl?" At least she didn't mind how she was addressed.

"Uff da," she replied. *"Det gjør vondt."*

Thorstad feigned a sympathetic smile, as if he had understood the Norwegian words. Her scalp was showing through her thinning white hair, and her eyes were puffy and skin splotchy, yet oddly wrinkle-free. He cringed to contemplate decades more of ministering like this to the halt and the lame before he reached retirement age. "Are you feeling any pain?" he asked.

"What else does *vondt* mean?" Lydia snapped and plopped herself down into a wingback chair.

Mrs. Bergdahl smiled at him with disarmingly kind, milky-blue eyes. An old mantle clock atop the television whirred and struck out the hours. While he waited for it to reach nine and stop, he glanced away from Mrs. Lundstrom's varicose veins and stifled a yawn. This exhausted after only a ten-mile run Saturday? As a St. Olaf undergraduate and later in the St. Paul seminary, such distances hadn't fazed him.

"Reverend Thorstad," Gladys said, giving his title and surname both a Norwegian lilt. His own mother was too genteel to exude such warmth, not that her nurturing had in any way been lacking. "Please sit down."

He lowered himself into an empty easy chair. Yawning again through his closed mouth, he asked, "When was the last time you saw your doctor, Mrs. Bergdahl?"

"She goes the first Tuesday every month!" Lydia blurted. "Same as ever. Judy takes her."

"God bless her," Mrs. Bergdahl piped up.

"Indeed," the pastor said, an odd lump forming in his throat. Somehow he would have to maneuver Mrs. Lundstrom out of here so he could get his first shut-in communion over with and then move on. Unfortunately, this part of his ministry was closer to logistics than pastoral care. Giving the sacrament to the two ladies together was out of the question, since Lydia was a renegade Lutheran, who to spite him for some imagined slight had abandoned her family's lifelong church and joined his rival Anderson's Methodists.

Bending forward with a groan, Lydia flipped on the television, and blaring soap opera voices came on. "It's our show, Gladys!" she shouted.

"Maybe we could skip it today," Mrs. Bergdahl told her. "Being as how the pastor is here and all."

Keeping her eyes glued to the screen, Lydia said, "Let's hope dumb Helen finally wises up to her two-timing husband."

Mrs. Bergdahl met Thorstad's scowl with a serene smile.

"Is it loud enough, Gladys?" Lydia shouted.

"Maybe it's too loud," Gladys replied. No matter, Lydia left the volume right where it was. "You know, Helen and Peter aren't really married," Gladys explained to the minister. "And those aren't their real names. They're what you call 'actors.'" Pronouncing the word as if it came from a language more exotic than Tibetan. "The show is so dumb that."

"I beg your pardon?" he blurted.

"The show is so dumb that," she said, repeating the peculiar syntax. Somebody gave the apartment front door a sharp rap. "Helen, you simply have to trust me," a square-jawed man intoned on the flickering Zenith screen.

Three more loud knocks sent Lydia reaching for her walker and cursing under her breath. "No, no, Mrs. Lundstrom," Thorstad said a beat too late. "Let me get it."

Out in the hall he found a gangly, gray-haired, red-nosed, sixtyish man, grinning as if the practical joke you and he had planned together was coming off without a hitch. "I'm Floyd Brennan," the man said, offering a bony hand. "I hear Lydia's got a leak." With an Irish surname like that, he had to be one of Father Kozlowski's flock.

"Eric Thorstad," the pastor told him. With every new interruption like this his schedule was falling further behind.

"I'm the new manager here."

Thorstad caught a whiff of alcohol on the guy's breath. "And I'm the pastor of the local Lutheran Church." In that moment he sincerely doubted that he was going to last as a minister. But what else might he do for a living? Wasn't he young enough to switch careers? Perhaps not with a wife and two small kids to support.

"I know who you are," Brennan told him with a chuckle. Like an angel of mercy he led Lydia away.

The clergyman soon was seated near the television on a chair still warm from Mrs. Lundstrom and bracing himself against a booming voice extolling the miraculous cleansing power of a detergent. Reaching for the volume control, he asked Mrs. Bergdahl, "May I?" No answer. Because she was already dozing on her couch. Gnashing his teeth, he snapped off the blasted contraption. Instantly the apartment grew silent, except for the gentle snoring of this elderly shut-in and the ticking of her mantle clock. It was so peaceful in fact it was unnerving. The idea of playing golf after finishing up pastoral duties here was stupid, wasn't it? When what he really needed was a long nap. But at this rate it'd turn dark before he ever departed the building.

Having to deal with the old and feeble like this wasn't why he had gone into the ministry, not that he had found doing so difficult. But then this career had never been an unquestioned choice. Whatever he was eventually going to do for a living, already at the age of twelve he had made up his mind not to follow in his father's footsteps by becoming a physician, not when that was his older brother's plan. It had always been impossible to outshine Leif, so why try?

When his simple childhood faith had collapsed soon after confirmation at the age of fourteen, it had left a hole in his heart he sought to plug with his head. While classmates busied themselves after school chasing girls and playing sports, he retired to his room and devoured the novels of Fyodor Dostoyevsky and Leo Tolstoy, two writers relentless in their pursuit of life's great questions. Their boldness in asking thrilled by itself, even if their answers never completely satisfied.

After high school graduation, he attended his parents' alma mater, St. Olaf, in Northfield, Minnesota. When it came time during his sophomore year to declare a major, he chose philosophy, the subject he was most enjoying. Soon he was immersing himself in Hegel and the Positivists, but before long became disenchanted with their self-blinkered refusal to consider reality in its entirety. Then came Professor Mollenhauer's celebrated course on Søren Kierkegaard. The great Danish thinker's eloquent rebuttals of all attempts to reduce the world to nothing but the rationally explicable deeply impressed him, even if they failed to fully convince. That was when he realized he could never bring himself to believe in anything his intellect didn't first respect. Soon he was shying away from all leaps of faith and instead preferring to let logic and reason strive to bridge every gap, even if such efforts often failed.

In time, philosophy's willingness to constantly raise questions without always reaching conclusions frustrated him. Then this irritation turned to disgust. And so mid-junior year he found himself looking for a more suitable field. Since he had been enjoying German every semester, why not earn a degree in that? And so he indeed had.

As difficult as this decision had been, choosing a graduate program was even more difficult, until one September day his senior year he dropped by Dr. Mollenhauer's office. In his incisive manner, his most impressive professor had gotten straight to the point: "Eric, what questions interest you the most?"

He was silent a long time before replying, "What are we? Where are we? Why are we here?" That was all Mollenhauer needed to hear before suggesting divinity school. Since that choice coincided with the fondest hopes of Eric's mother, that was that. Of course he made it a Lutheran seminary to stay within the traditional family church as far back as records in Norway went.

There in his second semester, the formidable Dr. Huss had introduced him to the writings of Rudolf Bultmann, the great German theologian from the University of Marburg. Bultmann, like many intelligent, reasoning Christians, was unable to accept the New Testament at face value, while never doubting its divine inspiration. So the scholar had set out to peel away the layers of myth and legend until only the kernel of truth at its core remained. This so-called demythologizing not only assuaged Eric's skeptical intellect, but gave him a workable faith, even if narrowly conceived.

His pulse quickened to recall the lively seminar debates during divinity school over which parts of the Gospels were holy truth and which were not. No one had been more ruthless than he had in paring revelation down to the minimum, and never before or since had he felt more highly regarded by peers. Hence those years remained the most glorious of his life, compared to which his actual ministry was about as exciting as mowing grass. At least of late, though it certainly hadn't started out like that.

Memories of Dr. Huss 's forbidding posture and precise elocution brought a grin to his face. No professor ever had been more intimidating, though when he invited another favorite student and him over for dinner, a little wine turned the guy into a smarmy teddy bear. When Thorstad chuckled at the memory, Mrs. Bergdahl coughed, but didn't awaken.

Even in her sleep this sweet parishioner had a beatific smile. And though far from tall, she still was a big woman, half again his own weight with a full, round face. That at eighty-four years of age her skin was still this smooth was uncanny. She must have truly led a carefree life. But hadn't somebody told him her husband had dropped dead decades ago? Or was that another member of his congregation?

All of a sudden pain stabbed his calf and he jackknifed double to massage the knotted muscle. A charley horse after all his conditioning? But there it was. When the spasms finally relented, he reached down and felt the throw rug beneath his wingtips. It truly was tied together from old nylons and rags. He bet Gladys had woven it herself, just as she had made the patchwork quilt resting under her head. Such frugality was touching in a quaint way. Once he had seen a photo in a magazine of how it was done. Two-by-four boards were propped up atop chairs and tied together into a square, while women sat around the outside, chatting and merrily working away. A quilting bee, they called it. From a long gone way of life. No jogging those days, no tennis, no golf, not anywhere near this neck of the woods.

His gaze came to rest upon Gladys's hands clasped over her ample stomach. The chafed, stubby fingers hinted at hardships her unlined face concealed. So maybe she had hit a few bumps along the road after all.

The wall behind her was decorated with religious kitsch, dominated by a portrait of a walnut-haired, azure-eyed Christ, as if Jesus had been Nordic, when he probably had looked more like the Palestinian leader Yassar Arafat. Alongside it hung three pairs of folded hands made of plaster of Paris, and what had to be the Lord's Prayer in Norwegian. Though Thorstad could read the Bible in the original Hebrew, Aramaic, and Greek, and Bultmann in German, he couldn't read this plaque despite his Norwegian ancestry. The language was just too minor to bother acquiring.

On the far wall hung a dark, grainy photograph under a cracked glass. He got up and took a closer look. Black scratches and splotches obscured a lanky boy of about sixteen and a little, pig-tailed girl of perhaps twelve, holding a baby.

The phone rang, and Gladys's eyes popped open. Still supine, she fumbled behind her head till she grasped the receiver. "Hello," she greeted, putting a Norwegian lilt even into that short a word. "Oh, Lillian, it's you! *Tusend takk* for calling! I was just visiting with my first-born, John Irwin. He's so happy that."

Didn't she realize he was still there?

"Oh, I'm pretty good," she went on. "My heart skips sometimes, you know, and I get so played out I can't hardly get up. But how are you?" Thorstad kept standing frozen in place. "Now, Lillian, you ask the Lord to help you accept Elmer's suffering. There's a good reason for it. It's not for us to understand." Mrs. Bergdahl switched into a soft, melodious Norwegian, one so full of sympathy and concern that the pastor's eyes teared up. The only word he understood was the repeated

Herre, meaning "Lord." It had been bullheaded of him never to have learned this language of his ancestors, hadn't it? "I'll remember you both in my prayers," Gladys said in English and hung up.

The pastor cleared his throat and stepped into view. "Now Mrs. Bergdahl, as you know, the reason I came here today"—a knock on the door interrupted. Gladys's warm, blue eyes met his, and without a word he hurried to answer it.

"Pastor Thorstad!" Judy Melby greeted, panting from a bulging grocery bag that she was carrying. The forty-year-old woman, her husband, and two children belonged to his congregation, though it had been months since he had last seen them in church.

"Hello there, Judy," he brittlely replied. Moments too late it occurred to him to take the bag from her. When he brought it into the kitchenette, Gladys was waiting on her feet, clutching an aluminum walker.

Flushing with discomfiture, he began unloading the groceries onto the counter. "The bananas and pears go in the fruit bowl," Mrs. Bergdahl gently directed. He sighed with relief, when Judy returned with a second sack and took over. "How's little Emily doing, Judy?" Gladys asked her helper.

"The fever broke real sudden like last night," Judy replied, grinning through misty eyes.

"Thank God," Gladys said. Those words that rolled easily off people's tongues had seldom sounded less idly uttered. "Now Judy, you and Helmer be sure to pray for Elmer Jacobson. From what Lydia says, he's nearly gone."

The pastor was feeling such an ache in his cheekbones and nostrils that he sat down, took off his glasses, and rubbed his sinuses. And that's where he was still sitting when the apartment door clicked shut, and the slow thump of Mrs. Bergdahl's walker approached. "Are you all right, Pastor Thorstad?"

He slipped his smudged glasses back on, cleared his throat, and assumed a brave smile. "Sure, I'm okay. Just a bit tired is all."

"Do you sleep good nights?"

"Yeah." Pronounced on the inhale, like his grandfather did it. "But then I get up quite early."

"It's not easy raising kids."

Thorstad nodded. He bet it wasn't—for his wife, since he had turned the entire responsibility for rearing their two daughters over to Anna. "Are those relatives of yours in that photograph?"

Gladys's smile widened an extra notch. "That's my boys and my girl."

"You have sons?" Nobody had ever mentioned them.

"Yeah," she answered. "John Irwin and Richard Leroy. I had pneumonia when I was carrying John, and he died before he was ten months. That's how it went with blue babies those days. Richard passed away at home twenty-five years ago. Back when we were still living in the Grove. The next summer my husband, Teddy, passed away, too."

That terse explanation left Thorstad's jaw hanging. All that heartache described in such a blissful tone, as if she weren't in her right mind. But she sounded clear as a bell. And what was that about talking to John Irwin a few minutes ago?

"What about your daughter?"

"Mary Alice is married to a mailman in Corpus Christi. That's in Texas." The name of the state pronounced, as if it were as exotic as Timbuktu. "They don't get back here more than once every three or four years."

Thorstad looked Mrs. Bergdahl square in the face. Her joyful smile and sparkling eyes with her history of family tragedy gave him a shiver. As if she had lost touch with reality. But that wasn't it at all, was it? "I'm so sorry," he muttered.

"Pardon?" Mrs. Bergdahl said. Her gnarled hands gripped the walker, and she thumped it along to the couch and plopped back down there with a soft moan.

He flipped up his immaculate palms. If his inane words made even him cringe, how must they sound to her? Or for that matter to the rest of his congregation during his perfunctory sermons?

"Mary Alice was lucky to find herself such a fine Christian man," Gladys told him. "Some women don't, you know."

The pastor cleared his throat. "So Mrs. Melby brings you groceries?" He winced at yet another stupid remark from him. He didn't use to be this trite. What changed?

"Yeah. And she cleans and cooks and helps me out in every other way I need. Judy's a good Christian."

"She's not that great about attending church, however," Thorstad said. Or honoring her pledges, he might have added.

Mrs. Bergdahl gave the pastor a beatific smile that cut him to the quick. "You know her husband left her last fall," she said. "They couldn't get along anymore after he lost his job."

Flushing with embarrassment, Reverend Thorstad kept his tactless mouth shut.

"Judy means well. Every day I pray for her and her kids and her husband. Because now she's got it almost as tough as Floyd."

"You mean the drunk who manages this place?"

Gladys's radiant smile didn't dim one whit. "He never drank before the Air Force told him his son was no longer missing. They finally found Archie's bones over in Vietnam. Floyd means well too, the same as Lydia. She won't be grumpy like this tomorrow. Today's the anniversary of her husband Derwood's death. She hasn't had it easy either."

The pastor was surprised to find his hands folded as if in prayer. A jolly fellow student at the seminary in St. Paul sometimes spoke of angels without wings, walking the earth and carrying out the Lord's work. Might he this very moment be in the presence of just such a remarkable person—in the unlikely guise of a poorly educated, elderly shut-in? The longer he spent here the more he sensed something very special about this parishioner. Her joyous smile despite all the pain suffered during her long life stirred something deep inside him. Is this what genuine faith can do for a true believer?

"Lydia misses being a member of our church," Gladys went on. "She'd like her funeral to be the same place where she got confirmed. But she's not going to ask you about it. You have to ask her."

"Mrs. Bergdahl," the pastor said, "what about you? What about your life?"

Gladys took her time before replying. "Sometimes I get kind of sad, when I think about the olden days over home. There was twelve of us kids, you know, and I was the oldest girl. All of us older kids had to help with the washing and cleaning and cooking and taking care of the little ones. When I turned fourteen, Pa got me a job as housekeeper with the Bahnub family the other side of Taylor, so I went to live with that them and do chores. The only pay was room and board. A couple years later I moved on to the Overliens and did the same thing. Only they paid me a couple of dollars a month too."

"But what about school?"

"There wasn't time for schooling once I turned ten."

"Two dollars a month?"

"Yeah. Then I met Theodore and it was love at first sight. Pa and my brothers didn't like him much, but Ma told them if Gladys and Teddy love each other, you'd better not stand in their way. There wasn't any money for a church wedding, so he drove us to Winona, Minnesota in his Model A, and we eloped. It was the Depression those days, you know, and everybody was poor." She was smiling through glistening eyes. "Maybe we had less money than other folks. Maybe we had more sickness. But one thing we always had plenty of was the Lord's blessings."

"But—but you had it so rough."

At those words Gladys's lips narrowed to a tiny slit, splotches of red popped out on her face, her chest heaved, and air whistled through her nose.

"Mrs. Bergdahl?"

She mumbled something in Norwegian that sounded more earthy than scriptural. Her tone close to a snarl, she said, "*Nei*, it's not for us to question God's will."

Chills went up and down the pastor's spine, and hair stood on the back of his neck. As frail and bloated as Gladys now was, as weak as she probably always had been physically compared to him, she was tougher inside than he could even imagine. Despite all his exercise, all his fitness, all his health foods, he could never have endured a tenth of the hardship and suffering that she had overcome. He squeezed his intertwined fingers more tightly together. But then it wasn't toughness on her part at all, was it? He felt a nearly overwhelming urge to weep, but controlled himself.

"Reverend Thorstad, will you give me communion now?" Mrs. Bergdahl asked, her tone tentative and humble, as if he just might refuse.

"Certainly," he whispered, at last getting to the purpose of this visit. He grabbed his briefcase and pushed its two buttons, but they refused to unsnap. Her sudden grave tone unnerved him, as if she were about to draw her last breath. He pressed harder, but the snaps still wouldn't budge. Finally, in exasperation he let go, and the briefcase popped open.

He removed the vestments and carefully laid them around his neck. Mrs. Bergdahl struggled to rise from the couch. "I don't think I can get up," she said. "My back hurts so that."

"Please stay where you are then, Mrs. Bergdahl."

His right hand grasped the well-worn Bible his parents had given him on his tenth birthday, and he got down upon his knees on the throw rug beside her and closed his eyes. He felt her warm hand rest upon his shoulder and took comfort in it. And as this remarkable woman held on to him, he sensed powerful energy rising from deep inside his being and spreading throughout his mortal body to his fingertips and toes, thereby genuinely experiencing the Holy Spirit—for the very first time ever.

Verses from the Book of Matthew came to mind as if flowing from a spring of living water. *"Blessed are the poor in spirit: for theirs is the kingdom of heaven. Blessed are they that mourn: for they shall be comforted. Blessed are the meek: for they shall inherit the earth."* One by one the beatitudes of Christ's immortal Sermon on the Mount filled his heart and soul. And from this moment hence the no longer skeptical pastor recognized now and forever more that no one but the Son of God Himself had expressed these eternal truths.

Of course God intervenes in earthly affairs—how dumb to have questioned that—and not just through believers inspired by their faith to do good works. Because what intervention was greater than the key event in the entirety of human history—Christ's sacrifice on the cross to save believing sinners. *"For God so loved the world, that he gave His only begotten Son, that whosoever believeth in Him should not perish, but have everlasting life,"* as John had so beautifully summarized it in his Gospel.

"Reverend?" this wise parishioner said.

Okay, on to the Sacrament of the Altar. Only Thorstad had trouble getting started. He took one deep breath and then another to calm himself, before reciting the most profound text in the entire Lutheran liturgy, words he had learned by heart already as a youngster: *"Almighty God, our Maker and Redeemer, we poor sinners confess unto Thee, that we are by nature sinful and unclean, and that we have sinned against Thee, by thought, word, and deed. Wherefore we flee for refuge to Thine infinite mercy, seeking and imploring Thy grace, for the sake of our Lord Jesus Christ."*

"I confess," Gladys echoed and halted.

He opened his eyes to make sure she was all right. Their misty gazes met, and she nodded. After which he proceeded to recite from Paul's First Epistle to the Corinthians, *"Our Lord Jesus Christ, in the night in which He was betrayed, took bread; and when he had given thanks, He broke it and gave it to His disciples, saying, Take, eat; this is my body which is given for you; this do in remembrance of Me."* The pastor took a deep breath before continuing, *"After the same manner also He took the cup, when He had supped, and when He had given thanks, He gave it to them saying, Drink ye all of it; this cup is the new testament in My Blood, which is shed for you, and for many, for the remission of sins; this do, as oft as ye drink of it, in remembrance of Me."*

"Amen," she said.

The pastor's trembling fingers reached into the rustling package inside his pocket and grasped a round, thin wafer. "This is My Body, which is given for you," he said and placed this host on her eager tongue. He paused while she chewed and swallowed. "This is My Blood, which is shed for you," he then added, poured a shot of red wine into a thick one-ounce glass and brought that to this blessed parishioner's thirsty lips and helped her down it to the last drop.

Still kneeling, he took back the empty glass from Gladys, who folded her stubby fingers, pressed her chin into her chest, and in a clear, resonant voice recited the Lord's prayer in Norwegian, her native language. After she had finished, he said, "Amen," reached for a second wafer, placed that precious morsel on his own tongue, and also devoured the body of our

Savior in spirit. Then he poured himself a shot of wine and also drank—lest he should drop dead on the spot with his many, many sins unforgiven.

Fugue

Mark Prentice is a bastard.

All men are bastards. Mark Prentice is a man. Therefore, Mark Prentice is a bastard. I used to think he was a human being.

Bruce Ripkin is a bigger bastard. He's head of the School Board. He's on the City Council. He's my ex-husband's lawyer. His divorce settlement screwed me over bad. But now he's screwing me over even worse. I used to think he was a human being.

Gary Johnston is the biggest bastard. He used to be my husband. He used to be my lover. He used to be a father to my son. But he gave that all up for good to become a drunken lout. I used to think he was a human being.

All men are bastards. Big, bigger, biggest. That is the only question. Get used to it.

My son Matthew is a boy. My son Matthew is a human being. One day my son Matthew will be a man. My son Matthew is not a bastard, but one day he will be I'm afraid.

I used to think Mark Prentice was different. He and I used to be the best of friends. Last Monday he calls me up like he used to every other day. He says, Kate, how about another lunch? Just like old times?

Another lunch? Like we'd been getting together all along? Like nothing had happened in between? Like we'd stayed best friends? *Another* lunch? After five years without a word?

I show up at D.K.'s exactly on time. No sign of him. I grab the last booth. I order coffee. He doesn't come. I get a refill. I twiddle my thumbs.

Finally Mark strolls in. Finally. Only forty minutes late. Only. Just like old times.

He slides into the booth. So how you doin', Kate? he says. And he winks and he smiles. No apology at all. None. Nada. Zero. Zilch. So how you doin', Kate? he says. Like he hasn't seen me in a week. Not even a hint of an apology.

And he keeps on smiling. And then he starts sneaking peeks. All around my face. Like I was a Michelangelo in a museum. But I have forehead wrinkles. I have crow's feet. I have laugh lines. A Michelangelo is a statue. I am a woman. A woman is not a statue. Therefore, I am not a Michelangelo.

He grins. He winks. He keeps sneaking peaks. Like my wrinkles are the biggest news in years. He chuckles. You're looking good, Kate, he says. The liar.

He looks good. I don't. *Another* lunch? After five years of fighting to keep the house? After five years of raising Matthew all by myself? After five years without a word? I don't look good. Not any more. Not after five years of lonely hell.

He smiles. He chuckles. Cat got your tongue? he says. He stares. Does the bastard actually expect me to look the same?

Say something, he says.

Something, I say.

He chuckles. He shrugs. He sneaks another peek. Really, you look nice, he says. The liar.

I look nice? Some compliment. Kind of modest. Kind of meager. Kind of pathetic compared to saying I was the most beautiful woman he'd ever met. Like he always did before.

I glare. I grind. I gnash.

He grins. Are you mad at me or something? he says.

Or something, I say.

He laughs out loud. He says, I mean it's not like I could have done anything to hurt you, since I haven't even seen you in what—my goodness—it must be five years.

Right, asshole. Rub it in.

He smiles. He stares. He says, sounding merry and nonchalant, I'm sure you heard I finally found that good woman I was looking for. And you know, ever since, everything in my life has fallen into place.

Right, merry, nonchalant asshole. Rub it in.

Mark Prentice is an asshole. Bruce Ripkin is a bigger asshole. Gary Johnston is the biggest asshole. Or is it the other way around? Big, bigger, biggest. That is the only question. Get used to it.

He smiles. He stares. He says, Ellen and I will have to invite you over. You won't believe how she's fixed the place up. And she's a big jogger. Just like you.

Just like me. Right, bastard, asshole. Rub it in.

He grins. He says, So, Kate, you been dating anybody since your divorce? Just like the liar really cares. He stares. At my forehead wrinkles. At my crow's feet. At my laugh lines. Like I was a Michelangelo in a museum.

I don't have time to date, I say. I've got a fulltime job. I've got a son to raise. And I've got a house to keep up.

He chuckles. He says, Isn't Matthew old enough to take care of himself yet? What is he now, fifteen?

I glare. I grind. I gnash. Sixteen! I say. My son! My house!

He laughs, sounding merry and nonchalant.

Mark Prentice is a prick. Bruce Ripkin is a bigger prick. Gary Johnston is the biggest prick. Or is it the other way around? Big, bigger, biggest. That is the only question. Get used to it.

He gives me a grin. He sneaks another peek. He says, Hey, Kate, it's okay not to date. But it'd be a snap for a woman like you to find somebody else.

I glare. I grind. I gnash. Why'd I ever think Mark Prentice was any different from the others?

Honestly, he says, it'd be a breeze.

Honestly, he lies. Honestly, he sneaks a peek. Like I was still beautiful. He smiles. Like this is just another lunch. Like we had stayed best friends. *Another* lunch?

You know, he says, I've been wondering if you'd like to meet my new colleague. His name is Tom Davis. He just got divorced. He's tall, dark, and handsome. And a whole lot of fun. What's not to like?

Me like a bastard, asshole, and prick? I glare. I grind. I gnash.

What if I have Tom give you a call? he says. Just like the liar really cares.

I already know all I need to know about this Tom Davis. Because all men are bastards, assholes, and pricks. Tom Davis is a man. Therefore, Tom Davis is a bastard, asshole, and prick.

He smiles. He says, Now, Kate, this is going to sound strange, but I'm getting this distinct impression I've offended you somehow.

Right, bastard, asshole, prick. Rub it in.

He stops grinning. He stops sneaking peeks. He says, Now, Kate, are you going to talk to me or what? If not, why did you agree to another lunch?

Another lunch? I glare. I grind. I gnash.

He frowns. He folds his arms. He says, Speak up, Kate. What's on your mind?

I say, All men are bastards, assholes, and pricks.

He laughs, sounding merry and nonchalant. He says, All men? You're not being rational.

Mark Prentice is. Gary Johnston is. Bruce Ripkin is. Tom Davis is. Because all men are. Because all men are men. I'm being perfectly rational. Big, bigger, biggest. That is the only question. Get used to it.

He furrows his brow like I'm not making any sense. Like he doesn't mind getting wrinkles. Like the liar really cares.

You know, Kate, he says, you're not making any sense.

I say, My ex and his lawyer are taking away my son. And now I have to put the house up for sale. My son! My house!

He blinks.

Were we not best friends? I say.

He shrugs. He frowns. We were, he says.

Were we not closer than best friends? I say.

He shrugs. He frowns. We were, he says.

Were we not affectionate friends? I say.

He sighs. He frowns. We were, he says.

Did we not avow our love? I say.

He sighs. He frowns. He looks away.

Did we not make plans? I say.

He frowns. He folds his hands. He looks down.

I glare. I grind. I gnash. I scream, Mark Prentice, you're a bastard! And an asshole! And a prick! You avowed your love! And then you backed out!

He makes a face like he's worried about me. He says, You know, Kate, I'm worried about you.

I shout, Bastard! Asshole! Prick! My son! My house!

He shakes his head like I'm out of touch with reality. You know, Kate, he says, you sound out of touch with reality. Sure, we were close friends. And affectionate friends. But.

Close friends? Affectionate friends? But? Close, yes. Affectionate, yes. Friends, yes. And so much, much more. We phoned. We talked. We teased. We hugged. Again and again and again. We never wanted to let go. Our hearts were in tune. *Our* hearts. Ours, ours, ours!

He shakes his head.

Liar, liar, liar. Big, bigger, biggest. That is the only question. Get used to it.

You know, he says. And he stops. I don't know, he means. You know, he begins again. I don't know, he means.

Liar, liar, liar. Bastard, asshole, prick. Punch him, kick him, smash him! Get used to it! I shriek.

He makes a face. Are you okay, Kate? he says. Just like he really cares.

Bastard! Asshole! Prick! I shriek. Liar, liar, liar! My son! My house! Punch, kick, smash! Get used to it!

The waitress rushes over, the child-woman, without one wrinkle, without one crow's foot, without one laugh line. Not yet. Is something wrong? she says.

He gives her a grin. He sneaks a peek. No, he says.

She says, sounding merry and nonchalant, Will there be anything else?

He gives her a little wink.

I shout, Bastards, assholes, pricks! Mark Prentice is! Gary Johnston is! Bruce Ripkin is! Tom Davis is! Because all men are! Because all men are men! I'm being perfectly rational! Big, bigger, biggest! That is the only question! Get used to it!

She gives me a little wink.

Fifty-fifty

What won't a man do to win a woman he can't live without? How close can he come to the edge of a cliff and not fall off? When does murder become no crime at all? So many questions, so few answers—as yet.

A guy's gotta do what a guy's gotta do, my neighbor tells me. You are who you are and you ain't who you ain't, another friend advises as well. But how could I be the same dorky Dave Schroeder in South Milwaukee, pitching Little League baseball? Or the middle-aged desperado breaking into a house? Thank goodness I remember everything that ever happened to me. What I've lacked in intelligence, I've more than made up with memory.

I just fed the six-legged black beasties living in my desk drawer another sugar cube and left a plate of mints out for the shyer insects lurking in the basement. Go to the ant, thou sluggard—or, for that matter, to the bee or wasp. None of us know where we shall encounter our pricks of inspiration, our stings of motivation, our points of light illuminating the way. The wise man sees the spirit made flesh wherever his gaze happens to rest.

Larva, pupa, imago. Heel, hermit, socialite. The woolly worm roams the cracked driveways under the cooling fall sun, dreaming of the summer nights when it will flit about in the moonlight as a tiger moth. The cycle continues without end for us as well as our segmented kin. Without my precious little friends, I wouldn't have survived the past two years. Though I haven't managed to grow feelers, my once pathetically thin skin has finally thickened into a veritable exoskeleton.

The past can be a nightmare from which we awaken to sleepwalk till our dreams end once and for all. A wiser man than I said suffering ceases to be pain once we form a precise picture of it. No mystery was ever unearthed without first scratching the surface—or sharpening a pencil and scribbling it dull again and again.

"What then is language?" I hear myself recite without a glance at my notes, crinkling on the lectern like so many November leaves. "The modulated flow of consonants and vowels," I reply with a smile. Linguistics lectures become rote when repeated every school year here at tiny Calypso State in Appalachian Ohio. Actually, my specialty is phonetics, the discipline's least respected and most obscure branch. In front of every class, my lips and tongue caress the stream of air resonating past my humming Adam's apple, as if giving my words the most soulful kisses. Let their written representations relate my tale of woe, wending its way relentlessly toward bliss.

I'm all right now. I mean, really. Glenn says so, and Sonia and Eric agree. But for a while there I most definitely was out of whack. But now I'm back to being as rational as ever.

Did you ever hear of a dinner party ending like a train wreck? One did at our house on Memorial Day weekend of 1989, the same year broccoli's implacable foe, George Kennebunkport Bush took over the White House from Ronald Bedtime-for-Bonzo Reagan, and the Iron Curtain was lifted in Europe to stay, and China's Democracy Movement perished in a fusillade of bullets on Tiananmen Square.

Just after lunch that Friday the phone rang in my campus office. "You got it, Schroeder," Dean Birch told me tersely and hung up. The Dean of Arts and Sciences had approved my tenure? Finally. After six tense, long years of probation. Whoopee! I jumped up and slapped the ceiling for joy. No more flooding the nation with résumés only to win at best another temporary reprieve. No more opening my mailbox with trepidation for fear of further rejection. No more job hunting again. Because at the ripe age of forty-two, Dave Schroeder's gypsy scholardom had ended for good. Would I ever have a better cause for rejoicing and revelry?

Three quick phone calls and a soirée was arranged for that night at our place. I buzzed my wife to relay the fantastic news. "We have to talk, David," she told me.

"Ruth, I did it! They gave me tenure! We won't have to move!"

"Great," she muttered as if I'd told her about unplugging a sluggish drain. "Could you meet me right now?"

"Honey, I have two more classes to teach. And then my office hour. Ruth, did you hear what I just said? I. Got. Tenure. We are set. For life."

"David, what I have to discuss can't wait."

The bell signaling the start of another class rang out in the hall. I told my better half I'd hurry home as soon as I could, though she shouldn't expect me before late afternoon. And I said that I'd invited our old gang over that evening for dinner. Meaning the Goughs, the Tischlers, and Skip with yet another mystery date. Maybe it wasn't our turn to host but who had a better reason to celebrate?

"No way!" Ruth snapped. "Not tonight."

"But—but," I stammered. "Okay, honey, we'll have that talk first thing when I get home."

As soon as I hung up, I realized that landing this permanent job meant Ruth and I could have that baby we'd been wanting—finally! If we had to phone in pizza to feed our guests that evening, who honestly cared?

I was just locking up my office when it hit me what Ruth might want to discuss. Could she already be pregnant? Just last week she had mentioned her period being late, and so maybe she was shying away from a party because expectant mothers shouldn't of course drink. If it'd make her feel any better, I'd hop on the wagon for the duration, too. Hey, now we truly deserved a soirée. I marched off to phonetics class that proceeded with uncommon glee. To finish the period's instruction with a rousing flourish, I asked my rowdy students, "How many vowels are there in English?" A favorite trick question.

Nothing but smirks and rolling eyes in response. Until one game youngster ventured, "Five. Namely, A, E, I, O, and U." His too obvious answer elicited groans and smirks.

"You're correct, Brian, that there are five vowel *letters*," I told him with a wry smile. "But I meant how many different vowel *sounds*."

Now only dumbfounded gawks and evasive stares.

I precisely enunciated, "Who would know aught of art must learn, act, and then take his ease." Which I explained were all words of one syllable apiece, each with its own unique vowel sound—for a grand sum of fourteen. Diphthongs of course excepted.

My audience acted duly impressed. A few students even clapped.

After the bell rang, I raced to the departmental lounge to join two dear faculty colleagues for a cappuccino—in honor of my promotion to associate professor. Not that my wife was missing anything here, since Ruth never could abide the company of eggheads. Not that I was one myself, not as an intellectual jack of all trades, master of none.

For my three o'clock History of Language course, I delivered a brisk talk on how a mongrel mix of Celts, Romans, Saxons, Angles, Jutes, Vikings, and Normans had developed a bastard

Low German dialect over centuries into the glory that is today's English. Not that I presume to wield it so ably as some, but still better than many. Well, at least my bright-eyed kids relished my presentation. Or my students I should say. I call them my kids since Ruth and I still had no children of our own.

After an uncommonly busy late afternoon office hour, I moseyed across campus, for once barely minding the oppressive southeastern Ohio swelter, long since returned to linger till fall. I not only reciprocated each and every passing student's friendly grin or greeting, but, at the intersection of Court and Union Streets even winked at a fetching coed, who smiled back. Life was indeed sweet.

Soon I was hiking up the narrow brick thoroughfares of hilly college town Calypso toward Buckeye Street. One last corner and there it stood, perched atop a ridge, the white American Four Square that Ruth and I called home. If Ohio wasn't Wisconsin, the state where I was born and bred and still felt attached, here we shared a good life that a child would only complete.

On the breakfast nook table in our glistening, newly redone kitchen, I found booze, mix, limes, glasses, and a paring knife neatly arrayed. And eight places immaculately set at our antique mahogany dining room table. Could there be any doubt? The impractical phonetician, Dave Schroeder, had married a master of logistics in Ruth McDaniel. The woman had kicked into gear once I announced our impromptu soirée. But then she'd been hanging out at home of late, sewing and moping, ever since the restaurant she'd helped run had gone belly up.

"Why didn't you get the air conditioning fixed?" a note scrawled in Ruth's loopy script read on our upstairs bathroom vanity. I chuckled. God knows I'd tried, but I couldn't get a soul to come look at the contraption before the long holiday weekend.

I tossed my sweaty shirt and slacks into the hamper and slid in beside my beloved spouse, napping in bra and panties atop our king-sized bed. One good look at her long legs and curvaceous behind sprawled so invitingly, and I ached for more baby-making on the spot, even if I'd already succeeded. Not that I would ever interrupt my wife's sleep. Like me, Ruth needed the rest to be at her best that night. Which explained in part why no couple in the county made better guests or hosts—or so our friends attested. Though one-on-one I had to admit she and I had been having a few squabbles.

I had no sooner dozed off despite the whine of a hornet probing a bedroom window screen for a breach than a shrill buzzing rudely jarred me out of a lustful dream. "Shut that darned thing off," Ruth mumbled into my ear. I peeled my cheek off the damp sheet and reached for my wife's tempting thigh, but she pushed me away. The buzzing persisted like a dentist's drill. "Turn that fricking thing off I said!" The bed jiggled as she shifted her weight. I stretched and poked the alarm button in.

The late May air felt stickier than ever. Lying there soaked in sweat, I cursed our broken central air conditioner under my breath. After sitting idle throughout another rainy, occasionally snowy, slushy, even icy, southern Ohio winter, it had worked fine that spring till quitting on us just that week.

"It's half past six," Ruth muttered, yet neither of us moved. Already since my departure from campus, my nostrils had swollen themselves shut and my sinuses ached. Sensing a yearning my sexy dream had only whetted, I grasped my wife's knee.

"Stop that," she snapped, slapping my hand away.

"But, honey."

"David, get up. We have to get ready for your guests."

"Our guests, you mean."

"Up, up," Ruth said, springing out of bed. "It really takes some gall on your part to expect me to do so much work just to entertain *your* friends."

"Since when aren't they your friends, too, honey?" I replied in my most conciliatory tone, ogling my wife's willowy five-foot-ten-inch frame. So our marriage wasn't ideal? So we'd been having a few spats? Once our baby showed up, I bet we'd be laughing about these petty quarrels. I wrapped the pillow around my head to sleep a bit longer.

I was just dozing off again when I jerked upright with a scream from a shock to my genitals. "That should cool you down," Ruth teased, towering over me with a bitter smirk. "Your coffee's in the john beside your Irish on the rocks."

I gingerly reached inside my underpants, pulled out the offending ice cubes, and eyed her own glass of brandy, already half gone. "You know, Ruthie," I said, "you really shouldn't be drinking."

Her milky blue eyes narrowed.

"I meant not now."

She took a hearty swig. "But we always have a stiff one before parties."

"Sure, but in your current condition?"

"Which is what?" She downed the rest of her drink, flipped on the vacuum cleaner, and attacked the already immaculate upstairs landing.

I moped to the john, washed the offending cubes off under the sink faucet, and added them to the highball awaiting me. "Because alcohol might harm a baby on the way!" I hollered to make myself heard.

The irksome whine of the appliance abruptly quit, and my gaze met her glower. "I'm not pregnant, thank God," she told me.

At that, my joy shrank by half. "But we could have a baby now," I muttered. "Since Calypso State just granted me job security for life."

With a snarl Ruth resumed sucking up dust that wasn't there. "So what did you want to talk to me about?" I yelled over the din of the blasted vacuum. If I had made such a stupid guess.

Again, the infernal noise ceased. "Why didn't you get the lawn mowed?" she said. "Our yard looks like a hay field. Here when you don't even have a full-time job."

At that jibe my temper flashed, but like a hammer striking a dud round didn't ignite. At least I was bringing in a steady income, but knew better than to voice that. I took a big swallow of my mellow Jameson's. "Are you trying to get my goat?" Like she was working herself up to some painful announcement. The only way Ruth could ever act tough was to get ticked off first.

"'Are you trying to get my goat?'" she mimicked. "Sometimes you sound just like your mousy father."

My temper again sparked but still didn't detonate. "You sure know how to hurt a guy sometimes."

"Bullshit. You're the expert at hitting below the belt. What really pisses me off is how you get away with your oh-so-innocent act."

Here we go again? No, here we don't. Because no matter how hard Ruth might try, this time I refused to fight. Not that I didn't feel sorely provoked. "The mower boy's been sick," I lamely explained. "As for me, I've been too busy."

"Doing what? Reciting A, E, I, O, U?"

I forced a chuckle. Did I really care that my wife didn't respect my work? Me, I was darned proud of my linguistics career. Okay, maybe I wasn't much of a scholar, but I sure could teach. Well, if I wasn't exactly a master teacher, I was at least a solid journeyman. How about the fine job I'd done in class that very day? Might it be the oppressive swelter souring my beloved's mood? Though she'd been oddly edgy like this for weeks.

"Why'd you have to go and invite that marriage wrecker Christine tonight?" Ruth asked, her face flushing a lurid crimson.

"We could hardly have a dinner party right next door to the Goughs and not invite them? It'd hurt their feelings."

"What about *my* feelings?"

"Ruthie, be rational."

"The only reason you even want this fricking party is so you can flirt with Christine yet again. That's how you two date, not counting your tipsy lunches together. Remember our last open house? A hundred guests showed up, but you spent the entire evening drooling over that slut. I felt so humiliated."

"This conversation is getting more illogical by the minute."

"Listen to me, David. I can't stand the sight of that anorexic whore. God, her throat must get raw from all that puking."

"Honey, calm down. Christine and I are just friends. Like you and Skip." What else could I say to such paranoia when everybody in town knew Christine was happily married to Glenn? Just as I dearly loved my own wife. Okay, maybe not in the sense of desiring the woman day and night. Still, Ruth was my spouse and, with a little luck, the mother-to-be of our child, too. Though there was no denying that I did glom onto the belle of every party and flirt outrageously, not that I indulged in any actual affairs. In my defense, my attentions were never unwelcome—as if I weren't the only person whose flagging ego craved flattering in the face of creeping middle age.

"Remember the last time we had the Goughs over and Christine danced with her hands above her head?" Ruth ranted on. "You ogled her every bump and grind like you were going to cream your jeans. When she starts strutting her stuff, you act like a tomcat getting a whiff of chicken."

"A well-fed kitty doesn't sniff around." Big mistake.

"There's more to marriage than fucking! David, you are obsessed with sex!"

"Maybe because I hardly get any." Bigger mistake.

At that remark Ruth balled a fist and threatened to punch me right in the kisser. I braced for impact, ready to give her the first blow, but she wisely refrained. "Do you have a death wish?" I said, my voice calm and steady. "You sure can tell you didn't grow up a boy. I wasn't very far along in grade school before I learned never to start something with anybody bigger than me. Unless I wanted the crap kicked out of me." Absurd talk, to be sure, coming from scrawny, mild-mannered Dave Schroeder.

"You're sinking so low you probably would hit a woman."

"Never have, never will. But that doesn't give you the right to take advantage of my chivalry. Come on, Ruthie. Cheer up. Our party'll be a blast."

Empty glass in hand, she stomped downstairs. I shut myself in the bathroom and took another swig from my highball, its cold fire burning all the way down. Its sweet barley aroma evoked the bibulous joys of a dozen great parties just that past year—as the hoppy aftertaste of a good German lager always recalled festive get-togethers during grad school back in Madison. Not that those days weren't ancient history.

Once fully unclothed, I checked myself out in the bathroom mirror. Blue-green eyes. Long, narrow face. Strong chin. Slender torso. Scrawny limbs. Medium-brown hair with red notes. The same as I'd looked since childhood except for graying here and there in the temples now. Which I loathed.

I turned the shower on icy cold and endured its bone-chilling stream till I'd sung every last stanza of *"Du, du liegst mir im Herzen."* After toweling off, I grabbed barber scissors, and leaning close to the mirror, cut out gray hairs from my temples one at a time as best I could. While trimming, I stretched my face every which way in the attempt to firm aging flesh.

Detecting motion out of the corner of an eye, I glanced out the window. Upstairs at our neighbors, a woman was standing buck naked, as if showing off her lovely derrière. Who else, but Christine Gough, starkers yet again? "Damn it," I cursed when my scissors nicked an ear and a drop of blood oozed out. I slapped a tissue against the tiny wound, keeping my gaze glued on Christine, now merrily toweling her hair and jiggling her breasts. "Holy shit," I muttered.

"What are you cussing about in there?" my better half teased from the landing. A new playfulness in her voice told me the booze was finally mellowing her out. Ruth barged right in, a refill of her own favorite rocket fuel, Corbel's brandy, in hand.

"I cut myself," I said, backing against the venetians and closing them behind me.

"What do you expect, cutting your own hair? Isn't it falling out fast enough for you as it is?"

Dearly welcoming this mocking tone, I smirked. Perhaps our soirée could still be the splendid success I had hoped.

"Your hair is probably turning gray over worrying when to fall out," Ruth said. "And would you please get rid of that spider up on the ceiling?"

I looked up at the tiny auburn creature hanging upside down, its eight legs curled close to a rotund body alongside a dead bug neatly bagged and tied for future consumption. "Why? It's not harming us."

"Day-vid," Ruth cooed. "Get rid of it now."

I thrust my jaw out as far as possible to stretch my too puffy cheeks.

"Who fed you that crap about a natural facelift anyway?"

Thanks to Ireland's finest overlying my flammable blood like a film of incombustible asbestos, I merely shrugged.

"Stop being so vain, David. You won't lose your good looks for at least another year. By the way, you do have to kill that thing up there. We don't want our guests thinking we're living in a tenement."

"I'll kill to protect myself, but that little critter is no threat."

"Day-vid," Ruth pleaded. Every passing minute was dulling her edge, and a heavy-lidded grin replacing her former scowl—thanks to Bacchus' favorite fruit and a skilled vintner. Was there any doubt why we often drank so much if good cheer like this was the result?

I took a good look at the fuchsia summer dress cinching my wife's narrow waist over dramatic hips. Was it too late to bag our celebration and get to work on the family we'd long planned? "Ruthie," I said, exaggerating my leer.

A hardness lingering in her bloodshot gaze told me this truly wasn't the right time. But we'd still have the rest of the long holiday weekend. I grabbed another tissue, climbed onto the toilet seat, gently swept the web and its creator off the paint, and flushed them to oblivion. God forgive me for the evil done for no decent reason.

"You know, David," Ruth said with a wistful smile, "you're not genuinely happy."

I downed another swig of my smooth irish.

"You pretend to be so light-hearted," she went on. "But you and I both know you aren't. Otherwise why would you drink like a fish?"

"Are you kidding? I'm very happy. Hey, they gave me tenure today. So if ever there was a time to party hearty, tonight is the night."

"Why'd you close the blinds?" Ruth leaned close and reached behind me. "Without the A/C, we need all the breeze we can get."

I rested both hands on my spouse's fetching hips to distract her. "What do you think I should wear?"

"How about pants and a shirt?"

Excellent advice, since what else did I ever put on? But then women have so much freedom of dress they can hardly imagine men's limited choices.

"That fricking slut!" Ruth suddenly shrieked. At least Christine had donned bikini panties in the meantime. "Okay, that's it, David."

I blocked Ruth's further view of our neighbor's sexy antics. "Honey, I'm being serious now. Can we talk about all this tomorrow? And have a nice, romantic day together? Just you and me?"

"Tomorrow my ass." She stomped off downstairs, cursing under her breath. I cringed at the pinkness visible in my own eyes and resumed trimming out the gray till curiosity about my wife's vague threat got the best of me.

From the upstairs landing I could overhear her on the phone in our foyer. "Dick, this is Ruth McDaniel," she was saying. "I typed that list up like you said. Now I'm really anxious to get things rolling. Please call me as soon as you can."

Dick? But we didn't know anybody named Dick. Or Richard, for that matter. Not counting my brother, Rick, of course. No way could Ruth be talking to him.

The front screen door snapped shut with a bang from its strong spring. I hurried to our guest bedroom window and spotted Ruth out front, assaulting the sidewalk with a broom. Could she go on the rampage whenever cleaning. I quaffed the rest of both my irish and coffee, slipped on a clean pair of khaki slacks, a navy blue polo shirt, and the new leather sandals, of course without socks, hustled down to the foyer, and hit the phone's memory key. After five rings, a recorded baritone voice said with a southeastern Ohio drawl, "You have reached the residence of Richard Ross."

I cut the connection. Why would my wife be contacting Dick Ross, the most ruthless lawyer in Calypso County? Picturing the dark, hairy egomaniac, I couldn't help but gnash my teeth. Most likely, slimy Ross couldn't come to the phone because he was too busy diddling his girlfriend of the week.

Ruth charged back inside, brandishing the broom overhead like a shillelagh.

"Ruthie, what if we cancel the party? So you and I can talk."

"But then you won't be able to flirt with that fricking Christine." She hustled into the kitchen and attacked our already spotless sink with a scouring pad.

Ruth wasn't having an affair with that prick lawyer Ross, was she? "What in holy hell is all this about?" I suddenly screamed, surprising myself with my vehemence.

She set her jaw, yanked open the top drawer of our Hoosier cupboard, and snatched out a piece of paper. "Take a gander at this," she said, thrusting the sheet at me. It consisted of two long columns, headed by the words "Ruth" and "Dave," listing all of our possessions. "That's about as close to a fifty-fifty split as you're gonna get," she told me with a resolute smirk. "You and I are through, chump."

The doorbell chimed.